Born in London to a runaway teenager, Rosie has always been a cuckoo in the nest. She is an eclectic writer and performer, ranging from singing in Goth band The March Violets; through touring with the Subversive Stitch Exhibition in the 90s; to her current incarnation as Rosie Lugosi the Vampire Queen: cabaret chanteuse, incomparable compere and electrifying poet. She has published five solo collections of poetry; and her award-winning short stories, poems and essays have been widely anthologised. *The Palace of Curiosities* is her debut novel.

THE PALACE OF CURIOSITIES

Before Eve is born, her mother goes to the circus. She swears she hears the lion sigh, just before it leaps . . . and nine months later when Eve is born, the story goes, she doesn't cry — she meows and licks her paws. When Abel is pulled from the stinking Thames, and the mudlarks search his pockets to divvy up the treasure, his eyes crack open and he coughs up a stream of black water. But, how has he survived a week in that thick stew of human waste? Cast out by Victorian society, Eve and Abel find succour from an unlikely source: they soar to fame as star performers in Professor Josiah Arroner's Palace of Curiosities. And there begins a journey that will entwine their fates forever . . .

ROSIE GARLAND

THE
PALACE OF
CURIOSITIES

Complete and Unabridged

CHARNWOOD
Leicester

First published in Great Britain in 2013 by
Harper
An imprint of
HarperCollins*Publishers*
London

First Charnwood Edition
published 2014
by arrangement with
HarperCollins*Publishers*
London

The moral right of the author has been asserted

This novel is entirely a work of fiction. The names, characters and incidents portrayed in it are the work of the author's imagination. Any resemblance to actual persons living or dead, events or localities is entirely coincidental.

A catalogue record for this book is available
from the British Library.

ISBN 978–1–4448–2020–1

Published by
F. A. Thorpe (Publishing)
Anstey, Leicestershire

Set by Words & Graphics Ltd.
Anstey, Leicestershire
Printed and bound in Great Britain by
T. J. International Ltd., Padstow, Cornwall

This book is printed on acid-free paper

*For everyone who believed
I would get here,
even when I didn't*

EVE

London, November 1831

Before I am born, my mother goes to the circus.

She has smelled sweat before: she knows the stink of mouldy cloth, meat left too long, the mess kicked into drains. But tonight, the world is perfumed with fairy tales. She gulps down its promise and a rope tightens across her stomach, causing her to stumble against Bert.

He doesn't notice. He pulls her up the theatre steps, head turned away, hair sleek black ink. She feels like a princess, even if she is being dragged headlong to the ball. She's no idiot: she won't let go of this charming prince come midnight.

Bert pays for them both as if sixpences are a trifle, and bustles her through the crowded foyer so fast the gilded plaster and frosted glass are a blur. She grips his arm above the elbow and he doesn't push her off. He is a good one: a stopper, a stayer-in. How he will love her! He flings his arm round her shoulders and squeezes her into his buttoned-up jacket.

'Now, girl,' he rumbles. 'Mind how you go.'

He will ask her that very night, she knows: will ask the question she's been working up to for three months now. She is seized with such a fierce certainty that it makes her dizzy. She does not realise it, but this commotion bubbling through her veins is all in preparation for me. The velvet drumbeat of her heart and the fanfare of her gasps are heralding my arrival. I have never kept an audience waiting.

Bert pushes them to the front row of benches. They are full, so he flaps his hand and the people already seated there shuffle up a little, but not enough. He curls his hand into a fist: they shrink away, and he and Mama sit down.

'This is the best place,' he says loudly, although no-one seems about to disagree. 'I would not sit in the galleries. No, I would not.'

He pauses and stares at my mother.

'You are right, Bert,' she says, for an answer is needed.

She gazes up at the tiers of seats climbing the walls towards a roof she can barely pick out in the darkness.

'Batty's Amphitheatre is far grander,' he continues. 'There is a chandelier with a thousand crystals.'

He is so close she can feel the feather of his breath stir the down on her cheek.

'Oh?' she whispers, and it takes a moment for her to realise he is still waiting for a response — a good one. 'This is marvellous, Bert. All I could want.'

The sun comes out in his face when he smiles. He is as tall as a statue in a park, and certainly as good-looking. But there is no more time to adore her new idol, for a gentleman appears in the

2

circle before them, eyes ringed with black, lips and cheeks rouged.

'Gentleman!' he cries. 'And ladies!'

This creates a swell of merriment, and Mama thinks it best to smile also.

'Tonight we have mirth!'

A cheer bursts out.

'Wit!'

Another whoop.

'And jollity!'

Mama joins in the cheering, and for once no-one tells her to be quiet. The Master of Ceremonies strides about the arena, brandishing his hands.

'You have come on a very special evening!' He grins, eyes gleaming. 'How happy I am to welcome you to this Palace of Delights on such an auspicious occasion! What Luck! What Serendipity! What Felicitous Providence!'

There is a hum of appreciation. Mama wonders why he is stretching his words out so, pulling at them so hard they are in danger of breaking.

'We humbly offer, for your discernment, Wonders Unparalleled! Incredible Feats of Daring! Please welcome the Italian Fairy, lately arrived from Milan, the Empress of the Air! Signorina Chiarini!'

A storm of clapping breaks over their heads. From the muddy dark of the carved ceiling a rope uncoils, lowering a hoop studded with rubies and emeralds more precious than those kept in the Tower. Balanced there is a magical creature who sparkles even more brightly, thighs bulging with diamond garters, beautiful as a fairy. She waves at my mother, winking at how clever she is to have such a handsome young man on her arm. Mama leans into Bert's shoulder. *My hero*, she thinks.

The lady does a swift pirouette, somersaults on to her hands, kicks up her heels and swings backwards and forwards on the golden ring. She strikes pose after impossible pose, accompanied by the gasps and moans of the crowd, for she plays so close to the brink of letting go. The whole time her grin is as broad as the street outside. My mother bites her lip: *She smiled at me*.

Then the acrobat climbs the rope, hand over glittering hand, wrapping it around her leg and dangling upside down, spinning like a whipped top. She spreads her arms; she falls. Mama is deafened by shrieks of dismay, only to hear them transformed into cheers of astonishment as one ankle is caught in the cord, cleverly twisted. The signorina swings, a gemstone on the end of a chain.

★   ★   ★

In the intermission, Bert buys her a penny twist of coloured sugar; she licks a finger and sticks it into the sweetness. She remembers she must not appear selfish, and offers him the paper cone, waiting for him to push his finger into the dint she has made. Instead, he grabs her hand, presses his lips around her fingertip and sucks.

'You're sweet enough for me,' he says.

She feels herself colour up like rhubarb and

4

wishes she could be one of those nicely brought-up girls who blush delicately. As she turns to hide her embarrassment, a new lady steps into the light, wearing a tight dress that shows off most of her titties. She sings a song about her sailor boy, and it is a good song, and many voices accompany her during the chorus.

As she trills up and down the scales, a number of low stools are carried out and placed in a circle around her. The painted gentleman appears from the side and bows her off, to whistles and shouts.

'Ah yes! The Fair Clara!' he simpers. 'The Most Dainty of Girls, lately from her Mother!'

The crowd roar once more.

'Be assured she will return. But now, it is time for stronger meat. Ladies and gentlemen! I require of you to engage your sternest courage! I ask you boldly: are you prepared to be petrified?'

'Yes,' they cry.

'Are there any amongst you of fragile disposition?'

'No,' they declare.

'No cowards?'

'No!'

'Brave men and true?'

'Yes!'

'Are you stout enough to come to the aid of any delicate creature who may faint and fall gasping into your lap?'

At this, there is howl of laughter Mama does not quite understand.

'Yes, indeed!'

'Can you view the most monstrous potentate

of the animal kingdom without fear?'

'Yes, oh yes!'

'I present to you, brought in at great expense from the Savage Heart of Africa! A Monster Forged in the Heat of a Merciless Sun! Gentlemen! I call upon you now to protect your lady companions!'

'Hurrah!'

'Behold then, the Fearsome King of the Beasts, the Ethiopian Sovereign, Djambo! And his Master, that most courageous of men, Mr Edwin Phillips!'

As the crowd applauds, a lion is hauled out on a chain and padlocked to one of the stools. It has been beaten bald as an old carpet. Its face is swiped with ancient scratches and one flank sports a hand's-breadth of dull pink skin. Mr Phillips cracks the long tail of his whip and Djambo staggers onto the seat. He slashes again, adding a fresh welt to the tip of the great cat's nose.

'Ho!' shouts Mr Phillips.

Djambo yawns. Mama is close enough to hear the lion-tamer hissing, 'Move, you scabby bastard, or I'll make a rug out of you.'

Djambo opens his eyes and looks directly at my mother. She feels like a package of pork, wrapped in brown paper. Mr Phillips is sweating. A moustache of dirt creeps across his top lip.

'Ho, Djambo!' he cries, bringing down the lash.

Very slowly, the lion moves his gaze from my mother to Mr Phillips.

'Now! I command you! Jump!'

6

'Yeah! Jump, why don't you!' bawls someone at the back.

'Hey, Puss! Didn't get your saucer of milk this morning?' chirps another wag, to great amusement.

'Boo!' says Bert, and a few pick it up.

The lion ignores them all and opens his mouth wide, gusting Mama with a reeking gale of dead breath. She claps her hand over her nose, but it is too late. Deep in her belly, the clot of blood that will be me in under an hour has smelled it, too. Mr Phillips whispers, 'Move, for Christ's sake, or I'm finished,' and they're the last words she does hear him say. He lifts his arm, flogging the beast again and again with the leather strap. The straggle of catcalls gains strength.

Mama is sure she hears Djambo sigh, just before he leaps. The chain rattles, tightens, but stretches far enough. The lion peers into the eyes of its torturer, and grins. For a moment the candles around the circle burn as bright as the hot bronze of an African sky; the baying of the audience is translated into the filthy laughter of hyenas. Then Djambo opens his jaws and closes them tight. The hyenas start to scream like women, and the sky flickers back into black.

The lion shakes his head from side to side, and Mr Phillips swings also. Three men with clubs race into the circle and wallop the beast until he lets go of the dying man, who slumps to the floor, a cat-o'-nine-tails of blood spurting from his neck and lashing the air. Djambo turns up his muzzle to catch the crimson rain beating down and lets loose a roar. Mama feels her face speckled with a spray as fine as drizzle. The lion's cry thunders down her throat; a raging tide of blood carries its essence into her womb and I stir.

She sits quiet, still. She has never felt so calm. But around her, the world is going mad. The mob is on its feet, and everyone's feet are in the way of everyone else's; the air is raw with screaming at the sight of a man's head bitten off. Bert is gone from her side. Mama stands, spies him a way in front of her and panics into movement, afraid of losing him, tonight of all nights. She races after his shining head, bright as a billiard ball on the tide of terrified bodies.

The wave spills her on to the street. She doubles over at the sudden stitch in her stomach as I dig in my claws and take root. She falls onto all fours, fingers squeezing the safety of the gutter muck. Dirt, she knows. Dirt, she understands. But just now she needs something more than dirt, something to swill away this new pain I am causing her. She crawls into a side-alley and hugs the wall, panting.

Bert appears, towering above her. She looks up, wondering how he found her, for it seems a very long time since she saw him last. There is such an uproar at the bottom of her belly, such a storm. He pats her on the back, very gently.

'Here, girl, here,' he says. 'You all right?'

She lurches to her feet, grabs his wrist, pulls him towards her. Now she understands why he is there: she needs him to flush me out.

'Bert,' she says. 'Now, Bert. Do me now.'

He makes a show of pulling away, but his

heart quivers. He flicks his eyes left, right, but the alley is empty enough for no-one to take notice.

'Oh Bert. Help me, Bert.'

She drags his hand up her skirt, points the way up the road he didn't think to find so easy; she pulls at his buttons and he's hard already, for doesn't he know women change their minds in a second? He pokes between her legs and finds the soft ready core of her. They rock me in the cradle of their rutting.

Not that I need the swim of his seed: I am already made. I am nothing to do with him and everything to do with snips and snails and lion's tails. I hunker down for my nine-month wait. He's done quickly; looks to see if he read this right but she's smiling, wider than she's ever smiled.

'Oh Bert,' she says, and will not let go of his hand. Her eyes are inky with pleasure.

'You all right, Maggie love?' he says.

'It was wonderful,' she sighs, unsure if she means what he has just done to her, or the lion.

ABEL

London, October 1854

Eyes closed. Waking. Hands upon me. Voices swarming into my ears. They start with my pockets, ferreting their fingers deeper and deeper into the ruins of my clothing.

'Not much here,' whines the voice of a boy. 'Not so much as a bloody wipe.'

'Nothing.' This sounds like a woman.

'No use.' And this, a girl.

'It was nice, his jacket, but it's finished.'

'Waste of bloody time.' This, another child.

'Now that's where you're wrong,' says a deeper voice, a man. 'There's a good doctor at the hospital as will give a few shillings.'

It seems there is a crowd gathered. I can hear the gentle prowl of the river draining towards the sea. Fingers lift my wrist, let it fall.

'Doctor? Too late for quacks. He's stone cold.'

'He's not breathing.'

'He's a dead one.'

I wonder if I am the dead man they are talking of so freely. My eyes are sticky with some insistent glue, my mouth also. Neither will open.

'The doctor I know will take a gentleman in

10

any condition, if you get my meaning.'

'Ooh, that's not right, George. Not decent.'

'What's he to you, all of a sudden?'

At that moment my body chooses to unseal itself: eyes crack open, mouth gapes and I cough black water. They spring away: the corpse they thought I was is suddenly too lively for comfort.

'He's alive!'

I vomit again, to prove the truth of it. My vision is unsteady. I am surrounded by vole-faced creatures with yellow teeth, breath hanging before them, the bones of their faces harsh. They are the colour of the mud in which they stand.

'Not a chance.'

'Got half the river in him, George.'

'Enough to fill the Fleet ditch.'

'He'll be a stiff soon enough if he's swallowed any of that.'

'He's coming round.'

The man they call George detaches himself from the pack; lowers himself to my side.

'Give this man his boots back,' he says.

'They're mine,' whines a skinny boy.

'Give him his trousers, at least. Can't have him walking around with his crown jewels up for grabs.'

'Fuck you.'

'And your sister.'

Small hands lift me out of the peaceful cushion of slime. I retch with the movement.

'He stinks.'

'So do you.'

'What's your name, man?'

'Where are you from?'

11

'Pissed, were you?'

My head swims with the need for words, for a mouth to form them, lungs to squeeze air, a tongue to shape the sound. There are so many tasks to perform and it is too much for me. I try a word, drawn up from deep inside the well: it meant a greeting when I used it before. They look from one to the other, raising bony shoulders.

'What's he saying?'

'Don't ask me. Some wop nonsense,' says George.

'What are you trying to say? Say it again.'

I choose a different word. Their eyes remain blank.

'Still a load of codswallop.'

'Here. He's that Italian fellow. That nob as went missing.'

'Yeah. Look at his eyes.'

'Jumped off Blackfriars Bridge.'

'They said he was shouting, raving. Ladies were screaming.'

'Sank like a stone.'

'But it was a week ago. A week, in that shit? Can't be him. Can it?'

'Rich bloke, I heard. A real swell.'

'I told you his jacket was nice.'

'Rich? Ooh. They'll want him back, then.'

'They'll be grateful, like.'

The ring of eyes glitter diamonds. One small creature — male or female, it is hard to say for its hair is a felted mat obscuring the face — raises its paw to touch my face, only to be clouted away. It whimpers, but almost instantly reaches out again, to be smacked off as fiercely.

'Grateful to them as found him.'

'Them as *saved* him,' corrects George.

I want them to go away and leave me here. I want to worm myself back into the mud and pull its blanket up over my chin. I am filled with the feeling that I have not been dead long enough. I do not know why, but I want to be dead a good while longer.

'Come on, sir. Say something else.'

I search for sounds to please them. 'I am drowned,' I say.

'What's he on about?'

'He says he's drowned.'

'That's English. Doesn't sound wop to me,' says George.

'Well, he looks Italian.'

'Maybe that's just dirt.'

'He's got to be that rich dago. There's no money in it if he's just some English bastard.'

'Can't we just say he's that Italian, George?'

'Don't be so bloody stupid.' The man puts his face close to mine. 'Who are you, then? Eh?'

'I don't know,' I reply.

'What's your name?'

I scrabble for the answer, paddling in the gutter of my mind, turning up nothing. I try harder. It is not a blank wall I come up against: there is no wall, no structure of any kind. I am void, featureless as the thick stew of human waste in which I am lying. They look at each other across my body.

'He *ought* to be a goner.'

George snorts, placing his hand upon me. I

13

see a bird made of blue ink flap its wings in the space between his thumb and forefinger.

'Bird,' I whisper.

'He's a nutter,' someone laughs.

'He's not *right*,' is the opinion of another.

'No one could last a minute in that, let alone a day.'

'He looks like he's coming out of the mud.'

'Like he was buried in it.'

'He ought to be dead. Why ain't he?'

'Something's not right.'

They begin to shrink back, all but the tattooed man, who regards me with thoughtfulness rather than fear.

'Come on, George. Leave the likes of him be.'

One of the women throws my trousers back at me; spits.

'I don't want nothing of him. Ooh,' she whinnies. 'I *touched* him.'

She wipes a hand on her greasy skirt. The boy holding my boots shifts from sticky foot to sticky foot.

'I'm keeping these,' he mutters defiantly.

George grins. 'Up to you, mate, but I'd not walk one inch in this man's shoes. He's not got the decency to die when he should.'

The lad chews the inside of his mouth awhile, and then hurls my boots into the muck.

'Fuck you, George.'

'And your sister. Your mother and all. And when I did, they didn't charge me, neither. Which is not like them in the least.'

George places his mouth close to my ear.

'Now. You tell George here your little secret. I

14

can spot a queer one when I see it. How come you're not dead?'

'I do not know.'

Again, it is the truth. I cough up another mouthful of the river and it dribbles down my chin.

'Could be worth your while. And mine.' His eyes gleam like sovereigns. 'I think you'll be coming with me, Lazarus.'

He grasps my hand, winches me into a sitting position. I heave, spill more oily slops down my chest. It seems I cannot stop leaking.

'Ooh,' squeals a girl from her safe distance. 'George is touching him.'

The words do not make George let go. I look at the way his fingers clasp mine, the ruddy glow of them against the bleached grey of my sodden flesh.

'I should be dead,' I whisper. 'Why am I not so?'

'That's what I'm going to find out, Mr Lazarus,' says George, showing me two rows of even teeth.

'What's he saying?' calls out one of the mudlarks.

'Nothing you lot need to know. This is man's business.'

'Talking up horrors, that's what they're doing,' wails a female voice.

The clacking of a rattle winds its way into the space between my ears.

'Fuck me, it's the Peelers.'

'Stay where you are,' yells George. 'We're breaking no bloody laws.'

'When did they ever care about the law?'

'Stay if you want. I'm legging it,' says the boy who gave up my boots.

I hear the suck and slather of mud as they hurry off. George looks from me to their retreating backs to me again. The rattling grows louder. He chews his lips.

'Fuck. Fuck. Fuck. Fuck the Queen and her fucking consort too.'

He lets go of my hand and I fall back. I stare at the sky. My thumbs dig into the soft quilt of the filthy ooze, and I let myself slide into the comfort of its tight wet mouth. I am lullabied into a drowse by the slurp of their footsteps retreating, the moist tread of other men approaching.

EVE

London, November 1845

They say when I was born I didn't cry; I meowed and licked my paws. They say that the midwife dropped dead of fright. They told a lot of tall stories but none of them were as tall as the ones I told myself when I looked in the mirror. Mama said I shouldn't look in mirrors: it would upset me. What she meant was, it upset her.

Other girls look in the mirror and see the fairest of them all. I saw a friend. Her name was Donkey-Skin. I can't remember when she came to me, only that she was always there. My only companion, born of imagination and loneliness, which is a hectic brew for a child. What did it signify if no one else could see her? I liked it so. She was mine and mine alone.

I did not want to share her with another soul, so I kept our conversations whispered, our games quiet. When Mama asked me whom I was talking to, I said, 'No one!' in my most innocent voice. She took it for another sign of my strangeness and it was not long before she ignored my chattering. Donkey-Skin wove herself from all the things I hid from my mother, knitting herself from the truths Mama would not tell me but I found out anyway.

Donkey-Skin was ugly: even uglier than me, which was quite something. If I was hairy, then she was as furry as a cave full of bears. If I was a freak, she was a cursed abomination in the sight of God. If I was lonely, she was abandoned on a hillside for wolves to devour. She was different because she did not care. Her life's work was to teach me not to care either.

When we were alone she murmured, *Kitten, kitten, my very own pet*. Her lullabies rang over the terrifying stretches of the night as I rested my cheek on her breast, safe under the press of her arm. She loved me because of my thick pelt of fur rather than despite it. Only she could sort my tangles. I purred beneath her gentle comb as she groomed my baby hair.

Of course, Mama was having none of that. Every day she reminded me that God made me foul-featured for a reason: punishment for a sin I could not remember and she never revealed. It could have been so much worse, she said. I was lucky, she said. Was I beaten? No. Was I fed? Yes. I had a roof over my head; I had a mother who was respectable. I should bow my head, keep my eyes down, keep the peace, be sweet, be grateful that someone cared enough to put bread in my mouth. I could have been sold to trim fur collars or made into a muff. I could have been tied in a bag and dropped in the Fleet.

My earliest memory is of Mama shaving me. She sat me upon the table and I kicked out my heels. She caught my foot and kissed the only part of me that was smooth and counted out my toes: 'This little piggy went to market, this little piggy got shaved.' Or was it 'saved'? I do not remember. Her songs were hopeful spells to make the fairies take pity and return the pretty pink and white babe they'd stolen from her womb. There was no escaping the truth of it. I was a changeling and as furry as a cat.

She doesn't want a baby, Donkey-Skin whispered in my ear. *She wants a piglet.*

I giggled.

A naked pink wobble of a thing, with that sore scalded look of them, tiptoeing as though the ground hurts and makes them screw up their eyes.

You are not a piglet, said Donkey-Skin. *Don't be one, not for anyone.*

Donkey-Skin was right; I did not want to be a piglet. Piglets grew into pigs, fat overblown pillows slathering in their own muck. Pigs were dinner. I had no wish to be sliced, smoked, fried, salted, stewed or pickled.

Mama grasped the kettle and heaved it from the mouth of the range, poured a bowlful and soaked the dishcloth. A cowlick of steam curled off the face of the liquid. She folded the rag in half and hung its hot wet curtain across my face.

'Mama?' I whimpered. 'Mama?'

'Is it too hot, little one?' she said.

She pulled the flannel away and I tingled with the sudden cold. I grabbed at it, but my reach was far too short. She picked up a jug, took the brush, dipped in the bristles and swiped foam across my cheek. I giggled and wiped it away,

19

slapping the white mess on to the floor.

'No,' she said and sopped my other cheek.

I wiped that away also, squeaking with delight.

'Stop it,' she said, louder, and I squealed louder, to match her.

She aimed quick blobs at my chin, my cheek, my forehead. I could not get enough of this new game. Even when she held my wrists with one hand and soaped my face with the other, I wriggled free.

'I am making you beautiful,' she snapped, and started to cry. 'I'm doing this because I love you.'

Then she smacked me. I had been stung far harder in the past, and deserved it too. This small slap spelled me into stone.

'Stay very, very still'

I sat obediently and let her lather up my whole face and neck. She unfolded the razor, stropped it keen and laid it on my forehead. I quivered under its chilly stroke, stranger than the licking of a cat. The blade came away loaded with scum, and more. With each scrape the water grew dirtier, clogged with brown silky threads which collected in thick clots. I grew cold. When she finished, she kissed me and tickled my hairless chin.

'Now you're my pretty girl, my real girl, the girl I should have got, the one who loves her mama and will never leave her side.'

★   ★   ★

That night, Donkey-Skin visited me as I undressed for sleep.

20

'Mama's made me pretty,' I sang, spinning in a circle to show off my new nakedness.

Pretty? she snorted. *She's made you ordinary.*

'Mama told me I am a real girl now. It must be true.'

You look like all the rest of them: simpering, feeble, wet-wristed, snickery-whickery, snappy-snippy little girls made of milk and money.

'Then what is a real girl, Donkey-Skin?'

It's a long story. I have plenty of answers. We have time.

Every week Mama shaved me. When I was old enough, I said *no.* She did it anyway. I grew and still she shaved me naked, until I was tall enough to smack the razor from her hand.

'You'll look like an animal,' she wept. 'Is that what you want?'

I stood in front of the looking-glass and admired myself. My moustache wormed across my lip, the tips lost in the crease behind my ears. My eyebrows met over the bridge of my nose and spread like wings up the side of my forehead. My chin sprouted a beard the colour of combed flax, reaching to my little breasts.

You are my very own princess stuck in the tower, whispered Donkey-Skin.

I laughed. 'A very small tower!'

Donkey-Skin tugged my moustache.

I will spin you into gold. Weave a happy ending with a handsome prince . . .

'I will weave my own story,' I replied, and she smiled.

'Listen to you talking to yourself!' cried Mama. She wiped her nose. 'Look at you,' she

21

sneered. 'You're not even human.'

I stuck out my chin and my beard swung backwards and forwards.

'I know that I am different. How could I not? If God intended me to be this hairy, I shall find out the reason, however long it takes me.'

'Do you think this is a game? You're only safe out there on the streets because I make you look like a real girl.'

I crossed my arms.

'People know who I am. Whatever I look like, they'll say, *There goes Eve, Maggie's daughter.*'

'You are stupider than you look. And you look particularly stupid. Can't you see my way is better?'

'I shall prove you wrong,' I said. 'Today, I shall take the air.'

★ ★ ★

I opened the door and stepped into fog as thick as oatmeal. Dim hulks of buildings swam towards me as I strolled along the pavement. No one pointed at me. Shadows tiptoed past, hands on the wall like blind beggars, and at first I was comforted by the thought that I was walking unseen, and therefore in safety. This soon changed to frustration: I would have no proof that our neighbours did not care what I looked like. I wanted to show Mama that I could be seen and accepted.

I kept walking, picking my way carefully, and did not realise how far I had come until the gate of the Zoological Gardens gaped before me. I strode past the ticket office, and smiled at saving sixpence. The mist had cleared a little and I found myself in front of the lion's cage. The great cat lolled within. A raven pecked at its beard.

The dark form of a man appeared next to me. He lifted his arm and threw a stone at the lion. It bounced off the animal's head.

'Oh, Harold, don't carry on so,' said a woman's voice.

His answer was to throw another.

'Oh, Harold,' she simpered.

A small crowd began to gather. More stones were thrown, until the lion was surrounded by a ring of pebbles. It continued to ignore us. Then a boy spotted me.

'Hey, look!' he squealed. 'Look at that, will you!'

Every nose swivelled to follow the compass point of his finger. There was a pause. I smiled. What better place to prove I was no animal than here, where the dividing line was drawn so clearly? They were in cages, and I was not. The mist grew thinner. I held my breath as it peeled away.

'Oh, Lord, will you look at that,' said the first of them.

'That's not right.'

'It's not *decent*.'

'If that were mine I'd never let it out.'

'If that were mine, I'd never of had it, if you get my meaning.'

Their eyes poked knitting needles at me. I took a step backwards and felt the bars of the cage.

'Shouldn't be allowed out. Should hide itself away from decent folk.'

'Mind you,' chirped one wag, 'right place for it, ain't it? You know, the zoo, like,' he said, in case they missed the joke.

They did not. There was a rattling of unpleasant laughter.

'Here, monkey. You a monkey or what?'

'Even a monkey ain't that hairy.'

'It's a dog.'

'Nah. Dog is man's best friend. It ain't no friend of mine.'

'Perhaps it's an exhibit got out of its cage.'

'Can't see no park-keepers,' one growled.

There was another pause as they ran out of amusing things to say. A boy bent down, picked up a stone and let it fly in my direction. It was weakly thrown and wide of the mark, in that way of first stones. I waited to see if anyone would tell him off. No-one spoke. In their eyes I read drowned cats, kicked dogs, rabbits skinned alive. I saw my own pelt stripped off and spread like a rug before the kitchen fire.

There was no point in searching for escape. The moment I looked away I would be piled up with rocks high as a hill. The cage pressed its bars into my back, too narrow to slip through. Then I felt the sweltering breath of the lion on my neck. I waited for its claws to rake me open, but instead my skin was sandpapered with a tongue the size of my foot.

'Look! Even the bloody lion thinks it's a cub!'

'Freak!'

The stones had started as a drizzle, but now

turned to rain, bouncing off the bars. One hit the lion on the face, and its roar boomed like thunder over the heads of the mob, which turned and ran. I reached into its prison and scratched the top of its head. A purr rumbled in its throat. A man in a peaked cap came running up to the enclosure.

'You bothering my lion?' he panted; then he saw my face and stepped away. 'Oh. Sorry, miss.'

'I won't bite you,' I said, but he muttered an excuse and left.

I did not cry. I would not shed tears. I took myself back home bent double with my shawl tied round my head. Mama did not say a word, but she smiled for the first time in many months.

Donkey-Skin was my only comfort. She called me all the names they shouted; all the cruelties made of words. Hours and hours we played the game; for days, for weeks, for years; until the words were mine again, and I was not just *bitch*, but the queen of all the bitches: not just *freak*, but empress of all the freakish, with a dazzling crown.

She told me new stories: of a prince clever enough to spot a princess through her wrapper of dirt, who would kiss the beast to make it beautiful. A fearless man who would fight through the bramble forest a hundred years' thick, past the wolf at the door and the witch at the gate. My fur was my protection. Only the most true of heart would find their way through.

There is a man for you with knife in hand to cut through the world's binding. A man of blood and flesh and bone and strange in all of them.

Keep an eye out for him. Watch carefully. You may not know him when he appears.

I am Donkey-Skin. Peel away this fur and I am as pink as you. The blood in my veins is as crimson. If you flay me, we stand equal. Beauty is truly skin-deep. We are all horrors under the skin.

ABEL

London, January 1857

It's not like waiting up. I'm awake already. I have been somewhere. Like sleep, but not. My body rocks backwards and forwards. Something has hold of my shoulder and is shaking it, vigorously.

'Wake up, Abel,' a voice whispers. 'It is time.'

'Time?' I ask, and forget everything.

I open my eyes. The first things I see are blocks of grey. They move: to and fro, up and down, side to side. A dark column hovers before me and I hold my breath. It leans over my bed, a swirl of mixed brightnesses. It touches my arm, and speaks.

'Wake up. Are you awake?'

With the words, the ghost becomes a man.

I answer, 'Yes.'

The smell of dried blood is on his shirt, under his fingernails, on the soles of his boots. I know this smell, for I have it on myself.

'It is time for work. Come now.'

I look about me, and see blotched and crumbling plaster above my head. Narrow slots pierce one wall close to the ceiling, letting in a dribble of pale light. I am surrounded by a multitude of pallets, packed close together. The spectres rising from them become other men. I inhale the comforting stink of my own body and the warm reek of the others crowded into this place; a morning chorus of belching, hacking, spitting and farting giddies me with happiness. I remember: I sleep here. It is my home.

'Shift yourself, Abel. You're like this every morning.'

His name will come to me in a moment. The man waking me works with blood. I sniff again: animal blood. Meat. A butcher? No, a butcher has his own business, and does not need to sleep in a cellar. Then I know: he is a slaughter-man. We work together. This reasoning takes very little time, but he is impatient.

'Abel, get bloody moving.'

It is my name. This man is my friend.

'Yes, yes,' I say cheerfully.

'You're in a good mood. Move, you old bastard.'

I am already dressed in most of my clothes. All I need do is put on my cap and boots. I get them from under my head, where I have been using them as a pillow. My friend pats me on the shoulder and smiles. We climb the grimy steps out of our cellar and join the troop of men lining up to pay the tallyman, who leans against the door-jamb, book in one hand, pint bottle of tea in the other, and a stub of a pencil behind his ear. Many of our companions thumb their caps and promise to cough up that evening. But we pay our sixpence on the spot for the next night's lodging as we leave, and I recall that we do this each morning, at my friend's insistence.

'We must pay one night at a time. A man never knows what might happen,' he says.

The moment the words come out of his mouth his name comes back to me, making me suddenly joyful at the gift of remembrance, at the realisation that he returns me to myself thus every day.

'Alfred,' I say. 'You are my friend.'

He laughs and calls me an old bastard once more.

★ ★ ★

We step out on to the street and my breath catches at each new sight, which stops being new the moment I look at it. I wonder how I would find myself in this blur of grey and brown if it were not for Alfred, shaking me into wakefulness, striding at my side, half a pace in front, urging me on, drawing me out of my drowse and into a beginning of myself.

The world reveals itself to me piecemeal: the flat surface at my side becomes a long terrace of filthy brickwork interrupted by black holes, which resolve themselves into doors and windows. One of these doors leads to my cellar. I gape at how similar it is to all the others, how simple a thing it would be to confuse one door with another. I lose myself in the contemplation of this wondrous revelation and Alfred grasps my elbow, steering me away from the ordure running down the middle of the street.

'What would you do without me?' he says.

'I do not know.'

I blink at this new world, which of course is the same world as yesterday, only somehow mislaid by me overnight.

'You'd walk through shit the whole time, that's for sure!' He laughs, and I understand that it is a joke, and that he does not realise what he means to me. I feel an urge to thank him, but I do not.

At this early hour the rough sleepers are still piled up in doorways, wrapped around each together against the chill. But Alfred and I are different: we are men of purpose. Men like us stride swiftly to a rightful place of employment. We have work to attend to, work that directs our hands and steers our feet, that fills our bellies with food and drink, that shakes us awake and tires us so we sleep deeply; work that gives us the money to pay for a place that is warm and comradely, a place where one man shares his good fortune with another, and where Alfred and I are often the men with that good fortune, for the pieces of meat that we bring.

Work prompts me with a purpose, with something to remember every morning. Without work I would be empty. I shake my head, and with it that unpleasant notion; I am not empty. I have work, I have food, I have lodging, I have Alfred. I am a happy man. There is no more contentment for which I could ask.

A coal-train heaves itself across the viaduct and we pass beneath, the vaulted arches shuddering a rain of soot on our heads, which Alfred dusts from my shoulders with many jokes about how I look even more like a gyppo when I'm blackened with smuts. The first criers are about, shouting, 'Milk! Watercress! Hot bread!' Carts jolt past, the iron clanging of their wheels dinning in my ears, bringing me further back into the glove of my senses. We cross over a stream of raw sewage.

'I don't know how you manage it. The smell,' says Alfred, voice muffled by the kerchief he has clapped over his mouth. 'What are you about? Make haste.'

I pause and look down at the mess. Not a whit of movement.

'It does not trouble me,' I say.

'Now I know you are lying,' he replies, uncovering his mouth when we are clear of the sewer.

But I am not. It is an aroma, that is all. I stand a while longer, but then realise that Alfred is no longer by my side. I glance down to see what my feet are about, and they are still when they should be moving. I have been looking down too long; when I look up Alfred has drawn some distance away. I command my feet to pick up their pace and keep up with him, for his legs are transporting him very swiftly, his body slipping neatly between the other men passing to and fro along the thoroughfare. I quicken my pace and after some shoving I draw level.

'You not awake yet, Abel?' he says. 'Come now, buck up, or there'll be no time to eat.'

My mouth waters at the thought of food.

'Ha! That's put a spring in your step! Sprightly, now.'

We bound forward. With each stride, I am

31

bolder and the world takes on more solid form. Each step breathes fire into my legs; the flagstones thump back at my heels, prickling my skin with wakefulness; my liver and lights quiver with the blood pumping around my veins. The jostling and jarring of the passers-by returns the awareness of my arms and ribs; the screaming of this waking city brings back my ears. I smile at every assault, for each serves to remind me of my flesh, my meat, my muscle, bone and blood. I am a man again, not the phantom I was upon waking.

A boy passing to my right shrieks the news so piercingly I clench my teeth: *'Savage Murder! Shocking Discovery!'* Alfred sees my grimace.

'You all right?'

I nod.

'Loud, isn't he?'

I nod again. 'I am very hungry,' I say.

'Ah! A fine suggestion.'

He claps his hands together in the cold. We stop at a stall, which I know is the place we usually take our breakfast, and the man shouts his halloa, handing us fat bacon wrapped in a square of dirty bread; a pint of tea each. I shove all into my mouth, and Alfred laughs.

'Your stomach, the great pit!'

The vendor roars at the joke. I smile through my bread, spilling some, filling them with even more merriment.

'You will make yourself sick, you silly bastard,' says Alfred. 'Yes, we must hurry, but not that much.'

It occurs to me that I am never sick, but I do

not say as much. It comes to me that I have tried to explain this before; but such things confuse him, and confusion takes away his cheerfulness. So I continue to play the fool, and he is happy. The grease sticks to my chin and I wipe it off, licking my fingers.

'Good stuff?' says Alfred through his bread.

'Good stuff,' I reply.

'That's you fixed up.'

Right away I know he is speaking the plain truth. The sticky bacon weighs me down into the earth. I pat my chest, feeling the smoke of the chimneys clogging each breath; rub my belly, testing the ballast of the half-loaf within.

'Thank you,' I say to him. 'You are my friend.'

For a moment, his face changes, and I recognise the look. Suddenly I am aware that I have seen it before, over and over. How I know this I do not recall, nor who has looked at me thus: only that many have. I search for names and faces, but find none. It is most confusing. Alfred pushes the last of his bacon between his lips and is once again my gruff companion.

'It's only breakfast,' he grunts. 'Any pal would do the same.'

The day is no warmer when we hand back the tin mugs; indeed, it is still dark, but I no longer care for I am hot inside. We bow into the wind and head past the tannery and turn left. As we walk through the gate a church clock somewhere begins to strike the hour. I count five.

'It is the best part of the day,' Alfred says. 'And winter too: the best time of year for men like ourselves.'

We strap on our leather aprons, and are ready. I know why I am here. I am a slaughter-man.

*   *   *

The first bullock of the morning is brought in. It is barely through the rectangle of the door before Alfred lifts his hammer and strikes the blow. The eyes roll and it falls forward on to its chin, grey tongue flopping between its teeth, gentle eye dim between the stiff, gummed lashes. Alfred shouts a brief huzzah at such a clean start and grins.

'Barely twitching!' he exclaims.

Two fellows hook the hind legs and winch the carcase upwards. Their names have not yet returned to my recollection, though I should have them before another hour has passed. I grasp the soft, warm ear and strike the knife beneath it; blood pours.

'He never misses,' mumbles one of the winchers, still chewing on his breakfast, a piece of bread clamped between his teeth.

His name surfaces in the mud of my mind.

'Yes, William,' I agree, pleased with myself.

'There is a man at peace with his labour,' says Alfred, and smiles. 'I can see William snoring in long, untroubled sleep. Can't you?' He looks slantwise at me. A blade scrapes against bone. 'Just like us, eh, Abel? You're not disturbed by what you see here. Are you?'

'Me? No.'

'Good. Me neither. Steady hands and a steady stomach. That's the two of us.'

The beast starts to kick, and Alfred frowns,

but it is only a brief show. I raise the blade and watch it fall, guided by a precision I possess without knowing how as it strikes the exact midline of the belly and splits it open; the insides begin to cascade out in a sodden fall.

William and his companion heave out the innards, briefly sorting through the coils for any obvious signs of sickness. They are quickly satisfied, and I slice away the heart, liver and lights, giving a final grunt of exertion as my blade breaks through the cartilage between the vertebrae. The skinners set to work straight away. Three lads carry away the pluck; four others slop the black waters away continuously, bent into their work, never looking up to see whence comes the thick dark stuff they push into the grille of the drain.

I delight in the handsome geometry of the beast: the soft handshake of the intestines coiling about my arms, humid from the belly, delicate green and blue; the perfect smoothness of the liver; the pink and grey lungs, matched in wonderful symmetry and nesting the heart between. There is no time to ponder each marvel, for we have many beeves to work through.

'This is a hungry city,' says Alfred.

Each carcase I split open reveals the same beautiful workings, each with their particular differences: a larger pair of lungs; a surprisingly violet twist of gut. But these small variations only seem to further underline the natural majesty of them all; I cannot avoid the sensation that I am close to some revelation about myself. Why the mysterious insides of beasts should make me feel thus I do not know, but they draw me with an uncanny power that here I might solve some riddle. I push towards the answer: I am a man who knows the mystery of beasts.

I see the way they come in after hours of stamping down a hard road: their ankles gone, hooves raw; driven, beaten, thrashed and pushed towards their deaths — and any man who says a beast doesn't know it is a fool. No fellow-beast comes back from the killing to tell them, but they guess it true enough.

They smell it on the road. Keeping their heads low: not sniffing for grass to chew, but getting a sniff of those who passed before, the excruciating spoor of that last drive, the screaming muscle, the aching bones. Most of all they smell the fear.

And if they are bad on the road in, that is nothing to how they are when they get to the yard and are left standing, listening to the sharpening of blades. They smell death before it happens; hear the thump of the stunning blow before it cracks the first skull of the day; taste the blood of their brothers misting the air from the day before, when their guts spilled out of the bag of their bellies.

The fear of beasts. It is a fire that runs between them dry as tinder. When they get it in them the worst things happen. So I strive to make it quick. Today, we are unlucky.

Alfred raises his hammer with a good will, but when it falls some agency turns it awry and it falls to one side, a feather's width only, but enough to inflict pain without release. The bullock rears up, its skull caved in. How can a dead animal leap up? When they are hammered, that should be an end to it. But I've seen what I've seen. Slaughter-men know these things.

It pauses, hanging in the air. We are fixed also, though we must clear out of its way for the plunge that will follow: it wants to take us into that animal darkness, and Heaven help anyone in the way when it comes crashing down. I have seen a man lose an arm, torn off at the shoulder by those fiendish hooves, and heard the beast give a last moan of delight to hear its murderer scream.

It falls, staggering. Alfred tries a second blow, but it swings its head despite our attempts to hold it steady, and this blow is worse than the first, breaking the bone beneath the eyes. The screaming starts: a sound no-one would believe who had not heard it. Women have it when they push a child out of them; beasts have it when we push the life out of them, and do it badly.

It is dead enough to fall to its knees, undead enough to thrash out when the hooks dig through its tendons and the hauling starts, so it takes four men to get it up there, the four who should be mopping the floor, so now we are slipping in the bile it has spewed up. I cut its throat right across, more than is needed, to sever the windpipe as well as the vein, and air whistles out, but at least it is a hiss and not the awful keening.

Finally, we tie it off: heels up, head down, tongue licking the floor; and still struggling. The blade is in my hand. My fellows are getting angrier, and I am the only one who can do a thing about it. I lift my hand; the blade falls and

I have some comfort that this stroke at least is deep and true. I lose myself in the sight of its guts, gushing out in a smooth clean tumble. I do not let myself see its juddering terror as I kill it for the last time. I will not let myself think of that at all.

The hauliers are bringing up the next beast, shouting, 'Get a move on, you fuckers. How long does it take to kill a bullock, for Christ's sake?' Their charge is restless: it can smell and hear and taste and see what is before it, and knows its share. Then it is in, stamping out its complaint, and we must continue. I look at Alfred: he is sweating, his hand unsteady. The hauliers hate him, the winch-men hate him, the sweepers hate him, the animals hate him. His day is already bad, and the only direction it can go is to the worse.

'Alfred,' I say.

I hold out my hand and he places the hammer into my grasp. The bullock looks at me with wet brown eyes, and I look back; I lay my hand on its flank until it grows still. Then it happens: it stumbles forwards, as though kneeling in prayer. I am to be its killer, but I am kind, each blow struck by me being on the mark. It knows it will be fully dead when it is split open. I am the only one it can be certain of. Other men try but I succeed, every time. It closes its eyes, knowing I will be quick and sure. It is my nature.

I do not disappoint: neither the beast nor my companions. They see my kindness, and each of them pauses, even the most brutish of the hauliers, and breathe out their relief.

'You're a good man,' says Alfred, and rubs my shoulder, swabbing it with blood.

His voice snaps in the middle, dry and thin. I return the hammer to him.

*   *   *

The day swims past, and I drift upon its languorous current. My arm continues to rise and fall and I am drawn into a drowse by the movement, by the length and silkiness of black hair flowing in a stream from wrist to elbow, the veins standing out along the length.

With each fall of the blade the muscles of my hand and thumb stiffen and relax, and I find myself thinking how simple a thing it would be to make a vertical incision upwards from the wrist; how soft the curtains of skin as I part them, warm as the inside of a mouth, revealing the workings of the body within.

I see myself slip a flat-bladed knife beneath the *musculus coracobrachialis* and *biceps brachii* — for these notations are suddenly known to me — and raise them slightly from their accustomed bed against the bone of my upper arm. I do not want to fix my gaze anywhere but on this work, which terrifies me yet is familiar, and comforting in its familiarity.

I am opened up, and am possessed of a knowledge that sparkles through me. My heart soars: I *know* this. For what are men but hills, swamps, sinkholes, deep abysses, flat plains? I understand now. This is no gazetteer of any country; it is the terrain of man's interior

39

geography, and I am a geographer of that body for I know the mountains and rivers, the highways and cities. I gaze at my flesh, opened up so beautifully. It prickles, quickens. I behold the *mappa mundi*. All I need to know is here.

I feel wetness on my cheeks, hear a cough and the softness flies away, as though I have been roughly shaken from sleep. My heart beats fast, and I am filled with a fear that I shall find everyone looking at me, somehow knowing my strange imaginings, but the sound is one of the sweepers. I examine my arm: it is untouched. My body is quiet again.

I shake my head and empty it of what I have just witnessed. I do not know whence it came. I have been affected by the terrified beast earlier, that is all. I am a plain man and do not know such long words, nor such an overwhelming philosophy. It is nothing. I press my knowledge into a deep well.

★ ★ ★

At mid-morning my companions lay down their tools and go out for a mug of tea and piece of bread.

'I shall stay,' I say, for I desire a peaceful spot in which to gather up my ragged thoughts.

'Come now, Abel. You've earned a breather.' Alfred grins.

'You more than any of us bastards,' adds William, and they laugh.

'One-Blow Abel, that's you!'

I make my mouth smile also.

'There is but one carcase needs finishing off,' I say, lightening my voice to make it careless.

Alfred dawdles.

'I shall stay also. We shall follow presently.'

He grins at me as they depart.

'Just the two of us, eh? Best company a man could have.'

I set myself back to work, striking the carcase before me; but my hand trembles and I only split it halfway. I try again and strike untrue, jarring the bone so hard my shoulder numbs, and I drop the axe. The steel rings against stone, and Alfred calls out.

'Abel?'

'Yes,' I reply.

'What is it?'

'I have dropped my blade.'

'Dropped it?' His voice sounds with shock, and he pushes through the curtain of cadavers to my side. 'What ails you, Abel?'

His eyes search mine.

I shrug. 'It is nothing.'

'Well, then,' he says. 'Very well.'

He coughs, busying himself in picking up my blade and placing it into my hand.

'See,' I say. 'I am steady again.'

I make another stroke to prove my words, but it is a poor effort, shearing away and striking my forearm, and I am sliced to the bone. For an instant, all is peaceful as we stare at my arm, the dark crimson of muscle within. He speaks first.

'Christ, your arm.'

'Yes,' I say.

It is true. It is my arm. He, like me, can see the

41

sick whiteness showing at the heart of the slit. I should be afraid, but I am not; I feel no panic as I watch the wound fill with sluggish blood. I wait for it to commence pumping, in the way that kine do when I cut their throats, but it does not. The liquid rises partway to the brim and then pauses, small bubbles winking on the surface. As I watch, I am aware of another sensation: my soul begins to beat sluggish wings, unfolding them after a long sleep. My body tingles, stirs.

'Christ,' says Alfred. 'Dear, sweet Christ.'

He sits upon the floor, not caring about the stickiness and filth.

'Sit down, man,' he croaks.

'Yes,' I say, lowering myself to sit next to him. He is trembling.

'You are dying. You will die. What am I to do?' he stutters. 'You will bleed to death. You are slain. What can we do?' His hands patter all over his apron, wringing the corners. 'I must get help,' he says, but does not move.

'Yes,' I agree, and do not move either, for my eyes will not leave the sight of my inner workings revealed in this impossible fashion.

I am surprised, but not in that way of a new thing, a never-before-seen thing. It is the stillness of curiosity. I ache to dip my thumb into the dish of the wound to see if I am warm or cool; indeed, I lift my hand to do so, and only hesitate because Alfred is shaking violently, small sobs coming from deep within his chest.

'I must go. I must go and find a doctor,' he says, over and over, not stirring. 'I should not have spoken to you. I distracted you. This is my fault.'

42

I want to say, *It is not*, but I am lost in contemplation of this phenomenon.

'I am not bleeding,' I muse, and find I have spoken aloud.

Alfred is sitting quite still. 'Dear Christ,' he breathes. 'You are not.'

It is the truth. The injury is full of blood, but is not spilling over.

'I wonder why,' I say, for it holds me in a fascination.

I am a slaughter-man: I know well the fountaining of heart's-blood when an artery is severed.

'Sweet Jesus,' repeats Alfred. 'Look.'

I look. The blood is sinking, and as it subsides the edges of the wound begin to close together very slowly, but fast enough that it is possible to observe the motion. I am held in the grip of a terrific stillness, so entrancing is the sight of my body re-sealing itself. After minutes I forget to count all that can be seen is a red seam along my forearm. I flex my fingers, and they move: I can bend easily at the elbow. Nothing is damaged. Alfred gets to his feet, staggering backwards.

'You . . . ' he says, his eyes wild. 'When a man is cut, he should stay open. You close up. It is not right. You should be dead.'

His gaze darts up and down and from side to side; everywhere but at me.

'I am not,' I say simply.

His breathing is rough. 'I do not — ' he begins, and stops. 'I do not know you.'

He walks away. I inspect my miraculous arm, twisting it about and watching the line where I cut myself grow smooth and pink. After a while I pick up my axe and continue with my labours. I am determined to concentrate, for I do not wish to slip into another bout of this dangerous half-sleep. The others come back in; Alfred also, but he says nothing, and will not look at me.

I set my teeth and apply myself to my labour. *I am a slaughterman*, I say to myself. I cut open the bodies of beasts. They stay open. I was cut, and I closed up. I did not bleed. I shake the troubling thoughts away. I must have been mistaken: I cannot have cut myself so deeply. These things are not possible.

★ ★ ★

The remainder of the day is simpler. Each beast waits patiently in line, and the greatest noise we hear is the sigh of each giving up its spirit gladly. At the end of the day, I walk out of the gate to find Alfred waiting.

'Let's be walking home, then,' he says grudgingly.

He keeps half a pace ahead of me, and looks back every now and then, as though expecting something, eyes sliding to my forearm. I wince with the knowledge of my body and how it healed; and how he witnessed it happening.

'Alfred?'

'What?' he growls.

'You are my friend,' I mumble.

'Yes, yes,' he mutters. 'So you keep saying. Give it a rest.'

He thrusts his eyes ahead, walking faster so that I have to quicken my step to keep up with him. I chew the inside of my mouth until I taste iron. I hold out the package I have been given as my day's perk: I bear the prize of an entire head, brains and all, *for the way I turned things round,* the gaffer said.

'I like brains,' I say. 'Brains are tasty.'

He breathes out, slowing down so that I do not have to rush so.

'They are,' he agrees, and we fall back into step.

The evening is chilly: he is wrapped up in his coat like a boatman, breath standing before him, humming some tune I do not recognise. I try not to interrupt him. It is difficult. At last I speak.

'About today — ' I start.

'It is of no consequence,' he snaps, picking up the pace again.

'But it was — '

'It was nothing!' he cries. 'It was a difficult day. That bullock! God, how it wouldn't die! Enough to make any man see things.'

'But, Alfred, at the slaughter-house — '

'I do not want to talk about it. In fact, I remember nothing.'

'Alfred — '

'I said, I do not want to talk about it. Get a move on,' he grunts. 'It is time to get some food inside us.'

'Oh.'

My mouth fills with water.

'That's the job. Think of that. Nothing else.'

'Yes. You are right.'

He breathes out heavily, clouding the air around his head.

'Of course I am. No more rambling. I'm freezing. Let's get back and get this lot cooked. Of a sudden I have a powerful hunger upon me. Think how good it'll taste. Any meat you've had a hand in is a clean and cheerful dish.'

He slaps my shoulder. I know that the events of today have brought me close to grasping something, but it is already beginning to slip away. If he would talk to me, maybe I could fix my understanding. But he will not.

We walk in silence to our lodging house, a narrow squeeze of a building caught between the muscular shoulders of the tenements to each side. Ours is little different, except the bricks are perhaps grimier, the steps to our cellar a little more slippery with spilt beer and bacon fat, the straw in our palliasses a little older. But there are just as many folk squeezed into the upper floors — three families to a room as I hear it. Their babies squall as lustily; their men and women argue just as cantankerously. It is our crowded ark, one of an armada of vessels crammed thick with humanity. I have no desire to move from my cellar, where everything is cosy and peaceful by comparison.

A woman from one of the upstairs rooms cooks the meat, and there is plenty to share. All the cellar-men fill up the kitchen, joining in the feast of my good fortune. One man brings beer, another, bread; for this is our way of a night. We eat until Alfred's bad humour is quite taken away, and we are friendly once again. When we have finished, we return to the cellar and Alfred finds our pallets as sure as a seagull finds its nest from the hundreds on a cliff. I stretch out, cradled in the comfort of my companions patting their stomachs, smacking their lips and wiping gravy off their chins.

Alfred lolls on his elbow, picking at his buckled teeth with a straw. His rough sandy hair stands up in surprised tufts. He shifts his thin hips, cracks out a fart and laughs at the sound. His mouth is soft, for all his endeavours to hide it beneath a broad moustache.

'You know what, Abel?' he muses. 'When we strike it rich, we'll be out of here. Get a nicer room.'

'Why would we want that? There are so many friends here.'

He scowls. 'So I'm just one of many, am I?'

'Not at all, Alfred. You are my dearest friend.'

'Ah, get away with you.'

He is pleased, and I do not know why he demurs. It is true: I would not find my way through each day without his guidance. The thought is alarming, so I push it away. He clears his throat.

'Time to reckon up, Abel.' He rubs his palms together in pleasure. 'Our little ritual.'

And I remember: every night before we turn in, I count out our wages.

'This is for lodging,' I say. 'This for breakfast. And midday food. This for drink. And this left over.'

'More drink?' says Alfred.

'Hmm. No. I need better boots.'

'That will not buy you boots.'

'Then I shall save each day until I have

enough.' I hand the money to him. 'Will you keep it safe for me? I lose things, you know. I will forget where I have put it.'

Alfred laughs. 'You'd forget your head!'

'Yes, you're a wooden-head, and no mistake!' calls a man further down the row of sacks.

'Old dozy!' another man takes up the cry.

'It is true,' I say, for so it is.

'Come on, lads,' mutters Alfred.

'Oh, we like him, Alfred; even if he is tuppence missing.'

'You know there's no harm in it.'

One of them punches my upper arm. 'You're our lucky charm.'

'Not one of us has got hurt since you joined us.'

'So we're not going to chase you off, eh?'

'Not our Abel.'

'You're a bit of a miracle, as I hear it.'

'Fished you out of the mud, they did.'

'You were mostly mud yourself.'

'You should of been a goner. By all accounts.'

'No-one as goes in the river comes out. Save you.'

'Got a bit of luck you'd like to rub off on me?'

'Come on, Abel, how about a good rub-down!'

They roar with laughter and I decide it is best to join in. I ache for them to say more. To paint in the blank picture of my forgetting.

'You were in the papers and everything. Come on, Alf, show us.'

Alfred unbuttons the neck of his shirt to a scatter of playful whistles and draws out a much-folded sheet of newspaper. He lays it across his

48

knee, smoothing out the folds carefully.

'There you are,' says one, leaning over Alfred's shoulder and jabbing at the page.

'Watch it, Pete. You'll tear a bloody hole in it.'

'Look, Abel. That's you, that is.'

I squint at the small engraving: a man's head; nose prominent, eyes dark and deep-set, a shadow of hair on the chin. Below, a cluster of uniformed men around a prone figure. They look very pleased with themselves. *Mysterious Gentleman Rescued*, reads the headline. *Startling Discovery, of Particular Interest.*

'You can read it?'

I realise I have been speaking out loud.

'Didn't know you were educated.'

'Neither did I,' I say.

They laugh, and are easy with me again.

'You can see why they thought you were that Italian.'

'Go on, say something wop. You know you can.'

I do not have to think: the words fly easily to my tongue. '*Piacere di conoscerla.*'

'He's a living marvel!'

'Yes, but not that posh one, as went missing.'

'They found him with his throat cut.'

'And his trousers down!'

'So you're common as muck, like the rest of us.'

'Better off with us lot, eh, Abel?'

'I am,' I agree, and it pleases them greatly.

'Why did you jump?' says one, more thoughtfully.

'I do not remember,' I say. 'Maybe I fell in.'

'Lot of drunks fall in. No offence.'

'I am not offended.'

'You don't seem like a drunk.'

'Well, you weren't in the pudding club. That's why the ladies tend to take a late swim.'

They chuckle again, and after a while Alfred shoos them away.

'Don't chase them off.'

'Only trying to help out a pal.' He sulks. 'Give you a bit of peace.'

'I know. But I like to hear them talk. Truly, I don't remember.'

'Remember what?'

'Any of it. Falling in the river. Being pulled out. Anything before this cellar.'

'Now you're pulling my leg.'

'Alfred, I am not.'

'Abel, I know you're a wooden-head at the best of times . . . ' He stops. 'You *mean* it?'

'I want to remember. I can't. I look into myself and find nothing. Each morning I wake up . . . '

He looks worried. I decide to stop. The look changes to thoughtful, and then he smiles.

'It'll come back,' he declares, with a certainty I do not share. 'Big shock, that's what it is. Thing like that'd scare any man out of his wits. Make him imagine all kinds of nonsense.'

'You are sure?'

'Course I am. Wouldn't lie to you, would I?'

'No. You are my friend.'

'You keep me straight, Abel, you do.' He smiles, and grasps my shoulder.

'Right, listen up!' bawls one of the cellar-men. All heads turn. 'I am chief bully for the evening, and I have a treat for us all.'

50

He flourishes his hand towards a woman at elbow. There are a few whistles and rumbles of approval.

'Some of you know her, some of you don't. Not a tooth in her head. Eh, May?'

The woman grins, demonstrating the truth of his statement.

'So, steady up, lads, finish your idle chatter,' he says. 'A gobble for sixpence; a helping hand for three.'

They gather into a knot and lay out their coins. She seems unconcerned by the number of acts they are negotiating, eyes brightening only when the take is firmly stowed in her bodice. She leads the first into the corner. The rest turn their backs and share a pipe, acting as though they cannot hear his shallowing gasps.

'You've got a bit left over, haven't you, Abel?' says Alfred casually.

'I have,' I say.

He waves towards the female, who is already taking her next customer in hand. I consider her fingers working at my body in a similar fashion.

'It's there for the taking.'

'No,' I decide.

He smiles. 'Me neither.'

Although I do not wish to participate, I find it difficult to take my attention from the hunched bodies in the darkness. One of the men, satisfied now and lounging on his mattress, notices the direction of my gaze.

'Come on, cold-fish,' he shouts. 'You can have one on me if you like.' He tosses a few coins in the air. 'It'll make a man of you.'

He laughs, not unpleasantly, and those men who are not distracted by the woman turn to regard me.

'You have *got* one, haven't you?'

'Maybe it's a tiddler,' chaffs one, waggling his little finger.

'She doesn't mind small fry, do you, May?'

The woman hoots, washing down her most recent bout with a mouthful of beer and scratching at her skirts.

'Maybe it's as lifeless as he is. That soaking in the river has made it as much good as a herring.'

'The river'll do that to a man. Turn his every part to mud.'

'Don't plague him so,' says Alfred, and their eyes turn from me to him. He is examining the laces of his boots as though they are fascinating objects worthy of deep study.

'Only our bit of fun, Alf.'

'He doesn't mind, do you, mate?'

'No,' I say truthfully.

One of them thumps me on the back.

'See? We're only jesting.'

'You're all right, Abel, even if you can't get it up. Anytime you change your mind, though, first one's on us. Right, lads?'

They murmur assent, raising their smokes and cups in a toast. Then, finished with their companionable teasing, they settle to the more stimulating activities of the evening. After some time, the woman completes her labours and departs.

It occurs to me that I have heard taunts like theirs before, and I scrabble in my head for when it might have been. Last night? Last year? The harder I search, the more elusive the answer. I close my eyes, and it comes to me: I stand encircled, hands bound. My mind stirs unpleasantly and I shake my head. Perhaps I do not want to remember, after all. But now I have called them up, they will not leave me.

Dead fish.

Dead man.

Corpse-kisser.

I have heard every name before and they do not sting. My mouth fills with bile. I blink, and am back in the cellar. Alfred is peering at me closely.

'You all right, Abel? You look like you've seen a ghost.'

'I am well,' I lie.

'They don't mean anything by it,' he says, and pats my knee.

'I know.'

'Don't pay them any mind.'

'I shall not.'

'Some men are so,' he reassures me.

'Yes.'

He is sitting so close his thigh is pressed against mine.

'Alfred,' I say quietly.

'Yes, Abel?' he breathes.

'Please let me speak to you.'

'Is it about today?' he grumbles.

'Yes.'

'I am tired, Abel. I do not wish to talk any longer.'

'Please?'

'Go to sleep, Abel.'

53

He turns, curving his back away from me. The cellar quietens into sleep.

* * *

I am left alone, now that there are no distractions. I roll up my sleeve, uncovering my left arm. It is the same shape and colour as it was this morning, the hair as dark, and sprouting a thick trail from elbow to wrist in the same fashion. It matches the right arm perfectly, except for the scar: now a pale silver trail.

I struggle to believe that it is a part of my body; yet when I cut into it, it was as familiar as looking into a dish of potatoes. I try to make sense of this, and tell myself it is because I spend my days and nights cutting open beasts, and am used to the sight of muscle, bone, yellow fat, grey slippery organs. I am not convinced. It is not the same. My flesh is quick; the beasts are dead.

How could my body accomplish such a feat of healing? I puzzle over this riddle but find no answer. Only a creeping fear: no true, honest man heals like this. Therefore, I am a monster.

My mind strains to escape from this terrible conclusion, for how can I live with such knowledge, with myself? I desire an answer, and for that answer to be that I am mistaken. My most sincere wish is to be man and not miracle. There is of course only one way to prove that I am a simple fellow who bleeds and heals in the slow, painful way of ordinary folk. I must cut myself again, and prove it wrong.

With a stolen candle stub in my pocket, I take

myself to the yard privy. Alfred does not wake to ask me what I am about. I get out my pocket-knife. My fist closes about the handle, the blade hovers; I press the point into my forearm, where the last trace of the scar remains. I will cut myself in the same spot, and it will bleed, and I will have to bind it up. Yes. I will prove it was nothing more than a freakish mistake.

I draw the blade along my arm in a straight line, and my skin separates as it should. I close my eyes in relief, but when I open them once more I see the gash beginning to draw shut. It is most curious. I run the blade along the new join and tease it open. My body obeys, and parts its lips, only to begin closing once again the moment I lift the knife away.

A shallow cut proves nothing. I dig a little deeper. There is pain now, but one that rouses me to a strange wakefulness. As a man swimming underwater breaks the surface and feels breath fly back into his body, so do I fly into myself. My body sparks into liveliness, including that masculine part of me, which also raises its sleepy head. I grind my teeth: how can I possibly feel arousal with the cutting open of my arm? It is shameful. I would rather be the piece of dead meat that everyone calls me than this degraded creature.

I examine the wound, excitement mixing with horror. It gapes, and I can see through to the dark red within. I have seen enough meat cut open to know there should be blood, and now. Tentatively, I push the knife back in, draw it out once more. This time I should leak, but I do not.

I turn my arm around in the small light, wondering at this mystery. The candle shows me what I do not wish to be real: other than a moist smearing on the metal itself, all is dry.

I stare at my disobedient arm, and once more the ragged edges of skin begin their drawing together. I push my finger into the hole to stop my body re-forming itself, but the flesh closes, pushing me out with a firm pressure, like the tongue of a cow. It takes a little while longer, but there is no halting the knitting-up of the slit.

I shake my head and tell myself that this is not a proper test. Perhaps only my left arm is possessed of these strange qualities. I should cut a different part of my body — but not my other arm, for that is too similar. I roll up the leg of my trousers to the knee, select a spot on the calf and push in the point of the blade.

A drop of blood trickles down, catching in the mat of hair. My heart leaps with joy; *I am bleeding*. But no more follows and already the cut is barely to be seen. I jab at a different spot and feel a fresh surge of hope when a fat red bead falls as far as my ankle. A second drop spills from the wound, followed by a third. Breath gathers tightly in my throat. I am a normal man: I bleed.

Then the flow thickens, and stops. The wound blinks its eye, and closes. This is not possible. I must be normal; I *have* to be. There must be some place on my body that does not heal. But where? I drag my trouser-leg up as far as it will go and poke the blade into the pale ochre skin of my thigh. There is barely a smear of scarlet for my trouble. I try again; healing occurs straight away.

Maybe I need to go faster, to beat my body at its game of healing. But however quickly I jab the point of the knife, each cut starts to close up before I have time to make the next; the quicker I stab myself the quicker the doors of my flesh slam shut, matching my frenzy for hurt with a frenzy for healing. My breath scales a ladder of panting gasps as I climb closer and closer to myself. I am — I am — I am not Abel. Rather, I am not merely Abel. I am broad as the desert, tall as the sky, deep as the ocean. I know the answer to all my questions. It is all so clear, so simple. I am —

So close. I soar towards the sun of understanding. As my body heals, heat sears my wings and I plummet into familiar darkness. There is no attainment to be found: my hand wearies, and I cease my battle. The knife is barely marked with moisture; the skin of my legs and arms flecked with creamy marks that fade as I watch. A few moments more and they are gone. My ribs heave up and down, and I realise I am weeping. The candle gutters and goes out.

I do not understand what manner of man can skewer himself with a knife and shed not one drop of blood, and have his body remake itself. I look like a man. I eat, drink, shit, sleep, lift and carry, the same as every one of my fellows. But I am unlike them. I do not know who I am, or what I am.

I hide a great secret, one that marks me as grotesque. Am I man or animal? I can no longer call myself either: I do not have the comfort of calling myself a beast, for a beast can be butchered for the use of mankind, and I cannot serve any such purpose. Nor can I say that I am a man, for no man can do what I have done: cut myself and heal, against nature. It is terrifying. It raises my hopes towards understanding only to dash them most cruelly. It thrills and humiliates me. What kind of creature am I? I have no answer.

★ ★ ★

I stumble back to the cellar, crawl back to my mattress. Alfred is humped beneath his jacket. I want to shake him awake, and smile, and call him slug-a-bed, and thereby assure myself of my humanity. But it is the middle of the night. I close up the knife and put it under my blanket. There is nothing left to do but attempt to sleep.

My eyes bore into the darkness. I see my work: carcases swaying from the ceiling, each one cleanly cut, ready for the butcher's slab; I know they are all my doing. I am proud and slap the nearest, feeling the cool clean flesh against my palm. I know this: it is what I do. I name each part: the shank, the loin, the flank, the rib, the wing, the blade, the clod, the words sinking into some deep, comforting place. I am a slaughter-man. It is all I am. A plain and simple man.

Let sleep come, I beg the night. *The soft delight in which I take such pleasure. Where there is neither fear nor worry.* It does not hear my prayer. The questions torment me. Why do I not bleed? How can I heal like this? I feel the granite ice of my mind begin to crack with such a groaning that it rends me head to heel. A cleft appears and light spears through the chink, casting fearsome shadows. I want to force myself shut, return to that safe vacancy where all is quiet. Yet I am also ravenous. I hunger to know what is in that great light, what I might discover when I shine the lamp of understanding upon myself.

I struggle with the need to know and the need to run. I blunder into nothingness: a dark room, darker than the inside of closed eyes, where I hold out my hands and pat the black air, afraid of stumbling into walls, or ditches, or worse. A day ago, I was a wiped plate. I was empty, clean, untouched. Now, I stand in the slaughter-house and see my body cut open, peeled by my own hand and yet healing. I do not want this body. I am too frightened to close my eyes again, for fear of what I might find there.

★   ★   ★

The next morning, Alfred does not need to rouse me, for I am already awake.

'Let's get to work,' he grunts, and it is all the greeting I have from him.

I want his smile, the warmth of his eyes when I call him friend, the easy way he guides me into the day. We walk in silence, the air freezing between us. I try to think of a topic of conversation that does not involve cutting. I fail, so great is my need to be unburdened.

59

'Yesterday. It was — strange,' I try.

'Indeed? I don't recall,' he snarls and hides his face behind his collar.

'But, Alfred — '

'Oh, can I have no peace? There's nothing to talk about, Abel. Nothing.'

I grasp his shoulder and swing him about. All I want to do is talk to him. I do not understand why he will not listen.

'Abel, get your hands off me. You're really pushing your luck.'

'Alfred, I am . . . '

My voice quavers, and his features soften. He takes my arm and pulls me to the wall, glancing up and down the street.

'All right, all right; if you are truly that upset. Let me help you, then. Tell me.'

'In truth? You want to hear?'

He sighs. 'Yes, I do.'

'Yesterday, when I cut myself . . . ' I gasp. 'You saw it. I healed.' I chew on the words, straining to free themselves from my mouth.

'Very well. I saw it. But it wasn't so deep. Perhaps.'

'I did it again,' I breathe.

'Oh, come now. No you didn't,' he says, forcing a brightness I do not share. It does not ease my confusion.

'Last night. While you slept.'

'You're mistaken. Maybe you had a nightmare. Don't carry on so.'

'Alfred — '

'This is too strange for me, Abel. You're a man like any other.'

'What if I am not?'

'You are. Think it and you can make it so. Come now, give me a smile and leave it be.'

'But don't you ever have strange thoughts about your body?'

'Thoughts?' He looks startled, and draws closer. 'I don't know what you mean.'

'But, Alfred — '

'But Alfred, but Alfred,' he sneers, in a mincing mimic of my voice. 'Let's get breakfast and drop this.'

'I am not hungry.'

'Christ, I thought I was in a bad mood,' he snaps, and sticks his hands into his pockets. 'But you take the bloody biscuit.'

We walk on in silence. I wish I could take back my words.

'Alfred. Please do not be angry with me.'

'Shut up, Abel. You're tiring me out and we haven't even started work yet.'

★　★　★

It is a long walk to the slaughter-house. From the first beast brought in, I find myself looking over my shoulder, starting at every twitch of thought, wary of where my mind might lead me. However, no fearsome pictures come to plague me. I would like to be sure it is the force of my will that keeps me free, but I cannot be sure.

I lift my arm, let it fall, and another carcase splits down the middle, the meat pale in the weak light. I push it aside and they bring in the next. It is easy work, the easiest I know. For all that I try to lose myself in the raising and falling of the cleaver, the line of uncountable carcases waiting to be split by my firm and unerring blow, my mind will not let off its needling.

I am steeled to drop my blade and run at the first intimation of strangeness; I keep my sleeve buttoned at the cuff. I do not want to be catching sight of my healed arm all the time for it continues to fill me with a sick feeling.

I do not want to drowse, do not want to be taken to any place but here, do not want to see the things I have seen. I press my attention to the slaughter-work with a great passion, and in under an hour every hook is hanging with the carcases of the beasts I have killed. My companions are delighted with the speed of the work, and go outside to smoke a pipe. For all their friendliness, I do not wish for company, so I busy myself cleaning all of the cleavers.

I am confused. I should be dead. Every beast I have ever slaughtered tells me the plain truth of it. When a man is cut, he should stay cut. But I heal; and even more disquietingly, I do not even bleed. When a man is drowned, he is drowned. But not me: they tell me I was as good as a drowned man when they pulled me out of the river. I am no better than any other man.

I have heard over and over how I am a miracle: spewed up on to the banks of the Thames. How no man comes out alive after supping on its liquor, but I stood up from my bed after three days, was working in less than two weeks. I do not disbelieve the tale; but it could have happened to a different man. I cannot remember

62

my tumble into the river, nor anything before: nothing of home, father, mother.

Alfred tells me it will return to me in time. But what if I am concealing some terrible secret from myself? I fear what I might have forgotten. Is that what I was so close to discovering when I cut myself last night? Am I running from some ghastly crime? Am I evil? Maybe I am a thief, a footpad, a murderer and do not know it. I shake these wonderings from my head: I do not want to fall into distraction and cut myself again.

Why not? breathes the voice in my head, quite calm and reasonable. *You will heal. You have seen it.*

I look at myself in the bright edge of the steel blade. I see brown eyes edged with dark lashes, a beaked nose, a broad mouth. Not the face of a wolf, or a bear. A man.

This is what you are, says the voice. *However different or strange, you are a man.*

I am not convinced. I shake the voice away, for all its kindness, and examine the sides of beef, hoping the sight of their symmetry might calm me. As I watch, the nearest carcase starts to sway in a current of air I cannot feel, gently back and forth.

The meat grows darker, oozing with moisture. The ribs swell out, only to be sucked in. It is breathing; air whistling through the severed windpipe, the stump of its neck twisting from side to side, searching for its missing head. Then the forelegs start to twitch, straining to touch the floor; the hind legs kick out to free themselves from the meat-hook.

Then they all begin: every dangling carcase dancing, thrashing back and forth on the hooks; fighting to free themselves, to find their scattered parts and knit themselves back together.

I hack at the monster that began this vile waltz; but with each slash it grows ever more frantic, as it fights to be free. I do not know what to do — there is no throat to cut nor heart to slice out, these things having been done already — yet I strike and strike again at the dead thing for there is nothing else for me to do, but it will not lie still, and I weep with the ghastly hopelessness of it. A hand grips my shoulder and the axe falls from my hand.

'You, man!' shouts a voice, and I turn to see the face of my pay-master. 'What are you doing?' he bellows.

I open and close my mouth.

He presses his face close to mine. 'I said, what in damnation are you doing?'

My mouth is empty.

'Look!' he bawls, punching me so hard I stagger backwards. 'Look, you bastard!' he shouts again, and I do look: at shredded pieces of flesh and bone on the floor, the remains of the carcase hanging before me. All is still.

'Waste my fucking meat, would you? You fucking lunatic. Get out of here and don't come back.'

I stare at the floor, at the quiet bones.

'I said, sod off.'

He thumps me again. I slip on a piece of fat and barely save myself from falling. He picks up my blade, brandishes it.

'Now. Get out. Unless you want to replace the carcase you've just ruined. I always knew you were trouble.'

I run. On the street I drag off my apron and let it fall into the gutter. I stare at it a long time. Alfred finds me there when he leaves work, for I have forgotten the way back to our lodgings. We walk in silence. When we arrive, I do not know what to do except lie down.

I barely have time to close my eyes before the silt of my mind stirs and a picture floats up, urgent as a stream of bubbles from the bottom of a pond. I am scrambling over coiled rope, thick as a man's thigh, headlong to the stern of a boat, its deck treacherous with oil and lurching from side to side in mountainous seas. I'm almost thrown off my feet as the hulk heels sharply.

I grip the iron railing and peer into the dashing spume of the sea, far below. *Jump*, commands the voice of the waters. *My arms await you.* I haul myself up the rungs to sway on the topmost bar.

'Wait for me: I am coming!' I yelp into the filthy spray.

The wind smacks the words back into my mouth.

Hurry, I will not wait.

Suddenly there are other voices: men approaching, screaming. I know the words mean *Stop, come down, madman.* I shall not be turned aside. This is not madness. This is escape. If falling onto land cannot kill me, then perhaps the death granted by water might.

I jump, and am sucked down into a darkness

65

cut into small flickering pieces; my jaw falls open at the hinge, mouth taking in a slow river of silt, filling my lungs with cold hard fists. Weed slops around my tongue like a woman's hair; the water is a stone in my lungs but there is no pain, no fire.

I move a piece of wood and it is my arm; I beat it against my face until the bridge of my nose swings towards my left eye. My arms do not break the surface; they stir the rusty mud and hide the broken window of the light, burrowing me deeper and deeper into the long night of the ocean.

The mouths of fish flay me to the bone; as fast as they nibble the fruit of my flesh, it restores itself. They return to feed on me, over and over. I beg the sea to grind me into mulch, for I ache to lie still for ever. *I shall not come out*, I wail. But it pushes me away. Throws me out, onto earth. I surface from tea-brown water, flesh boggy from its long stewing, gasping for my first breath as the new air slaps life into my lungs. *But I want to die*, cries the voice of my soul.

The heavy embrace of the river resolves into the hands of children searching through my pockets, fingers boring holes into my shoulders as they strip me. My ears unlock to their complaints.

Not much here.

Not so much as a bloody wipe.

Waste of bloody time.

He's a dead one.

I want to be a dead one for them. Blood settles in a slow night-fall into the pouches of my cheeks. The muscles of my face remember; begin to knit and heal and make me whole again, and they are never tired. I am already forgetting that I have done this. My body remembers, and keeps it secret. I go forward into darkness, into the fear. To find that light I saw and lost.

EVE

London, March–April 1857

Mama and I thought the knock at the door was the man come for the collars I had sewn; but a stranger's voice gusted down the passageway to my customary sheltering place in the crook of the door, out of sight of the street.

'My dear madam, forgive this intrusion,' said the voice.

I could sense Mama's eyes creasing at the corners, the marbles of her thoughts clacking together. *Who is he? Do I owe him money?* The air rippled as he raised his hat; the stitching in his coat creaked as he bowed politely. I heard him say, 'Is your sister at home?' And Mama's surprised, 'Sister? I have no sister,' and only then halting, realising it was flattery.

She brought him in, and he bloomed to the very edges of our meagre walls. He was of middling height, but held himself taller; of a middling girth, but bulged himself fatter. He pigeoned out his chin, which was shaved so close I wondered if he hated his own beard and moustaches. He looked at the small table and the sewing laid upon it; the truckle-bed huddled in the corner

— everywhere but at me.

Mama stared at his waistcoat, a gaudy affair of vermilion brocade before which I could have warmed my hands. He turned this way and that, the fabric gleaming, complimenting Mama on the tidy industry of the room, the delicate embroidery of the collars, and every sentence held an apology for having so intemperately disturbed the retirement of her afternoon. His hands peeped from the tight cuffs of his shirt, soft as a midwife's; there was a shine on the seat of his trousers, a stain of sweat creeping around his hat-brim.

Think of him peeled from his linen, his wool, his velvet, whispered Donkey-Skin.

I shushed her, and the noise made him turn, as though he noticed me for the first time. He bowed, very slowly.

'Dearest miss,' he breathed.

I dropped my eyes, tried to find a place to conceal my paws, and settled for behind my back.

'Do not be alarmed, dear miss,' he said. 'I mean neither you nor your mother any mischief.'

Don't be alarmed, sneered Donkey-Skin through her nose. I giggled: she was a very good mimic.

'Have some manners,' hissed Mama, and I was quiet.

'Do not scold her on my account,' he said. 'It is fitting for a young lady to be shy in the presence of a stranger. Therefore let me introduce myself, I entreat you.'

He cleared his throat, and puffed himself out some more.

'I am Josiah Arroner. Amateur Scientist.

69

Gentleman of Letters. Entrepreneur.'

Taxidermist? murmured Donkey-Skin. *Careful, girl, or he'll skin and stuff you before you know it.*

Mama was already bustling about him, offering him the sturdier of our little chairs, bleating excuses for the lack of tea, lack of sugar, lack of milk. He took out a sovereign from his pocket with the carelessness of finding a coat-button there and shone its little sun upon the dullness of our room.

'Ah, the labours of a caring mother. They are never done, are they, madam? Pray do send a boy to bring us tea, and milk, and sugar — plenty of sugar.' He smiled. 'And a penny for the lad himself.'

'Oh no, sir, I could not,' Mama lied.

'You are right. How unfeeling of me to expect you to work whilst I rest! No, it is not fitting that you should prepare tea for an unexpected caller. I observed a restaurant on the corner as I came this way. Pray, send the boy there instead, so he may fetch a can of good sweet tea ready-made, a plate of bread and butter and some slices of beef. I declare I am a little hungry and would not eat alone.'

Mama paused for precisely as long as was necessary to indicate her treasured respectability; then raced down the passage and bawled to the woman upstairs for her eldest to run an errand, now. I stared at my lap and counted the seconds before she returned and resumed fussing once more about our guest's comfort. I was the one hairy as a dog, but I believe she would have

70

rolled on her back and stuck her paws in the air if she had thought it might please him.

★ ★ ★

I watched him through my eyebrows, simpering at my mother, making little jokes at which she tittered. When the food arrived, Mama left the room to argue about the change and he occupied himself gazing at the tobacco walls, the empty grate, the unlit gas-bracket, the cracked picture of a cow up to its hooves in a puddle, once again avoiding the sight of me. I folded my hands, stroking the fur on my knuckles and wondering why my breathing seemed so excessively noisy this afternoon.

The boy followed Mama into the room, his right cheek glowing with the pinch of her fingers. Mama scurried like a girl-of-all-work, finding a plate here, a cloth for the table there, chasing the lad upstairs for a third chair, because our visitor refused to stay seated whilst one or other of us remained standing. At last the tea was poured, the beef slapped onto a little plate beside the bread, and all of it sitting between us, curling at the edges.

'Take some,' Mama urged me, 'and do not be so ungrateful.'

I took the largest slice of meat, rolled it into a cigar and placed it in my mouth where it collapsed deliciously on my tongue. The more I chewed, the more delectable it became: I could not remember when I had tasted anything so good. We dined in silence, Mama and I endeavouring to

71

eat as slowly as possible. The plate emptied. Mr Arroner cleared his throat once more.

'Dear ladies, I hope you will forgive such a rude invasion into the peaceful business of your lives.'

He sipped at his tea with feminine delicacy.

Donkey-Skin snorted: *Why does he not growl, and toss it down his throat? Why does he not drink it like a man?*

I ignored her. He turned to Mama.

'With your permission, I would present myself as a friend to you, madam. And may I blushingly say it, to your delightful and most remarkable daughter.'

Delightful? said Donkey-Skin, pretending to search the room. *Remarkable? Of whom does he speak? You? Ha!*

He put down his cup and pressed his hand to his breast. 'Ah. Dear madam, I can dissemble no longer. I am a simple man and your wits have found me out: I confess it is indeed your daughter with whom I wish to be more closely acquainted.'

Mama's tea-cup paused partway to her lips. 'My daughter?'

'I have heard of her. By reputation.' He coughed gently. 'I have also heard of certain cruelties visited upon her person. I declare this has moved me deeply. Ah! To hear of the callous spite of those who neither understand nor appreciate that which is truly gifted, truly different, truly extraordinary! I resolved that I would visit and offer myself as a kind soul possessed of fellow feeling. One who might dare to offer his hand humbly in friendship.'

Mama blinked at this vision. He scraped his chair to face me directly. I raised a lavish eyebrow. Moisture gleamed each side of his nose and upon the thick curtain of his lips.

'My dearest miss, I entreat you, do not dismiss me as incapacitated with impetuous foolishness. It will be clear to you that I am no longer a young man. However I do declare that it is most distracting to find myself in such an intimate setting with you.' He took a deep breath and bowed his head. 'I hope you might forgive such a passionate outburst.'

I picked up the last slice of bread and beef and began to devour it.

'Ah. I have said too much.'

I looked at him, in agreement for that moment. Mama kicked me under the table, and it wobbled.

Donkey-Skin laughed, and then grew quiet. *He's lying*, she whispered.

I know, I thought in return, but discovered that I was blushing. I swallowed my mouthful.

'Dearest miss, I can see by your bashfulness that it is true. I have spoken too hastily, and have offended your modest nature.'

I wondered if he thought he could read me through my fur.

Perhaps he is not lying, suggested Donkey-Skin.

Mama's hands trembled; she could not lift the tea-cup to her lips.

'What a fool I am!' he continued. 'Why should you trust me, when you do not know who I am? When I have not shown you my recommendations?'

He reached inside his coat and brought out a

73

folded paper with fine scrollwork at its head, declaring itself sent from the Royal Society of Philanthropic Science. Mama crabbed her eyes at the scramble of fancy letters, taking in the sealing wax and the quality of the ink.

'Read the whole, madam. The whole, I beg of you. I have nothing to conceal. I am a scientist, it is true; but alas, not wealthy. My studies are of the unrecognised kind. There is a fearful prejudice against men such as myself: men possessed of intelligence and skill, but lacking the requisite high birth. It is the greatest scourge and scandal of this society we live in.'

Mama nodded as though she understood what he was talking about.

'However, there are gentlemen who recognise the talents of a man who does not have Lord So-and-So as his father, nor Lady Blank as his mother. Upon them do I rely, and to them I turn for encouragement and honest employment.'

Mama chewed her lower lip. 'It is a fine document,' she pronounced, when enough time had passed that our guest might think she had read it.

I scanned it carefully; it was a fine piece of work, full of phrases praising his tact, extolling his intelligence, his application, his scholarly virtues.

'You appear before us a paragon,' I said, when I had read enough to get a taste of the whole.

Donkey-Skin read it over my shoulder. *Too princely*, she tsked. *He is lying after all.*

He rocked back, and I hoped the chair would not faint beneath his well-fed shoulders.

'So do men find me. I would not be so bold as

to heap such compliments upon myself.'

He bent forward, bringing his face very close to mine. The chair groaned.

'My dear miss, I desire most earnestly that you might trust me.'

He smelled of tea and beef and something else, some underlying spice I knew but could not name.

'In some small way I know what it is to face the hurts of the world. A world which turns aside that which it does not comprehend. I offer you the hand of comradeship, and a fine understanding of the world's wounds.'

He made one of his deep inhalations and my breath was sucked into his nostrils.

'I know what it is to gird on a sword and buckler to withstand the onslaughts of society. I know the daily battle — the loneliness of the fight!'

He leaned back then, and I steadied myself from tumbling into his wake. Could *he* be the prince Donkey-Skin told me about? She wasn't answering. I glanced at Mama, her tea growing cold in its cup, and saw the famished look written on her: hungry to be rid of me, to walk out of the house without the thought of me warming the shadow of her steps. She seethed with hope, and guilt, and fear; and though he saw less than half of it, I knew he saw enough to wet her, stick his thumb into her innards and spin her like a pot on a wheel.

'Dear ladies.' He stood, squeaking back his chair. 'I have taken up too much of your valuable time. I will leave you now.'

He stood before me, and I dropped my eyes to the floor. His boots gleamed. I thought of his elbow, in and out, in and out, pumping a shine into the leather. He lifted himself on to the balls of his feet, lowered himself, and then rose again. My neck ached from staring at the rug.

'Madam,' he coughed. 'You have a jewel here. A pearl of great price.'

I lifted my head at last, to snort a laugh into his face, but a fire had been lit in his eyes and it quenched all my sharpness. I had a sudden fancy he intended to swallow me up, then and there, thrusting his teeth into the pit of my stomach. I found myself quivering.

'I have stayed too long. I should not wish to tire you or your esteemed mother any longer with my tiresome chattering.'

Mama jumped up, begging him to stay, but he would go with the most earnest politeness. I stayed seated, and did not speak a word to hold him. Still he paused, holding my eyes with his.

'I beg your mother's permission to leave you a small gift. Perhaps you would look upon it kindly after I have gone?'

He did not place it into my hand directly, but laid it on the table.

'This token is for you,' he said. 'Open it later and think of the giver.'

Mama stood behind me and twisted the hair on the back of my neck so that I had to grind my teeth against the pain.

'Thank you, Mr Arroner, for your kind attention,' I squeezed out.

'Dear madam,' he said to Mama over the

crown of my head. 'I thank you for permitting me to visit you and your enchanting daughter today. Most devoutly I hope you might permit me to call upon you at a future date? If that does not inconvenience you overmuch?'

I felt the tremor of Mama's frantic nodding. He gripped the brim of his hat and tipped it to me, flapped the tails of his coat like a ringmaster. I looked down straightway.

'Dear ladies. I will now take my leave, and wish you a pleasant afternoon, and a more pleasant evening.'

His feet crossed the floor; the door opened, he stepped through it, and the door closed.

★　★　★

I hovered my hand in the empty space where he had stood only a few moments before and felt the air that had just now lapped his cheek.

Mama returned. 'Well, then?' she whispered.

'Well what, Mama?' I yawned.

'The gift. What has he left you?'

'I had almost forgot it,' I lied. 'I suppose I must see what it is.'

I stood and walked to the table very slowly, for all that Mama would not stop clucking for me to hurry. It was a kidskin pouch, glazed to a top-of-the-milk sheen, the breadth of my palm and containing something square and unforgiving: a piece of slate, perhaps. I lay my hand where his had been and took the pulse of whatever lay within, testing the beat of its tiny heart. I undid the string and ferreted my hand into the smooth

77

dark burrow, soft inside as it was outside.

Donkey-Skin was whispering: *Tight as a purse and you are the coin inside. Are you so ready to be spent?*

My palm dampened inside the tight grip of the bag. It could almost make me believe I was hairless. I felt him watching me, so close his breath warmed my ear. *Slip in your hand*, he said. *Discover what is within the suppleness of this little pouch. Think of me as you do it; for I am watching the expression in your remarkable face as you draw out the treasure I have given you.*

Blood crackled in my veins; my fingers closed around a hard object and I pulled out a looking-glass. It froze at the sight of my face and leapt away from me, clattering against the skirting board.

Mama shrank away. 'It is a vile thing!' she cried. 'What a cruel gift. Throw it away!'

I bent and picked it up. It had not suffered the smallest chip. I looked at it more carefully: it did not jeer *ugly, ugly, ugly*. Did not wink its broad silver eye and hiss, *Who are you to crack me from side to side? How dare you look into a glass? Leave mirror-gazing to pretty girls with plump pink cheeks.*

Instead, it shimmered with admiration at my hair: how it waterfalled down each side of my nose! See the curls twirling on each temple! It admired my beard: oh, the softness! Those honeyed lights shining like a twist of caramel sugar!

Who gave you that? asked Donkey-Skin, peering over my shoulder. She picked at a lump of mud in her hair.

I smiled. 'No one important.'

She laughed, and her teeth rattled in my ears. *The Cat-Faced Girl has got a beau! At last, at last, Beast has got a Beau. Let Heaven rejoice! Ma can be shot of you.*

I had to smile. She was my friend. 'I think it's time for you to go,' I said, not taking my eyes off the mirror.

When I was a child, I had Donkey-Skin for my friend, a thing sewn from raw-headed scraps of dreams and rag-tag stories, knitted out of all the words my mother could not say, from the grandmothers I never met, the fag-ends of fathers who never stayed long enough for me to know their names. Now I was a woman. It was time to put away childish things.

Me? Go? she hissed. *Now? Not likely. You need me more than ever.*

★ ★ ★

That night, as I lay in the bed beside Mama, I was glad that it was warm; it meant that she curled away on to the far side of the mattress, and I desired greatly to be alone. I stretched out on my back, listening to her mutter herself to sleep, about how hot I was to lie next to, why did I heat the bed so, it was impossible to sleep with such a hearthrug next to her, and over and over, *ungrateful child, thoughtless and uncaring, to forget all the years I have protected her from mirrors,* until the words drifted into deep breathing.

I allowed my thoughts to creep out and fill the room: thoughts so thrilling and wicked I was

79

sure they would wake her. I imagined Mr Arroner coming back into the room, standing at the foot of this very bed. He shucked off his clothing, piece by piece, and I watched him the while, my excitement growing. Then all at once he sprang: leapt on to me, pressing his face deep into my belly and biting me fiercely, teeth sharp as knives, but not fiercely enough to satisfy; not fiercely enough to tear my hide. I wanted him to rip me open, and my voice begged him, *Harder. Bite me, my love, harder. Harder.*

In the morning Mama sighed and held her aching places, as though the holding might make them sting the less. I feigned sleepiness, which was not difficult, because I had had so little in the night. She called me lazy.

'Do you wish the world to wait upon you?'

She was angry. I did not care. I was courted. I offered to rub her feet.

'I am not helpless yet,' she grumbled.

'I will have him,' I said to her and tried to make it sound like submission and not greed. 'If you will allow it.'

I tipped my head to one side, playing the shy maid at the thought of marriage, a ring on my finger, a handful of hurled rice. A wedding night.

'You'll leave me,' she said. 'Then what will I become?'

I had stopped listening. I dreamed of a priest with a swim of lace around his throat, four white horses pulling my carriage, hymns sung, bells rung, a fat cushion of orange-blossom in my arms; breakfast after, with beer for the men, tea for the ladies. I pictured myself swathed in a sumptuous gown of the latest organdie, primped with tulle so fine as to be almost invisible, a veil of tambour lace floating around my head.

Donkey-Skin leaned on her elbow, yawning at my fancies.

'Are you not excited?' I gasped.

Lace tears easily, she said, digging in her ears with a long fingernail. *And you can never get the stains out of organdie. I'd rather have a sturdy pair of boots and a five-pound note tucked inside them.*

'You don't have a breath of romance in the whole of you,' I sulked.

Good thing too, she said, drily.

'Won't you be happy for me?'

There was no answer.

'Glad to see the dirty back of you!' I shouted into the emptiness. I would not let her spoil my day.

★ ★ ★

Mama begged and borrowed plates and saucers from every room in the house, so that my wedding feast was served on a higgledy-piggledy mismatch of crockery and all of it chipped and cracked. I barely noticed. I believe Mama could have poured tea from a leather bucket and I would not have cared.

All morning she was a fury of bread-buttering, slicing it so thin you could have hung it at the window and seen through to the houses opposite. There were three vast pots of tea, a whole cup of sugar. She kept muttering 'Friday for

81

losses' until I had to tell her to keep her empty-headed superstitions to herself. I was gaining a husband.

I stood at the window, pulling on my gloves only to draw them off when my paws grew too hot, which was very quickly. I kissed the soft lilac leather, for surely he had touched it when he picked them out for my trousseau. There was no extravagant gauzy bridal gown, but he had bought me a pleasing and practical costume: a going-away dress in dark lavender, a pretty hat and new boots made for me alone. It was very kind of him.

I paced up and down so that I would not sit creases into my new skirt, screwing my head first to one side and then the other so that I could keep my eye on the street. It had to be the most long-drawn-out morning in the history of the world. Surely the moments had never ticked by so slowly.

'Mama, I think the priest is late.'

'Eve, sit down. You are making me dizzy with all this to-ing and fro-ing.'

'I cannot be still.'

'It is unladylike to bustle about, and in such a nice dress. You will become overheated.'

She could not bring herself to say the word 'sweaty', but it was true: my fur was clinging to the inside of my blouse.

'Mama, do not fuss.'

'Do you want to faint away? That'd be a fine business, if the priest asks you to say 'I do' and I have to fan you awake with a hymn sheet.'

At last the wedding party arrived, to a fanfare

82

of much rapping at the outer door. I fought to stand still while Mama went to greet them. Mr Arroner was first through the door, greeting my mother with loud declarations of apology for his lateness. He burst into our room and bowed deeply, heaping me with tender compliments and presenting me with a small posy of violets to match the dress. He was followed by a priest and two plainly dressed strangers who stared at me and my not-quite-yet husband back and forth until I thought their heads might grind their necks down to their shoulders.

There was no Order of Service, no hymn sheet, no hymns of any kind; only the briefest of prayers and I do not remember a word of them. The only words worth treasuring were the ones which dropped from his lips when he said he would have me as his wife.

'Do you take this woman?' said the minister, too hastily for my liking.

'Indeed I do.'

They were the sweetest sounds I had ever heard, so delightful I half expected doves to fly out of his hat. He could have stood before me in sack-cloth for that vow clothed him more royally than any king. Then the minister blinked at me.

'Do you take this man?' he said, unable to keep a curl of distaste from his lips.

'I do,' I said, boldly.

Holy eyes flickered between my husband and myself.

'Yes, she can speak for herself,' said my new man, and I squeezed his arm for the champion he was.

I went to throw my arms around his neck, but his eyebrows climbed so far up his forehead I thought they might drop off. Mama also shot me a look, and I tempered my behaviour. We would be alone soon enough: I could wait for marital embraces a little while longer. I dropped my head and made a courageous attempt to behave decorously, as befitting a bride. I clenched and unclenched my fingers around the spray of flowers so often that I quite strangled them.

My mother did not cry. We signed our names and my man gave a coin to the witnesses: they were quick to leave and I did not see them again. It was not a grand ceremony, but it was good enough. I had the greatest prize, a husband who had already taken up a shield in my defence against the world. I loosened the word 'girl' from my shoulders and dropped it at the side of the front door.

★　★　★

Mr Arroner took me then into my new home, *our* new home: a palace with high ceilings and five steps leading up from the pavement to the door and a pink-and-white maid who bobbed her head and called me 'mum'.

'You will want to prepare for bed, Mrs Arroner,' he said as soon as we were through the door. 'As shall I. I shall be in my dressing-room.'

'Yes, Mr Arroner,' I said, delighting in the words.

He was mine. I followed him up the stairs; he showed me into the bedroom and left me there.

My head swam with the notion that he had an entire room in which to dress and undress, for it was thrilling enough that there was a room set aside for sleeping. Of course, not only for sleeping: there were the other things husbands did with wives in their bedrooms.

I flushed beneath my fur and began to undo the buttons at my cuffs, but discovered those running down the back of my blouse were out of reach. Mama had fastened me into my clothes that morning, which seemed a very long while ago. I was not sure what to do next. I looked around the room: a small fireplace, a jug and basin on the chest of drawers, the window shutters closed tight, a cheval-glass leaning into the corner.

He did not return. I did not know what mysteries husbands engaged in to prepare themselves for their wedding nights, and the room into which he had retired was very quiet. I thought of how he had looked earlier that day, not yet my husband, and I not yet his wife: his polished hat, new stiff collar, bright waistcoat and gloves so fresh they were not yet rubbed from holding the head of his cane. I had tried diligently to be as nervous as a virgin should be, but I could not stop my eyes from wandering over his body, even when Mama pinched me.

Still he did not come. There was no clock ticking, but it was my opinion that enough time had passed for him to remove his clothing. Perhaps he was smoking a cigar; perhaps he thought me so timid that he wished to give me time to compose myself. But I was not composed: I was sitting with my cuffs open and no other preparations made. I tried once more to reach the buttons laddering down my back but failed. It was easier at home: my clothes were simpler and I had Mama to help me. I slapped away the ungrateful thought. I was wearing the beautiful clothes he had picked out with his own hand. They were just troublesome to get out of.

Then it came to me: perhaps he did not want me undressed at all. He wanted to do it himself. I was deeply stimulated at the thought of him standing behind me, unlooping each pearl button from the nape of my neck down to the dip where spine flares to hip, pressing his palms on to my unclothed shoulders, weaving his fingers into my hair and pulling me towards him for our first wedded embrace. My pelt prickled, imagining itself ruffled up under his hands. These imaginings were no longer sinful, for I was a married woman and such thoughts were permitted.

My stays were very tight. I hoped he might come soon, for I needed loosening and a tickle of sweat was stirring between my breasts. I wondered if he was shaving himself; I thought how grand it would be to say to him, *Now you are my husband, I wish you to grow a beard*. I itched for him to open the door.

My delicious dream returned, that he had chosen me because he was hairy too, just like Donkey-Skin said he would be, but he shaved and kept it secret. Now he had me, he would no longer need to do so for I would throw away his razor, tie up his wrists with his handkerchief and feed him soup as I waited for him to sprout the

86

bristles hidden in the gift-wrapping of his skin. Days would pass, and he would sigh, *Oh, untie me, do. Set me free, my love*, but not angrily, and each day with less conviction.

I imagined his hair set free from the confines of his clothing: wandering up and down his breast from navel to neck, spreading its paw-prints over his shoulders and down his back to the sweet damp crease of his buttocks. He would be my faun, my Pan, the Lord of my Woods, and I would be his maenad for he was the strange prince Donkey-Skin had told me to look out for. He must be.

The handle of the door turned; my heart leapt. I looked into my lap, I looked at the bedspread, at the ewer, the bowl, the wallpaper, the window-shutters. At last I looked at my husband. The dark rug between us seemed the width of a continent. He smiled.

'My dear wife!' he said. 'Dear little wife!'

He crossed the space in three strides. He was dressed in a smoking jacket which reached past his knees, his oiled-down hair catching the light from the candle. His chin was smooth.

'Dear little wife!' he said again. 'Or should I call you Mrs Arroner?'

'Wife is a very good word.'

'Is it not? A capital word! To me you are wife; to the world you are Mrs Josiah Arroner. What status! What gravitas!'

'Yes, my dear.'

I thought it a little overwrought, but tonight I could allow him any of his fancies.

'Come now, Mrs Arroner.'

He took my hand and patted it; I lifted my golden wrist to his chin and he pecked at it with dry lips.

'My name is Eve, dearest.'

'It is indeed. The sweetest of names to my heart from the day I met you.'

He leaned forward and pressed his mouth to the velvet of my forehead. A deep thrill swept from that spot down to my inmost parts until I was running over with richness, churning instantly from milk to cream.

'Oh, Josiah,' I breathed, and snatched at his coat, pulling him towards me.

The weight of his breath warmed the crook of my neck, perfumed with coffee and tobacco. I wrapped my arms around him and we rocked backwards and forwards. I rubbed myself against him, purring. Unsheathed my claws and dug them into his back, chewing on his neck.

He shoved me hard; my eyes sprang open to find him breathing in short bursts, his collar awry where I had torn it. He staggered to the mirror where he examined the spreading wine-stain of my mouth on his throat, and began to tie his cravat very high, to cover the dark spot. I watched the way his fingers slipped the silk over and about until he was satisfied with his handiwork, devouring his every gesture. However, I was confused, for I would be proud to have his mark on me — would parade our passion without shame. Then I understood: he did not want to share our secret. I giggled.

'Was I a little rough?' I simpered. 'You will forgive me?'

He turned, eyes wide. 'What are you staring at?' he wheezed.

'Just you, my dear Josiah.'

I tried to pull him towards me again in this newly-wed game we were playing, but he slipped out of my grasp.

'Dear wife,' he said.

'Yes?' I smirked, looking up at him through my eyelashes.

'Dear Mrs Arroner. You will be tired, my pet, after such an enervating day. I shall retire and allow you to rest and restore yourself. As any gentleman should.'

He clicked his heels together, and was gone.

★ ★ ★

The room was suddenly very empty, the walls too far apart. I cursed myself for being so forward. I should have let him take the lead, should have held myself back, acted the bashful maid. But I would bring him back to me; tonight, even. How could he resist my bounty? I was his harvest-home, safely gathered in: a full larder that would never be empty, a heaping board, cartwheels of cheeses, thumbed loaves, oozing cuts of crackling pork, dishes of plump curds. I would gorge him. I could not understand why he would not taste me. All he needed to do was gather me in for year after year of happy ploughing, seeding, cropping.

I would purr spells to bind him to me. Witch words no-one taught me. I would draw them up from the secret book of my body, written during the long years of want and wanting. An alphabet of need, spelling an A-B-C of *love me, need me, want me, hold me*. He would want me. Would not be able to resist.

I would make my own fortune. I did not need any of Donkey-Skin's bewitching flummery. A hairy gentleman with sword in hand? No. I would settle for this man of solid flesh, not some childhood fancy. Tellers of fortunes were tellers of lies. Butcher, baker or candlestick-maker, Josiah Arroner was the only one to come wooing. In this hand I had been dealt there were neither princes nor glass shoes. He was married to me: that would serve me well enough. And what did I care if he was as close-shaved as a peeled boiled egg? If that was as close as the prophecy got, it was sufficient.

'You were wrong,' I said to Donkey-Skin.

Well, she said. *I wonder.*

ABEL

London, May-August 1857

I am deafened by the shouting of commands. The boat heels sharply to the side, ropes groaning, planks straining against each other. Vast sails slap as they are taken by the wind.

I look about and see for the first time manacles upon my wrists and ankles, a chain which leads from the cuffs to an iron ring nailed into the deck. I have no time to wonder at my situation, for all about me are naked men chained in the same fashion in the belly of this leviathan. The stink of shit and sweat makes my head swim. A man dark as a tanned goatskin squats before me, holds a ladle to my lips and I drink thirstily. I smile but he is gone down the line, to desperate entreaties of 'Water! Here! I beg you!'

We lean forwards as one body, shoving the tree-trunk of the oar; at a yell from the steersman we haul backwards. Beneath me I feel the huge vessel slip through the water to the chorus of oars moaning in their rowlocks and the grunting of my fellows. So it goes on: I rock to and fro, faster and faster, my breath catching, head ringing with the stench.

I am shaken by the movement of the body next to mine, and tumble into wakefulness.

'Good morning, Abel,' he says, pulling on his boots.

I rub the crust from my eyes. I was on a boat, and am now in a cellar. This man is smiling at me. His name is . . . His name is . . . I will have it in a moment.

'It's Alfred, you dozy bastard,' he laughs. 'Rough night?'

I shake away the dream of the boat, seep back into myself. Of course, this man is Alfred. Truly, no man has such a friend. My dull soul awakens and rubs a bleary eye as it comes forth into light. I owe Alfred everything. There is no gift too precious to repay all he does for me. I smile, stretching my limbs into the warmth of the morning.

'Is it time to get up?'

He looks away. 'I am going to work,' he says.

Yes, of course. We work together: we are slaughter-men.

'Wait, I shall be ready straightway,' I say.

He pauses in the lacing of his boot.

'Abel, you cannot come with me. Don't you remember?' he sighs. 'Every morning you've forgotten and I have to tell you afresh. It's been weeks and weeks now.' He tightens the kerchief around his neck. 'The carcase. You must remember.'

He makes a stabbing movement with his bunched fist. The trickle of memory becomes a flood and I see myself hack the carcase to pieces, hear the angry shouts of the gaffer. Most vividly, I remember my body, monstrous in its ability to heal.

Alfred is still occupied with his laces.

'What will you do today, Abel?'

'I do not know.'

My hopeful mood melts away. I think of the hours until he returns: this room, my mattress, the swelling tide of pictures I do not want; images of myself cut and healing, rising from a river that refuses to drown me.

'Will you go and find new work?'

I am intrigued by the idea. Although I remember that I am a slaughter-man, I do not recall how I rose to that state, nor what else I can do.

'Maybe I could be a surgeon?'

I do not know whence comes the notion, but the word slides easily into my mouth. Alfred guffaws.

'Bullocks are a bit of a different matter to men!' he crows. 'Though you'd not think it, by some of the sawbones I've seen.' He finishes fastening his boots. 'You must find work, Abel. You have no money.'

I think of my plate, full each night.

'But I have plenty to eat.'

'My friend,' he continues, without meeting my gaze, 'I cannot pay your food and lodging as well as my own. I would if I could, I swear to you; but I cannot. Not any longer.'

His voice quakes.

'Oh, Alfred. I did not realise.'

I grasp his shoulder and he allows my hand to

rest there briefly, eyes darting left to right. After a moment he springs to his feet.

'I must go. I shall see you later. Find work, Abel.'

I lie there and think about the rightness of his words. It is true; I must find work. I cannot expect Alfred to pay for me. I am ashamed that I did not realise this was happening, and curse myself for being so addle-brained. Any fool should have known that something was amiss when there was always food.

The ceiling extends grubby plaster above me. It is high enough for a man to stand, but not much more. It is stained with tobacco smoke and patches of mould spread their dark continents across its map. I consider what I know of the world beyond this room. Alfred wakes me each day; he goes to work; he returns. Sometimes he goes out drinking and I go with him, and drink also, and we return together and sleep. The next thing I know is Alfred shaking me awake once more.

I wonder how I might go about seeking employment. Minutes pass. Weak daylight grows stronger through the barred windows high in the wall. Further down the line of pallets a man is stirring, and when he stands up I call out to him.

'Are you going to work?' I ask.

He does not answer, sliding into his jacket and coughing as he does so. I ask again, a little louder.

He turns in my direction. 'Oh, it's you. Are you talking to me?' He coughs again and his lungs rattle.

'Yes.'

'Well, I am, then.'

'Do they need men, where you work?'

'Not likely. More men than jobs. You work with Alf, don't you? Down the slaughter-yards?'

I am surprised by his knowledge, but answer yes quickly enough.

'So you've got work.'

'Not any more.'

'You lost it?'

I nod.

'How?'

I do not want to tell him what happened, but I cannot think of what else I might say.

'You are a fool, then. And with something to hide. Don't want one of them working at my place.'

He hacks, spits and grunts with satisfaction at the black oyster of phlegm on the floor. With no farewell, he leaves the cellar. I watch the rest of the men get up from their beds, one by one, until only the smallest handful of us remain.

★ ★ ★

I dread the day before me, wondering what I can do to fill up the hours, where I might find employment for my hands, for already they are raging in my jacket pockets, clenching and unclenching, worrying at loose threads in the weave, scratching, pulling, needling. I beg them to let me sleep away the time but they rove over the blanket plucking at lice and crushing them so intently I believe I kill every bug in my bedding.

When that is done they trail at my sides, picking at splinters in the floorboards.

My mind wanders as aimlessly as my hands. I could follow someone to his place of employment and ask the gaffers if there is need for another man. If they say no, I can come back. I consider what might happen if they say yes. I know how to loll beeves: I do not know anything else. Will they, too, ask how I lost my job at the slaughter-house? My mind scrambles in search of answers, clattering inside the empty tin of myself until I am exhausted.

At last I fall into a drowse and am suddenly in a small room which sparkles with colour and prickles my nose with the scent of oil. Although it is not the place I sleep, it is very familiar. I feel a rippling run down my spine, and look down at my body, convinced I will discover some change, but I am the same. The walls are lined with clocks of all sizes and types: beehive, carriage, crystal regulator, Vienna regulator, drop trunk, lantern, long case, ogee, skeleton. I know the name of each one, and it fills me with the same pride I felt when I was One-Blow Abel.

I walk amongst them, stroking each cool face of glass, listening to its particular music. There is other music from the street outside: the voices of passers-by sing greetings to each other for such a delightful morning, and I understand each alien word as soon as it is uttered. There is the creaking of great wooden carts, air deliciously soft with the clean scent of horse dung, and further off the smell of a broad river, aching towards the sea.

I am entranced by these distractions but a moment, for a table appears before me, a common wooden thing spread with a smooth black cloth, and upon it lies a selection of wonderful objects: small wheels of brass, tiny golden cogs, miniature spindles and springs, and each thing sparkling in the sunlight which glances through the window.

I hunch over these treasures and place a glass lens over my eye, squinting my brow so that it does not fall. The objects leap into clear view, transformed into giants, such is the marvellous power of the eyepiece through which I peer.

My hands hover over the scattered pieces, tweezers poised. There is no anxiety, only an ache to be started. *Begin*, says the voice of my mind, and they fly to their work. I watch in amazement as they dart this way and that, full of deft comprehension. A wonderful machine forms itself on the table. I know the name of every part I place in its correct setting: engine, fusee, spring, pivot, curb, detent, verge-escapement; and in what seems to be a few moments the watch lies finished upon the tablecloth.

A gentle stroke and it begins to tick, a sound as musical as the voice of an angel. My mouth widens into a smile; my hands dance with pleasure, and the golden workings dance in turn. I need no other to admire my work, to partake in this pleasure.

I see the universe in miniature spin its orbits: as above, so below. A happiness soars within my breast: I taste delight, peace, understanding, and in it I find myself complete. It is brief, however. The eyeglass drops onto the table and I return to my habitual blank calmness. I sit thus a few moments longer, and then it occurs to me that I must be dreaming; but if so, why do I not awaken? I consider this, looking at the tobacco-stained walls, the chair in the corner which I do not favour because it rocks on the back leg; and it strikes me that this is no dream. I wonder what it might be.

It is a memory, speaks the voice. *Like everything else.*

★ ★ ★

A hand shakes me; I turn and am returned to the cellar.

'Alfred?' I say, for there is only one man who does this, and I delight in my cleverness in recalling his name so readily.

'No, it's bloody not. Shut your racket, shit-head. Going on with yourself like that. I've been slaving all night. Some of us want to sleep.'

I do not recognise the angry face pushed into mine; I sorely wish to return to the quiet room where I was happy and my hands knew what they were doing.

'I am sorry,' I say.

'All right,' he mutters, his anger spent. 'Just keep it down.'

A clever thought comes to me. 'What was I saying?'

'Don't know,' he shrugs. 'Wasn't English. Thought you were English.'

'I am,' I say, and wonder if I am lying. 'I have been to many places.'

This seems a safer answer.

'Haven't we all,' he snorts. He returns to his mattress and is snoring within minutes.

Once more I am reduced to staring at the crackled plaster of the ceiling. Men come and go: the fellow who shook me out of my reverie leaves some time later with a comradely grunt in my direction; others return and sit about smoking, talking and sleeping. I wait for Alfred, full of excitement at the news about myself that I itch to tell him. At last he returns, his boots smelling of meat.

'I am glad to see you,' I say.

He smiles. 'You seem happy: have you found work?'

'No.'

'Oh.' The grin drifts from his face. 'What have you done all day?'

'I have been thinking.'

'Thinking? Christ, Abel, you need money, not thoughts.'

'But I have discovered something. It will bring money.'

He sighs. 'What?'

'Give me your watch.'

'What? It has not worked for years.'

'I want to look at it,' I lie, and turn my face away.

'Hell's teeth, Abel,' he moans, digging into his shirt and pulling out the battered creature.

He tosses the watch into my lap. It is not a costly piece, but it is the thing Alfred values most, and he keeps it close by him always. I prise it open, unscrew the plate with my fingernail and spill the parts on to my knees.

'Abel!' he shouts. 'What in Christ's name have you done? You bastard. It was my — '

His voice breaks off. I look at the confusing mass of metal pieces and feel a fearsome bafflement. What was I thinking? How can a slaughter-man understand the workings of a timepiece? All I have done is make my friend angry.

Then my hands stir, moving so fast I can barely make out what they are doing. I try to shove them into my pockets, but they will not obey me. I watch in amazement as I begin to put the pieces back together; blowing away dust, plucking a stiff straw from the palliasse beneath me and poking it into the little machine. I tell myself I must be making a mess of Alfred's watch, and he is already furious. After a short while my fingers cease their movement, and before me lies Alfred's watch, reassembled and ticking.

'I believe it is working again.'

He stares at it. 'I believe it is. Damn you, Abel, where did you learn this?'

'I do not remember.'

'This is a great skill. I always knew you for a clever man.'

He does not ask me any more difficult questions; he simply smiles.

'Abel, I've got an idea. Let us begin straightway.' He clears his throat and shouts. 'Does any man here have a broken watch?'

Most of them laugh, and remark how it would be a fine thing to own such a treasure, broken or not; but one of them approaches us.

'It has never worked,' he says, turning the object over in his hand. 'And the man I got it from told me it never worked for him, neither.'

He rolls it over again, rubbing the scratched and cloudy glass with his thumb.

'Do you wish to see a fine thing?' says Alfred. 'Give me the watch.'

The man is reluctant.

'Come,' Alfred encourages him. 'There is no harm in it. I shall not spirit it away.'

The man gives up the watch, and Alfred passes it to me.

'What?' he exclaims. 'You didn't say anything about *him* touching it.'

'Trust me.'

'You, Alfred, I trust. That friend of yours . . . well, that is a different matter.'

'I have seen him do this.'

Alfred places the watch in my hand. My fingers take this as permission and spring forth, pressing themselves about the silver case, finding straight away how to open it, tapping and coaxing and stroking the tiny brass wheels.

Once again, I watch my hands at work, moving with such confident facility that my eyes can scarcely follow. At one flick of my fingernail the wheels recommence their miniature revolutions. Alfred and the man gasp, for they have both been holding their breath. A crowd of men have gathered around, and one of them whistles. I cradle the machine a moment, for I am filled with an affection that is entirely familiar; it is a few moments before I can bear to close the case and return the watch.

'It's working!' its owner exclaims. 'I am sorry for doubting you.'

'Thank you.'

'I wouldn't of thought it.'

'It's worth something now,' says Alfred.

'I'd best sell it then, before one of you bastards pinches it.' He laughs, and we all laugh with him.

★ ★ ★

Alfred is cheerful for the rest of the evening. He stands at my side as I pay sixpence for my next night's lodging: the fourpence the man gave me for mending his watch, and the twopence made up of the farthings other men in the cellar gave me — 'for the entertainment', as they put it. He goes out to bring in a jug of beer to celebrate my new-found skill. 'And a special gift,' he says. While he is gone, a stranger seats himself beside me, on Alfred's mattress. He pushes out his hand, and I take it. He speaks in a language that I do not know.

'*Hoe gaat het?*' he says.

'*Alles goed?*' I reply, without thinking.

'At last!' he declares in his rolling tongue. 'We are countrymen.'

'Perhaps,' I say, for it is best to agree with strangers for as long as is possible. 'What makes you think so?'

'I heard you talking in your sleep today. And now you greet me, and we are speaking. Where do you hail from?' he continues.

The word appears in my mouth as soon as he asks the question. 'Nijmegen,' I say.

'Ah, so beautiful,' he sighs. 'I have an aunt there: she married well'

'Ah,' I agree, and nod. 'Good luck to a woman who goes east.' The proverb comes easily to my lips, though it is the first time I have heard it.

He laughs, wiping his eyes. 'Good God, I've not heard that in years.'

'Ah,' I say again, with a lift of my eyebrows that I hope appears clever rather than confused.

My mind is tumbling. I am speaking a language I do not remember learning, and claiming to be a native of a foreign town I have never visited.

He continues to grin. 'So what brings you to this place?'

'Work,' I say, more confidently. 'I am a slaughter-man. I *was* a slaughter-man,' I correct myself.

'Ah, indeed?' he says, smiling. 'We are men of the world, are we not? You need say no more. These are troublesome times.'

I nod again, not understanding what is so troublesome.

'I can mend watches,' I offer, hoping to steer the conversation to an easier place.

'A clock-mender! Of course, that is why you were in Nijmegen. You are a clever man, then!'

'Such is luck and life,' I say, the queer words coming easily to my mouth.

He pauses a little, as though to grasp what I am saying; then he laughs again, very loudly.

'You are cheerful,' I remark. 'Every word I say, you laugh.'

'My friend, please do not be offended. I mean

no harm. It is a pleasure to speak with you. Truly, truly. It is just that you speak a little oddly.'

'How so?'

He fights his smile. 'I did not think Nijmegen so backward. No, I mean no insult. It is amusing, simply.'

'In what way?'

'The way you speak. It is so formal, so old-fashioned: many of your words have fallen out of use. I can understand you, but it is like listening to my grandfather. Did the Kabouters carry you away to their kingdom under the hill for a night that lasted a hundred years?'

'Perhaps,' I say, not having a better answer.

Alfred returns with the beer and a parcel under his arm. He stands to one side and clears his throat. The Dutchman looks at Alfred; Alfred looks at the Dutchman; and after a while the latter bids me a farewell, and stands.

'I am going to have a pipe of tobacco. You are welcome to join me.'

'I shall,' I say. 'In a little while.'

★ ★ ★

Alfred sits down.

'Look. Take them,' he says softly, pushing the bundle at me.

I open the sack to find a pair of boots.

'They will fit. I took your old ones for size.'

They are dark brown, with new laces. The heels have been mended; the leather gleams with careful oiling.

104

'Do you like them?'

'They are very good.'

'Look,' he says. 'They've been broken in. All the hard work's been done for you. They'll not pinch. The perfect boot.'

'The perfect boot,' I agree, and turn them round the better to inspect them.

'And the heels.'

'Yes, the heels. I believe the heels are the best part.'

His teeth shine in the lamplight. 'Try them on,' he gasps; then he adds, in a sterner voice, 'To see what they are like.'

They fit well, and I say as much. Alfred rubs his hands together.

'Oh,' I say. 'I am very stupid. I owe you money.'

'No, you don't. You gave it me to save up, don't you recall?'

'But these boots are very good. I did not give you this much.'

'I got a good bargain on the old pair, once I'd polished them up a bit.'

'Oh.' I twist my feet around, enjoying the feel of these fine new boots. 'But these are — '

'I did not steal them, if that is what you mean.'

'I did not mean that at all.'

His forehead is deeply creased. 'Very well,' he mumbles. 'I put in some of my own money.'

'Why would you want to do that?' I ask.

'Why? Is generosity against your sodding ideals, Mr High and Mighty?'

'Shut up, you bastard,' comes a shout from a few yards away.

Alfred peers into my face, sucking on his bottom lip. 'I'm sorry,' he says.

I do not understand what he is sorry for, but I know it would be a bad idea to ask. Then the right words come to me.

'Thank you.'

He grunts, but will not look at me.

'You are my friend,' I add, laying my hand on his.

'Not here,' he growls.

I wonder where would be better. Again, I do not ask.

'Anyhow,' he says. 'What was all that about before? What were you saying to that fellow? I didn't understand a word of it.'

'We were talking about Nijmegen.'

'What?'

'It is a town, in Holland. I lived there.' The words become truth the moment I speak them. 'That's where I learned how to mend clocks.'

'You never told me that. Why did you not tell me?'

'I did not remember until today.'

'But I've heard you speak Italian — all the men here have.'

'They have.'

'So, which is it? Dutch or Italian?'

'Both?'

It seems true. He looks at me awhile.

'I do not understand you, Abel. Sometimes I do not think I know you at all.'

He drinks the beer and we do not speak again that evening.

I lie awake, staring into the darkness, listening to the snorts and grunts of my fellows, breathing out heavy night's-breath. They have no trouble remembering who they are and where they are, for they never stop talking of wives, lovers, whores, children, themselves as children, their homes. But my mouth struggles to shape the words. It is as though I have never had to use them.

I consider the discoveries I am making about myself. I drowned in a river and lived against all the odds. I cut myself open and healed straight away — indeed, it seems that however mortally I injure myself, I heal. Now I seem to have found recollections of a life as a clock-mender in Holland. I have no idea how I came from that country to this, but I reason that because a sea divides one from the other, then I must have travelled by boat.

I push and the memory pushes back, forcing me away. I feel a stirring of fear that there is more to be uncovered: I know not what. I am swelling up with secrets and wonder how much more I can be filled before I burst. I wish Alfred would listen to me.

At last my eyes close and I am carried beneath the arch of the sky to a narrow flight of stone steps, my feet pounding up a staircase of stone, one of those tight spirals that wind up the corner of a tall narrow tower; I am climbing ever higher, higher, with an intensity of purpose I do not recognise, panting for breath, hand clapped over my heart, for it seems it might beat its way out of my chest. I am a mild man, yet in this dream I am in a torrent of desire. I wonder what this longing might be: is there a woman at the top of the staircase and I am late to meet her?

I cannot stop climbing, cannot stop putting one foot in front of the other, staggering towards something I know awaits me, and for all that I wish to stop, I cannot, my breath ragged, lungs shrieking for rest; and then suddenly there are no more steps to climb. I cling to the wall, wind tugging at my hair, and then I step out on to a walkway circling great bells hanging down from massive beams. I do not pause to admire them, but pace up and down, wringing my hands together, wiping sweat from my top lip. There is no lady here: I am alone, and in a torment, my breath hammering in my ears.

I jump up onto the ledge, and suddenly realise what this is: what I am doing. My heart catches — both here, now, on my pallet in the cellar; and there, then, on the highest part of this tower. I stretch out my hand to pull myself back, comfort myself with words of love, save myself from the horror I know awaits me. I fail.

I jump; I fall, see the ground rush up to meet me, feel the agony of bones breaking, my heart bursting with the hope of dying; gasping, 'Yes, yes.' Straight away I am surrounded by the thump of men's feet, quick hands that lift and carry me, voices that whisper of miracles. *Let me die*, I pray. But my body does not listen. The blood in my gorge shrinks back; my ribs withdraw their spears from my insides; my lungs start to sew up their spongy bags.

An uneasy truth scratches at the door of my mind: *This is no dream.*

* ⋆ *

I wake to find Alfred seated cross-legged on his pallet, smiling at the little machine in his hands, holding it to his ear to capture the gentle ticking. He looks at me, but I am still gripped by the terror of jumping from a tower — and healing, even from such a fall.

'Are you all right, Abel? You were crying out.'

'I was?'

'Yes. Bad dream?' he asks.

I shudder. 'I fell.'

'Must be dreaming of when you fell into the river. Told you it'd come back, didn't I?'

'I fell off a tower.'

'No towers by the river.' He smiles. 'You're panting like a Derby runner.'

'Oh.'

'I hope you won!' he chuckles.

'Won?'

'The race!' He waves his watch at me. 'It's still working,' he says. 'I'm sorry.'

'Sorry?'

'I was in a poor temper last night, my clever pal.'

Then I remember myself the previous night: picking open the case, dismantling and removing the parts and replacing them, each in its rightful place. Alfred was angry, yes, but it is difficult to recall exactly why. I try to remember the whole of yesterday, and slowly it returns. I mended watches, I spoke to a Dutchman, I ate, I drank. But each meal is so much the same it is as though I have only ever eaten one meal and drunk one glass of beer.

The memories stumble back: the town I lived in; the Dutch tongue I can speak; the clock-mender's work; my work as a slaughter-man, before I lost my job. Before I discovered my frightful talent for healing. One night's sleep and it seems I am in danger of losing everything without Alfred at my side to remind me. I wonder what else I forget after a night's sleep.

Alfred alone has prevented me from losing this completely. I wonder what it would be like if I were to wake one day and find him gone. How I would find myself? Who would I be? The thought is terrifying: more terrible even than the memory of my arm cut open. I need a place to keep this new knowledge, a way of keeping it beside me always.

'Is it time for you to go to work?' I ask.

'No. Not for a while.'

'Will you show me the way to a stationer's?'

'Going into the scribbling trade now?' He laughs, but takes me anyway and pays for a sheet of cheap paper, pen, nib and watery ink.

'You'll pay me back soon enough, now you're a clock-mender,' he says, grinning, pointing me back to our lodgings.

I do not know if I can write, for I cannot remember ever doing so, but the moment I dip the pen and set it to the page it forms words well enough. *I am a slaughter-man.* I correct myself: *I*

110

was a *slaughter-man. My friend is Alfred.* I pause, and wonder what to write next. It seeps into my remembering.

Before I came to London, I was a clock-mender in Holland, I write. *In Nijmegen. I have a wonderful facility for mending time-pieces.* I pause. *I can speak Dutch,* I continue. *I can speak Italian. I ran up a tower. I wanted to jump.* Then I write, *When I cut, I heal.* I do not wish to record this, but it is true. I think of that other thing that happens when I cut myself, but it is too shameful to put into words. Finally, I write the date at the top of the sheet: *14th May 1857.* It seems very important. *Written by my own hand, Abel.* I fold the paper and tuck it inside my shirt. The day passes.

The next morning I wake early and lie a moment, gazing upwards and waiting for my eyes to bring the room into focus. Something scratches at my left armpit. I draw a piece of paper out of my shirt, and as I hold it I remember that I placed it there. I unfold it. Only a few lines, at the top of the page, in writing that I know is my own, though I cannot swear that I recognise it. I am intrigued. What message have I left myself?

I note the date first, and of a sudden know it for yesterday. Then I read my words, and with the reading, remember. In a few lines of ink I make my history mine once more. I am filled with terrible relief, and clutch the paper to my heart. I know who I am. However strange, I have not lost myself overnight.

Alfred continues to be happy. I bury myself in the busyness of repairing watches. Men bring them broken; I send them away restored; they pay me. I give Alfred the money I owe him for lodging and food, and he tries to refuse, but in the end accepts the money, somewhat ill-humouredly.

Customers come in greater and greater numbers as word of my skill gets about. One regular visitor brings a small bag each time, four or five of them. I say how fortunate he is to own such a quantity of timepieces, and wonder why he has need of so many.

'I am a lucky man.' He laughs in a way that is difficult for me to copy, and pays me fourpence for each one I mend.

Alfred suggests we look for better lodgings, but when I ask why, he claps my shoulder and calls me his dear innocent friend.

'Right now,' he says, 'we're in a doss-house cellar. But put a bit aside and who knows? We'll get a room upstairs where there'll only be six of us. And up and up till we have our own room.' His eyes sparkle.

'I am very comfortable here, with you.'

'Where's your ambition?' he exclaims. 'Think of it! The peace and quiet!'

I do not want it quiet. My memories crowd in far more insistently when all is calm. I grit my teeth against the word 'memory'.

'I like a bit of hustle and bustle.'

He chatters on as though I have not spoken. I

want to understand: what could be better than the place I live now? I have a mattress to sleep on, a roof to keep off the rain, a friend to wake me each morning. I am not lonely, for the cellar is full of comings and goings. Alfred's companionship steadies me. I have discovered a new talent, and the labour binds me to each day with a sense of purpose. Even more delightfully, the more I work, the less I reflect upon the more frightening aspects of myself.

I have my paper to remind me who I am each morning, and it seems that with each day I am less dull, less stupid. I have the clever idea of recording the street names of my neighbourhood until my document is a map: a thread through the labyrinth not just of my cluttered inner lands but also the heaving world outside. It is almost as though I have forgotten that time of disturbing dreams of towers or rivers, of cutting and healing and the shameful and demeaning way in which my body flares into arousal when I slice myself deeply. I push the thoughts away. I shall work and work, and not think about any of that at all.

★ ★ ★

With each morning the weather becomes warmer, the cellar stickier until a fug of sweaty heat hangs over us in the evening. One afternoon, late in the summer, Alfred returns from work with a look of excitement on his face.

'Fancy a bit of fun tonight?' he asks.

'Where?'

'It's the tenting season. There's a bit of a do

113

up Mile End way. Plenty to see, plenty to eat and drink. Come on. Shake a loose leg, Abel. It'll do you good.'

When we step up to the street it is late enough in the day to be early evening and the city is gilding itself with the lowering rays of the sun. I sigh, caught up in its unaccustomed beauty.

'Are you tired? If you are we don't have to go,' says Alfred.

'I am not tired.'

'Good.' He smiles. 'We deserve a bit of a knees-up.'

We make our way in warm comradeship. Every few paces Alfred opens his mouth as though an idea has come into his head, but at each turn he is confounded, either by some drunken fellows staggering past, or by a cart rolling by, its wheels shrieking from lack of oil, till at last he gives up, grins and drops his chin to his breast. We settle into a comfortable rhythm, steps matching and our breath also.

'Just like our old walks to the slaughter-house,' he says in a brief moment of quiet. 'But this time it's sport we are headed to!'

He is in such a good humour I wonder if I might be bold enough to ask him once more about my strange dreams, but each time I open my mouth he makes some joke, or points out an interesting sight. Indeed, he is so cheerful I fear that my thoughts would serve only to dampen his spirits. So I chew my tongue and we walk on.

We turn a final corner and find ourselves at our destination. It is crammed with booths advertising wonders and wrestling matches, fortunes to be told, prizes to be won. Swing-boats squeal; hawkers shriek out their wares just as noisily. The aroma of grilled pork tickles my nostrils, and music weaves with shouts and laughter into a tapestry of sound and scents. A boy passes with a tray of cups slopping with gin and Alfred seizes two, throwing down coins with a tinkle.

'Let's drink to us!' he shouts, shoving a cup into my hand. 'Down in one, Abel!'

I peer at the liquid, and pour it into my mouth. Straight away, my eyes spring water at the rough brew.

'Another?' he asks.

'Not yet,' I wheeze.

He takes my cup, laughing, and returns it to the boy.

'So then,' he asks, rubbing his palms together, 'what shall we do first? Knock down a few skittles?'

Two gaudy females swagger across our path: one has pale yellow curls and a length of lace tied around her eyes; her companion has thumbed a line of rouge along her cheekbones, as scarlet as her hair. Both are sweating out strong spirits, so that standing close to them is as intoxicating as taking the drink itself.

'Give us a kiss, lads!' they howl, and press their faces to ours, smearing us with red grease, before leaving to claim more embraces. 'First one's on us!'

Alfred looks as though he has been slapped.

'Are you ill?' I ask.

'People do not kiss me,' he mumbles, 'as a rule.' Another gin-seller passes, and he grabs three glasses, swigging two of them. 'Pay me no mind. It is nothing.'

He passes me the remaining glass and the searing mouthful brings on such a fit of coughing that he has to slap my back. As we make our way deeper into the multitude, a thin arm snakes out from a gypsy's stall and catches me by the wrist.

'Come now! You're a fine gent!' she cackles. 'A silver coin, one sixpence only, and I shall uncover the secrets of your future!' She digs into my palm and spreads the fingers wide. 'A fine fortune for you, sir! Yes, I see good fortune, and wealth!'

'Leave him be,' Alfred grunts, taking my free hand and pulling me away.

'A fortune, a good one!' she rattles on, not letting me go. She rubs the stub of her thumb into my flesh, as though searching for a way in. 'Good health, and — '

Her hand springs back, dropping me as you would a hot coal. I stare at the reddened skin.

'Ha!' Alfred crows. 'Too much for you? I told you to leave off.'

'Get him away from me,' she hisses, all her showy patter stripped away. She horns her fingers and shoves them at me.

'You? Frightened of him?' Alfred laughs. 'My pal, of all people? That's the funniest thing I've heard in years. Come on, Abel. Let's get away from the old bitch.'

'Yes, Alfred.'

I am still entranced by the bruise.

'It'll fade,' he says, taking my hand in his, inspecting the darkening spot. 'Come on. Plenty to do. Indeed, look. There is a dancing bear.'

The creature is a sorry sight, with a shaved snout and a tattered bonnet strapped to its head. It keeps swiping at it with clipped paws, missing each time. It peers about, as though searching for something it knows is close, but unattainable, and at every blink its keeper jerks the chain, chafing the metal collar deeper into the welts about its neck.

Alfred squeezes his nose.

'Christ, it stinks!'

He has to shout, for the crowd are clapping and chanting, throwing apple cores, urging the beast to sprightlier movement. It opens its maw and groans a gale of cheap beer.

'Come on. Let's go. This is no fun.'

I nod and walk at his side. I shudder; I see myself bound, dragged to my knees, a metal collar about my throat, chains linking me to the man in front, the man behind, throat parched, muscles shrieking. I shuffle forward, head bent under the burden of a blazing sun, ears ringing with shouts that urge me forward: a foreign tongue I understand although I have no reason to.

'Abel? You're as pale as a ghost.'

'It is nothing,' I lie, stumbling against him.

'Do you want to go?'

'I am well,' I say.

A knot of children dashes past, squawking, and one clouts Alfred on the side of the head with a pig's bladder on a stick.

'Little bastards,' he says good-naturedly. 'That's kids for you.'

117

A skinny boy bobs before us, pulling a square of paper from the sheaf hanging over his arm.

'Here you go, mister,' he says politely, pushing it towards me. 'The Wonders of the Age! Come and see the only true and genuine Lion-Faced Woman, Star Attraction at Professor Arroner's Marvels!'

Alfred plucks the playbill from the boy's hand and snorts with laughter.

'Coo, that is one ugly sight,' he declares and passes it to me.

The youth shrugs. 'Please yourself. It's not for the faint of heart,' he says with an innocent air. 'No, definitely for brave men.'

'You cheeky little shit — ' starts Alfred, but the boy has gone, skipping through the mob.

I examine the paper. Bold lettering at the top of the page announces her as *The Non-Pareil of the Female Sex*. Beneath is the crude engraving which so amused Alfred. Her hair cascades in a veil down her face, locks brushed carefully away from her eyes and curling to her shoulders; the eyebrows combed upwards; the beard tumbling as far as her breasts, a luxuriant braid hanging out of each ear. There is not one spot of naked skin to be seen. Alfred yanks my sleeve.

'Come on,' he says, taking my arm and tugging it roughly. 'Enough of gawping at monsters.'

'She is not a monster,' I say. 'She is just not . . . ' I search for words.

'A woman?' he suggests. 'Bloody right.'

'She is a woman. But not the same as any other.'

He hoots, slaps his thighs. 'You never said a

118

truer word! What a freak!'

'She is different.' I do not mirror his smile.

'Oh, come on, Abel. Humour me. A bear is a bear and can't help stinking. A female should be a female. Not something halfway between, like that.' He stabs a finger into the playbill.

'But I am different also,' I say. 'Is that what you think about me? A freak?'

We stare at each other for the length of time it would take to fill a pipe of tobacco. He chews at his moustache, casting his eyes about.

'Don't take on so, Abel. Only joking. Don't pay me no mind. I've had a few.'

He snatches the advertisement from me, and I make a grab for it. He shoves me away, tossing the paper to the ground.

'I want to look at it.'

'No,' he grunts. He puts his foot upon her face and grinds it flat. 'I'll not see you get mixed up with circus folk.'

'Nonsense. Give it back.'

'You're a good man, but a simple one. They're a bad lot.'

'Bad? How?'

'Thieves. They'd have the shirt off your back as likely as not, and wouldn't even take off your jacket to do it.'

'No, you're surely mistaken. She looks — '

I want to say *unafraid*. It is not the right word to say to Alfred.

'Vile habits, too.' He hawks and spits mightily. 'Perversions you can't imagine. They're *filth*.'

'I want to look at the picture,' I growl. 'Why shouldn't I be interested?'

119

He takes my shoulders and shakes till my head snaps back and forth.

'Listen,' he hisses. 'Pay attention for once. There's nothing wrong with a bit of good honest dirt, but they wallow in cesspits of their own making. Fucking *animals*.'

He hangs on to me. I do not want to look at him. Gradually, his breathing slows. 'You see? I'm quite the poet when I get started. Anyhow, you wouldn't quit your old pal Alfred, would you?'

His eyes are fearful.

'No! Why would I do that?'

'You were drooling over that ugly bitch for long enough,' he grumbles.

'I said she was different. Not that I wanted to marry her, you idiot.' I smile.

He smiles back. 'Well, then.'

He squeezes my arm and is his playful self again, pulling off my cap and waving it out of reach till we are almost breathless with our game of tag.

'I need another drink now!' he gasps. 'A good long beer. What say you?'

'Yes,' I say, and his grin broadens.

'Let's find a tapster, then.'

'Yes.'

A barrel organ cranks up a few paces away.

'That's more like it!' he cries. 'This way.' He takes my arm and drags me towards the sound. 'Don't be angry.'

'I am not.'

'Let us not fall out with each other again.'

'No. Let us not.'

The smile remains upon his lips. We buy two beers and drink them swiftly, and then knock back another two.

★ ★ ★

A rabble of women are kicking up their feet to the racket. I spot the pair who embraced us earlier, laughing raucously and swishing their skirts up to the knee as they scissor their feet in and out. They flick their eyes about the whole time, calling to any man who catches their attention, beckoning to him, calling out 'dearie', and 'husband', and enticing him with lewd gestures at their private parts.

'You had your free kiss!' the pale-haired one bawls at me. 'Come and get the full works!'

'You and your mate!'

'We can take two in hand, no trouble!'

Alfred shakes his head. They shrug and turn to seeking out more interested parties.

'Did you want to . . . ' he starts.

I think of the Lion-Faced Woman. She piques my interest far more.

'No,' I say.

'No. Not to my taste, neither.'

We watch a while longer.

'Do you dance?' he asks, nostrils twitching.

'I do not know.'

'Oh.'

'I mean, I don't remember.'

'Perhaps it is another of your hidden skills, Abel.'

The tune flourishes, finishes; ragged bows are

made. A large man peels away from the dancers and approaches me, his arms broad enough to heft beer barrels with ease. He bows very neatly and makes a show of doffing his cap, at which the women applaud.

'Charlie's the name,' he says, his voice oddly sweet for such a huge frame. 'I'll have this dance, if you're not taken.'

I glance at Alfred, but this drayman grabs my hand and hauls me away to join the throng, beaming at me cheerfully. My breath catches and all at once my feet remember what to do: I find myself rising up on my toes, drawing first my left boot and then my right in a curve across the dirt, hands on my hips. *I know how to dance*, I think. *Is there anything I don't know, anything I've not done?*

I spin Charlie beneath my raised arm, my other hand pressing lightly into the small of his back; for less than the space of a breath he hovers close to my body, then I swing him out to the end of my reach, steering his steps with confidence.

My heels spark fire from the stones. I hurl myself into lively twistings, skipping and hopping like a child; each time we circle each other I leap a little higher. I hear cheers that seem timed to my cavorting, and I realise the crowd's approval is for my efforts. It spurs me to greater feats, and by the time the dance finishes I am breathless with delight at this discovery. I bend forward with my palms splayed on my knees. Charlie pounds my shoulder and I wheeze.

'I'll have you as a partner any time!' he crows.

'Never had a finer!'

Without thinking, I drop into a curtsey, to the great amusement of the onlookers. I stiffen, waiting for the taunts, but they are good-natured, clapping me on the back.

'What a frisky dancer your pal is!' grins Charlie at Alfred.

'I'd curtsey to him and all!' laughs the red-cheeked woman, snapping her kerchief across my buttocks.

'He's a good pal,' says Alfred, very quietly.

The cry goes up: 'Let's have another!' and coins are thrown into the organ-grinder's hat. The pipes squeal, and I take Alfred's hand and pull him towards me. For an instant he hugs himself into my arms; then he pushes me away.

'Get off me!' he declares. 'What do you think I am, some kind of molly?'

The music stutters, the laughter stops, and the air is suddenly cold.

'You got a problem with mollies?' sneers the fair-haired female.

Alfred shifts from foot to foot. 'What, me? Got the wrong man.'

'Nah. I heard you.'

'Seems to me he doesn't like our Charlie.'

She jabs his shoulder with a sharp talon. The other women cluster around Alfred, joining in the poking.

'Charlie's all right.'

'Looks after us judies, he does.'

'We look after our own.'

'Hey, Charlie!' one shouts. 'Someone here's got a problem with your new dancing partner.'

Charlie lumbers towards us.

'He needs sorting out, seems to me.'

It is as though I am seeing Alfred for the first time: the sunken cheeks, hungry eyes, shrivelled frame. He chews his moustache nervously.

I step forward. 'Alfred,' I declare. 'We should go, dear boy. We have a long walk ahead of us.'

All heads turn in the direction of my voice.

'My dear boy,' I repeat. 'It is late.'

I link my arm through his, carefully. They look from me to Alfred, and back again. Charlie is the first to laugh. He grabs Alfred's hand and shakes it energetically.

'It's all right, mate,' he purrs. 'I won't steal your boyfriend away. Just let me have a little polka with him every now and then.'

The women hoot with merriment.

'They're together!'

'He's jealous!'

'That's what it is!'

One of them pats Alfred on the cheek.

'Aw, my pet. You should of said!'

Alfred's face is crimson. The women giggle at him, their anger melted away.

★ ★ ★

The music starts up again and they caper off, leaving us alone.

'You can stay with your new friend,' he mutters, 'if you want.'

'Oh come off it, Alfred. You know that you're my friend.'

'Suppose,' he grunts in reply.

124

A snail of doubt uncurls from its shell: *Without Alfred, how would I find my way?* I look around at the unfamiliar sights, unfamiliar buildings.

'Also,' I add, 'you can lead me home.'

At this, he smiles. 'Same old Abel. But I think you will have to lead me! That gin was bad. My eyes are swimming like eels in a tub.'

'You are tired. Let us go.'

'Oh, I am not so tired,' he protests, staggering against me.

He attempts to straighten up, but the drink cuffs him on the jaw and he stumbles into the circle of my arms.

'You are a good dancer,' he murmurs into my shirt-front. 'Oh.' He clutches the side of his head. 'Help me, Abel,' he slurs. 'I can't hardly walk.' He topples against me, legs buckling. 'You're right. I'm more tired than I think I am. I mean, than I know I am. Oh, Abel, you'll have to be the clever one tonight.'

'I shall help you home.'

'You will?'

'Of course.'

He grasps my arm in gratitude, running his fingers up the sleeve, squeezing the muscle within.

'I could end up anywhere,' he hiccoughs.

I put my shoulder in his armpit to lift him, and am buffeted by the stinking punch of his sweat. We sway in and out of the gutter, Alfred heaping drunken thanks on me at every step, breath thick with belched-out gin: he calls me 'mate' and 'pal' over and over, as though it is some urgent truth he must share. The moisture from under his arm soaks through to my shoulder. It takes a long time to get to our door, because I know only the streets close to our building and Alfred takes the wrong turn many times.

'I can't feel my feet,' he groans. 'Will you help me in?'

'Of course.'

I lift the latch and we almost fall inside, but I catch him and guide him to the empty kitchen, our shoes clattering on the tiles: the room is stifling with trapped heat and the odour of singeing tallow. I set him upon the bench, pushed up against the wall, and light one of the candle ends rattling in his pocket. He clasps his hand across his eyes, breathing heavily.

The flame hollows his cheeks and eyes, giving him a famished look. He claws at his cap, dragging it away from his glistening forehead, dropping it to the floor. I bend to retrieve it and a hand swipes the back of my thigh, curving round my hip so briefly I cannot be sure if I felt it.

'Alfred?' I say, turning quickly, but his fingers are at his throat, worrying at his neckerchief.

The tip of his tongue runs from one side of his mouth to the other; his lips appearing bruised in the uncertain light, livid against the dark graze of stubble on his chin.

'Alfred. You're ill'

'My stomach is heaving,' he moans. 'My own fault. Too much cheap gin and no food. Look at me. What a picture I make.'

'You'll feel better if you lie down. Come now.'

I begin to lift and carry him to the cellar. He grabs my collar.

'Not yet,' he growls.

I am surprised, for Alfred is always telling me to leave off and get some sleep. I sit next to him, and his body tilts towards mine. He picks at his cuffs; then his hand finds my knee and rests there the space of a long breath. It lifts away briefly, lands again, clasps the bone.

'We're pals, aren't we, Abel?'

'Of course,' I say, wondering why he needs to ask a question with such a clear answer.

He twists his face to look up at me.

'You drunk, Abel?'

I test my senses for light-headedness, but there is very little.

'No,' I say.

'I am,' he slurs. 'Can't hardly think straight.'

There is a pause. He is so still it occurs to me that he has fallen asleep.

'Alfred?' I say, quietly.

'Abel,' he blurts out. 'I am not a good man.'

He hugs my knee.

'You?'

'I lied to you.'

'When?'

He hiccoughs, and slides his fingers a few inches up my thigh.

'Do you remember,' he sighs, 'a long while ago? You asked me if I had strange thoughts?'

I frown with the effort of recollection. Then it comes to me.

'I do!' I smack my palms together. 'I do remember! I'd forgotten; but when you said the words, it came back to me.' I realise I have spoken too loudly. 'I am sorry, Alfred. I am excited. You know I can never remember anything.'

I brim with delight. I am holding on to memories. Perhaps I am not so irretrievable a dullard after all. Alfred stares into my eyes a long while, on the brink of speaking.

'Alfred?' I say to encourage him.

'Oh. Yes. Sorry, Abel.'

'Sorry? What for?'

'My friend,' he breathes. 'Yes. Strange thoughts. Well.' He runs his finger round the inside of his collar and undoes his shirt buttons. 'It is so hot.'

I smell his musk, the scent of trapped meat. I look at him closely. He gazes back with a curious expression on his face. My hopes wilt. Perhaps I have been mistaken.

'If you have changed your mind we can talk another time, Alfred.'

'No!' He grabs my hand. 'No,' he says, less urgently. 'Let us talk a while. You're my pal. I want to tell you. I do have thoughts.' He coughs with the effort of speaking. 'About — things I am afraid to tell.'

'You are afraid, too?'

It rushes in upon me: all the frightening memories I have hidden from him, afraid to reveal them for fear they might become more real, more uncontrollable, more unbearable. How I have tamped them down, week after week, in fearful isolation. When, right before me, he was alone and hiding secrets too.

'I thought you might hate me,' I confess.

I think of the occasions I tried to tell him, how he shrugged me away. I was so afraid. But he is not shrugging me away now; his hand is hanging on to mine, tight.

'Abel,' he murmur's.

'I thought you did not want to know,' I say. 'I tried to tell you before.'

'Oh, Abel.'

He presses into my side, eyes swooning with drink; chucks his knuckles beneath my chin. My mind wavers in that way it does before I am plunged into a memory. *Please: not now*, I think. *Not when I am so close to unburdening myself.* I wipe at my face and my hand comes away clammy. It is exceedingly warm, for all that the fire is out: I open the neck of my shirt to the navel. His nostrils flare and he shuffles closer.

'My memories plague me, Alfred. I cannot sleep. I cannot think right. Sometimes I am close to understanding, then all is snatched away.'

He breathes deeply, fingers tracing the edge of my cheek.

'I can't think right, neither. It's the drink.'

'I have such thoughts.' My voice cracks. 'So many pictures.'

I try to shake them out of my head, but now that I have opened the door to their knocking, I cannot close it again. His hands slide up my arms, cup the bones of my shoulders and squeeze.

'Shhh,' he says. 'Hush now.'

He brings his face close to mine, eyes flicking over me like a tongue.

'Help me understand,' I hiss through clenched teeth.

'Yes,' he whispers, his features tight. 'Hush

now. You'll wake the house.'

I clutch my arms around him, and cannot tell if he is feverish, or I am.

'Yes. Help me,' I say. 'I'd give anything.'

'I am so drunk, Abel. I believe I could *do* anything.'

He heaps his weight against me and we slide off the bench onto the floor. I try to get up, but he holds me down, teeth working their way up the column of my throat, hands grabbing the hair at the nape of my neck, and pressing his face to mine, sticking his tongue between my lips.

'Alfred — ' I try to say, but his tongue is in my mouth and I cannot get the word out.

'Shhh,' he wheezes.

He grips my hand, squeezing so passionately I wince; he guides it between his thighs and rubs my palm against the firmness there.

'Oh, Abel,' he pants, breath faint and fast as a rabbit, clutching me against the hardness, jerking my fist up and down in faster and faster strokes. 'God, no,' he whimpers, and hangs on fiercely.

The rubbing becomes ever more frantic; he groans into my ear, grasp tightening as his body begins to wind its spring towards release. Then he pauses, seizes my arms and flips me over, nose-down on the stamped-in grease of the floor. His fingers scrabble violently at the waistband of my trousers. I do not know why he feels he must force me. He could simply ask. I take a breath to tell him that I am quite willing, breathe in dirt and dust and hair and start to sneeze, my whole body racked with noisy spluttering.

As I catch my breath I become aware that

Alfred has stopped grinding against me. I twist round to face him, straddled across my thighs.

'You may continue, if you wish,' I say.

'What?' he stutters.

He gawps at the palms of his hands, then at their backs, as though they are those of a stranger and he is discovering them for the first time.

'You want this. You are my friend. I'll give you anything, body and soul, if it's your desire.'

I resume my prone position, propping myself on my elbows so that I do not breathe in more dust and set off another fit of wheezing.

'No!' he gasps. 'You are shameless.'

'There is no shame.' I smile over my shoulder. 'It is the pleasurable joining of bodies. You do not need to coerce me. I have done it before.'

'Done it before?' he repeats, slowly.

'Of course!' I laugh with the sudden flood of happy memories. Flesh sticky with joyful excitement, the delicious parts of women and men. 'Many times.'

'*Many* times? How — you — '

His face twists, untwists and twists again. I did not think it possible for a man to reveal so many warring emotions in so short a time.

'You — you — ' He gathers in a deep breath and then hurls it out. 'You bastard! You filthy sod! This is not my doing,' he gulps.

He looks at his body as though it is suddenly foreign. He sees the tent in the rough fabric of his breeches and his fingers fly to cover the evidence of his arousal.

'No. This is not what I want.' He slams a fist

into his groin and whimpers in pain.

'Alfred, you are hurting yourself.'

'This is *you*,' he snarls. '*You* make a man do things he does not want to.'

I raise myself into a sitting position and lay my hand upon his shoulder.

'Alfred. I am happy. Be happy with me.'

'Let go of me, you bugger.' He wipes his mouth with the back of his hand, turning away. He will not look at me. 'You're evil. A perversion of all that's clean and good.'

'Please. Talk to me.'

'Talk to you? You fucking nancy-boy.'

'Alfred? You are my friend.'

'Don't say that. Never. Do you hear? Never.'

'I do not understand.' I try to hug him closer.

'What are you doing?' he gulps. 'You're fucking hurting me, you shit-stabbing piece of filth.' He raises his fist and thumps me on the side of the head. I let go and he scrambles away. 'You disgust me.'

'Alfred, why are you being like this?'

'Like what? Nothing happened here, and don't you ever dare say any different.'

He tidies his trousers where they have fallen open and staggers to the cellar door.

'Alfred,' I call.

'Leave me alone.'

I say his name again, but he is gone. I follow him down the dark stairs to my empty pallet. There is nowhere else to go. Alfred is breathing heavily on the mattress next to mine. I do not understand what has happened. I have no words to bring my friend back to me.

I lie down, open the gates of my being and wait for the pleasurable images to return, but the door swings loosely on its hinge. Nothing. I am an abandoned house, my lustful ghosts gone for the evening. No. Please. I want them. I can make them happen. I can bring them to me.

Fill me, my soul cries.

My voice rings against the walls. I shall bring my dreams to me with the force of my will; they are mine. I grit my teeth. I had so many delightful memories. I want them, now! If I am tormented so often with pictures of death, why should I not have the comfort of lascivious thoughts also? It is the cruellest trick. I scrabble in my mind's pond.

Perhaps I can find my other recollections. There was something about steps. Was I running? The more I try to remember, the more impossible seems the task. Something about a clock; but there are no clocks in this cellar. So why am I thinking about clocks? Or was it a knife? I tumble into a void, and it holds no comfort.

EVE

London, May-July 1857

Mr Arroner pushed open the double doors.

For the first month of our marriage he had kept this one particular room locked and was most coy when I enquired what lay within, lifting his eyebrow teasingly and counselling patience. How anyone could stay patient I did not know, for day after day fresh deliveries were swallowed by the mysterious doors and I was ordered upstairs so as not to spoil the surprise, as he put it. However far I leaned out of the window I could never see enough to quench my curiosity. I was on the verge of imagining him to be a true Bluebeard when he called me downstairs.

'Dear wife. I hope you are not disappointed. I know this salon is a little cramped. You deserve finer, I know.'

'Finer?'

He did not seem to understand why my chin was slack with wonder. The room stretched the entire width of the house. The fireplace bristled with fire-irons, the mantelpiece with candlesticks, and windows stretched all the way from the skirting board to the plaster cornice. Even the wallpaper was alive, flapping with crimson birds.

'Oh! My dear!' I gasped, struggling to find adequate words.

I dared not move, scared that if I placed one foot over the threshold the spell would be broken and this vista would shimmer and wink out.

'I hoped to impress you with this wedding gift. But it is a sorry sight, is it not? Soon you shall have grander apartments. Forgive me, Mrs Arroner, do.'

I seized his hand with such excitement he flinched a little.

'Oh, my dearest Josiah!' I breathed. 'This is wonderful!'

He patted the top of my head. 'I knew you for a kind creature from the moment I met you. How tenderly you preserve your husband's pride.' He swept out his hand. 'Dear wife, it would please me greatly if you would enter.'

I took a deep breath. Spell or no spell, this was mine. I stepped inside, hungry for more of the room's delights. There was so much space between myself and the walls; even between myself and the nearest piece of furniture. I wondered if this was how the Queen lived. I doubted it: she had palaces, and a stream of servants; but all the same, I felt like a princess. I walked in boldly, my toes brushing against Persian carpet at every step, and stretched out my hands; whirling around till my skirts flew up in a dance of their own. At last I stopped, giggling with dizziness. My husband was looking at me with a small smile on his lips.

'Dear, sweet wife,' he said calmly.

There was a podium of sorts set against the furthest wall, covered with a broad rug. At its centre stood a carver chair, plump with red and cream striped satin. Before and below it were a quantity of smaller chairs arranged in a half-circle; not close enough to touch whoever might be sitting on the dais, but near enough to see the rise and fall of their breathing.

'What a curious arrangement,' I laughed. 'Are you going to invite a musician to entertain us?' Anything might be possible in my grand new world.

'Ah, my dear! That chair is for your comfort alone. Here is where you shall receive our guests. You must be eager to welcome my friends, must you not? For they are full of eagerness to meet you, my wonderful new wife.'

I gazed up at my Adonis.

'But, my love, must I sit alone?' I asked.

He tickled me beneath my chin. 'Dear, foolish child! I shall not leave your side for an instant!'

My natural curiosity would give me no peace.

'But, my dearest Josiah, is it not a little strange for me to be so raised above your friends? Will they not think me proud?'

'Of course not. It is the done thing, in fashionable society. It is how ladies of finest breeding receive visitors.'

I looked at my paws: I knew nothing of breeding. I desired to ask more questions, but he was already describing the wallpaper, and how much it had cost him. After some minutes spent thus, he smiled very broadly, and his eyes glittered.

'We shall begin this very afternoon. Many of my most intimate acquaintances ache to see you.'

* * *

He was distracted throughout luncheon, glancing from his pocket-watch to the wall-clock, only speaking to press me into eating my plateful of eggs poached in butter.

'I am too excited to eat,' I said.

'It will make your hair glossy,' he replied. 'Drink your glass of milk.' He checked the time once more and this time it satisfied him. 'Enough. We must make ready.'

'Dear husband, no-one has arrived.'

'You must be seated when they call.'

He placed me on the chair, angling it sideways to the window so that I could not gaze out upon the street. I faced the empty rows of seats.

'May I have a book to read until they are come?'

'Later. Indeed, that is a good idea. It will impress them.'

He took a step back and regarded me. I smiled.

'Raise your fan.'

I did as he asked.

'Better. Yes, that is better. Have you learned 'Alice, Where Art Thou'?'

'Yes, I have it right.' I yawned.

'My dear Mrs Arroner, please be a little more ladylike.'

'I am sorry, dearest Josiah.' I giggled. 'Those eggs were very rich.'

'Yes, yes. And please call me Mr Arroner.'

'Dearest?'

'Before our guests. It is more seemly.'

The sun gushed through the glass and my armpits were threatening to trickle.

'Dearest — Mr Arroner. It is very warm. Would you close the window shutters?'

My husband laughed. 'No-one has died! What notions you have.'

There was a thunderous knocking at the door, and he raced to answer it. I sat quietly, wondering how I might ease the growing cramp in my calves without getting up and skipping about on the rug. I simmered in the sunshine, stiff in my new whalebone.

A crowd of gentlemen walked in, looking about and making loud comments about the quality of our furnishings. My husband ducked like a coal-heaver, hand hovering halfway to tugging his hair in gratitude. He showed our visitors into their seats, calling for tea, for coffee, and drawing attention to the little biscuits made from almonds, and how costly they were, to be sure. I smiled at his unaccustomed deference.

To begin with, our guests paid me no attention. They chattered like ravens on a roof-ridge about the best horse to wager upon, the best tailor for waistcoats, the best for trousers, all the while sipping noisily at their coffee. I felt like a bird of paradise, stuffed and mounted on a twig, a glass dome rammed down over my head.

However, they could not keep their eyes from me for long, and after a few minutes I spied them sneaking glances over the brims of their cups. I wondered when one of them might remember his good manners, step up, kiss my hand politely and ask me how I fared. I flapped my fan and grew stickier.

'Gentlemen!' my husband cried, and their clucking stopped. He stepped into the centre of the room and made a deep bow. 'I welcome you all to my humble abode.'

There was a fluttering of amusement and he bowed again.

'Permit me to make the correct and proper introductions, for which I know you are most keen. My wife,' he said and made a flourishing gesture towards me. 'My dear and most precious wife.'

I heard a few gasps and grinned, covering the smirk with my fan.

'Is it an automaton?' said one. 'I have seen the new French creations.'

'It is much larger.'

'These Frenchies are capable of anything.'

My husband coughed. '*She* is no clockwork creature,' he said, pronouncing the word 'she' with great emphasis, for which I was grateful.

'I am sure I spy a key!' laughed one wag. 'Let me wind it up and watch it dance!'

'No, there is no key.'

'Ha! I declare there is one hidden up its skirt! Let me show you.'

The fellow stood up, and my husband patted him on the shoulder so heartily he sat back down again. He laughed along with their laughter, complimenting them for being such 'brave fellows, oh yes, fine fellows, men of distinction and discrimination!' until by and by the thought of peering up my dress was forgotten.

'Oh! That I have been blessed with such a jewel for my wife!' he exclaimed.

The gentlemen cheered gleefully, whereupon my husband removed his hat and lowered his voice to a conspiratorial hiss.

'Ah, yes! This unusual creature you see before you was brought into London at great expense from the broad savannahs of Africa! From the establishment of a certain lady of such high position and royal connections that discretion does not permit me to elaborate further.'

He winked, prompting one man seated on the front row to whisper in the ear of his neighbour, who exclaimed, 'No!' in disbelief.

'Tut tut!' chided my husband. 'Such tittle-tattle, I never did!'

The company sniggered.

'Suffice it to say that said lady was startled by a ravening lion and was rescued from the jaws of death by her brave husband. Nine months later she brought forth the miraculous child you see before you.'

I ducked behind my fan at hearing such an exaggerated account of my beginnings. I felt no shame about my humble origins, and I wondered if he did, for it was such a mesh of lies he was spinning. I had no desire to be thought showy. But he was already speaking again.

'This gentlewoman entrusted her unusual babe into the care of others, who brought her to our fair isle to be educated in seclusion. For beneath her savage and terrifying appearance quivers the heart of a true Lady. Who can estimate the delicacy of emotion, the tenderness of expression which is concealed behind such a savage visage?'

He pointed at me. Their eyebrows climbed up their foreheads.

'Shall I prove she is a creature of flesh and blood, gentlemen?'

He walked to my side, leaned to my ear and hissed, 'Now, my dear.' I grasped the arms of the chair and raised myself slowly, closing my fan and resting it upon my breast.

'Gentlemen,' I said. Quietly, but each could hear me, for I declare a thick silence had fallen. 'I am delighted to meet you.'

'It speaks,' said one, in a small voice.

'Indeed, that is true,' I said. 'I speak. Shall I also sing for you, dear guests?'

Their heads nodded, stiff-necked. I had their attention now, however much they wished to dismiss me.

I began, and they held their tongues, and there were no more smart answers:

'The birds sleeping gently,
Sweet Luna gleameth bright . . . '

At the end they patted their hands together, which I thought kind, for my voice is not the most melodious.

'Ah! Is she not unique?' cried my husband, striding forwards. 'The best of her kind! Never seen before! How fortunate you are to be

141

granted this rare opportunity to study such a sport of nature, and thereby to speculate on the mysterious Hand of God working through His creation!'

After a further selection of songs and a more detailed elaboration of my qualities, our visitors began to file out, pressing money into my husband's hand.

'Tell all your acquaintances!' he called after them. 'She is the only true and genuine Lion-Faced Woman. We are at home every day from two o'clock until six o'clock. Two shillings and one for children.'

After they had departed, he was smiling in a way I had never seen before.

'We are rich,' he grinned, bouncing from foot to foot.

'Are we, my dear? How so?' said I.

He waved a bag, and it clinked.

'Is this not wonderful?' he crowed, unable to help himself.

'It is wonderful, Mr Arroner. How did we come by such fortune?'

'You, my dear little wife! You are my fortune!' I must have looked confused, for he patted my head again. 'Ah! Such a sweet girl, I declare. Our visitors were rich, my dear, and have bestowed some of their wealth upon us. Simply for the pleasure they have experienced today, of meeting such a treasure as yourself.'

'That is very generous of them.'

'Indeed! It is capital,' he crooned, cradling his newborn wealth. 'I shall deny you nothing. Ask anything.'

I opened my mouth, but he filled the space before I had a chance to speak.

'Anything. New dresses, new fans, new hats; ah yes, indeed — new hats!'

With each afternoon my husband's description of me grew more and more outlandish until I was transformed into a creature I barely recognised: I became 'morally uplifting; the most prodigious creature ever examined by Europe's leading men of Science and Philosophy; offered to the general populace for the further edification and education of Mankind'.

★ ★ ★

Donkey-Skin remained my sole night-time companion.

See how they struggle with pity, horror and amusement, she said. *How terrified they would be if they looked into the mirror and saw you instead of their own milky faces.*

You are what they fear they might truly be. When they have snuffed the bedside candle, you are there. You are the darkness that swims over them, and drowns them.

'Oh hush,' I said to her. 'You are always so dramatic.'

I grew tired of listening to her poetic ramblings, so I resolved to go to my husband and discover what so occupied his nocturnal hours. Taking a candle, it was not difficult to find him in the room at the top of his house that he described as his Chamber of Retreat. The door was ajar; through it I saw, first, shelves lining the walls, stacked with yards of morocco-bound books stamped with brassy tides. I had never seen him read any of them. A narrow bed constructed of broad oak planks was shoved against the wall. In the centre of the room was a desk, over which bent my husband, lit by a bulb-stomached oil lamp. He was counting coins into neat piles. At the satisfactory completion of each heap he scribbled in an open ledger, the stub of his index finger keeping the place.

The word 'dearest' was less than one-half out of my mouth when his head spun in my direction; at the same moment he brought his arms around the coins and cradled them to his breast in a motherly gesture. It lasted less than two ticks of the wall clock; then he straightened up and began to adjust his cufflinks.

'Ah! Dear wife. So you find me at my labours.'

'It is late, Mr Arroner.'

'This is necessary toil.' He pointed at a small metal box, attached to the leg of the bed by a sturdy chain. 'Safer than the Bank of England,' he beamed, giving the chain a powerful tug. It responded with an obedient rattle. 'Guaranteed fire-proof. And I have the only key.'

'Are you not tired?' I asked hopefully.

'I am never tired when it comes to securing our financial future, Mrs Arroner.'

'Oh.'

He leaned towards me and planted a kiss on my forehead.

'Off with you, dearest heart. Take your rest and do not fret over your beloved. He will be thinking of you every minute.'

144

He turned away and resumed counting. I returned to my bed and stuffed my fingers into my ears so that I could not hear a word of Donkey-Skin's *what did you expect?*

★　★　★

The next day brought more callers, the day after more again, until I thought the walls would burst with the heap of them: the men bringing with them their women, who giggled and contrived ladylike fits of fainting, and their children, who yelped and hid their faces in their mothers' skirts to the greater amusement of the crowds.

I was made giddy with the ceaseless bustle, the endless coming and going of visitors. Each time I asked my husband to temper his exuberant descriptions of me, he brushed away my concerns, showering me with costly trinkets and new songs to learn. I grew so enervated that one day over luncheon, after we had been married for three months, I asked him to send the guests away — just for one afternoon.

'It is not merely for my well-being,' I reasoned. 'They fatigue you also.'

'Not so!' he said. 'They give me the greatest satisfaction.'

'Dearest husband, we spend no time together.'

'We are always together. Every day. I do not leave you for one minute.'

'But we are always in the company of others.'

'Yes, dear Mrs Arroner. Is it not wonderful?'

I searched for words to say how I longed for his kisses, his body pressing against mine, but could find nothing that was not indelicate.

'Do you not like my friends? Is their company not to your taste?'

'It is not that, Mr Arroner.'

'Would you choose different friends for me?'

'Of course not, dear husband.'

'Then I declare myself confused.'

'I would be with you, that is all.'

'So, I do not pay you enough attention, is that it? Is it not enough that I shower you with every gift a woman could desire?'

He stood up, gripping the edge of the table, crumpling the cloth in his plump fingers.

'Of course: it is more than enough.'

'Clearly it is not. You are ungrateful. Unnatural. I do not see you casting away your new dresses and declaring, 'Oh, please give me no presents; give me no pretty things.''

He clapped his hand over the place on his waistcoat beneath which his heart beat and rolled his eyes to the ceiling.

'Mr Arroner, I did not mean to sound ungrateful. I am most grateful.'

'Are you? Are you indeed? It seems to be doubtful. Do I ask a lot of you? Do I desire you to sweat in a factory, or work your fingers to ribbons with a needle?'

He thumped at his chest as though trying to dislodge a piece of gristle stuck in his gullet.

'No, sir, you do not.'

'No, indeed I do not. Did I not rescue you from just such an estate?'

'You did. You did.'

'I am hurt, Mrs Arroner.'

146

He placed his free hand over his eyes, and I took the opportunity to lay my own small hand upon his elbow.

'Please do not turn from me, dear husband. It wounds me so.'

'Mrs Arroner, I am the wounded party. I strive only for your comfort. Comfort such as this takes money.'

'I know.'

'And money comes from our guests. No, it flows from our guests.'

'I know.' I bowed my head.

'If you would send our guests away you would send our money after.' He waved his arm towards the window. 'Farewell to comfort! To fine clothes! To fine food!'

'Dear husband, please, I do not wish our visitors sent away.'

'You do not?'

He peered at me and sat down slowly.

'No,' I sighed. 'I am content with the busyness of it. I am used to labour.'

'Yes,' he said, as though he did not fully believe me.

'I will do as you wish. We are wedded together, so we must work together.'

'Yes.'

'All I ask ... ' Still the words eluded me. ' ... is to be your wife. Truly. *Fully*,' I added, heavily.

'My wife? Of course you are my wife! Ah, dear Mrs Arroner! I see it now. You think my eye is dazzled by our prettier guests?' He tugged the hair on my cheek.

'No,' I began, but he held up his hand.

'I have been a foolish man,' he said. 'Gifts are not sufficient.'

At this he fell to his knees and clasped my paws in his huge hands.

'Dear wife!' he bellowed. 'I am yours and yours alone. You are more dear to me than life itself! More precious than a string of pearls!'

'My love, there is no need — '

'But need there is! You have gifts: but be assured also of my devotion. Undying! Unwavering!'

He turned my hands over and pressed his lips onto the palms. As he lifted his face I leaned forward quickly and planted my mouth upon his, and felt him shudder away. His face pursed up as though he had bitten into a piece of bread and found it mouldy. It was a second only, and then he gathered himself, muttering how the girl was late in clearing away the luncheon plates and how he must make preparations for the afternoon's callers. Then he was gone. I knew what I had seen; I knew what must be done.

★ ★ ★

I went to my bedroom and sat on the edge of my bed, gazing into the little mirror he gave to me on his first visit. The girl reflected on that day was radiant as a princess, her hair a halo the sun blessed with its radiance. Now she was reduced: the gold had tarnished into brass, the brightness of her eyes had dimmed. It was confusing: I had a husband, a grand home, a stream of fine

148

visitors; I did not even have to trouble myself to answer the door, for my husband did that himself.

I had everything a wife could wish for. I tried to tell myself I was being ungrateful, but I did not believe it. The gifts meant nothing: I had a husband, but I did not have his embrace. Donkey-Skin looked over my shoulder.

Dear girl, she murmured. *Dear lost girl . . .*

I will not tell you to give up.

I will not advise you to be an obedient, quiet wife.

I will not tell you how many more nights of weeping you have left to live through.

I will not say: I told you so.

I will not say: I told you to be watchful for the right man.

Remember what I said about knives? It does not get better. But it does not get worse. It gets different. Exciting. Terrifying.

Be brave.

'I can't,' I sniffed. 'I want him. I would give it all up for a kiss: the house, the servant, the dresses, even the hats and fans. For him to take me into his arms, truly, as a man does his wife. For that, I would sacrifice my fur.'

The girl in the mirror shuddered.

What are you thinking of? said Donkey-Skin. *Have you forgotten all the battles with your mother? With the world?*

This is the mark that makes you the princess you are. How can you even think of giving that up?

Why do you wish to be the same as every

other girl in the world?

I would not listen to her: my mind was made up. I grinned bravely, and the girl in the glass gave me a small smile of permission.

I can't believe you're considering this.

'But I must have him. I will do anything. Yes, even cut my hair.'

I don't believe you.

'Believe it. You're the one who started me thinking about knives. That was your prophecy, and he is a man with a sharp razor: I shall take it to myself.'

Do what you must, tutted Donkey-Skin. *Twist my fortune-telling if it pleases you. But don't expect me to tell you the story of Samson and Delilah with a happy ending.*

I crept into his dressing-room and found the razor and strop, the soap and bowl. I began on my arm, sopping it wet from wrist to elbow. For a moment I worried that I might have forgotten the way of it, but as soon as I held the handle I remembered how Mama stroked it against the leather, and I angled the blade against my skin and moved it till I heard the sharp, eager swishing of the edge through sticky hair.

My naked arm prickled into goose-flesh; I ran my finger over my uncovered flesh, smooth as a doll's arm and twined with tendrils of red and blue veins. With a stroke of the razor I was turned into a girl, a real girl, just like a trick from the shows when the magician pulls away the silk square and the dove is changed into a kitten. Now the prestige was played turnabout: the kitten was turned into a dove.

I shaved around my throat, down to the brim of my corset and across my shoulders till only my beard and moustache remained. I nodded at the looking-glass, and then stripped off cheeks, chin and brow.

'Look,' I said to Donkey-Skin. 'I am a true girl. Cinderella cleaned of her grime and ready to meet her prince.'

She would not answer.

Then I thought: What if my husband saw me so transformed and wished to take me straightway into his arms? I was only half-shaved; all the hair on my breasts and body covered me still. I blushed at my imaginings and was alarmed to see how I betrayed my feelings with crimson. I had always been able to hide behind my hair.

I peeled off my clothes and made quick work of my legs, belly and breasts, thwarted only by my back, which I could not reach. I would have to keep my face turned towards him; it would not be difficult. I would teach the kitchen girl to shave my back, or beg my husband for a maid all of my own. We were rich. I blinked at the glass. I was thinner than I remembered, my face pale as a water-biscuit. I pinched the blood back into my cheeks.

'What a princess!' I said. 'What do you think?' I cried as I twirled myself around, feeling my skin brave and cold against the air.

Donkey-Skin was silent.

'Come! Don't be like that. I am pretty, aren't I?' My voice echoed off the walls.

'Where are you?'

I let her sulk. I knew what I was about: no

longer a child in need of fairy stories to make sense of my world. Mumbo-jumbo predictions about dark strangers were for empty-headed girls. I was a woman, and a wife with a marriage to save. Her spell over me was broken.

No empty-headed hoping and wishing would ever draw my husband to me. I had the means to bring him to me all the time, but was too giddy-headed to see it: of course he did not want a beast, but a woman; and that is what I had made of myself. I was done wishing for him to be the phantom prince Donkey-Skin had dreamed up for me.

I dressed — the cloth oddly rough against my new nakedness — and took myself into the reception room, sat on my stuffed satin throne, and waited. He would be home soon, and I longed to see his surprise. Now I was shaved clean, I could permit myself to think back to our wedding night when I had seen distaste — disgust — in his features. My stomach turned over in a corner of itself. Well, no more: that was finished with and I would have my husband.

The outer door opened. There was the rattle of his cane in the stand, the click of his heels on the tiles. Then it was quiet, for I always ran to him at this moment. He would be standing in the hall, expecting me. I was blushing again, so hid behind my hands.

'Mrs Arroner?'

I held my breath, squirming in my seat.

'My dear?' he cried, a little louder.

I could wait no longer. 'I am here, my love!' I called.

Even my voice sounded clearer. Would he recognise me, so transformed? I found myself chewing on my lower lip. Of course he would, I chided. No other woman would answer to Mrs Arroner.

'Why are you in . . . ' he began to say, opening the double doors and stepping into the room.

His lips stopped moving, his body also, as if one of my old spells had finally begun its work. It lasted only the briefest moment.

'What in the name of all that is fucking holy have you done?'

I had heard the profanity before, but not from his mouth. He crossed the space between us in two or three strides. He grasped the arms of the chair and pushed his face into mine. 'What have you done, my *dear?*'

His voice was very quiet. I knew the answer, but could find no words. I stared at him, wondering when language might return. It seemed a long way distant.

'Would you make a pauper of me? Would you have us thrown out on to the street? Well? Well?'

I could do nothing but stare at him.

'Do you want all your pretty trinkets sold to buy us bread? Do you hate your husband so?'

This last freed my body from its frozen state. I jumped up and ran down the hall and out of the house, along streets I could not name, my corset pinching my ribs so badly that I had to stop to catch my breath. I glanced up and saw myself reflected in a shop window: face pale as a punched loaf, eyes two dints where the baker had thumbed the middle. Behind me, men and women drifted past grey as Monday soup, and I was indistinguishable against the flock of dim faces.

I had made myself beautiful for my husband, and could not understand why he did not want me. I did not know I could feel like this: to ache for him to put his hands upon me, touch me here and here and here. Did not know how much I could need a man's grasp. I had lived with the smoothness of my mama's arms and now desired his rough hands, the crisp burn of his chin against mine, the tobacco bitterness of his tongue in my mouth, the weight of him on my small bones.

'I am beautiful, aren't I?' I whimpered to the pane of glass, but Donkey-Skin had not followed me.

There must be a man who would delight in my loveliness: why not my husband? A dark sleeve brushed mine and I stumbled.

'I am sorry, miss,' said a man I did not recognise, touching his hat.

I looked directly into his face, and waited for his eyes to widen, the ink of his eyes to bloom in approval at my new good looks. But he snatched himself away and continued, barely breaking the rhythm of his stride.

I had nowhere to go. I could not go back to my mother; to her smile of victory as she opened the door and found me on the step, the way she always wanted me: broken, beaten, biddable. Never.

There was only one place to go, and that was back to Mr Arroner. I knocked at the door, for I had no key, and the maid answered, with a smile on her face I did not like. I tilted up my nose and strode past her, catching my face in the hall mirror; saw how I was the startled white-green colour of milk left standing too long. My husband was seated in the breakfast room, with a pot of tea and one cup.

'Ah, dear Mrs Arroner. You are returned. Let me call for another cup. I did not expect you so soon. Mary!' he shouted. 'So. You are refreshed after your excursion?'

'Josiah, I — '

He held up his hand. The girl brought a second cup and saucer, bobbed a curtsey and left us.

'I apologise for my previous outburst, Mrs Arroner. I was angry. But I have reflected upon your words and believe that I understand you.' He spoke as if his words were chicken bones and he must not snap one of them. 'You are lonely.'

'I am,' I whimpered. 'For you.'

He poured me a cup of tea and added four sugars.

'You have me always. I am your husband.'

He patted my cheek. I pushed my sleek skin into his palm.

'Dearest husband, all I want is for — '

'Yes, yes. I have decided. You need company. Company that will make you feel more comfortable in your delightful strangeness. You will grow your hair back. Everything will be arranged.'

ABEL

London, August 1857

I wake up with a gasp. As soon as there is enough light I read my document, frightened that the words will have been sweat-washed away in the night. But it is whole and, as I read, I remember. My belly urges me to go to the privy, but as I stand my trousers fall partway to my knees, to the amusement of those men who are already awake.

As I wonder why half the buttons are opened, I recall last night, and Alfred: the brightness that burned between us. I turn to find him looking at me slantwise.

'I was drunk last night,' he says firmly. 'I believe you were, also.'

'I was not.'

'I remember nothing. You remember nothing,' he declares. 'You never do.'

I draw close to him and lower my voice. 'Why are you being so out of sorts with me? We are friends.'

'Don't know about that any more.'

He turns over on his mattress and refuses to speak any further. I look at my hands. After the time it would take to drink a cup of tea, he rolls over and regards me strangely.

'You still here? Can't a man get a bit of peace?'

'I have nowhere to go.'

'Hanging around me like a bloody shadow. A fellow can get tired of it, you know.'

'Shadow? That's unfair of you.' I search for the word to describe all that I owe him. 'You are my anchor.'

'So, I'm a millstone, am I?' he snaps. 'Drag you down to my depths and hold you there, do I? If you're so far above me, then fly away. Cut the chain that weighs you down so inconveniently if that's what you want.' He flaps his hand, almost striking me on the cheek.

'I did not mean that, Alfred. You do not weigh me down.'

'Seems I bloody do,' he mutters.

'You hold me steady. I am adrift without you.'

'Oh, will you shut your row!' He buries his face in his hands. 'Nag, nag, nag. You're worse than a bloody woman. My head is thundering.'

'Shall I fetch you some food? A drink?'

'A drink? Oh, piss off, Abel.'

'Alfred, please,' I whisper.

'I said, hop it. Get out of my life. I never want to see you again. Got that, thick-head?'

I lace up my boots. Alfred watches through his fingers. I stand and he rolls away. I stagger up the stairs, on to the street and am assaulted by the rough noise of the city going about its business; once a pleasure but now painful, as though I have been stripped of more than flesh. A wagon carrying barrels drives by so close I can smell the beer within.

'Are you blind?' yells the drayman.

Before I can shout an apology he whips the horses into a lather of speed and is away. Alfred is gone. In moments his friendship and desire burned away to be replaced with hatred. I do not understand why. I refused him nothing. Yet he turned away from what he wanted. My mind aches with confusion. And more.

Each step I take is one further from his anchor fastening me to my being. I scrabble at my shirt buttons, feverish with worry that my paper might have deserted me also. Its reassuring crackle greets my fingers as I draw it out and scan the words hungrily. *I was a slaughter-man*. The past tense carries a weight of story. Ah! I have it. I lost my job in the slaughter-yards because . . . My recollection stutters. Because . . .

I read on, the bare words reduced to splinters of driftwood on a stream which grows muddier with each line. *My friend is Alfred*. Yet he is no longer my friend. If my own words can lie to me, how can I believe anything I have written? The paper shakes and I fight the urge to crumple it into a ball and throw it far from me. Why did I not write more when I had the chance? I had something near, close. I can almost taste it. Truly, I am a fool.

I am terrified that I will lose everything. I cannot let myself slip back into the void. My dreams and memories are the key to myself, but without Alfred's friendship to tie me to each day how will I turn that key and find my way through this gathering darkness?

I wander for what seems like hours and find I am back at the fairground, drawn by something more compelling than the scent of grilled meat. I dawdle with my hands in my pockets, listening to the crowds making merry and wondering how I might find what I am seeking — anything to divert me from the terrifying confusion that is creeping upon me.

The bear remains, or one much like it: as miserable, as bruised, as battered. There is a barrel-organ also, and a knot of women kicking their heels about. They might be the same but I do not recognise them, nor they me. They are as gaudy as before, but it is half-hearted stuff. In the daylight some glaze of enchantment has been rubbed off, leaving a child's playthings cut from bright paper. There was something else. I am already losing what it was.

The revellers flicker in and out of my line of sight, in and out, in and out, dizzying my mind so much that I have to lean against the wall. I close my eyes to gather up my wits and am carried to another fairground, another square, where I am watching a different group of females pace the flagstones, their dresses bright as ink poured. They turn this way and that, and their skirts swing about, as though a hand churned that ink for marbled paper into swirls of vermilion, carmine, indigo. They promenade up and down, fluttering their fans, hiding their faces and showing them and hiding again, like a child playing peek-a-boo with its nurse.

Their dance begins. Step and pause and step and pause, the iron taps on their shoes striking stars, a troupe of dancing princesses stepping perfectly in time, hand over hand, the powder on their wigs trickling onto their shoulders and breasts, breath shallow inside their tightly sewn bodices. I think of them under their clothes, beneath their powder and paint, and feel neither embarrassment nor curiosity. I know they expect me to be bewitched, but I am stone.

My eyelids flutter and I return from my drowse. They have gone, of course. I sigh. Another dream: but as usual I am not sleeping. Another troubling thought surfaces through the sludge of my understanding: my memories are of people dressed outlandishly in the costume of many years ago. I yearn to return to Alfred, to talk to him. Beg him to be my friend again. Ask him to help.

I do not notice the old man stagger out of his patched booth until he tumbles over my feet, belching beer. He clutches at my coat, steadying himself, and peers up at me. The booth's sign reads 'Arturo the Astonishing, Fortune-Teller to Royalty'. He points at it, hiccoughing.

'That's me, kind sir!'

'You are not astonishing,' I say, trying to shake him off. 'Let go of me. I don't like fortune-tellers and they don't like me. And you stink like the dancing bear.'

'Oh, it's all in the smell, isn't it!' he cackles. 'Everything in the smell!'

He shoves his face into my sleeve and inhales a lungful of air; then he leans back, smacking his lips.

'What are you doing?'

'Oh, I can smell you out, sir! Your scent betrays all your hopes and dreams!' he leers.

He fumbles in my pocket, but it is empty, my small store of money being tucked into my boot.

'Are you a fortune-teller or a thief?' I ask, pushing his hand away.

'Both, I suppose,' he shrugs, and takes a slower sniff of me. 'Now, you are a curious one. I'll not let you go just yet. You smell lucky for me. It's all aromatics, sir: a man gives away his secrets through his sweat.' He snuffles at my elbow, grasping a piece of my shirt in his fist. 'Will you give me a few coins for what I can discover?'

His eyes scuttle over me; he blinks, suddenly confused.

'You smell deep. You're a special one and no mistake, are you not? Will you let me read you like a book, sir? Open you up? Watch you heal back up again?'

He affects a mime of unbuttoning his belly and spilling his innards on to the ground. I grab his shirt and shove him back through the tent-flap.

'How do you know?' I growl. 'How can you see this?' I tighten my grip on his throat, watch his pupils bloom into soot. 'Tell me now.'

I squeeze, feeling the flex of his windpipe under my fingers. He splutters, breath rattling in his gullet, nodding his head wildly. I let go of him and he bends over, coughing mightily.

'I am sorry,' I say. 'I was angry. It is spent.'

He rubs his neck tenderly, tips his head on one side and shows an uneven hedge of teeth.

'Of course. I shouldn't have surprised you. Skittish as a foal. Still, you can't hide from this nose.'

He taps the organ in question, leans close once more and flares his nostrils. I lick my lips, for they are suddenly dry.

'Sir,' he says kindly. 'I shall not insult you with my old schmatter. No lies about bags of gold at the end of rainbows. In faith, I shall not fleece you. Come now. I believe I can help you.'

He coughs, spits phlegm on to the floor and kicks dirt over it with the side of his foot.

'Help me?'

'Yes. It is what you most desire, is it not?' He grins through battered teeth. 'Someone who will listen to you? Someone who'll understand?'

It is suddenly the hardest thing in the world for my legs to hold me up; I collapse on to a spindly chair. It creaks a little, but holds.

'You have me, Signor Arturo,' I sigh. 'I shall not hurt you again. I don't believe anyone can help me, for all you say you can. But I have no one else.'

'Not even Alfred?'

'What do you mean?' I demand. My stomach leaps. I grasp his tattered neckcloth again to pull him close once more.

'Enough. Let me go, please!'

I release him. It seems my anger is itching to be set free.

'How do you know his name?' I demand.

'Sir, listen. I can smell him on you.'

'Alfred was my friend.'

'I know. And you have had so many.'

'I have not. Alfred was my only friend.'

As I speak the words, I know them for a lie. But I do not know what the truth is.

'Don't you remember?'

'Remember what?'

'Don't you know where you have been?'

'I don't remember anything,' I grumble, crossing my arms across my chest.

'You must. It is not possible. You see nothing?'

'I see — things,' I mutter. 'I do not wish to.'

'What things?'

I dip my fingers into my shirt and extract my paper, clear my throat and recite its secrets.

'I was a clock-mender, in Holland,' I say. 'I can speak Dutch, and Italian. I see myself at the top of a tower. I — fall. When I cut, I heal'

I fold my document and replace it. The old man's mouth hangs open.

'Is that all?'

'What else can there be? Isn't that enough for one man?'

He breathes me in again, as though I am the finest array of dishes ever laid before him.

'It is not possible. One like yourself, to be so blind. Sir, do you truly not know who you are?'

'Who am I?' I cry. 'Tell me now!'

'You are . . . ' He pauses and takes a deeper inhalation, fanning his hand to scoop my scent deeper into his nostrils.' . . . unplumbable. A well I could never drain dry. A mine whose gems I could never exhaust. Ah!'

He takes my hand and kisses it, snuffling as he does so. His eyes glow, and for an instant he is glamoured with youth.

'Oh! If I began merely with the list of your names — the names men have given you — I should be here a hundred nights! You are perfumed with so many pasts. I have never dined upon such a banquet as you! I could take years, tasting your delicacies.'

He stoops, taking sniffs of air around my body with little cries of pleasure.

'Here is a fine dance, with music and ladies dressed for the carnival! And here, a horse galloping across a broad plain and you upon it, spear in hand. Here, a swift ship creaking beneath your feet. Here, the hand of desire upon your breast — and a kiss! Such sweetness! So many loves!'

'You see all these pleasures?'

'Of course.' Arturo opens his eyes very wide. 'Do you not see them? Their fragrance is so deeply grained into you. Ah! To glimpse into your unbounded soul, to be lifted into your great expanse of lives.' He sweeps his hand so that it brushes the canvas sky of the tent. 'You are the Morning Star: a bright comet fallen from Heaven, carrying light into the darkness and illuminating all around you. Who would not fall in love when touched by your spirit?'

His cheeks are wet.

'If I glimpse happiness, it lasts but a moment. The only constant is pain,' I say, my voice snapping like dry twigs underfoot.

'Pain?'

'Whatever injury I do to myself, I heal straightway.'

'Is this not a source of joy to you?'

'I ache to die. I cannot.'

'You want to die? You think that is possible?'

'You are not listening,' I cry. 'I drown myself, yet do not drown. I cut myself, and do not bleed. Over and over I climb to the top of a building — a tower, a house, a church — and I jump. I fall. I feel my bones break. They mend themselves. Is that not terrifying? Maybe I want to stay broken.' I lower my head for shame of hearing my voice speak such words of despair.

The old man pats my shoulder. 'Dear boy,' he murmurs. 'So inconsolable.'

'I am not a boy.'

I make an attempt to shake him off, but the warmth of his hand pierces the fabric of my coat and I cannot bear the thought of losing this small comfort.

'I am sorry,' he says. 'I do not mean to sound cruel. But, surely — '

'I am lost: lost in the forest of my thoughts. I close my eyes and am swept into bloody nightmares of falling, breaking and healing.'

'You think them nightmares?'

'No,' I whisper. 'They are memories.'

I have spoken the truth I did not wish to admit. It is a relief. I take a strengthening breath. 'I want to understand what they mean; why they plague me so.'

He clasps my hand. 'Listen, Abel, if that is your name now. I can tell you everything; it comes to me through the sweat on your palms. I can scent out your entire history and where it has led you.'

A strange sensation possesses me: I stand on the step of a great house, grasping the door handle. All I need do is turn it and open the gateway to myself. The old man bounces from foot to foot, as though the earth is burning the soles of his shoes. He rubs his palms together, eyes sparkling.

'So. You will scoop out my stories.'

'Yes, yes!' he cries, cracking his fingers.

'Will they not fill this tent, this fairground, this city? If I am as full as you say, will it not be so?'

'Of course,' he gasps. He scratches at my sleeve and pulls me close, trembling, his palms clammy. 'Give yourself to me.'

'And when you have taken everything out and laid it before me, what then?' I ask.

He blinks. 'All will be well. Come now.'

'Wait. How will I put them back in? How will they all fit?'

'Do not worry about that.' His eyes are famished. 'Let me have your stories.'

'No!' I shove him away but he hangs on, greedy as a leech.

'Please. Just one good sniff. That's all I ask; nothing more,' he whines.

It comes to me that I have heard lies such as this before.

'How can I trust your words? You wish to open me up, gawp at my insides and then leave me spread in pieces like a broken watch.'

'But I can tell you what you are,' he wheedles. 'Stay with me. We shall have such adventures.'

'Get away from me!' I cry. 'No more lies!'

All he wants is to satisfy his own need; slake his thirst on my soul, feeding and feeding. I thrust out my hand and he falls; I do not look

166

where. I shall pretend I have not met this man. I will not write it on my document. I will forget him. I plunge out of the tent and run into the noise of the fair, grateful for the screech of peddlers, the sour puddles of beer, the pattering hands of whores.

⋆   ⋆   ⋆

At last I am far enough away to stop. My breath returns to me slowly. My mind spools in circles. At my feet are scraps of paper, trodden into the churned earth. I pick one up and see the picture of a girl entirely covered in hair, and straight away recall her strange image from the previous night.

I recognise her with an eye that is not one of common sight. It is an odd sense of communion: we are both different. Hers is the first thing people remark upon: she is never free of her distinguishing strangeness. Mine is less easy to find out, so that I can pass as a man amongst men. Yet both of us are shackled. I wonder if we have met before. I forget these things.

I try to smooth out the creases, but the paper is dirty, the words smudged. What if the same should happen to my document? I pat my breast and feel it rustle against the skin. I breathe in relief.

A man comes barrelling up to my side.

'No need to pick up the leavings! Here's a fresh bill of fare. The most astonishing aggregation of human curiosities gathered together in one place!' he yells.

I take one without thinking overmuch. As he pushes it into my hand I see a scrawl of dark paint on his hand: a tiny indigo bird in the V between thumb and forefinger. A memory stirs. He notices my hesitation and peers at me more closely.

'I know you.'

He stares a long moment, and then lets out a long whistle.

'Well, well. It's *you*. Mr Lazarus himself, risen from the mud. Wondered if I might run into you again sooner or later. Fuck me and no mistake. You've had a bit of a wash and brush-up, haven't you?'

I blink at him, trying to make sense of his words. The memory is very close: he said mud. Yes, I am lying in mud . . . He wiggles his thumb in front of my eyes and the inky bird flutters.

'It is flying!' I cry, and the attempt at recollection flutters away.

'Ha! Given you a taster, have I?' He tugs back his cuff to reveal a tangle of flowers. 'That's not all,' he whispers. 'I'm covered, here to here.'

He indicates neck and ankle.

'Why?' I ask.

He lays a lazy arm across my shoulder, hugging me to his breast in a sudden friendliness that serves only to remind me how friendless I am.

'It is a passion. After the first I had, I could not rest until I had a second. Then a third. My skin hungered for them. Of course, I look at the old ones and find I grow dissatisfied with them for they bleed and blur. But I can have their lines redrawn, have them turned into something else. But I keep this first one untouched.'

He points to the swallow soaring in its sky of naked skin, as though the surrounding ink is pushed back from its minute power.

'I will not cover it.'

He rolls his sleeve up further to a banner unfurling around the blooms, etched with the word 'Mother'. Above, a scarlet heart drips blood on to the scroll.

'Why do you have Mother tattooed on to your skin?' I ask. 'Are you afraid that you will forget her?'

He smiles and twists his arm so he can see the riband. With the tip of his finger he traces the outline of the letter M. He notices me observing him, and shakes off the softness with a burst of angry laughter.

'Do all your tattoos bring such an excess of feeling?'

'Feeling? I don't know what you're on about! Her? Clouted me if I so much as begged a crust.'

He crooks his elbow, swelling the muscle of his upper arm, and the heart starts to beat in a steady rhythm.

'When my mother died, she left me her heart,' he sneers. 'It is a joke; a bit of patter,' he adds in a whisper. 'Keeps the paying customers happy. Got to keep them happy, eh?'

I think once more of my document fraying and softening against the rub of my skin, ink blurring when I sleep on it. How fragile it seems of a sudden. What if I were to lose it? I think of the word 'slaughter-man' inked on to my arm, where

169

it would draw no attention to itself. I could record only what I wish and not a word more. I think of the fortune-teller and shudder.

'Can a man have anything tattooed?' I ask.

'Here's your answer,' he says, and removes his shirt.

The flowers at his wrist bloom into an abundance of stems and branches weaving up his right arm and across his breast, green-leaved and hung with swollen orange fruit, succulent and enticing me to bite into them. A striped cat roars, leaping across his stomach, and on the other side a warrior brandishes a silver sword before the great yellow fangs.

'You've seen nothing like it before, have you?'

I begin to say no, but as the word forms and falls from my mouth my mind sparkles with pictures, each small as a pinprick and as long-lasting: I see an ochre-skinned fellow, face swirled with dark waves; a woman with swollen indigo lips; an old man inked with furrows of dots punctuating the body's meridians. I blink them away.

'No,' I say firmly. 'I have never seen anything like this. Ever.'

'Of course you have not.'

He wraps his arm around my shoulder.

'Now. You come along with George. I'll not be letting you out of my sight so fast this time.'

'Where are we going?'

'To be entertained!'

He speaks this last very loudly, and heads turn. He stands, twisting himself in a way that makes his back appear broader. He winks at me and swoops his shirt in the air.

'Watch this,' he hisses. 'Yes!' he cries. 'You have before you the Encyclopaedic Man! The Wonder of the Taboo! Every forbidden enquiry satisfied! With illustrations,' he croons.

Soon, he has an audience of eager listeners.

'Here I stand, chief wonder of Professor Arroner's Astonishing Marvels! Inked with every story from the *Arabian Nights*, illustrations both saucy and satirical!'

He grins and twirls about some more.

'For you, gentlemen, and fine ladies of distinction, I think something salty shall suffice. I shall tell the 'Tale of the Mermaid'.'

He contorts his body into various postures, swelling first the muscles of his arms, then his thighs, then his shoulders. As he does, the pictures step forward for attention, or stand back to let another take prime position. The small crowd oohs and aahs. He bends his left arm at the elbow and a woman jiggles bright pink breasts and flicks an emerald tail.

'I caught her in the South Seas, when I was fishing for turtles. The native sailors would have gutted and pickled her — but not me! She was the greatest prize a sailor could ask for. They told me she was cursed! That I was a fool! But did I listen? Do you think I listened?'

'No!' sings out the little gathering.

'No, indeed. Think of it: at sea for six long months without a woman's touch.' He winks again. 'Ah! She was fishy!'

He sniffs loudly and the men snigger; I am not quick enough to accompany them.

171

'Fishier than a dockside trollop!' he cackles, to an answering chorus from the women, and this time I am faster.

'But, oh, she had skills that would put the most seasoned whore to shame. She was flexible as a flounder! Lascivious as a lamprey! Tight as a turbot! She'd take it any way I wanted.'

The snickering grows in intensity.

'A woman's touch! When your only companions are cannibals! Demons in human form!'

He turns about and shoves down the waistband of his britches, baring his left buttock to reveal a devil's face, all teeth and long scarlet tongue.

'A portrait,' he whispers. 'Your actual portrait, taken from life, of one of my companions!'

There are exclamations of disbelief. He stops his narrative.

'Would you hear more?'

They rumble approval.

'Then, gentlefolk all, you may view me in greater detail, and hear even saucier tales each night as one of Professor Arroner's Anatomical Marvels on Cockspur Street. Not just me. You will have heard, of course, of the infamous Stomach-Dance of Salome, to which no ladies of a nervous disposition are admitted? Oh, sirs, a treat for the eye, and the body also!' He guffaws, flashing bright teeth.

He hands out the playbills, crying out their merits as he does so.

'And that is not all! See the India-Rubber Boy, brought lately from the Malay plantations! View the most true and genuine Lion-Faced Woman!

172

What does she hide beneath her hair? What indeed!'

As he speaks, he holds out his cap.

'Thirsty work, kind sirs. Thirsty work indeed.'

Farthings and halfpennies tumble into his hat, and he nods at each small generosity; smiling as broadly at those who shrug and give nothing, muttering, 'Purely voluntary, sirs, purely donatory.' When he is satisfied that all forthcoming monies have been gathered in, he stands at my side once more and struggles back into his shirt.

'Does it hurt?' I ask.

'Hurt?'

'The tattoos.'

'Every one of them!' He laughs. 'It is a manly sport. The pain is not for weaklings.'

'I would have one. Like this.' I point to the word 'Mother', near-hidden in the flashier illustrations on his arm.

'I shall take you. This is indeed my lucky day: my prodigal friend returned; money in my pocket; and business to conduct.'

★ ★ ★

He leads me to a modest tent in the midst of the fair. The tattooist greets George warmly, enquiring how the latest piece of work has settled. George rolls up his trouser leg and points to a dragon looped around his ankle, and they hem and haw over the alacrity of its healing and the particularly fine detailing on the drops of venom trickling across its scales. I amuse myself looking about the booth at the neatly drawn

173

designs pinned to the canvas of anchors, snakes and ships.

'So, what is it for you, sir?' enquires Ivan smiling, for we are introduced to each other. 'This is your first?'

'Yes.'

'Then you are in the right place. More than your standard ritz.'

'I want something like this,' I say.

George's arm is covered, so I point to a design of a curling ribbon bearing the legend 'Your word here'.

'A nice banner. A fine choice, if I may say so. Nice fine work, and easy on the body.'

'And not too expensive,' adds George.

'Of course! Hygienic and good prices. What size shall the banner be?'

'I just want words,' I say.

'No ribbon?'

'Just words.'

'Please yourself. Names, are they? Lady friends? Any name you like. Priced by the letter.'

I turn over the coins in my pocket, and wonder where to start. I get out my paper and take a peep at it.

'Slaughter-man,' I say.

The tattooist glances at George, who shrugs.

'It's a long word,' says Ivan. 'It'll cost you.'

'That is of no concern.'

'Each to their own. Let's be started, then.'

He selects a needle from the cabinet at his side and waves it at me.

'Sharpened and cleaned fresh this morning,' he says proudly, and begins.

He holds the skin of my arm tightly stretched out; inks the needle-tip; lowers it into my skin and scratches; wipes; sits back. Scratches once more, poking and hammering the colour into my shoulder. I listen to the clock of needle striking bone.

Pain wells in my arm, as though a thousand inquisitive teeth are edging questions into my body. I find myself sliding into a drowse. I know the feeling, know that in this swim of pain I grow closer to a bright understanding. It is something I have always known, yet lost the knowledge of, and the pricking brings me back to it. I close my eyes and drift on the delicious feeling, when suddenly it is cut short by a muttered curse.

'I do not understand. What's wrong with you?' says Ivan.

I blink at him.

'What's up?' says George.

'The ink won't stick,' Ivan replies. 'Look.'

I feel the stab of the needle and its withdrawal. I look at my arm and see the shape of an S in dark blue.

'I'm needling him; I'm writing it. I get through the skin and the ink comes straight back out. Look.'

He takes a rag and wipes his work. The ink comes away, leaving a faint half-moon of pinpricks. As we watch, they heal.

'What in damnation is that?'

'Oh,' I say. 'I heal quickly.'

'You're telling me. You should be leaking blood and water. There's nothing. Not a drop.'

175

'Can you try again? Perhaps faster? A larger needle?'

'It'll hurt.'

'Please?' I say, and he lifts his eyebrows.

'You're the boss.'

He digs into me, hard. As fast as he inks me, my body matches him for speed of healing. After many attempts, he throws down his tools.

'I can't do anything with you. No man should knit up like that.'

'He's a queer one,' remarks George, his eyes taking on a strange light.

'I've seen something like it before,' says Ivan.

'You have?' I sit forward, eager to hear if there are other men like me.

'A Negro. Said he wanted a lion. I told him it wouldn't show up on skin as dark as his, but he said he knew it would be there, and that was the important thing. Couldn't do a bloody thing with him. Wherever I stuck my needle, his flesh came up in lumps, like I'd stuck peas under his skin. He didn't mind. Said his grandfather had a row of them across his forehead, so he'd have a band of them round his arm. You'll be like him, I expect.'

'Oh,' I say. I sit back. It is not like me at all.

'Some men have strange skin.'

'Can't you try again?'

'I've tried enough. I'm not blunting my points on you.'

'Come on,' says George, taking my wrist and drawing me out of the chair. 'Pay Ivan for his trouble. Then let us go for a walk.'

★　★　★

176

The tattooist is happy enough to take my money, and George seems in a hurry to bundle me out on to the street.

'Yes, you're a queer one indeed,' he says.

'Am I? It is something that happens to me. I am used to it.'

'What?'

'I cut,' I say in a dull voice. 'I heal. No blood.'

I want to be in my cellar, with the man I once called friend. His name dangles just out of reach.

'What — like with a knife?'

I shrug. 'Knife, blade, anything.'

'And you heal up, quick as you did just then?'

I shrug once more, waiting for the exclamation of disgust. It does not come.

'I knew you were special, first time I clapped eyes on you.'

'The first time?'

'On the river-bank. You were dead. Or should of been. Fished you out, I did. That makes us mates, right?'

I want to be away from this inquisitive man walking beside me, from the troublesome questions he keeps asking. I do not know these streets, for they are not recorded on my document.

'I must get back to my lodgings,' I say, keeping my voice as calm as possible. 'Will you walk me there?'

'Of course, of course. Plenty of time for all that. But first I must introduce you to a good friend of mine. A man of fine discrimination who would be most interested to make your acquaintance.'

'Why would he wish to meet me?'

'He is interested in marvels, and it seems that is what you are.'

I think of my comfortable bed. 'I am very tired.'

'It will take the briefest of moments. Today is not just my lucky day. I believe it is yours, too.'

'How so?'

'Listen. Do you fancy some easy work?'

'I have easy work.'

'No, listen. Real easy. Like me.'

'What do you mean?'

'All I need do is take off my shirt, show off my pictures, and that is the extent of my labours.'

'Men pay you for this?'

'They do. I am a marvel of ink and needles. But you are far more marvellous.'

'I am?'

'When I am pricked, I bleed. You do not. Your body is as coy as a virgin. It will not open its holes for any man.'

He chuckles, and I echo the sound, for it is expected.

'I saw an Indian like you. He danced on nails, and I swear he was not injured. Are you a Moghul? You look as dark.'

'No. I am from Holland. Or Italy. They say.'

I do not want to say, *I do not know*.

'Ah, well,' he shrugs. 'That is a shame. They love a bit of the exotic.'

George walks us through a maze of looming buildings, leading us down so many alleyways and up so many flights of steps that I declare even a man with the keenest recollection would become lost. After what seems like a half-day we

178

find ourselves in a neighbourhood I do not recognise. The streets are swept clean of the smallest speck of dirt; the gutters do not run with filth. Tall houses with gleaming white faces regard me haughtily.

He leads me boldly up steps I would not dare to climb on my own account, down a broad hallway and through a pair of polished doors into the grandest room I have ever seen. I scrape off my cap and hug it to my breast. His gaffer is a short man with a sticky hat pulled tightly on to his head. He looks me up and down.

'So, George. What can this one do? Seems less than nothing to me,' he sniffs.

'Just you wait. Go on,' George says to me. 'Show the miserable old bastard what you can do.'

'Watch it,' says the greasy man, but without anger. 'Let us be civil.'

George hisses 'Cut yourself' in my ear. I roll up my sleeve and take out my pocket-knife. I rub the handle with my thumb. It is so long since I marked myself with this sign of horror and shame. I have shied away from its strangeness. I taunt myself with the hope that I might bleed like any normal man, but I know the truth. My hand hovers. George digs me in the ribs. I snap awake.

'Who is this ruddy fool?' cries the short man.

'Wait; he is ready now,' says George and widens his eyes at me.

I place the blade on my forearm and make a shallow cut. The skin prickles with anticipation.

'Is that it, George? You have brought me a man

179

can take a knife to himself and not scream like a baby?'

'Watch.'

The wound heals slowly. The little man sighs impatiently.

'Still, I say, is that all?'

George waggles his hands at me.

'Come on, Abel. Make an effort,' he says urgently.

I press the knife until the skin opens; I draw the sharp point towards the crook of my elbow, revealing the tangle of veins, the dark crimson of my inner surfaces. I smile at their welcoming familiarity.

'Fuck me,' shouts the man. 'Fucking fuck me.'

'You see? Told you he was special.'

'He's not special; he's a bloody lunatic. He's killing himself, and me a part of it. Get him out of here,' he shouts.

'Wait,' shouts George. 'Look, he's not done.'

I close up my knife and gaze at my arm. My skin is beginning its graceful reconnection; my head swims with the fleeting delight I have experienced. It takes only a moment, and my body has sewn itself back together.

'Christ,' breathes the man.

'Now do you believe me? Have you ever seen the like?'

'George, you are right. A marvel. A true marvel.' He rubs his palms up and down the front of his waistcoat.

'How about a finder's fee then, Mr Arroner?'

'How about I kick you in the balls, George?'

'How about I take him away again, and myself

too? I could start my own company with someone as extraordinary as him.'

I let them argue, drowsing in the comfortable numbness of myself knitted up, of their exclamations of approval rather than rejection; revelling in the momentary respite it brings me. I pull down my cuff and feel the crackle of my document in my armpit. All is well.

'Well, Abel, if that is the name you wish me to call you by . . . ?' The gaffer winks at me.

'It is my name,' I say.

'Ha! Good man, good man.'

He slaps my shoulder, with a little stretching on to the tips of his toes.

'So, tell me about yourself, Mr Anatomy.' He squeezes his chin between thumb and forefinger. 'No, that is not right. There is no poetry to it. Tell me, sir, would you like better lodgings?'

I think of the cellar, the warm press of bodies. 'I am happy enough,' I say.

'Ha ha! You are a clever man.'

'I do not think myself overly clever, Mr Arroner. Though I can mend watches.'

'Can you indeed? Well, well. I can offer you food, sir. You eat food, do you not?'

'Yes, Mr Arroner.'

'Like beef, do you?'

'I do, sir. I can cut it, too.'

He does not seem very interested in my skills, and dashes on.

'Then beef you shall eat, if you work for me. Beef and bread and beer, every day, till you beg me to stop.'

'Why should I wish you to stop?' I ask, and

George nudges me in the ribs again.

'Fine lodgings. Good company. And money, too. Do you wish to make your fortune, see your name painted in letters two feet tall? I can do that for you. You shall want for nothing. Just like George here. Don't you agree, George?'

'Indeed, Mr Arroner.' My new companion coughs. 'We eat well, and live well. Though it would be a benefit to see more money, Mr Arroner, sir.'

The short man laughs. 'Then we must attract Abel into our circle, must we not? Is he not prodigious?'

'He is.'

'Is he not new? Never seen before?'

'He is.'

'Then consider that, George, and think how the money will come.'

'I do, Mr Arroner. I do think of that.'

George scratches at the fruit inked onto his arm. Our conversation seems to have put the oily man into a very cheerful humour.

'How fortunate I am!' he cries. 'How blessed you are also, to meet me at this juncture when I have need of men with talents such as yours.'

He takes a step back and regards the whole of me, sliding his eyes from my toes to the crown of my head.

'Yes, this is an auspicious day for you, my friend.'

'Mr Lazarus, you should call him,' says George.

'Oh no, George. I fancy something far more refined. Rhetorical.' He sweeps his hand across the air as though wiping dampness from a window-pane. 'I see it now. I shall call him the Marsyas of Modern Times.'

'Massy what?'

'Marsyas, my oafish friend. Flayed alive by the god Apollo for . . . ' He pauses. 'For stealing a golden apple,' he continues quickly. 'Now. To business, my fascinating new employee. A new suit of clothes. At my expense — I insist.'

George winks at me over the short man's shoulder.

'Very generous, Mr Arroner.'

'I know, George. I am a fool to myself.' He wags his forefinger at my feet. 'But those boots will not do. They will not do at all.'

'But they are good,' I say.

'Good? Bless you. Hear that, George?'

'I do, Mr Arroner.'

'The poor wretch, that he considers such battered specimens to be worthy of the epithet 'good'. See, the soles are nearly come away; the leather is almost worn through at the toe.'

'New boots would be just the thing.' George grins. 'What luck, eh, Abel?' He turns up his thumbs. 'Told you he was a good gaffer, didn't I?'

'Kind words, George, kind words. I am most affected. Well, Abel, you must stay with us, I declare.'

'I cannot,' I begin. 'I have another — '

I want to say, *I have another job*, but I know it is not true.

'Of course, another job,' says the short man, waving his hand. 'Besides, from one look at you I should imagine you lodge in a most foul and disgusting cave.'

'It is a cellar,' I say, to correct his mistake.

He continues as though I have not spoken a word.

'Dirty work. A dirtier life, wouldn't you say so, George?'

'Oh yes, Mr Arroner. All that dirt.'

'Think of it, Abel. You would never have to labour so again. You would sleep on clean sheets.'

'It is not so bad.'

'Pah! I won't hear of it. You shall lodge with us.'

'But Mr Arroner, sir — '

'Ah. I see it now. You have debts and obligations which worry you.'

'No, that is not it.'

'Some dear lady to whom you must bid a tearful adieu?'

George snorts and the short man shows his teeth. 'You see it too, George, do you not? A string of disconsolate females, weeping into their handkerchiefs!'

They laugh very loudly and I know this is one of those occasions when it is wise for me to laugh also. The short man wipes his eyes.

'Enough. Well, Abel, there is no looking back. George has told me of your previous employment. There is no need for shame. I am an honest man and you will find me a fair one.'

I look at George, astounded that he should remember my old job, when I do not. I take out my document. *I am a slaughter-man.* The word has been crossed out and corrected to *I was a slaughter-man.*

'What's this?'

184

The gaffer waggles his finger at my paper.

'It is mine, sir,' I say, and push it back into my shirt.

'Ah! A love letter, no doubt. I'll not take that from you. Just your old boots.'

'Sir.'

'George! Take him downstairs this very instant. He looks set to faint away from hunger. I'll wager you need a good dinner inside you, eh?'

He smiles, and once again it is my turn to smile back. George pats me on the back and takes me below stairs to the kitchen, a room far cleaner than the one I was in this morning. A vast cooking-range spreads its bulk from one wall to the other. On it is a black kettle, exhaling long puffs of steam. Two women and a lad sit around the table, hovering over plates piled with food. My mouth waters.

'Look what I've brought home. Let me introduce you to Abel. A new friend for us to play with.'

His words are light, but the women do not smile. The woman-mountain — for such is the abundant hill of flesh she bears upon her bones — folds her arms and winches up an eyebrow.

'Have a care, George. If he's one like us, mind your tongue.'

'Oh, I'll mind it well enough,' he coos.

He raises his hand as if to cup her prodigious cheek, but something in her eyes arrests the motion partway: his fingers curl and he withdraws. He contents himself with running his tongue backwards and forwards over his lips.

'He's a succulent little morsel. Don't you think so, Lizzie?'

'Not to my taste. I only like them willing,' rumbles the big woman.

George fixes his eye upon the younger female, a creature covered entirely in long golden hair. The girl from the handbill. She seems smaller than I imagined she would be.

'Oh, I don't know,' he continues. 'I like my ladies to struggle a bit. Lets me know what I've got in my hands is flesh and not wood. Not that I've any problem with wood. You got a problem with wood, Eve, my kitten?'

The hairy girl crimsons through her fur. The skinny boy giggles.

'That's quite sufficient, George,' growls the one they call Lizzie.

'Yes, yes. We must maintain a polite and orderly house to impress this gentleman, must we not?' He leans close and snaps his fingers before my eyes. 'So, my fine friend. What does it take to rouse you from the dead, eh?'

'I am not dead,' I say. 'Quite the opposite.'

The two women laugh.

'He's got the measure of you!' cheers Lizzie.

George scowls. 'Has he indeed?'

'Don't mind him,' says Lizzie to me. 'Don't mind him at all. You'll do all right, Abel.'

She pushes a plate of sausages and bread into my hands and bids me sit. They fall on to their food, and I join them. I do not know where I began this morning. I grow less sure with each forkful of food I put in my belly; with each glance of these new folk and their puzzling conversations; with the deep thrumming of shared strangeness I feel each time I look at the hairy girl. My eyes are tugged sideways, and it seems each time they alight upon her I meet her gaze.

I feel myself sliding away from all I knew. I understood things about myself, but what they were has slipped away. If I am lost, perhaps it is easier to be so. I shall stay here. There is no better place to go, and no worse. Indeed, there is no other place at all.

EVE

London, October 1857

'Step up, step up, I say!'

My husband stepped forward with a lantern in his hand.

'All alive!' he cried. 'The most astonishing aggregation of human curiosities gathered together in one place! Are these creatures animal or human? Historical or mythical? Mineral, vegetable or fantastical? Discover the truth for yourself here, tonight, and for a limited engagement only!'

He swept off his hat, a black silk chimney-pot of a thing, and tipped it to the men seated on the front row.

'Yes, you have heard tell of our Pandora's Box of mystical entertainments. Prepare to be astonished by the India-Rubber Boy! Prepare to be scandalised by the infamous Dance of Salome, the exotic Eastern Beauty! Dazzled by her voluptuous secrets!'

I thumped the drum and Bill clashed the cymbals as he described the allurements of each act. I peeped through the curtain rigged up to conceal us when we were not on show. It was not a bad crowd this evening: well-dressed swells for the most part, for my husband still managed to maintain a precarious hold on the better class of men.

Still, we had our share of rough types in glaring checked jackets, and as for women — well, that was a different matter: dollymops full of oyster suppers, not to mention the night-stand women eyeing up potential customers. He had sacrificed any claims to educational improvement with the arrival of Lizzie and her particular talents in the stomach-dance.

'Prepare to be diverted by the entertainments of the Encyclopaedic Man, inked with every story from the *Arabian Nights*, illustrations both saucy and satirical! You shall view the most true and genuine Lion-Faced Woman! What does she hide beneath her veil? All will be revealed: here, tonight!'

I would be out front soon enough. For now I revelled in the delicious luxury of watching them rather than them watching me. I loved to see their eyes, darting to and fro, lips parted with excitement.

'Everything is genuine! No gaffs nor fake freakery in my famed establishment!'

He grasped the chair, rapping his knuckles on the underside of the seat.

'Hard, plain wood!' he yelled, so loud a man in the front row flinched. 'Solid! Here for your inspection! No hidden trapdoors! Let any man approach and test the veracity of this himself!'

They were quiet. One thin lad was jostled forwards by his companions, but shook his head, growing more and more red-faced.

'Not one of you?' said Mr Arroner. 'Your trust is admirable, gentlemen.'

He positioned the lantern beneath his chin and it threw strange darknesses on to his face.

'First, we have something rare,' continued my husband, dropping his voice to a fearsome hiss. 'The Great Non-Descript! You have heard about him. The rumours are about in every salon where men of discernment gather. In every coffee-house where the sensational is freely discussed.'

He lowered his voice even further and every neck craned forwards to hear.

'You have heard whispers regarding his special talents. You know not whether to believe. You will say it is not possible. But see!'

He stood up suddenly and bellowed, causing many of the audience to start back in surprise.

'And seeing, believe! Ah! This famed exhibition is for the stout of heart, not for swooning, weeping, cowardly types. These are wonders unsuited to fainting females and mewling infants! Strong resolve is what we ask for. Are you strong men, brave men, men of firm resolve, who will not flinch from the terrors displayed here tonight?'

'Yes,' they breathed.

'Are there any faint-hearted amongst you?'

'No!'

'Ah, indeed! You are all brave-hearted men. You are not afraid. Oh no, not you. Tonight, I present the world's strangest mystery. The Man With No Name! The Man Without a History!'

They thought it was flannel, but it was the only time I heard my husband approach the truth, and it made me smile. He waved his hands suddenly, shrieked, and everyone jumped, even Bill and myself, despite knowing his showman's style. The audience smiled, elbowing each other for being caught out in such foolishness.

'Ah,' said Mr Arroner sadly, dropping his chin and affecting a mournful expression. 'It seems I was mistaken. See how easily you are frightened. Maybe it is better if we stop this train of events now. There is still time. I shall give you back your money; we shall pretend we never met.'

They shifted uneasily in their seats.

'There is no shame in being too fearful to see this petrifying performance. You can call it off, and — perhaps — still call yourselves men. What do you say? Shall we shake hands and bid each other goodnight?'

He stuck out his hand; the room was quiet. He flexed his forearm and fisted the air.

'Or shall we stand firm?'

There was a rumble of assent. We were in luck; it was an obedient crowd. However, this answering murmur did not satisfy him, for he spoke again, louder.

'I said, are you men enough to witness Terror? Are you brave men and true?'

'*Yes!*' came the response, and he grinned.

'You are fine fellows all. And no monies will be refunded for any future sickening of the stomach,' he added quickly.

'And now! His strange fame has advanced before him. He is the Arcane. He makes the hidden revealed! Stir up your courage, and prepare yourself for the Flayed Man: the Marsyas of Modern Times!'

Abel was steered on to the stage by George, who struck a lucifer and lit the circle of candles, manoeuvring Abel into position in the middle, where he unbuttoned his shirt and removed it. My gaze was drawn to the slick of damp fur fanning across his chest and stomach, and I forced myself to turn away. It was nothing. My husband took the shirt and swung it around his head.

'See!' he cried. 'An ordinary shirt, such as any of you might wear!'

My husband had wanted to grease him with pig-fat and stick him with sequins, but Abel had said no in that quiet way of his, much firmer than any bluster. He did, however, ask for one of Lizzie's shawls to be bundled around his hips, although this seemed a strange affectation for one so plain in his manners.

George held his hand to his mouth in mock-fright, reached into his belt and drew out a knife. He waved it backwards and forwards in the flickering light so all might see the gleam of true steel.

Abel took it at last, lifted it to his nose, sniffed along its length, and then rested it gently at the bulge of flesh on his upper arm. His skin goose-fleshed: pocked as though he had once been plumed with feathers, and each one had been pulled out. He flattened the palm of his hand and pushed. There was resistance: he pushed again and the skin popped like the smack of opening lips, the tongue of metal slipping into this new mouth.

'Oh God,' gasped a voice.

Abel looked towards the sound, tipped his head to one side, and smiled. Then he returned to his arm, drawing a crimson line of agony from shoulder to elbow. Breath was sucked into a multitude of throats. Feet shuffled. This was the moment we always feared: the sparking of panic, shouts of *murder!* The whole crowd kicking back their chairs and running away.

'See!' roared my husband, pointing at Abel. 'There is no blood!'

They looked; they believed; they breathed out. A few souls made nervous exclamations of how they had not been afraid, *oh no, not them.*

'It's a trick!' ventured one wag.

'It is not!' boomed Mr Arroner. 'Observe!'

The knife finished writing its scarlet name along Abel's arm. He gripped the edges of the gash and pulled the book of himself wide open to a dark red page, lifting his skinned limb for the crowd's inspection. Then, with neither flourish nor showmanship, he placed the point of the blade on to his naked stomach and drove it in.

'He's a bloody marvel,' murmured Bill, with the fervour of a convert turning to his new God.

It was his silence that made it bearable. If Abel had flinched just the once, or drawn in his breath too sharply, it would have been too much. But he worked upon himself with the calm curiosity of a boy who opens up a box of promised sweets, and, finding them uncommonly delectable, must needs sit quiet awhile and enjoy them with his eyes.

So did he let us enjoy him. His calmness at opening his body allowed us to marvel also. He was not mysterious in that trickster way of many freaks whose act is only a flag of smoke: he was beautiful. My husband had taken me on his search for strange companions and I had seen plenty of show-folk stick skewers through their cheeks and tongues. For all their showy strangeness, not one of them matched Abel for oddness. To him, the cutting was as simple as drinking tea, but infinitely stranger.

As I watched, I became aware of a tightness in my throat as a thrilling sensation rose throughout my body. I should not feel this way. It was unbecoming. I was a wife — a good wife; I ought to feel this stirring for my husband and for him alone. I endeavoured to wrench my eyes away from the sight of Abel. I looked at the toes of my boots. I studied my nails. I finger-combed my beard, for it always tangled into snags at the earliest opportunity, and then did the same with the long tresses which dangled from my ears.

Whatever I did, I found my gaze drawn back. Although nowhere near as abundant as the hair on my own skin, his chest was covered with delicate black hair; I wondered if it was as soft as it looked. One might find out by touching. Once again, I forced my eyes away, a fierce wash of blood sweeping over my cheeks. I was never more grateful for my fur. I clenched my hands firm and still and waited for my embarrassment to subside. This was wrong. My mind reeled.

'Perfect,' hissed my husband through the curtain, and I startled awake.

'Yes,' I gasped. 'Oh, yes.'

'That's enough for now. Knock those cymbals

together, Bill. I'll not see him tired out. Nor our paying guests.'

He screwed his hat back on to his head and stepped back into the centre of the stage to a burst of applause at which he simpered as though it was for himself alone. He pranced up and down, making a fine distraction from Abel, who was gazing at his wounds like a mother on the face of her sleeping child.

I could not stop watching Abel. My imagination danced wildly, and there was a lump of shame in my throat, hard to swallow as a piece of pork gristle. Cheers and catcalls dinned in my ears as George bundled Abel off-stage and placed him on a chair at my side. Lizzie was getting ready for her dance, swathing yard upon yard of satin around her copious frame.

I filled a cup with cordial and offered it to Abel, my hands barely shaking. As I flustered, Abel seemed lost in his own quiet space. I wondered what it might be like to be somewhere so peaceful. He was tranquil, observing the cut on his arm as it healed up.

'Are you well, Abel?' I asked, my voice a little rough.

It was a foolish question, and I was grateful when he did not appear to have heard. I sat beside him, as enchanted as he by the knitting of his flesh, which was now much progressed. The edges of the wounds had joined and were now red welts, livid as the mark of a lash. A single drop of blood was oozing from the deepest cut on his stomach; he licked his thumb and wiped it away, sighing.

Lizzie swept up to us and twitched her scarf away from where it dangled from Abel's lap.

'You finished with this?' she asked, peering where it had lain.

He blushed, nodding.

'Yes, it seems you have,' she chuckled, and sailed away.

I did not know what she meant by this, but for some reason it created an echoing blush in my own face. I was glad it was obscured by my moustaches. I wanted to speak; I did not know where to start. I thought of the years I had been locked in my own incongruity; how I had yearned to escape that loneliness and imagined the day when I might meet someone as queer as myself. I had pictured the communion which might spring up between us, how we would need no words to explain our companionship.

In truth, there were no words here, but I was flooded with awkwardness. He was seated next to me, but was as distant as India. On the other side of the curtain, my husband was making Bill's pitch. Lizzie was on next, and Abel would need to be ready with his pipe.

'Drink up, Abel,' I said. 'You need to play for Lizzie in a moment.'

'Thank you, Eve,' he said, gazing at me with a warmth that unsettled me even further.

'It is nothing,' I said as carelessly as possible.

He grinned. His dark eyes continued to hold me, and of a sudden I felt as though he was running a wet finger around the sticky bowl of my mind, placing that finger into his mouth and sucking it finger clean. I shuddered. *I am a good*

196

wife, I reminded myself feebly.

Beyond the draped velvet, Bill capered across the carpet, stretching out the elastic skin of his cheeks and letting go with much play-acting of feigned pain, to the crowds gales of relieved laughter. Abel continued to stare at me.

'Have we met before?' he said.

'Indeed!' I laughed. 'This morning, in the kitchen!'

He looked into his lap, frowning with some effort I could not understand.

'No,' he whispered, intently. 'Did we not meet before — this? Before I came to the troupe?'

'No, Abel. I am sure I would remember meeting someone like you.'

I smiled to show that I meant kindness.

'I forget so many things,' he muttered. 'Sometimes I wish it could be everything.'

He shivered and examined his palms for something that was not there.

'Abel. Drink your water.'

'Oh. Yes.'

He drained the glass, and as I took it from him, my fingers touched his. The hair on the back of my hand began to stir at once, as though a breeze was running through it, swirling it into curls, and then sweeping up over my wrist, prickling each hair on my arm into a stand of attention. My eyebrows fluttered; my side-whiskers licked flames across my cheeks, pulling my mouth into the broadest smile I had ever known. I ached with pleasure, and clutched at his hand.

With the clasping of our fingers, the pleasure

197

soared higher. Beneath my bodice my hair writhed across my back and shoulders, over my breasts; my nipples pinked and sang. At any moment this champagne exhilaration would make my feet leave the ground and carry me across the floor and out of this house; up over the city and far from here: very far and very fast.

Every part of me was on tip-toe, the tingling eddying around my belly and then with the keenness of a blade swooping between my thighs: I gasped at the sudden deep sting and my hand flew away from him. My pelt settled by tiny degrees, flattening slowly against my skin. We sat facing each other, his face as surprised as mine. I had a thousand questions and did not know which to ask first.

'Abel?' I gasped.

My stays were exceedingly tight. I seemed to be struggling for breath within their steel cage.

'Abel's not bad,' said my husband at my shoulder, so suddenly it made me start. 'But we'll make a better showman of him yet.'

My breast heaved and I prayed he had seen nothing. But he was ignoring me. I was never so relieved. This evening could not be paralleled for strangeness.

★　★　★

Bill made his final bow, snapping the skin of his thighs and cartwheeling back behind the curtain to a burst of clapping. My husband nodded *ready?* at Lizzie. She nodded back, and he stepped out before the audience once more.

'Who is here for something *educational?*'

My husband winked so hard I thought his eye might disappear into the bowl of his head. The crowd raised their beer-pots and cheered.

'Who would enjoy something a little *edifying?*' he leered.

The roars grew in strength. Bill looked at me and pulled a face. Lizzie saw it and pinched his ear.

'Less of that,' she growled. 'I'm on. Get those cymbals ready.'

'Get off, Lizzie,' Bill yelped, clutching his wounded ear, but was quick to obey her.

I was glad everyone was so busy, for I was sure the delight I had felt upon touching Abel was written clearly upon my body, fur or no fur.

'A Bible story, perhaps, gentlemen? And of course, *ladies?*'

He steepled his hands in mock-prayer, and the laughter washed up to our toes.

'And now! Will you welcome the Mystery of the East! The Wonder of the Harem! The Voluptuous! The Murderous! Salome!'

Feet stamped; beer spilled; my husband sent George to the door so no late-comers might squeeze into the room and cheat him of a shilling. I picked up a tambourine and shook it, feebly, for my arm still tingled. Lizzie waded forward, head veiled and wrapped from chin to ankle in a length of red satin, the sort used for dressing lampshades. She seemed to stretch from one side of the room to the other.

She lifted her great arms, joining her palms in a point to the ceiling. Clapped her hands, and the chatter of the company was slapped in half. Clapped them again, and all held their breath at this woman-mountain come before them. Then she began to roll her hips in a slow circle. The men's eyes rolled with her, hooked to the bounty of flesh that quaked before them.

I counted four gyrations: on the fifth she slung her hip sharply to the left, and I smacked my tambourine; then she swung to the right, to another crash from me and a jangle from the heavy girdle of brass coins around her middle. The crowd huzzahed. She let them cheer; but before the noise had died clapped her hands once more and silenced them completely.

Next, she swiped away the scarf and revealed her face. They could not help it: all gasped at her. No mere fat lady of a hundred cheap side-shows but the true Salome: long ringlets trailing into the squeezed crease of her enormous breasts, jewels glued across her forehead, rouged lips, eyes smudged with black grease, face stained the brown of the richest gravy. I had oiled her hair, smoothed on her paint, rubbed sunshine into her cheeks, would have been speared with jealousy if she had allowed anyone else to touch her.

She held her audience an aching moment longer and then billowed forward. The satin trickled over her belly and made her breasts shimmer.

'I am Salome!' she roared. 'The Whore of Babylon!'

Here some wags whistled, as we hoped they might.

'I am the Woman Clothed in Blood!' she bellowed. 'Oh! See what I have done!'

Continuing to howl, she waggled her fingers behind her back.

'What great sin have I done! See my sin and tremble!'

Bill stuck his hand through the backdrop and put the paper mask into her hand. Lizzie waved it fast enough to hide the truth of its papier mâché and paint.

'See the dripping head of John the Baptist!'

She swung the grisly spectacle of the severed head, and those in the front row scraped their chairs back. A female voice cried out in horror.

'Ha,' said my husband, close to my ear, 'There is always one woman to get them going. There has to be — or else I would have to send you out there, my dear, to start the proceedings.'

Lizzie peered into the field of faces clustering before her.

'Oh, what have I done?' she wailed, and not one of them gave back a smart retort.

'Ha,' breathed my husband again. 'A good night. It is a good night, indeed.'

I counted the long seconds of the crowd's held breath.

'Aaah!' shrieked Lizzie, now transformed into a frightful red spectre.

My husband nodded at Bill, who waggled a tin sheet, and at once the room boomed with thunder.

'Oh! How the Lord moves the Heavens!' she keened. 'Hear how I am cursed!'

Bill crackled the metal back and forth. Another gesture from my husband and I picked up the bucket of pebbles and shook it up and down.

'I hear the vengeance of God approach me!' bawled Lizzie over the ferocious din.

She dipped into her girdle and drew out a knife to swipe the air.

'I am cursed!' she yodelled, and brandished the blade in their faces. 'I have killed once! Shall I not kill again? Who shall I slay! I must have blood!'

She showed her teeth.

'Shall it be you?' she hissed, stepping forward and leaning over a scrawny man. 'Or shall it be me?'

His mouth slackened, Adam's apple ratcheting up and down his throat. She pointed the tip against her right teat, where the nipple pushed out the satin.

'Or shall I dance one final dance before dying? Shall I dance the dance I danced for Herod?'

'Yes!' cried out a brave soul, and the call was picked up by the rest of the rabble.

'How I danced before Caesar! How I danced before Herod! See me now as I dance before you!'

The air was hot with breathed-out beer; the men polished up their faces and took hopeful steps forward. One leaned into his tart's ear and spoke some lewdness; she laughed, slapping him gently enough not to earn a slap in return.

My husband raised his hand and Bill picked up the drum and set up a slow thumping. Lizzie stuck out her belly and shook its weight from side to side. Her dress stretched tight; through the slick fabric she showed the deep cup of her navel. Out front, the men screwed their caps tightly on to their heads.

My husband pointed his finger at Abel, who licked the nib of the pipe and blew a whining note that looped a ribbon around my throat and grew tighter. Lizzie wound her hips in a broad circle, first one way and then the other; flicking her stomach forward in a shimmering wobble at the end of each sweep. I saw tongues lick lips, mouths fall open, cheeks flash with excitement.

Bill picked up the pace and she picked up her feet, stamping, switching up the hem of her dress to show the stretched skin of her ankles, and then her rippled calves as far as the dimpled hams of her thighs. The men could not keep their eyes from her, entranced by the spectacle of the dance. One woman tugged her beau's sleeve and he shrugged her away. She screwed up her face in a scowl for a moment; then squeezed herself into him again.

Lizzie's dress was no longer cheap satin. It was her skin, and her skin was a flame of fire licking the generous sweets of her flesh. She was Salome, dancing her feet to ribbons in the court of a merciless king, blossoming huge with untold sin, dancing for men who could never hope to quench her lustful appetites.

My husband motioned to Bill, who beat the drum faster, and to Abel, who was already piping an Arabian air, perfectly in time. I watched my husband's upper lip prickle with sweat; his tongue darted out and licked it away.

'This is better than the pantomime any day,' he muttered.

Lizzie was now swirling her enormous hips in

a figure of eight, the strap of brass coins clashing with each swing. Abel played faster and faster. The tune became an aching need for comfort, for touch. It was the stroke of a hot finger down the ridged walk of my spine, cupping the balls of my feet and tossing me into the swirling indigo of heaven, spinning me amongst the stars till I was flailed into milky rain, wet from head to foot. My breath fluttered tiny feathers inside the sparrow cage of my ribs; every hair on my arm stood to attention. I could have listened for ever.

Then I noticed Lizzie. The dress darkened beneath her armpits, across her stomach and then down her thighs. Her chins trickled sweat on to the swaying sacks of her breasts but the crowd bayed her on, clapping in and out of rhythm with the drum.

'Mr Arroner,' I whispered, tugging at his shirtsleeve. The sound of the flute continued to twine brambles between my ears. 'Is it not time to stop the dance?'

'What? Not on your life. Look at them. They will talk of this for days. I shall charge double.'

'My dearest, look at *her*.'

'What?'

'She is about to fall. Then there will be nothing to charge for.'

He grumbled at the truth of it and hissed 'stop' to Abel, who ignored him. He waved, but Abel continued. He stood in front of him, semaphoring a cut throat, but Abel kept playing, eyelids slumped, the slit of eye showing the white. Lizzie shot a look to the side, her breathing harsh. The crowd whooped.

At last my husband laid his hand on Abel's shoulder and the tune stuttered, then stopped. At once he drew his hand back as though bitten, though Abel did not so much as frown. Lizzie swung to a halt, panting. I watched the rough sea of her breasts heave up and down.

'More!' cried a hopeful voice.

'Now,' said my husband, and poked me in the ribs. 'Give them what you're good at.'

I let out a shriek that was taken up by every other female there.

'No!' yelled Lizzie.

With a great swoop she stuck the knife into the side of the head still dangling from her left hand: the bladder within burst and red liquid streamed on to the floor. She swung it over the fools who had crammed forward to see the dance, spattering them with paint, crowing with angry joy at the sight of their hands slapping away at the dark spots staining their shoulders.

'Blood!' she screamed. 'Blood!'

I smiled, for I knew it to be only tea, much stewed, and a little India-ink powder.

There was a final drum-roll from Bill; I twitched back the curtain and Lizzie was swallowed up in its folds. The crowd bellowed and stamped; Mr Arroner stepped forward and started on his dazzling chatter about how wonderful was the spectacle they had been able to witness, how this entertainment would be repeated the following evening at this same location at nine o'clock, ten o'clock and eleven, and how the finest beers and spirits were available at the fine public house along the street, at good prices, this very minute.

'Drink to our health!' he cried, and swept towards the door and the extra money.

★ ★ ★

'Get me some gin,' said Lizzie to Bill, 'I'm ruddy parched.'

We sat behind the curtain while Mr Arroner steered the audience outside, screwing out the last farthing he could on his way. I watched Lizzie smearing the coloured grease from her cheeks, becoming the woman I knew once again.

There was a cough from the edge of the curtain. The scraggy man stood there, circling his cap in his hands. His eyes followed the rag as Lizzie wiped her face clean and dropped it between her ankles.

'Salome has gone,' said Lizzie, surprisingly gently. 'She has flown to sin in the lap of Herod.'

'Oh,' he squeaked, the only word his unruly voice would allow him.

There was no magic any longer. All that was left was a crew of scarecrows pecking at a heap of coins. Lizzie was an ageing tart with hot eyes, George merely a fellow with too many tattoos, the India-Rubber Man a pimply boy; Abel was a smear at the corner of his eye whom he would not remember. And me? A cat stuffed into a dress.

'Oh,' he croaked, voice snapping like a pipe-stem.

He floated away. We turned back to the take. My husband returned, thumped a bottle and more money on to the table.

'A wonderful crowd,' he beamed. 'Lizzie, a wonderful performance.'

'Bloody hell,' Lizzie hissed at Abel, 'lay off that sodding flute, will you? I thought you were never going to fucking stop.'

'Watch your language, Lizzie. There are ladies present.'

'Watch the takings, Arroner. When there's a problem with them, I'll lay off the fucking language. All he had to do was play the tune, then stop. It's all he ever has to do; and he forgets it, every bloody time. Have Bill do it. Bill wouldn't dare make a mistake, would you, Bill?'

Bill shook his head vigorously.

'Lizzie, calm yourself.'

'Don't give me calm. Up yours, Arroner.'

'Lizzie, my dear. We shall make a great deal — '

'We all have a living to make,' Lizzie grunted, 'and I don't make much of a living from you. I need more than your money to plump me up into the delicious pudding you see. I need fruit. I need sugar. I need — '

'I know what you need.'

She raised herself, stamping a path to the door.

'Lizzie, will you not stay and count the money? There is much here which is yours by right.'

'I trust you, Arroner,' she called back to us.

George and Bill laughed. I laughed. My husband laughed. Even Abel laughed, one step behind the rest of us.

'I am hungry,' she said, at the threshold.

'There are pies ordered,' piped Bill.

My husband stood up from his seat at the head of the table and made his way to Lizzie; he laid his hand on her shoulder, and she did not shake him off.

'Not even pies, Lizzie? Rich gravy? And gin? Enough gin even for George?'

The men laughed again, and George belched; but through the merriment I heard Lizzie hiss, 'Arroner, I am *hungry*. And not for your bloody pies.'

'Lizzie. We have an agreement.'

'Then keep your troupe in check. I've danced a pail of sweat off me tonight.'

'Be careful, then.'

She glared. 'I am always bloody careful. You get your cut of everything.'

I chased Lizzie to the door. 'Don't go,' I whispered.

She tickled the back of my neck till I purred. 'I'll be back — presently,' she said. 'You'll not miss me.'

'I shall. Lizzie, I need to talk to you. It's about — ' Abel's name stuck in my throat.

'Sweet girl. Let old Lizzie go.'

'You're not old.'

But as I looked into her face, I saw it was true. Small vertical lines I had not noticed before were creasing her lips and eyes, and a grey tide crept up the shore of her neck.

'You see? Wait for me,' she said quietly, and squeezed my hand, and then shouted to the room, 'Save me some gin, you thieves!'

Then she was gone. My hand hung empty. My

husband raised a cheer.

'A drink, my friends and dear wife! A toast to us all!'

He uncorked the bottle and slopped liquid into our glasses.

'Here's to us! None like us! Eh? Eh?'

He jabbed his fingers at Bill, grasped the flesh of the boy's cheek and pulled, let the six inches of skin spring back with a snap. We raised our glasses and clinked them.

Who can match us?

None can match us.

Who like us?

None like us.

★   ★   ★

The pies could not make me happy. I made a face at my husband and said I must go and attend to a lady's business, and left the room as slowly as I could manage. I took the stairs down to the kitchen, where the girl was flirting with a gentleman who had his heels propped on our table. They were too busy piling bread and beer into their mouths to take any note of me.

Their talk was all of Lizzie, but the woman they spoke of was not present, so I continued along the narrow passageway leading to the cellar and the room where the men slept. The aniseed scent of her was unmistakable; she had clearly come this way. But there was no food in a cellar, and she had said she was hungry. She looked starved when she left the upstairs room. I would see her fed; then she would listen to me.

With each step downstairs the darkness squeezed my heart further up into my throat. There might be rats. My skin crawled. The men's sleeping room was empty. The door at the end of the corridor was closed. My fingers fumbled for the door-knob, but I stopped as I heard her laughter through the wood, and the answering rumble of a man's voice.

As my eyes grew used to the dark, I saw a tiny light dribbling through a knot-hole at the level of my elbow. I crouched, and lined up my eye. At first I thought the room was on fire, then I saw it was the guttering of a candle-stub flaring against Lizzie's satin wrap where it was spread out beneath her, flaming the room with its sunset. She was laid upon it, naked as a babe, but very much larger. And upon her, the bony man who had come to speak to her.

I felt my face flush. I had never seen a man so unclothed: the shrivelled thighs, the bunching of bone at the knee, the drizzle of hair at the small of his back, feathering down into the dark crack between his buttocks; the way he clutched his arms as far as he could about her gigantic body.

And I had never seen Lizzie so beautiful. Freed from the binding of her clothes, she unfurled in a great sweep of gleaming flesh, soft and white as the inside of a loaf of bread. As a child just born seeks warmth and home, the scrawny man made his way across her stomach and came to rest in the groove between her mountainous breasts.

I knew I should leave, but my feet disagreed. I watched him suck her great brown nipple into

210

his mouth, kneading at the other breast as she stroked the top of his head. I did not know it could be so gentle, so unhurried, and with the room lit. She was tender with him; he was tender with her. He could see the whole of her; she the whole of him: that such things might happen between a man and a woman astonished me. Then I heard him speak.

'Take me, Lizzie,' he said. 'Make it all go away. Make it quiet. Just for a while I want to dream of my girl come back to me. Our boys still living and not dead of the cholera.'

I was holding my breath so tight I worried I might betray myself with spluttering, so I forced myself to breathe slowly. Lizzie bolstered him between her breasts and he wet them with slug trails of weeping.

'Come to Lizzie,' she hummed. 'Come to comfort.'

She held the nipple back to his lips, the ring around it almost the size of the dish under a Christmas roast.

'Don't let me go.' His voice was the snipped-off whimper of a puppy.

'Now, now,' she clucked. 'I'm here.'

She took his hand and nibbled his fingers to deep sighs from him.

'Come on, Lizzie. Give a man what he needs.'

'Be sure now,' she mumbled.

'I'm sure. A man needs some peace.'

'Never had a one who wasn't sure.'

'Do it, Lizzie. Do me,' he bawled into the deep cleft running from chin to cunny. 'Quick; can't you do it quick?'

'We've all the time we need.' She giggled, and smacked her lips. 'Don't hurry pleasure. Of all things, there should be no haste in that.'

He clambered further up her hill, snuggling into deep soft valleys. Her head fainted backwards, raining laughter: bubbling, spouting out of her throat and swirling around the room. The ring of meat beneath her chin swung its heavy necklace. Yet hers was not a cruel taunting: she chuckled so sweetly it tugged a string at the pit of my stomach and I wanted to shove open the door and dive into her too.

'Mama,' I sniffed, despite myself.

Her belly was broad as a pale mattress. His hand drifted into her navel and was lost up to the wrist; she smiled with the tickle of it.

'No hurry,' she gurgled. 'There's no hurry, my little man.'

Very slowly, her breasts began to squeeze together. At first it seemed by some magical force, then I saw she was bringing her arms closer and closer to her sides, scooping up great cushions of fat as she did so. Gradually he became enveloped in soft flesh, beginning with hips and chest.

Lizzie looked down and their eyes met. All the motherliness and kindness in the world was in that glance. It seemed to last an hour, but I suppose it was no more than a quarter-minute. I pressed my hand to my mouth for fear I should cry out at the sudden realisation that no-one had ever looked upon me with such love. She spoke again, very softly, and I would have heard nothing if all my senses had not been so on fire.

'Be sure. Are you content? Is all quiet?'

'All quiet, Lizzie,' he murmured, wriggling deliciously into her softness.

There was no more talking. She flexed her arms, heaping up her breasts until he was covered, except for his spillikin ankles and the grimy soles of his feet. There was no struggle, no lacking. Lizzie let out a great sigh, as of some great labour accomplished. The candle flickered, making brief lunatic shadows, and went out.

On shaking legs I returned to my room and perched on the edge of my bed, unable to sleep. I wanted to cry, but could not. After a long while, I heard the unmistakable sweep of Lizzie's body ascending the stairs. I waited a little longer and then crept to her door. Through it, I could hear snoring. I tiptoed to where she was lying and tucked myself into the warm dough of her armpit; fell asleep with her yeast tickling my nostrils, thumb in my mouth.

ABEL

Every morning, I wake up on a broad new bed, in a broad new room. It is below stairs like the place I was before, but lacks the comforting fume of men's bodies, the rolling murmur of their voices at all hours, the warm security of Alfred's friendship in which I wrapped myself so tightly it gave me a sense of who I am. Who I was.

Here, I have a clean mattress that rests upon a frame with four legs, and there is a washing-day when the sheets are taken away and returned at night smelling hot and empty. In the wall there is a window with glass in it that gives out on to a well at the rear of the building, and if I look up through it I can see a square of sky. Light comes through at strange hours and troubles me. There are no constant smells, no constant sounds, no constant shadows in which to lose myself.

There are only two other men besides myself: a boy named Bill who whimpers in his sleep, a thin sound which peels the air raw; and George, who does not shake me awake in the mornings, nor suggest we breakfast together, nor visit public houses. I lie on my bed all day, staring at the lines of brick outside the window until someone yells down the stairs that there is food, or beer, or it is time to show myself to visitors. After I have eaten, drunk or displayed myself, I lie down once more. So the days pass.

I lie in the emptiness of this room, through the emptiness of the days. Eating takes up very little time before my belly is satisfied, and I find myself with a surfeit of hours lacking activity to fill up the time. When I mention this to George he calls me an idiot and tells me I had better keep such dangerous thoughts to myself.

'I for one can find a wealth of things to divert me,' he says.

I ask him what he finds to do when he is not showing his tattoos, and he laughs in a way that does not invite me to join him.

So I lie and read my document, there being nothing else to do. The paper is soft, the folds almost worn through. *I am a slaughter-man. I was a slaughter-man.* I had a job of work before I came here: it occupied me. When I think of it, I feel contentment: the carcases, swinging on shining hooks, each drained flawlessly, split into faultless halves by my hand. *My friend is Alfred,* reads the next line. My heart turns over, for I have lost that security. I move on swiftly. *Before I came to London, I was a clock-mender in Holland.* The pleasurable feeling returns briefly, but no-one brings watches any more.

I shake myself out of such self-pitying meanderings and chide myself sternly. Such

215

lolling about will profit me nothing. If there is nothing with which to fill the hours, why then, I must create useful diversions. I take myself upstairs to find George arguing with Bill in the hallway.

'But Mr Arroner told you to go,' complains the lad.

'I'm no man's errand-boy,' he sneers. 'Hop it.' He sees me appear and nods in my direction. 'Take him instead. It'll do him good to shift his arse for a change.'

'But — '

'Don't let him hold the purse. He's as like to drop it in a beggar's hat and think it well spent.'

'I'll go,' I say.

'I don't know,' says Bill, looking at me nervously.

George sticks his face very close to the boy's.

'Another word from you, you little turd, and I'll turn you upside down and use your head to mop out the privy. I've got a busy evening.'

He saunters away, whistling. Bill shrugs and we set off towards the market.

'All George does is prop his feet on the table and swig tea,' grumbles Bill. 'And gin. Lazy bastard.' He bites his lip. 'Begging your pardon.'

I laugh, and he relaxes.

'Just you wait,' he continues. 'I'm not putting up with him for ever. I've had offers,' he says proudly and sticks out his little chin. 'Don't tell anyone,' he adds in a whisper. 'Mr Arroner'd skin me. And George would hold the stone to sharpen the knife.'

'I'll tell no one, Bill.' I smile. 'George is no

particular friend of mine.'

'No, I suppose he's not.'

We walk through chilly streets. I decide that I must begin a new map to find my way about, so I note the name-plates as we pass, scribbling them on to my increasingly crowded document. Bill blows on his fingers.

'At least this bloody weather will keep the meat fresh. Arroner won't let me go early in the day.'

'Why not?'

He regards me as though I am rather foolish to ask such a question. 'It's a fair bit cheaper at the close of business.'

'Are we not wealthy enough to buy whatever we desire?'

He laughs. 'That's a good one, Abel.'

'But Mr Arroner talks of our wealth. Indeed, I would say he talks of little else.'

'You're not wrong there.'

The press of bodies, the creaking of loaded wagons to and fro, all the hustle and bustle reminds me of the time when I walked out every day during my stint at the slaughter-yards. I had forgotten how much I enjoyed the pounding of my feet along the cobbles, the drum of my heart beating a steady rhythm in my breast. I breathe in the scent of fresh horse-dung and scan the evening flood of workers, weary faces enlivened by the knowledge that their day's labour is done. The public houses are thronged, raucous with shouts for beer as men drown out all thoughts of returning to wherever they call home. I always walked directly home. Why would a man not go there straight away?

But I am falling into one of my reveries. I blink myself awake, and listen to Bill chatter about the list of items we are to purchase. He points out objects of interest in the shop windows: jewellery in one, ladies' hats in another. I do not remember looking so closely through their blank glass faces before. After many such diversions, we reach a street of butchers' stalls. To my eye, they are far more enthralling than a milliner or glove-maker.

The entire row is hung with carcases, festooned as though in preparation for some gay festival: a curtain of huge beeves suspended on hooks, accentuated by carefully arranged pigs; here and there a swag of furry coneys and a feathery pelmet of bantam hens, all hanging by their heels. Scrawny dogs skulk, ever hopeful, ever to be booted away with colourful curses. Costermongers' carts squeal along the stones, accompanied by cries of 'Sharp knives, sharp knives, fresh limes, ho!' Squat brown pots of rosemary and bay mix their fragrance with that of long-hung meat.

'Like lace on a turd,' giggles Bill.

I sigh in happy contemplation as we stroll along the shop-fronts, nodding at the butchers shouting out bargains to be had. Bill catches the eye of one, swathed in a rust-spattered apron, and points out a tired piece of beef dangling from an iron spike.

'Who cut that?' I remark. 'Looks like he used a fork and spoon.'

The butcher laughs. 'I'd like to see you do any better.'

'Just give me a chance.' I smile. 'I was a

slaughter-man,' I say proudly.

'Were you now.'

'Yes, at — '

I do not remember the name. Bill leaps in and fills the space.

'Now he's moved up in the world! He's a proper sensation, he is.'

I cover my embarrassment by prodding a slab of liver with my thumb.

'That's a nice piece. And those cow-heels,' I add. 'Make a succulent dish, they will.'

'Maybe you do know your stuff,' says the butcher. 'Best bits I've got left for such a price.'

He wraps them in bloody paper and throws in a slice of brawn for good measure. Bill counts out the coins with great care.

'You're a box of surprises, you know that?' says Bill as we carry our purchases away. 'I'd rather be with you over George, any day of the week. He talks to the traders like they're dirt on his boot. It riles them up and as often as not we walk home with sausages that are half off, or half straw. I'm looking forward to my dinner tonight.'

He skips along the pavement, dancing ahead a few paces and then back, singing snatches of the kind of songs that Eve performs in the show. I think of Eve and it is a pleasant occupation of my mind. Bill jumps up and down happily and it occurs to me that he is still a child. I wonder if I was ever that young. I must have been. How many lifetimes ago? I push the question away. Such thoughts make me weary.

★　★　★

Later that night, after the show is done, I lie on my bed, listening to George and Bill snore. I draw out my paper and spread it on my knee. I shall record each day, each memory. If I keep writing, then I shall build myself up, word by word, line by line, page by page until I fill a book. Who knows, one day I may find myself writing a line and I shall cry out, *Ah! This is the answer! I have found it!* And all will be well. The thought makes me smile. When I have finished noting today's events, I fold the paper carefully along its well-thumbed creases and put it back under my armpit.

My shirt pulls up from the waistband of my breeches and I look at my belly: silver lines radiate across its paleness where once it had expanded and now is shrunk, sagging between the heels of my hipbones like the collapsed skin of a milk pudding. Once, I must have been fat; now I am thin. When did that change? Why I should forget is still a mystery.

I look at my clever hands, crossed with lines, dark against the biscuit-brown of my skin. Something stirs; deep, close. I know this sensation, as familiar as breathing. I sigh, and wait. The pictures will come now. I fall into a drowse that is not sleep but a breathless lifting of myself to another place, immeasurably far from the bed on which I lie.

I smell blood, hear the rasp of sharp blades. At first I am confused for I see knives every day: pressing them into myself for the show and feeling their brief consolation. This is different, however. I gaze at the ceiling and am washed with light from high windows, the room suddenly pungent with the stink of dead bodies that I discover arranged around me in rows. My nostrils sting; yet somehow I know that in a few moments I will barely notice it.

A question stirs: perhaps this is where I will find an answer to my questions, for why else would I be brought here? I am sure that I belong in this unfamiliar place: I know with a certainty that my hands have laid out these corpses. I walk amongst them, brushing the cheek of one, stroking the hand of another, showing them kindness for they are gone into the slumber from which only God can rouse them.

I sense the stretch and bulge of muscle, the squeeze of lungs, the soup of the stomach, the purples and reds of their insides bound up in the perfect bags of their skins. My breath catches, and I wonder if I am sickening into a swoon, but it does not occupy my attention for long. I am far more intrigued by the scene unfolding before me.

I see a white-haired man, neither George nor Bill, standing beside one of the tables on the far side of the room. He is dressed in outlandish clothing: short breeches, tight stockings and a long waistcoat, and furthermore he is wearing not his own hair, but a wig, dusted with powder. Other men clothed in the same odd fashion surround him, and each of them watches his movements, intent upon his words.

He raises his hand, smiling, beckoning me. When he speaks it is not English, but another tongue I recognise instantly, full of poetry. I hesitate, for I think myself an observer, not one who can be observed; he speaks again, more urgently, and I understand he is asking for particular instruments, although the words are strange and I have no recollection of hearing them before.

But I know where I am: in the Museum of Anatomy, in Florence, the studio of Master Calvari. It is as sure as I knew the watchmender's shop in Nijmegen. I go straight away and find the blades, knowing that I have selected the ones he named; I return to his side and he nods at my correct choice. Warmth fills my breast: I have pleased him.

Our first cadaver is laid out in readiness. My master — for I know with a firm conviction he is such — draws back the sheet laid over her in an effort to preserve her modesty. Her mouth is still full of her last sour breath; her breasts are pale, the vital liquids within them long settled into the flesh of her back and buttocks; her belly thrusts upwards like a sack overfilled with beans.

'She will make an excellent model for our studies, caught so late in the pregnancy,' my master declares.

We gaze at her, not one of us showing any discomfort at her nakedness. My master points at various parts of the dead body, naming its function, even marking the small details of the *porta hepatis*, so easy to overlook. He turns to me.

'Lazzaro,' he says, for that, in his mind, is my name. 'You may make the first incision.'

My heart soars with pride. I take my knife and

draw apart the curtains of her body, cutting into her belly. I fish within and bring out the heavy loops of her greater and lesser intestine. I peer at the foam about her lips, the inky blotches on her breasts and upper arms; examine her stained and blackened hand.

'She drowned,' I say.

'Your reasoning?' he asks, forefinger tapping his great square chin.

'See, they had to cut a branch from between her fingers. She must have clutched at it when she cast herself into the water.'

My master laughs, pleased with my clever deduction. He presses his thumb into her distended uterus, exposed now that I have lifted out the reeking contents of her belly.

'Observe,' he declares, 'the condition which prompted such a desperate act. But it was not a whole-hearted decision, for indeed she reached out and tried to save herself. Sir, continue.'

My fingers peel back the *omentum majus*, and I open a window on to her womb. The manikin is wedged within, *umbilicus* fouled around its neck, grimacing in the agony of its final struggle.

'How precarious our coming forth into this world!' he exclaims. 'How the *umbilicus* must have tightened as it fought to be free!'

He snaps his fingers.

'Plaster,' he says, and one of the students dashes away to do his bidding.

I stand close by him, breath furring the frigid air, reading the lessons of the body and keeping private my store of questions. I watch him spread the mixing-plaster over the face of the unborn

223

child, his hands steady.

'We anatomists labour to capture the essence of our beautiful mortality,' he says in his musical voice. 'We are more beautiful than anything the Greeks carved from stone, for stone cannot breathe, however cleverly wrought and marvellously proportioned. I would have the beauty of flesh. Not marble.'

I am spellbound. He looks on me again.

'What do you think, Lazzaro?' His voice swells with encouragement.

'You understand!' I reply, a little breathlessly.

The students laugh, and I hang my head, for I fear that I have spoken insultingly. Of course he understands; he is my master.

'You are most complimentary,' he says, and I look up to see he is smiling. 'I hope your faith in me is not misplaced.'

'Yes, master,' I whisper.

He returns his attention to the corpse.

'This is death: putrefaction and stench,' he continues, pointing his plaster-knife at the body. 'We anatomists are sculptors. Artists. We seek out the wonderful workmanship of God in Man. We open His great picture book of Man. In it may we discover all that is remarkable in God's creation. Through study of the powers and functions of each of the parts, shall we know ourselves.'

I cannot cease from gazing upon him as he speaks. It is as though each word is meant for my ears alone.

'By understanding visible nature we may understand God's divine plan. Understand ourselves, and we understand the measure of all things. This is more than *anatomia normale*. This is the revealing of divine architecture.'

It strikes me then: here, in this reeking anatomy studio, I am close to my answer. I am filled with an unfamiliar emotion and slowly realise that it is happiness; I bloom under the tutelage of my master, studying the wondrous geometry of the human body, feeling it bringing me close to resolution, to insight.

My master knows: everything he says confirms that he could understand my secret. All I need do is ask the questions I have stored up in my soul, and he will tell me the answer, for he is the one who can teach me what I am. Hope makes me bold. At the end of the lesson I dawdle behind.

'*Dottore*,' I say when we are alone. 'I want to ask you something.'

'Indeed. Speak, man.'

I will ask him now. He will tell me.

'Then, master, let me ask: what ties a man to life? What loosens him into death?'

'Good questions, my dear man, most excellent!' he cries. 'What do you think?'

'Every living thing bleeds when it is cut,' I say, and drop my chin. 'That is the law of nature.'

'Good,' he says. 'You are an observant pupil. Every creature with blood, such as a dog, or a man.'

'Every man?'

'Of course.'

'And every man, when he is cut deeply, remains open?' I say nervously.

'And bleeds to death. The blood is the life, Lazzaro.'

I swallow a great lungful of air. 'What if a man was cut and did not bleed? And his flesh knitted up, and swiftly?'

I dare not look at him. He must be able to see what I am concealing: that I speak of myself.

'It would be a miracle.'

'Maybe I have seen such a thing, master.'

'Pah! A piece of trickery such as you may see in one of the fairground booths on Holy Days. Men who swallow swords, or toads. My good man, cast your mind solely upon science, not fakery and magic tricks.'

He turns to leave, but my questions are burning a hole in my tongue and it seems I must spit them out.

'Master. Does everything stay dead when it is cut?'

'You may be sure of it. A fatal wound will kill a man. When a man is dead, he stays dead.'

His eyes are friendly and it makes me bold enough to keep on pressing him.

'There are other things that trouble me.'

'Indeed? What?'

'I have thoughts I can tell no-one. Dreams. Memories. I want someone to help me.'

'Perhaps I can help,' he says, and starts to flicker, like the flame of a candle in a draught.

I clutch at his arm and cry, 'Master! *Dottore!*' I want to hold tight to the answers he possesses: they are here, in this place. I do not want to leave, but I am dragged away into darkness. Of all my desires, the one I most long for is to return.

A voice speaks: *Don't you understand? This is not a dream. You are not sleeping.*

I look around, trying to find the blackguard who is torturing me, but I am alone.

This is your answer, says the voice. *You do not want to hear it.*

'Shut up!' I cry.

You run from yourself, it continues. *But you are always at your own heels. There is no escape.*

There is a deafening thunder, bowling closer and closer.

'Please, stop. I can no longer bear it,' I shout, and I am returned to my clean bed.

★ ★ ★

Eve, the one they call the Lion-Faced Girl, is standing in the doorway, knocking on the wooden frame.

'Abel?' she says.

'Yes.'

'I thought you were asleep.'

'I thought so, also,' I say, blushing at the untruth.

'What ails you?'

'Nothing,' I lie once more.

'You are pale, sweating as though you are in a fever. You were crying out.'

'Was I? I think I have had a nightmare.'

'Indeed?' She flicks a voluminous eyebrow; her forehead shimmers. 'You are as bad a liar as I am, Master Abel.'

She is smiling; she means kindness. I struggle to catch my breath, to clutch at what I have just

227

seen: the anatomy studio; picture after picture, leading further into myself. Not dreams: lives, memories. Already I am losing the meaning of it. I scrabble inside my shirt and get out my paper. I press the pencil stub into it so hard it breaks off.

'Do you have pen and ink?' I say.

She laughs. 'No. What a strange request.'

'Please,' I say, my voice rising in panic.

Her smile fades away. 'I am sorry,' she mutters and disappears.

I chant, 'Anatomy, answers, memories,' over and over until she returns with pen and inkwell. I scrawl in a fury, trying desperately to remember more details before they fade.

'Abel?' she says. 'What are you writing?'

'I have dreams. But they are not dreams.' I point to what I have just written. 'I believe they are memories.'

The effort of saying this makes my teeth grind. If I tell her about my secret strangeness, she will draw aside from me. They all do.

'Abel, you look as though you are about to faint clean away. Wait,' she says, although I have no intention of going anywhere.

She returns a moment later with a glass of clear liquid, perfuming the room with the sharp oily smell of gin. She glances over her shoulder into the corridor before seating herself at the end of my bed.

'Thank you,' I say, and take the drink.

It fortifies me surprisingly well. She smiles, and the long moustaches framing her mouth quiver. There is a pause.

'You are stranger than the others, Abel.'

'Am I?'

'Yes. Can you not see it?'

'I do not know,' I say, turning away from her clever eyes.

'George has his wonders painted on to him. Bill? Well, he is a boy, and an exaggeration only. I never heard of any man who can do what you do.'

'No, I dare say you haven't.'

'I think there is more to you than that, even.'

'Yes?'

I endeavour to sound careless, although my heart is pounding with mixed fear and exhilaration that she can read me so clearly. She leans forward and takes my hand, grasping it firmly. As we touch, a profound sensation seizes me, as though my innermost being is reaching up towards her from a deep well.

'Oh,' she whispers. 'I did not expect . . . I feel . . . '

'What?'

She breathes heavily awhile, and then smooths out her ruffled face.

'You.' She smiles.

We stare at each other. I feel a tantalising hope that I may draw close to the shore of friendship and understanding. I do not know if I can trust her. I have been wrong before. I draw my hand away. She hangs on.

'No, Abel. Let me. There is such — '

'Confusion? As if I do not know that myself.'

'Far from it, Abel. I think I see . . . wondrous things.'

I am torn between my aching need for communion and answers, and the quaking fear of how badly it turns out. The hungry pawing of the fortune-teller is disturbingly fresh in my memory, as is the bewildering rejection of Alfred, a man who called me friend. My fear triumphs.

'Please. No more.'

'Why are you so afraid?'

'Mrs Arroner — '

'My name is Eve.'

'Eve, I am sorry. I am a coward.'

'Are you indeed?' she says drily. Her smile is warm. 'Very well. I shall never force you to anything you do not wish.' She busies herself with rolling a lock of hair round and round her finger. 'Let us talk of other things.' She nods at the document I still have in my lap. 'What *is* that piece of paper you carry about, Abel?' she asks.

'It is the record of who I am,' I begin. 'The thread which I pray most devoutly might lead me out of this labyrinth.'

'How very politely you speak, Abel!' She laughs, but there is delight in the sound rather than cruelty. 'I almost see you in a brocade waistcoat to the knee, doffing a three-cornered hat trimmed with feathers, like a prince from a history book.'

'I would bow as deep, if it should please you, my lady,' I say in an affected twitter, caught up in the easy playfulness that sparks between us.

'You are quite the dandy.' She laughs again and claps her hands softly. 'I believe you are rather droll, Abel.'

'I believe you may be right.'

We smile at each other, shyly at first, her eyes demurely cast down; then more boldly and freely until she lifts her head, tossing her abundant curls in a swinging cloak about her shoulders. Her eyes shine beacons into mine. Then her head turns quickly, and I hear it too: the clump of a man's feet along the corridor. She starts to her feet and is leaning casually against the door by the time George saunters in. He looks at her and then at me.

'Cosy little chat, eh?' he says, and whistles softly.

'Indeed not, George,' she replies. 'It is almost time for the show.'

'Already?'

'Yes. It seems one of my daily tasks is to rouse you men into activity. At least Abel is present.'

'Always ready and Abel?' he sniggers.

He stretches out and plucks away my document before I can stop him.

'What's all this then? Writing love letters to the lady of the house on the sly?'

'It's his, George. Give it back.'

'What? Not got a tongue in your head?' he taunts, waving the sheet just out of my reach. 'Want this, you meat-head?'

'Yes, I do.'

He squints at the crowd of words. ''I am a — ' What's this nonsense?'

'George, do you truly wish to reveal that you can barely read?'

'You bitch,' he growls, crumpling the paper.

'Oh no, George. The Lion-Faced Girl, remember? Most assuredly not a dog.'

'I'll show the two of you!' He scowls, striding out.

I spring to my feet.

'Leave it,' hisses Eve. 'Don't provoke him.'

I ignore her and follow George to the kitchen. He dangles my paper over the range.

'I knew you'd come. You have to see this.'

He drops it into the flames and I am on my knees straight away, hand in the heart of the fire. What I manage to rescue is charred beyond reading. Amongst the scattered words I pick out *slaughter, friend, speak, jump*.

'Fuck me.' I look up and see George, his features squirming. 'Your bleeding hand.'

The skin is sizzling, peeling into curls. He backs away, tripping over his own feet in his haste to be out of the room. I watch my flesh bubble: it begins as a tickle of warmth, the heat growing and growing until I look about me and discover myself in the heart of a conflagration, thrust into another of my memories. I smell the bitterness of burning hair; the crackling roast of my skin, which crisps without blackening; the fume of green wood stacked round my shins. I am not alone: I am surrounded by other men, bound like myself, and shrieking, for the blaze finds them delicious.

Flames tumble up my arms and I hold them before me, observing their fluttering. 'I am sweet!' I shout, my words parched to nothing in the heat; but the fire will not feast upon me, although I yearn for it to sink its fangs and taste me.

It shrugs me off, hovering but not devouring;

making a halo of gold to display my nakedness; consuming my clothes, my hair, all my externals, even the very air, but not my flesh. I touch the ropes binding me and they fall into cinders: I walk free, carrying the furnace from place to place, and am preserved within it.

I wake, the scent of grilled meat hovering in my nostrils, gasping with the shock of what I have seen. A hand alights on my shoulder. I look up into Eve's face.

'Abel, what is happening? Oh, your hand.'

I hide the vile flesh under my armpit. 'You are horrified.'

'No! I am surprised. That is all.'

Her eyes sparkle with friendship. I so wish to place my trust in her. But I have been betrayed, so many times.

'How can you want to draw close to a monster such as myself? You cannot understand. No-one can.'

Her eyes wince, and I cringe with shame at my rudeness: I did not think myself so cruel.

'I am sorry. I spoke harshly. I am not harsh.'

'No. You are not.' She regards me steadily. 'Show me.'

I draw out my hand hesitantly and she seats herself on the floor beside me. We watch my skin rekindle, grow back pink and shining. After the time it would take to eat a bowl of soup, I am whole again.

'Abel, I should count it a singular honour if we could be friends,' she says.

She gets to her feet, patting out the creases in her skirt, reaches out her hand and pulls me to my feet with surprising vigour.

'Eve,' I breathe, and squeeze her hand. 'I should value it above all things.'

'Thank you, Abel,' she says tenderly. 'And, in truth, it is time for the show.'

★   ★   ★

On the playbill Eve's face is flattened out like a dried splash of tea staining the paper. But when she steps before the lights she comes to thrilling life. The warm air rising from the candles causes her hair to float about her head as though she is being carried on its wings. Abundant tresses mass round her delightful face, tumbling over her cheeks like a stream over pebbles. She is afire in the candlelight, a tapestry of gold threads mixed with bronze. I did not think myself so rhapsodical. Spun gold and bronze? Perhaps I was a poet once. Not a very good one, if my art bent towards such over-burdened phrases.

Her whole body — or, at least, all that we are permitted to observe — gleams with smooth fur. I see how modestly she endeavours to veil her downy breasts, for they are in danger of toppling out of the neckline of her dress. It is cut very low at Mr Arroner's insistence: 'To add a bit of piquancy,' as he puts it.

A man at the front cries, 'Go on love, a bit more leg!'

She smiles at the audience, her teeth clamped together, and declines to accommodate the request. There is a growing chorus of wolfish howls.

'Show us your knees!' says another hopeful, only to be ignored.

Mr Arroner stands to the side, grunting with exasperation at such a missed opportunity. He waves his hands as though pushing up an invisible sash window, gesturing for Eve to lift her skirt. *Higher, higher.*

She promenades from right to left and back again, singing a pretty ballad about her true love, who is a dear sweet boy and surely will return to her at any moment.

'It's singing!' laughs one wag.

'Miaowing, more like!' pipes up another.

No-one seems particularly interested in her words. It is only when she swirls her petticoats in the chorus that they show any appreciation, and it is of a low sort. For all Mr Arroner's continual reminders of how refined and educational we are, I observe very little refinement or desire for learning in these groundlings. Before me are slack chins and looser minds; prurience that licks its lips and smacks its chops at the sight of her parading before it.

She pauses and stands with her fists on her hips, tapping her foot, as though considering a conundrum. Then she twirls her long moustache and throws the crowd a wink as she starts her second song, a well-known air. When she gets to the chorus, she sings 'I'm your own, your very own puss' instead of 'your very own girl'.

The whistles and catcalls fall silent for a full line of the next verse. She throws in a few more substitutions of 'cat' and 'puss', with a miaow or two for good measure, tossing her hair and

235

winking at the men who had hooted at her and are now struck dumb. The laughter begins; slow at first but building into a wave that rolls from wall to wall and back again as they celebrate her cleverness in bending the tune to her will.

Mr Arroner is at the side of the stage, arms crossed over the bulge of his stomach. I watch his sour frown smooth into surprise, then astonishment, then avarice. As Eve leaves the stage to a tumult of applause, he leaps on to the vacant stage.

'So modest a maiden!' he carols to the crowd. 'But who knows what tricks she might have for you tomorrow! Who can guess what she might be cajoled into revealing! There's always, something new and exciting at Professor Arroner's Unique and Genuine Anatomical Marvels!'

At this suitable gap in the performance, Bill squeezes between the shoulders of the mob, carrying a tray of pork fat cut into little squares that Lizzie fried crisp that afternoon. His cries of 'Fresh crackling, tuppence a twist' can be heard over the low murmuring of the audience. Mr Arroner paces in small circles around Eve, fiddling with the buttons on his waistcoat until I am sure the threads will snap under the strain.

'What a revelation, my dear. Indeed, how you take your poor old husband by surprise. But a fine idea.' He preens. 'A capital notion. I believe I shall rewrite more melodies for you.'

On and on he chatters, until I notice how it becomes his own invention and Eve's talent is quite overlooked. She sits, combing out the knots in her beard whilst he enumerates song

236

after song which could be adapted to her needs. At last, he bounds back before the crowd to announce my turn.

'Does it not bother you that he takes all the credit?' I ask.

'When he is happy, he is kinder,' she says. 'And is it not something to see me transformed from a spectacle of ugliness into the creator of mirth?'

With that, it is time for me to take my seat in the wavering light and rancid stink of the candles. I wind a shawl around my hips, to cover the shame of my unfortunate reaction to any deep cutting. My fingers tighten around the handle and lift the knife. What Eve has just said reverberates around my mind. It is true: here, under the eager eyes of the audience, I can act as lord of myself, even if only for a few moments.

I swing the blade in a mesmerising circle, round and round, watching light flash up and down the keen edge. At first, the movement is accompanied by the steady crunch of teeth on roasted pigskin. Gradually, the sound subsides. When I judge that I have their full and breath-held attention, I press the point into my forearm, beginning with feathery cuts which barely penetrate, flickering touches, cat's-tooth sharp. The watchers gasp a little, roll their eyes, but I am just begun.

I twist the knife upwards and my flesh opens. I plunge inside, hear the breathing of the whole room catch, for now they think the bleeding will begin. Of course, I know the truth. I thrust my fingers into the hole, drag the lips of skin to one side and spread my body wide: red-violet, soft enough to slide inside. To a mounting hiss of disbelief I push the blade in further, ramming it back and forth, groaning with each thrust, and begging the gods to make this pain so great it may finally carry me over the tantalising threshold to my soul. I strain into this great darkness: sweat-smeared, sticky, slashed, open.

I stick out my arm and display my secret, observing their eyes drinking me up. I reveal the crimson at the core of every man; I make what is hidden visible. Some step back in disgust; some step forward with the hunger of men who starve for strange meat.

'Behold, the Marsyas of the Modern World!' Mr Arroner bellows somewhere off to the side, reminding them of the wonders they are witnessing.

'Go on,' he grunts, urging me to further wounding. 'More!'

My mind sharpens like the knife I hold. I draw it across my stomach, slashing my flesh deeper and deeper, approaching wholeness only when I am cut to ribbons. Perhaps this time I will throw open all my doors and step into the daylight of full self-knowledge, stride through this sleepy world, awake at last. But all I do is stir my private parts into wakefulness, shaming me, grinding my nose in the truth of just how far I am from clean and wholesome manliness.

'Touch me,' I entreat, but they shudder, shrink back.

I lose the fight. The moment I cease my strife, I begin to heal. My eyelids droop and I feel rather than see a pair of strong hands lift me, carry me off-stage, seat me behind the curtain. At last, I feel nothing.

* * *

'It took me enough time to find you,' the man says, coming up to greet me after the show. 'It did not help that they're calling you the Man With No Name.'

He smiles, and pushes out his hand; I take it out of politeness and he shakes mine up and down, smiling all the while. I take the opportunity to examine his face, which has the greenish tinge of a man away from the sun overmuch, a thick moustache above a gentle mouth, cheeks thin as a weasel's. There is a smell of dried blood about him. His features shift in the silt of my mind, but I am sure he is not anyone of my acquaintance.

'So, how are you, Abel?' he asks. 'This new life suiting you?'

'Yes. It is good,' I answer, wondering how he knows my name.

'Plenty of excitement? Bit of a step up.'

I wonder what I have stepped up from, but I decide to agree with whatever he says. George has burned my document, and already I am losing the memories of my time before here.

'Yes. A step up.'

He seems so sure of me that I wonder if I do know him. He shifts from foot to foot.

'Still the big talker, eh?' he says, showing all the teeth he possesses in a broad smile. 'That's my Abel. Not changed one bit!'

He sticks his hands back into his pockets. I would do the same, but the britches I wear for the show have none. 'To prevent any accusation of fakery,' Mr Arroner says. I scratch my freshly healed stomach. He eyes the gesture.

'Hmm. You are more peculiar than ever, that's for sure.'

'How goes it with you?' I ask, hoping such a question might help me remember this gentleman. Perhaps he is a friend from — before. I concentrate all my faculties and his name poises on the very end of my tongue, eager to be spoken out loud.

'Oh, not so bad.' His eyes slide away from mine. 'The work's much the same. Although the beeves miss your aim. As do we all.'

The memory rushes in. My hand is raised. The hammer falls and a bullock staggers, falls, dies. My knife cuts it open.

'Of course! I am a slaughter-man,' I declare, and know the words as truly as if my paper were returned to me.

'Not any more you aren't! Far too grand for the likes of me now. Ran off, you did.'

He grasps the peak of his hat and pulls it tightly on to the top of his head.

'I ran away? Surely not.'

'Yes, well. It was a while ago. All forgotten.'

His face colours from greyish-green to pink. With a supreme effort I gather up my wits. Yes, I know this man: we lived together, laboured together.

'You are a slaughter-man!' I cry, and loudly,

for George and Eve glance up from the table where they are counting out the take.

'That's me. Couldn't be happier.' He nods at my feet. 'Those are fine boots you have on.'

'Yes.'

I look down at the gleaming new leather. He forces his fists deeper into his pockets. I know the gesture so well. He used to do it when he was embarrassed. This is most frustrating.

'No need for my old rubbish, I'll wager. Well, then. I must go. You are a busy man. Far too busy for your old pal.'

'I am not so busy.'

'Of course you are.' He jerks his head sideways to where the others are clustered. 'Off you go. Your new pals.'

With that slight sneer it comes to me, at last.

'Alfred!' I exclaim warmly. 'It is you!'

I take his hand and pump it up and down.

'Now, now,' he says, pulling away. 'That's enough.'

His eyes dart from one side of the room to the other as though we are overlooked by men who would do us harm.

'Please. Let us sit awhile. You are my friend.'

The words freeze as they tumble from my mouth. I stare at him, and remember. His embraces, his desire, how he thrust them aside and me with them, his vicious words. He *was* my friend.

'I shall not keep you,' he says quickly, not meeting my gaze. 'I must go.'

He withdraws his hand and I do not stop him.

'Yes, so you must.'

He turns and walks away, leaving me heavy

with memory. He was my friend, and then he was not. As simple as that. I wrote his name on my document. But as easily as it has been burned away, so is he gone. How many other times have I written the heart of myself on to a scrap of paper only to see it lost? I drift back to the table and my new companions. Lizzie is gone, as is her habit. Mr Arroner is leaning back in his chair and drawing on the stub-end of a cigar, talking at the top of his voice.

'Bill? Run and fetch a bottle, lad. On me. You've all worked very hard.'.

He spills coins into the skinny palm. The boy nods quickly and scampers off.

'Now I shall go and make safe the remainder.'

Mr Arroner pats the flank of the money-box and leaves the room. I take the opportunity to seat myself in the empty space beside Eve for, I declare, I wish to find more ways to be at her side.

'Off he goes,' grumbles George. 'To cuddle up with his one true love.'

Eve stares into her lap. When Bill returns, George grabs the bottle, measures out a glass for himself and one for Bill. He waves the gin at Eve and she shrugs, but pushes her glass forwards to be filled all the same.

She seems subdued tonight, which is not like her usual self. As they cradle their cups, I consider her muted brightness. Who would not be so if wedded to such a puffed-up bore as Mr Arroner? I sigh. We may pretend friendship but I know that I want more. I want communion, a far closer bond than any man may have with a woman who is another's wife.

Eve declares that she wants my friendship, it is true. But so did Alfred. So did the fortune-teller, in his twisted way. How many other so-called friends have I lost in the fug of memory? How often have I been spurned, betrayed? Why should she be any different? Perhaps I am deluding myself with hope and loneliness. I must be a fool to trust again.

These miserable thoughts transport me into a maudlin state, one in which I do not wish to dwell overlong. I consider how George and Bill cram their leisure hours with drinking, how merry it makes them, how swiftly they fall into the numbness of sleep. If they can drink themselves into a snoring oblivion, then so can I.

'I would like a cup of gin,' I say.

Their heads turn.

'What?' squeaks Bill, and George tugs his ear, stretching it out some distance.

'Now, Bill. Have a care. The good Mrs Arroner has instructed me to be philanthropic to our poor companion. Pour him a big one.'

Bill limps off to fetch a fresh glass, rubbing the side of his head. He presents me with a tin mug slopping with clear liquid, smelling of tar. I toss it back, pat my stomach and belch loudly.

'Another!' I shout.

'That's more like it!' George snickers. 'Why not get another one of them inside you?'

He makes a space for me at his side, suddenly companionable; feeds me cup after cup, his pleasure at my new-found thirst matched by my hope that it will make me forget how dear Eve has become, how impossible it is for me to trust anyone's offer of friendship.

'Down in one, Abel!' he coos. 'Come on, man. One more for your old pal!'

'George,' I hear Eve say, in the swooping to and fro of my drunken thoughts.

'Watch, everyone! Watch old George make this dead fish swim!'

'I am a happy man!' I shout, shoving my drink into the air, spilling it down my arm. 'Look at all my friends!'

George laughs as though I have made a wonderful joke, and quickly refills what I have lost. Somewhere in the midst of George's merriment I hear Eve say, 'Hold off, you'll make him sick,' but George ignores her and so do I. Later, much later it seems, Lizzie returns.

'Good evening, Lizzies both,' I slur, for there are two of her.

I wonder how they can both fit through the door at the same time, for she is a broad woman. Bill runs to her side and tucks himself under her arm, walks his fingers up her belly, finding the overhang of the first billow of fat and tucking his hand into the warm envelope. He sighs, burrowing his cheek into the comforting flab.

'Not too deep, now, William,' she says, softly. 'There, child; there.'

'I'm not a child,' he mews, without complaint.

'Be glad you are, Bill. Don't be in any hurry to become a man.' She turns her attention to George, then to me. 'I think he's had quite enough.'

'Oh, we're just getting started. Aren't we, Abel?' George throws his arm across my

244

shoulder and I nudge my head in the crook of his neck. 'You're my pal, aren't you now.'

'My pal!' I belch. 'Here's to friends! Best thing in the world!'

'What's he on about?' asks Lizzie.

'Who cares,' says George. 'But what larks I'm having finding out.'

'George, stop this. I know your ways.'

'Lay off, Lizzie. Just welcoming him into the fold.'

She stares down her many chins at him.

'Enough. It is time for us *all* to be abed.'

'Have it your way,' he mutters. 'Can't a man have a bit of fun at the end of a working day?'

She shoos us away, to the complaints of Bill and George, who swear they wish to drink all night. My knees loosen as I stand, so they crouch under my armpits and carry me swinging between them down to our sleeping-room and drop me on the bed. I roll on to my back, eyes blurring the walls into doubles of themselves.

'Look at me! The happiest man in the world!' I slur at them, and close my eyes.

★ ★ ★

This is when my pictures come and torment me. I want them to flood in upon me tonight, for nothing could be more cruel than the torment of knowing myself damned to an eternity of loneliness. But the gin seems to have sealed the jar of myself, and the horrors flap within, teeth pecking too feebly to effect an escape. I grind my teeth with hope, praying for wild dreams to rush in and blot out all thought of Eve and how unattainable she is. I close my eyes, and feel the sway of the great earth beneath my bones.

It begins, in greater force than ever: I am wrenched once again to the top of the tower. I cling to the finger-holds between the bricks, this hell I am returned to.

Go on. Do it again, commands the voice.

I look about me and see that the building I am about to throw myself from is different tonight. The houses below are tiled with black stone, gleaming in a spray of rain, and it is no tower: rather, I am scrambling on to the steep pitch of a roof. But wherever I may be, whichever one of the thousand roofs I have climbed on to, my purpose is the same, to grind myself to nothing.

I slip on wetness and my heel catches in the broad mouth of a leaden gutter, which gurgles a stream along the side of the building and spurts it out of the jaws of a stone demon carved at the gable end. The rain gathers force, soaking my hair on to my face.

You are alone. You are outcast.

'I know!' I yell.

Jump. Finish it off. Finish yourself.

'But this does not work. It never has.'

I laugh at the gargoyle, and jump. Feel the storm hammer my body down on to the flagstones. Hear the familiar breaking; the familiar prayer. *Let me be done with. Let it be the end, this time.*

It is said that a man finds himself at the bottom of a fall. I wish only to be lost, to die, to be human with its attendant bleeding, ageing,

246

gentle dissolution into dust. I yearn for brokenness, and as I leap I know it is the one thing I have been forever denied. My existence is a cycle of dying and healing. I can no longer avoid the truth of the countless times I have done this, in countless different places, how I have failed at every attempt.

I cannot count the number of times I have been compelled to climb, seeking a place I pray is high enough to kill me when I fall. There is nothing I cannot heal from. Nothing I can do to stop trying to find a way.

Try drowning! cries the voice.

I dive into a river. Water presses into my ears; I breathe in its sweet promise, but however hard I labour it does not want me and throws me on to the bank.

Or disease? Surely there is some sickness you haven't tried yet?

So I breathe in the corrupt air of hospital wards but remain uncorrupted; I press filthy bedsheets to my body, lick the sores of old men dying of fatal distemper, put my tongue into the soft green wounds of soldiers, taste the foul breath of cholera, typhoid, diphtheria and every other slime for which there is no name and still I do not sicken.

See how many deaths you have evaded!

I am stripped, a leather thong around my throat, thrown into the maw of the marsh, the sour water smacking its lips, sucking at me and then spewing me up. See! My belly crammed with poison. See! I sway on the end of a rope; I fall on to my sword; I am broken, burned,

247

drowned. And always healing.

I am surrounded by men and women who have found their way out of life and into death, when I cannot. It seems I have spent my life trying to do so, and a lot of time trying to forget. The dying is not successful; neither is the forgetting. I am remembering and do not want to for there is no comfort in it.

The pictures crowd me to the edge of myself, finding any space to push their way into me. They are memories: that truth I can no longer avoid. I have tried to run away from them and now they have caught up, mobbing me as small birds do a hawk, pecking until it tumbles from the sky: eyeless, its flight feathers ripped away.

Perhaps I was happy in my state of blank indifference, before I began to search for answers. Perhaps I was happy when I was the butt of jokes, the 'dimwit', the 'cold fish', 'the slack-jawed one'. Now I am intelligent and all I wish to do is return myself to my former state of childishness.

* * *

Light begins to seep through the window from a sky I cannot see. I cannot lose myself in gin. If I cannot finish myself off by hurling myself into rivers or off towers it was foolish to think I could do so by drinking. I rub my aching head. Eve offers me friendship. I am a mean sort of creature if I turn her generosity aside merely because I have been spurned or mistreated by others. *Away with such wallowing self-regard*, I tell myself.

I am a selfish wretch. I barely deserve to claim so much as a kind glance from Eve, yet she offers far more. Terror or loneliness, memories or nightmares, I shall go forward as I have done a thousand mornings before, and a thousand thousand mornings before that. Today, I will cut my body open, and it will heal and close up. I consider the dreams of last night and it comes to me that all I do is plough the same furrow of self-pity and self-torture, over and over. Perhaps it is time to lay off my self-entranced mirror-gazing and look into the face of the world.

EVE

London, June 1858

'You need a new name,' mused my husband, drinking his third cup of coffee that morning. 'The Lion-Faced Girl is not sufficient. We need a fresh twist. There is tea in the pot,' he added, seeing me staring at him.

'Why not use my real name? Eve is a fine name. It means mother of all.'

'Our paying guests do not want a mother. Not with a face like yours. They want something pretty. Dimpled. Helpless.'

'Medea?' I smirked.

'Sounds a bit grand. You are a fair English rose hidden in a bush. There's a thought. Your name must blossom too. Flora. Dora. Rosaletta. Doralinda.'

I let him play with his Floras and Doras. Despite his promises of travel once the winter became summer, we were still in London. Our address was now a little less flash: a medium-sized villa with no flight of scrubbed steps leading to a front door gleaming with a lion-faced knocker. There was now a cheap brass plate, a 'necessary disbursement' in the words of my husband. He

250

cleaned it himself every Sunday morning, rag in one hand, tin of polish in the other, smearing on the oily muck and then buffing it to a proud shine: 'J. Arroner, Esq. Entrepreneur. Exhibitor of Exquisites, by Appointment'. Bill was foolish enough to ask 'by appointment to who?' He never learned how to avoid getting his ears boxed.

We still had a fire in every room, although not all of them stocked with wood and coal in the colder months. And whereas our previous water-closet had sprigs of blue posies inside the bowl and was situated in a tiled room of its own, our new offices were of plain cream porcelain with a sturdy brown seat. At least we shared it only amongst ourselves and were not fallen to the penury of my childhood, when the yard privy was used by countless weary backsides.

My personal maid was gone, leaving us only a girl-of-all-work, for whom the word 'work' seemed a foreign idea. As often as not I drew the curtains, lifted the rugs, hauled them outdoors and beat them. And every morning I listened to my husband bluster about landlords milking our hard-earned sovereigns. His bedroom, still separate to mine, had become his Chamber of Retreat and his strong-box resided therein, chained beneath the bed like a chamber pot.

He glanced up from his newspaper.

'You have on a hat, Mrs Arroner.'

'Yes, my dear.'

'Are you dressed to go out?'

'Yes, indeed I am, Mr Arroner.'

'Are you well?'

'I am very well.'

'Hmm,' he said. 'Where will you go?'

'I am going to walk to the end of the street,' I said. 'And when I am there, I may turn the corner and walk to the end of that street, also.'

'Will you?'

'If the weather continues to be fine, I shall. I shall walk up and down the street and take the air.'

He smiled over the top of the newspaper he was pretending to read. He still believed I could not tell the difference between reading and peering at the shapes of words.

'An enchanting idea. You could perhaps call upon your mother.'

I clenched my fingers together so tightly I thought they might tear the stitching in my gloves. For months I had sent letters inviting her to visit us, and all of them had been returned. I half hoped she might come now we were in less impressive lodgings, but the letters continued to come back. I wondered if she was living a new life, one in which I had never been her daughter. I might be famous, but I hardly kept respectable company.

'No,' I said with a casual air, as though his words had made no impression upon me. 'I believe I shall call upon the Cow-Horned Lady who is residing in Goverton Square. I hear she is strange as am I.'

'Indeed, I have heard the same. It is a fine day. Very fine. You will have a long and pleasant walk. Will you, at least, return by evening?'

'I shall,' I whispered.

'For we shall want you for the show. It would

252

not be the same without you.'

'I have never missed a performance.'

'Of course, of course. But I do wonder if you might become enchanted by the sights you see. I fear some gentleman might tip his hat to you and you might be bewitched away from me.'

'How could that happen?'

'Oh, men of the world have ways to entice an innocent creature such as yourself.'

I hesitated. 'I shall return straightway, dear husband. Be assured of my devotion. There is no need to be concerned on that account.'

I willed him to raise his eyes and meet mine with a kind glance, but he was attending to the task of reading. One affectionate word was all it would take to keep me.

'I am not concerned. In any case, make sure they do not charge you the entry fee. Lift up your veil if they insist.'

'I thought I might not wear it.'

He looked over the top of the paper.

'Of course, that is your choice, Mrs Arroner. I am sure people are grown much kinder these days.'

'I am famous,' I hazarded. 'I am their own Lion-Faced Girl. They have taken me to their hearts. My only dilemma will be the signing of so many autographs.'

My voice contained a tremble I hoped he did not hear.

'Indeed, Mrs Arroner, you must take a pencil. I believe I have one you may borrow.'

I sat down on the edge of the fiddle-back chair and felt the seat sag accommodatingly beneath me: it would be comfortable to remain seated. I chewed my lip. Thought of the crowds: the line between affection and repulsion.

'Maybe it will turn to rain after all?' I said as though I did not care overmuch. I could just see the top of his head over the brim of the paper, his scalp gleaming through his thinning hair. 'These are new gloves,' I continued. 'You gave them to me.'

He did not lower the newspaper.

'I do so want to call upon the Cow-Horned Lady.'

'I will purchase her *carte de visite* for you,' he remarked, and then stopped, slamming the paper on to the table-top. The cups and saucers danced.

'Mr Arroner?'

'That's it? Of course! Capital! I am a genius! All the best people have these new cards, even the monstrous. It is just the thing we lack, and precisely the thing we need. Imagine it.' He wiped his palm across the air as though clearing a space on a bookshelf. 'Who is the fairest of them all? You! Ladies, we have proof irrefutable. Your photograph taken with the only true and genuine Lion-Faced Woman. Every lady a princess by comparison. Guaranteed.'

'You are very clever.'

'Clever? I am a wizard! A worker of miracles! What better than to be in at the start, when the rage for these cards is new and fresh. Imagine, dear wife, your face for sale, by the hundred-weight. Available for purchase, by high and low regardless.'

'Dear Mr Arroner — '

'She looks you in the eye! Dare you face Medusa's glare!'

I sighed.

'I am glad that you are happy.'

'I am delighted.'

His face gleamed. He grinned at me.

'I do not wish to spoil these gloves,' I declared. 'I shall stay here.'

'Will you?'

The smile teetered.

'Yes. Will you read to me from the latest news, my dear? We could spend a pleasant hour together.'

He placed the paper onto his lap.

'I should enjoy that very much, Mrs Arroner,' he said, folding the sheet. 'But I have a pressing engagement — the business of men. I declare, it fatigues me greatly. I should much rather spend the morning with you.'

He looked at his watch.

'Ah, it is almost afternoon.' He stood, crooked his forefinger into a hook and nudged me under the chin. 'How you would be lost and strayed without my guiding hand,' he remarked, chuckling.

He left the room. I listened to the pleasurable creaks of the chair released from his weight.

★ ★ ★

My husband returned that evening with a new dress of green satin to set off the spun flax of my hair. One thing which had not changed was his purchasing of clothing which I thought immodest.

'It is a little short, Mr Arroner,' I said, for it did not reach my ankles.

'It is what the most fashionable ladies are wearing this season,' he protested, not looking me directly in the eye. 'Besides, we have to keep tantalising them with the hope that you might lift up your skirts.'

He watched my eyebrows climb.

'Which of course you will not, Mrs Arroner.'

'I should hope not, neither,' barked Lizzie. 'Don't want her diverting any of my trade up her river.'

'Do not worry yourself, Elizabeth.' He smiled. 'You are our Whore of Babylon. There could never be any to touch you.'

Lizzie preened herself.

'There's a fair queue outside,' said Bill.

'This is two shows in one,' crooned my dear Mr Arroner. 'They come to have their pictures taken. They come to watch the pictures being taken. It is brilliance.'

★   ★   ★

There was the fraught silence of anticipation as Bill pulled back the curtain and we waited for the opening burst of applause.

'Step up!' bawled my husband, drilling the point of a walking stick at me. 'Step up and take a seat! Your picture with the Lion-Faced Woman! Quick as lightning by virtue of the Collodion Wonder of the Photographic Art! One shilling only!'

They were here to stare into my magic mirror;

256

for always I gave the same answer: *You are the fairest*. Even the ugliest could walk away satisfied that there was one woman more foul-featured than her.

'Is she animal or human? Her visage cries out *animal*! But her manners are those of the most tenderly raised female. Which gives great satisfaction to all who venture to see her.'

There were two seats set up, and I filled only one. Lizzie had brushed and combed me till I shone like the glossy cushion I crossed my ankles on. The drop behind me was painted like a forest glade, blotted with sunshine through sharp-edged leaves.

'Be not afraid. Be venturesome! Come, ladies, step forward!'

For all that I might work miracles for the hideous, no-one wanted to be first.

'We all know the story of Samson and the lion. Come and see this lioness made lamb-like! For out of the strong came forth sweetness, as was made clear to me by the Dean of Cologne, who travelled all the way from Germany to view this marvel! She is our Lion Princess. Our kitten, who will purr as sweet as any puss. Approach without fear!'

My husband stalked the length of the front row of chairs, and fixed on the plainest woman in the room, a woman who was fat whilst lacking any of Lizzie's pride. She tried to squirm away from his attention, but he had her in his sights.

'Ah! Sweet Cupid! You have stuck me with your dart!' he mugged, clutching his breast. 'I am slain!'

There was a ripple of mirth at the sight of my dandy-cock of a husband losing his heart to such a slab of flesh. He grasped her vast hand and lifted it to his lips.

'Such porcelain skin! Such maidenly modesty! Oh, how I am slain by the arrows of Venus!'

The ripple became a surge of laughter.

'Will you not step forward, dearest miss?'

'Madam, I think!' came the cry, and the audience hooted with delight.

'Go on, love, up you go,' yelled an encouraging voice.

'Ladies and gentlemen! Is she brave enough to hold the paw of the fearsome lioness?'

'Yes, go on, love!'

'Do it!'

She was pushed to her feet, made to gather up her skirts and sway across the space between us. The effort of those few steps up flushed her face with tough breath. She bared her teeth, displaying gums shrunk back from grey stumps, and lowered herself puffing into the chair beside me. I flashed my row of little pearls and she glared as though she'd like to skittle them down, one by one.

I nodded, and reached out to her, palm up to show the pad, pink and safe. Her hand edged across the space between us.

'Brave woman! Brave, brave woman!' bellowed my husband to the delight of the crowd. 'Ah! But will she bite? And will *she* bite too?' he added, pointing the cane at me again, to greater guffaws.

'I meant the beast, sir! Not your wife! You look nibbled enough!'

The audience cackled.

'No,' he continued. 'Our lioness is as gentle as a kitten. Look how she licks her paw!'

At his signal I raised my hand obediently to my lips, to *aws*, and *aahs*, and *isn't-it-pretty*.

'Are you ready now?' he said, half to the sack of a female by my side, half to the audience. 'Are you *ready*, I said?'

'Yes!' came the chorus.

'Are you ready, Mr Photographer?'

George waved from behind the great wooden box, the fancy equipment brought in as a favour from one of my husband's many associates. I clutched at her hand and set my teeth in a rictus grin. As I counted out the long moments of the exposure the strangeness happened, reminding me of when I had touched Abel's hand previously. I had thought that he was a fluke, that I could find my way into his inner world alone. But it seemed as though he had been the catalyst for a new skill. My fingers tasted the texture of her skin, the lines running back and forth across her palm. Gypsy-paths, my mother had called them.

I followed those paths as they led to her inmost secrets: I was singed by the heat of her tears as her son died two hours after birth; I sweated with the mortal fever of her daughter, five years before. I saw further back, to the unwelcome fumble of her father's hands; I heard her scream and no-one come; I swilled the beer she poured into the space in her heart to drown out all memory: all of it flooded into me, scorching hotter and hotter.

At last, George cried out, 'Done!' and I pulled my hand away from hers, whimpering.

'What's its problem?' she growled, wiping her face with a large yellow handkerchief. 'Aren't I good enough for it to touch? Airs and graces, that's what I say, from dogs what don't deserve them.'

The room swung around my head and I clutched my aching paw to my breast. Mr Arroner simpered at her side.

'Not a dog, dear lady!' he crooned. 'A sweet and harmless kitten!'

'Whatever you will,' sniffed the woman, hoisting herself from the chair. 'I'll have my picture, if you please.'

'And with our compliments!' he cried. 'Prepared and delivered to your door! Besides, we would not dream of requesting payment from such a kind lady as yourself.'

The walls continued to heave as she was bundled away.

* * *

'What was that about?' said my husband, when she was gone. 'You will not upset our guests, my dear.'

'No more photographs,' I hissed. My brain was hammering against the confines of my skull.

'There will be photographs, and plenty of them. Stop this foolishness,' he said.

'Then let me catch my breath.'

'Shut up, Arroner,' said Lizzie. 'Look at her, she's turning blue.'

'How can you tell through her bloody hair?'

'Look at her lips, you idiot.'

They pushed water down my throat, and fanned me with an advertising playbill. All I could see was my pinched face flickering back and forth before me. *Is she Beauty? Is she Beast?* I closed my eyes to shut out the sight of myself.

'I said, what is the matter?' cried my husband, to anyone who might attend to him.

Lizzie held her face close to mine. 'Are you taken, pet?' My eyes asked the question. 'Taken,' she repeated. 'In the female way.'

I turned my head slowly from side to side. She looked disappointed.

'It's a shame,' she muttered. 'You might keep him longer.'

'He does not touch me,' I whispered into her ear. 'Not at all.'

She hauled herself upright. 'Well, she's not in the family way,' she puffed.

My husband blinked.

Presently, I was able to sit upright and drink a little from the glass of spirits that was pushed under my nose.

'I will say again, what was all of that about?' said my husband.

'I could see. Things,' I said. 'It is the truth.'

'See what?' said Lizzie.

I still felt the dying child's fever in my blood. I shivered.

'I saw her daughter. Dead of typhoid. And her son. The poor little creature.'

'Whose daughter?' asked my husband. 'Whose son? For the last time, will someone explain what is bloody well going on?'

'That woman,' I said. 'The one sitting next to me. I knew what had happened to her.'

'How could you tell?' asked Abel, quietly.

'It was when I took her hand in mine.' I could not look at him, for I thought I might betray my desire to clasp him close and bury my face into his neck. 'It was all there. I could feel the fever. Feel the sickness.'

'Fuck me,' gasped George. 'She's a palm-reader. A sodding gyppo fortune-teller.'

'My wife is no such thing.'

'Plain fortune-teller, then.'

The room was beginning to slow its sickening waltz. My husband peered at me.

'Mrs Arroner, I will have you speak the truth. No trumped-up tales to get you more attention than is your due.'

'Leave her alone,' said Lizzie.

'Elizabeth, my *dear*, I would trouble you to mind your own business. A man has the right to know if his wife is deceiving him.'

'I am deceiving no-one,' I gulped. 'It is true.'

'Pah! It is a girlish whim, I say, to puff yourself up.'

'It is not!'

'I am your husband, and if I say it is trickery, then it is trickery. And I shall uncover what manner of trick. Come: if you are so gifted you shall read all our hands.'

'I am tired.'

'A fine excuse. We are all fatigued. Lizzie, come here. You will be first.'

Lizzie pushed the broad shelf of her hand at

me, placing her back to my husband and mouthing, *Be careful. Go easy.* I laid my palm over hers.

'That's not how you do it,' squeaked Bill. 'You look at it. That's what gypsies do.'

'Bill, shush,' said Lizzie over her shoulder. 'Our Evie isn't a gypsy, remember?'

I felt them grow quiet. I thought of what Bill had said, and lifted away my hand and examined Lizzie's palm. I remembered the great china hand I had seen at Bartholomew Fair with its simple lines thickly drawn. I recalled their names: the Lines of Life, Love, Fate; what faced me here was a cat's-wool tangle. Lizzie's palm was crossed entirely with thin red scribbles, not one line standing alone, for all were overlaid by fainter lines, and those by even fainter. The more I stared, the more I became confused: this was not what I felt when I held the woman's hand.

I closed my eyes and laid my skin against hers: straight away I began to tingle. I saw Lizzie grown into a giantess, towering on legs of white marble and straddling a world of skinny men queuing to taste her abundance; her head falling backwards, mouth open, quim shaking with laughter, joy bubbling up and raining upon the earth.

I saw the secret truth of her: Lizzie was the fairy hill made flesh, opening up to let each man live for ever. I heard her laughing when they clambered up her; laughing when they tumbled down; laughing at the coins they left. I opened my eyes.

'Well?' said my husband.

'Well, Evie love?' said Lizzie, widening her eyes in warning. *Take care what you say Please.*

'You are a happy woman,' I said carefully. 'You love the dancer's life. I hear much laughter.'

'Is that all?' snorted my husband.

'That's plenty,' said Lizzie, patting my shoulder and mouthing *Thank you.*

'Anyone could work out that nonsense,' muttered my man. 'It's trickery. I shall find out. You'll read Bill's palm next. That'll tell us if it's fakery soon enough.'

'She won't,' squeaked Bill. 'It's cursed stuff.'

'You'll do as I say, you little shit.'

'I won't,' he whimpered.

'You bloody will.'

There was a slap, and an answering squeal.

'She's too clever.'

'We'll see the truth or lie of that.'

'It's me, Bill,' I breathed. 'I am not going to hurt you.'

I squeezed the lad's fingers; felt the quick beat of his blood. When his body had relaxed I laid my other hand over his, poured calmness into the fear. His skin stretched out beneath mine.

I placed my index finger at the starting point of his Line of Life and slowly traced it to its end. It was long: a little frayed about the middle, but robust enough. I was relieved; I liked him, for he was not unkind in that general way of boys who are unlatching the door to manhood. I rubbed the spot and shivered as I saw him, much younger than now, lying on a thin mattress, gasping. Sweat oozed behind my ears.

'A fever,' I said. My mouth parched. 'Yes. You

had a fever as a child. You came through it.'

'Yes,' he gasped. 'I did.'

'Of course he did,' scoffed my husband. 'He's here, isn't he?'

Bill's soul flowered in my grasp, and gave up his secrets. The rest would be simple.

'This is too easy,' said my husband.

'Leave her be, Arroner,' grunted Lizzie.

'Put a cloth on his hand. Make her read it through a towel, or some such.'

'Oh, for the love of Jesus,' said George.

But a scrap of fabric was found, and laid between myself and the boy. It made no difference. His Line of Heart warmed into me; one tiny skip to the side his Line of Head rattled cheerfully — emptily.

'What are you smirking about?'

'Dear husband, he has happiness in his life. It would make anyone smile.'

'You can tell that through the cloth?' quivered the boy.

'Hum. It is all too vague. A happy life, a long life. Rubbish. Give us something we can hold on to.'

'Very well,' I sighed.

I pressed my finger firmly into the heart of his palm; heard his mother call him to her, felt the rush of him swept off his feet into the steaming valley of her bosom. She flicked her hair and sang, ''He is my lovely bonny, but he's gone to sea . . .''

'Your mother had brown hair — '

'As do all women,' muttered Mr Arroner.

' — which reached halfway down her back, to

her apron-strings; and curled; and when the sun caught it, there were yellow lights at the tips. She was a big woman who sang to you, 'He is my lovely — ''

Bill dragged himself away. 'She's a bloody witch!' he squawked and my husband clapped him round the ears. 'Ow!'

'Mind your language: there's ladies.'

Lizzie gargled her deep laugh. 'Ladies! Oh lah-di-dah.'

'Put your hand back.'

'I won't.'

'Is this true?' said Abel, quiet until now.

'Yes,' whimpered the boy, hugging his scalded hand to his chest. 'My ma's dead, isn't she?' he snuffled.

'She said there *was* happiness, did she not? And that your life has happiness to come?' Abel continued.

There was a pause. 'Yes, she did.'

'So.'

'Oh.' Bill's small paw grabbed at me. 'Tell me more. Please. I'm sorry I called you a witch.'

'Stop this now!' bellowed my husband. 'It's all trumpery nonsense. I'll prove it yet. The boy has no doubt whined to her about his bloody mother, and now she dresses it up and dishes it out like it's new, when it's left-over scraps.' His face pulsed anger.

'What shall I do then, Mr Arroner, dearest?'

'You'll wear a blindfold, that's what you'll do. I'll put something over your head so you can't bloody see who you're reading. And then we'll see how you fare. All fortune-tellers take their

266

cues from people's faces. I'll prove it's all a gaff.'

'Yes, my love,' I simpered. 'I will do whatever you wish.'

'I will prove you a liar,' he growled. 'No-one can read palms blind.'

'I am not making false claims. I see it in my head. It is not mysterious.'

'Not to you, perhaps.'

'Mr Arroner, sir,' said George. 'This might be a gold-mine. Think of it. Have your picture taken with the Lion-Faced Girl. Then stay and have your palm read by her. She's a genius. She just keeps coming up with grand ideas.'

'Genius, is she?' he rumbled, turning his wrath on to George. 'I thought I was the genius around here. Yes, I distinctly remember that I am the only one in this sorry circus to possess such a quality.'

'Arroner, George is right,' said Lizzie. 'The marks will pay. Do you care why?'

He glared at her, and she shook her chin, spitting out a rough laugh.

'I care that my wife is taking me for a fool.'

'None of us thinks you a fool,' said Lizzie quickly. 'Do we, lads?'

George and Bill said no, with much shaking of their heads, Abel a short step behind.

'I will be proved right.'

He stamped out of the room. I folded my hands on my lap and dropped my chin until the point of my beard brushed the buttons of my dress. Bill goggled fish eyes at me.

'Can't you tell me no more?'

'Not just now, Bill.' I thought of his foolish

Line of Head and wondered if it would undo his happiness. I hoped not. 'See how angry Mr Arroner is? Let us not vex him.'

'Oh. Yes.'

The door flew open and my husband reappeared, carrying a severed head.

'He's killed a man!' shouted the lad. 'We'll be for it, now.'

'It's a mask, you idiot,' hissed Lizzie. 'The one used for John the Baptist.'

'I will not put that on,' I said. 'I shall stifle.'

'You will not.'

'Why is a simple scarf not enough for you?' said Lizzie.

'She could see through it.'

'For God's sake, Arroner, you're torturing her.'

'I am a man of science, and this is my experiment. She is my wife. I shall do as I please, you will find, just as I should if you were mine.'

He bunched his fist and Lizzie laughed till her belly wobbled.

'Fat chance. You'd lose that in here.' She pointed at the expanse of her stomach and slitted her eyes. 'Swallow you up, I could.'

'Please, please,' said George. 'Let us be civil. We are become very serious all of a sudden.'

'I have spoken,' said my husband. 'She'll put this over her head.'

He ground the papier mâché down over my eyes. It stank of rotten rabbit skin: the smell of dirty words breathed into a child's ear.

'We are ready. Shall we start?'

'I have sinned!' cried Bill. His giggle was

snapped off by the sound of a smack. 'I only said 'sin'. Like Lizzie does. In her act,' he whined.

'Now, turn her round.'

I knew this voice was my husband, but he was far off, muffled by the stink of fish glue. I was spun round until I thought I might indeed lose all chance of breath. At last they stopped, and a hand guided me gently into the chair. Gradually head and body stopped swimming against the tide of the other.

'Now she will read a hand and not know whose it is. It might be George, Abel, or even Bill or Lizzie thrown in again to confound her.'

Someone grasped my wrist and hauled me forward. My fingers patted air for a few moments until I touched leather. It was a glove of heavy cow-hide, the kind used by barrow-men. I gritted my teeth at this fresh attempt to thwart my efforts. I would not be so easily shaken; it would simply take a little more concentration. I weighed the ballast of the hand, cupped in the cradle of my own palm. As I hoped, I could read through the leather. Here was a tense hand that only feigned repose.

'You find it hard to seek rest,' I began.

'Louder,' said a voice. 'Can't hear you.'

I thought it George, but through the stifling paper head it was hard to be sure.

'You do not sleep easily!' I yelled, and was met with laughter.

'It seems that is wrong,' said a man's voice.

'Unless you are lullabied with drink,' I added, and the snorting fell away.

'We all of us drink,' a man muttered, the ill

humour betraying the voice of my master.

It was time to begin, properly. I spidered my fingers delicately across the dish of the palm before me. The lines glowed their heat into my fingertips, showering constellations into the tar-scented night sky of the mask. I took in a deep breath. The lines were clear before me, as though I was looking at them directly. This was almost like cheating, it was so easy.

I smiled at the wicked pleasure of opening this person's most intimate treasure box, sliding my hands between the folded linen of their dreams and truths. I might not be able to see, but my finger could sense its way. My fur seethed in circles over my belly, tiny lightning bolts crackling up my arm as I danced over the Lines of Heart and Head.

I saw a blue sea shot with silver: upon it bobbed jolly-boats cut from red and white paper. The waves sparkled, and above all smiled a sun taken straight from the pages of a child's book. To my right, the chirp of a sailor's pipe; to my left, the gentle lapping of water; before me, a stretch of vermilion sand, soft and welcoming. Brightly painted beach-huts necklaced the horizon. I stretched out my foot, aching to run and dive into the water. My shoulders unloosed, and I laughed at such a pretty sight.

Then the beach rippled, yawned; the beach-huts lifted up their wheels and began to roll towards me, doors flapping open and gaping wide maws into a darkness that swallowed up the gay pictures. I tried to pull my hand away, but could not move.

A chasm opened in the sea and twisted itself into a maelstrom; out of the gurgling hole whiplashed a long tongue which wrapped itself around my wrist, dark blood pumping through the jellied-eel rope of it. It licked me, sucked me, gnawed the flesh of my arm to the bone until I was pulled apart with the shrivelled snap of a wishbone.

'You are trembling,' said a distant voice, and I flew back into the safe home of the mask.

'I am hot beneath this thing,' I snapped — quickly, so no-one would hear the terrified quake of my answer.

'Get on with it.' This was my husband speaking, surely.

'You have a long life ahead of you,' I lied, my arm still stinging with the slather of that horrible tongue.

This hand I was reading was sticky with death and would drag down others with it. *Be sure you are not one of them*, spoke my mind quietly.

'You are cleverer than men take you for,' I lied again, scraping my nail across the slimy palm.

The hand twitched in the sunshine of my flattery. So, he was stupid as well as self-opinionated. I knew it must be a man: it was certainly not Lizzie.

'You have a secret wish to go to sea,' I hazarded, remembering the little ships and praying he might one day drown himself in the whirlpool of his hatred, a fearful thing that would never be quenched, however many souls it drained.

My voice grew a little steadier.

'And, of course, you are loved and admired.'

I waited for the answering wriggle of self-satisfaction, and when I had it I added, 'So should you love more generously in return.'

I had to say something to avert this nightmarish vision. The hand stiffened: so be it. I could not work miracles. Still, the owner of the hand was not satisfied, and waited for more. I prodded it and continued spooning out untruths.

'There is success written here,' I said, knowing the terrain was blank. 'If you will trust others.'

I knew he would not.

'You will travel far,' I continued.

It was a safe guess, knowing what I did of all our histories and desires. I fought not to gabble, for I ached to drop this paw and wash myself in the hottest water in the house. I was a fool for thinking this new-found skill would be easy. A wicked pleasure? Far from it.

'Enough,' I panted. 'I shall burst.'

I withdrew, and managed not to wipe myself clean upon my skirts. I sat meekly as the mask was lifted away. Sitting opposite me, and unsheathing his hand from the leather glove, was my husband.

I arranged my mouth into a grin, made pretty jokes about the brightness of the light and the smell of the mask, and of course *that* was why my eyes were running with water, and I sneezed and twisted my nose daintily, and stroked my moustaches until everyone laughed.

'So, you are not false, my love!' he chuckled, tugging at my beard.

I patted his arm with great affection.

'Did I not tell you so? Can I not read you true?' I simpered.

He called me his special little pet, and how we should straightway make the mask a part of the show, and what a clever idea it was, so original, so indicative of greatness.

I took my hand away from him as slowly as I dared and waited for the easy knack of breathing to come again. I looked at him sideways, at his slick chin, the strangle of his cravat, the fatness of his fingers when he waggled them in time to the nonsense of his pronouncements. I swallowed a sour clot in my throat, there being nowhere to spit.

'Ladies and gentlemen,' he announced, thumbing the pockets of his waistcoat. 'I believe that good luck has smiled broadly upon our company. Did I not tell you what a genius you have for an impresario? What we have here is a new attraction. Think of it. The Mystical Lioness! She'll tell your fortune blindfold!'

We nodded our heads carefully, each one of us. Even Abel.

★ ★ ★

All I desired was to be alone, and after the night's show that came soon enough. The men were gone to their downstairs room, my husband and I to our separate chambers in the upper part of the house, and Lizzie no-one knew where. I ached behind my eyes.

I undressed and climbed into bed, but could not bear the weight of the blankets on my arm, for I could still not shake off the fancy that the foul tongue I saw in the palm-reading still slabbered over me from wrist to elbow. When I could stand it no longer, I swung my feet over the side of the mattress and pattered my toes about in search of the rug. I got up and stalked up and down until the prickling on my skin ebbed somewhat.

I lit the gas and thrust my hand into the pool of light, thinking that if I could make sense of others' hands, surely I could make some sense of my own. I closed my eyes and pressed my palms together, waiting for the surge of bright pictures, but my skin stayed blank and cool, however fiercely I rubbed. Nothing. No great insights. So much for my magical talent.

Any thought of sleep was impossible. Candlestick in hand, I tiptoed out of my room and towards my husband's. I wanted to see him in all his wobbling humanity: his moist pate, thinning hair, short and dimpled fingers, bulbous nose and stomach, and thereby reduced to a mere creature of flesh and bone, not the ravening beast I had spied within. His room was empty, the door standing wide open. Why I chose to enter and not return to my safe bed I do not know. But enter I did.

I was drawn to the tall-boy whereupon stood a small box of dark blue velvet. I opened it to find a ring resting upon the satin lining, a gold band set with a ruby flanked by two pearls. My heart leaped. I believe a herd of cows could have been driven through the house at that moment and I would have noticed nothing. I thought my husband lost to me. I thought him a Bluebeard. I cringed with shame for imagining such terrible things about him. Here was his first gift for a very long time. I did not count the dresses made for my performances. This was an intimate offering for my eyes alone.

A tiny scrap of folded paper was tucked into the lid. I paused. I should let him deliver this treasure to me with some of its secrets intact. But I ached to soothe myself with affectionate words; I had been so starved, and for so long. I told myself I could unfold and refold it so that no-one would guess it had been read. The paper shook as I opened it. There were seven words, and they changed everything.

To my Bet, from her naughty JoeJoe.

My fingers were as deft as I thought. They closed the billet-doux into precisely the same shape, and pressed it back into the lid. It looked exactly the same as a minute previously. I do not know how many moments I stood there, transfixed by the sparkling gems until they blurred.

However much I tried to put off the dawning of truth, I knew there was only one fortune for me: *fool.* I *was* a fool, for my husband would never take me in his arms, whatever I had dreamed of. I was his Golden Goose, and as long as I was careful to remain so, I would suffer neither the mistreatment nor the harsh words he dealt out to my odd companions. He would continue to laugh and call me his little kitten, for to him I was no more than an interesting pet who would bring fortune his way with my freakish talents, a helpless creature who would stray or be lost if it were not for his strong right hand.

I thought of the way he smiled when I wore a new pair of gloves, how he lifted his eyebrow at a new dress, a new hat, or a fresh determination to walk from one end of the street to the other. How he had slowly seeped away my will, watered down my confidence with his kindly glance. How could I have not noticed it?

I had been led astray by hats, and fans, and dresses. Blinded by my desire to escape from my cramped beginnings into a better life. Dazzled by the word 'husband' and all I thought it could mean. It was as brittle as the vision I had seen when I read my dear sweet husband's palm, and as false. Most of all, I had fooled myself with the stubborn hope that he might love me.

★   ★   ★

I took the jewel-box and raced back to my own room where I hauled open the door to the press, pulled out my show costumes and threw them on the bed. The green satin, so short it came barely halfway to the knee; the lilac stripe, trimmed with cheap lace and beaded edging on the bodice: glass, not jet. I had sold myself for a necklace of glass beads. I tossed the ring after them.

I hated them all with their feminine fussiness. I wanted long plain skirts and no corset to push my breasts up to my chin. I had had enough. No more pandering to his huckstering shouts: 'See how her natural daintiness is cursed! How her natural femininity is thwarted!'

It was long after midnight. I sat on the edge of

the bed and listened to the mattress sighing with me. Everything I owned was spread-eagled on the coverlet. I was decided: I would go. I would take away nothing of our married life. I pushed the dresses as far from me as I could and they slid into a rustling hill on the floor.

I was left with very little; only the mirror, small enough to fit my hand, but large enough to remind me that once I believed I was the fairest of them all. There was also the money I had saved, hidden when my husband was too busy being boastful: six sovereigns and the folded sheet of a five-pound note. I think I would have remained sitting there until the end of the world, staring at the heap of my life, if Lizzie had not passed by the door. I came out of my daze to the sound of her tossing coins from one hand to the other.

'Someone's got to show a bit of spark round here.' She grinned. 'We'll not get fed sitting round the kitchen table and moping over the teapot. Unless your palm-reading can sort me out with a few winners at Newmarket, eh?'

My answer was to hold out the box. The mattress sank as she planted herself next to me and examined the ring. She tipped her head thoughtfully.

'It's pretty. But you're not happy. There's a riddle.'

'It is a gift from my husband. But not for me.'

'Ah,' she said. 'Well.'

'Lizzie,' I said carefully, 'did you know?'

'Evie, my pet — '

'Don't call me that. It's what he calls me. Do

277

not console me with kind words.'

'I was not planning on doing so,' she snorted. She turned the ring round and about in the dim light, squinting at it. 'Pinchbeck.' She tutted. 'The stone is paste.' She placed it between her teeth with a crunch. 'Pearls as false as Bill's claim to come from Malaya.'

'Is that supposed to make me feel happier?'

She shrugged her mountainous shoulders and put the gem back in its nest. There was a tiny graze where her teeth had taken the nacreous paint off the bead.

'That is not something over which I have any power,' she said gently.

I sniffed. 'He'll leave me for her.'

'He will most certainly not. You are his gold-mine. He'll not throw you aside for some tart with big eyes, big tits and a big appetite for his money. He'll never give you up.'

'That ought to please me. It does not,' I said, so softly my moustaches did not even stir.

'Eve, he does not *love* her.'

'How can you know?'

She sighed and looked away, as though making up her mind how to explain an important yet uncomfortable fact to a foolish child.

'Who — or what — did you think you had married, Evie?'

'A husband.'

'And that you have. The piece of paper, the name, the shield of respectability.'

'I did not think you so cruel, Lizzie. George, yes; but you?'

She covered my little hand with the broad

expanse of her own. Her kindness insinuated itself through my skin.

'What I tell you is so that you may be armed with truth and be free of the syrupy entanglement of romantic lies.'

I hung my head.

'I apologise.'

They were the two most difficult words I had ever spoken.

'I am not cruel. And you are not stupid. This you must know. Arroner loves neither you, nor her, nor any other person who walks this earth. I strongly suspect he does not love himself, either. There is but one thing he adores and that is — '

'His money-box.'

'Ha! I'll wager he takes it to bed with him. I knew you were bright. Queer folk are by nature cleverer than the normal types, as a rule. Evie, I believe you are growing up.'

I rubbed my face into the warm cushion of her breast.

'Now.' She slapped her palms against her knees and the bed trembled. 'We must put the ring back where you found it, and tidy up in here.' She stuck out her chin at the pile of clothes on the rug. 'Were you planning on a moonlit flit?'

'I was going to leave.' I chewed my lip. 'And then I was not.'

'Sounds about right!' She let out a squeeze of breath and raised an eyebrow. 'All of us have dreams of our own salons filled with red velvet chairs and brocade curtains floor to ceiling and Indian carpets. But there's no point in running away in the middle of the night without a plan. A girl can end up in a nasty spot, and that's the truth.'

She pulled each of her fingers in turn, as though her skin were a glove which had wrinkled and she had to smooth it out.

'Lizzie, I do not know how much longer I can live with Mr Arroner and pretend.'

She touched her finger over my heart, and I slowed.

'It is important you should play him skilfully,' she said, adjusting her thumb. 'Tend his stupidity. Until it is clear to go — safely.'

'I do not know if I can.'

'You are far cleverer than your husband. His shallowness might save you yet. He is too thinly planted to take a root, his imagination being the sparsest of topsoils. He thinks himself intelligent and that is your great safety. But you must also be more cautious, If I have caught you looking at Abel, then so have others.'

'Abel?' I found that my heart was quickening, blood skipping into my cheeks. 'There's something about him.'

'There is.'

She tickled the back of my neck until I purred. I hugged myself into her flesh.

'I believe he sees me, truly.'

'Indeed?' She raised an eyebrow.

'I mean, through my fur. No other man does,' I mumbled. I grew bolder. 'I touched him, Lizzie,' I whispered.

'Did you, indeed!'

She held me at arm's length, bored crafty eyes into me.

'No! Nothing like that. Like when I read palms. There are pictures inside him. Wonderful things,' I moaned.

'Be careful, Evie,' she said. 'Not of Abel.'

'I know. It is my husband I must beware of.'

She pressed her soft cheek into mine and breathed liquorice into my ear.

'Return the ring. And the clothes, for now. When you leave, you will have no time for packing bags.'

'What do you mean?'

'Nothing, nothing. You'll know right enough when the time comes. Now, I must be off and find me a cup of gin. I believe I have the heartburn. Poor Lizzie! The heartache of others brings it on.'

She billowed me into her. I drowsed against the booming of her heart. With a final squeeze she bade me good-night and waded away.

I would not leave tonight. I could wait. It seemed that yesterday I had adored my husband; now I hated him, simple as turning a page. I had frittered away our marriage trying to read affection into his solicitous kindness, when it was bitterness enveloped in sweet words. He had snipped the tiny veins of my hope, small, sharp nicks but enough to bleed away my confidence; and each time I tried to sew up the shallow wounds made by the little razors of his mouth my head swooned more from the loss of it. Indeed, he had near killed me with his ever-hovering questions.

Are you well? Are you comfortable?

Do you want for anything?

Would you care for a sugared almond?

All I had ever desired was a kiss upon my lips.

Would you like a new pair of gloves? The new style, which button to the elbow?

My only dream of delight had been for him to take my hand and squeeze it with passion.

Take a bite of this marzipan: it is as sweet as you.

I lit another candle, and then another, until my room glowed. I stood before the dressing-mirror and assessed myself: my disordered hair, my rumpled night-dress, my eyes rough from weeping. Enough. I wet my hands from the ewer and smoothed droplets through my tresses. I scooped a handful of hairpins and stuck them between my teeth, looped a length of hair around my finger, wound it round and round and secured it close to my chin. Over and over I repeated the action until every hair on my head was clipped into curling-pins. It gave me the appearance of a startled hedgehog, but I was not planning on receiving visitors. It would dry into ringlets overnight. And in the morning, I would simper, toss my curls, play my part and my husband would be none the wiser.

He would never guess how sick I was of his cloying sugar. I ached to blunt the sharp edges of my girlishness. I wanted to take a bite of the salt and sour of a man, feel him fire me up, rub me, flint me into flame. I had kept my heart faithful even when I felt drawn to Abel. It was pointless to deny it. I liked what I saw in Abel, and not only that — although I did find him handsome. With each day he seemed to grow into himself as though his being was a murky pond and he was the creature surfacing from its depths.

I smiled when I thought of how I had dutifully tamped down all lascivious thoughts about him and crushed them flat when they tickled my ankles or blew softly upon my neck. How I had pushed away dreams when they blossomed into wild flights in the breathless forest of my belly: dreams wherein Abel stepped out from the trees, seething with hair, eyes glowering up and down my body and spreading me open for that first gasping taste. My Pan, my serpent.

I had throttled every wicked thought with wifely shame. I might as well have indulged my bodily imaginings and woken every morning with tangled sheets and a slack smile on my face. Yet this was no mere infatuation of the flesh. Abel spoke to me as one equal to another; both of us different, both of us travelling towards the city of self-discovery. Perhaps if I had met him when . . . ? No. I shook my head and scattered hairpins on to the floor.

No more. I would make plans and dream of the day when I would throw away my curling pins and all feminine fripperies. I would let my beard roughen and wear it like a sailor, tugged into two greasy points, tangled with bread-crumbs and beer. I would swear out loud and not just in the tent of my head; I would have a girl in every port, and remember not one of their names. And when I tired of mannishness I would be so voluptuous my swains would faint away at the sight of me; I would braid ribbons into my beard, file my teeth to glittering points and hunt men for sport; pluck a hundred peacocks and sew their eyes into my coat; plume my dress with the sapphire sheen of magpie tail-feather. I would be the Woman Beast, fearful and beautiful.

I could not tell this truth, for it would make gunpowder of the air between Mr Arroner and myself. I feared the spark that would light the touch paper, set off a thundering show and burn us all to ashes. I would bide my time: be sweet and quiet as a kitten. Lap at my saucer of milk and pretend myself browbeaten, meek and obedient. I would slump round the table, pretending to look for hope in the bottom of a glass of gin. I would beat him at his own game. One day I would run, beating out the sweetest rhythm with my feet, the pounding percussion of escape.

One day I would do it. Not yet.

ABEL

London, September 1858

The front door slams.

'We're ruined!'

Arroner's roar of despair thunders down the hall, down the stairs and into the kitchen. I am sitting with Eve and George, hoping that George will leave for I wish to speak to her alone. I have so much to say that the words sizzle on my tongue. George is sipping his tea from the saucer more slowly than I think it possible for a man to drink, glancing from Eve to myself and back again, a crafty expression on his face. Arroner storms into the room, brandishing a crumpled sheet of paper.

'Look!' he screams. 'The conniving, thieving bastards!'

'What is it, dear husband?' asks Eve mildly.

She gets a fresh cup and pours tea into it.

'What is it? What *is* it? Nothing but our entire collapse and ruination. All my years of careful labour turned to sand in the space of a moment!'

'I'm sure it is not as bad as you think, dearest. Tell us what ails you.'

'What *ails* me?' he shrieks. He shoves his face

285

close to hers and she draws away the smallest fraction of an inch. 'Look!' he continues, spittle spraying from his mouth and hanging in drops from her moustache and long eyebrows.

With the word he slaps the paper on to the table. It is a handbill. Thick black letters in bold script declare an invitation: *The New Sensation! Greater Than Any Seen Before! The Two-Headed Nightingale!*

'*That's* what ails me, you stupid woman.'

The picture beneath the trumpeting headline is of a young woman with two heads, both mouths smiling. Or rather, it is two girls, pressed closely together at the hip, their four arms in an affectionate embrace around the other. She is — or rather, they are — in dresses so short all four of their legs are clearly displayed. Something within me stirs damp wings: she seems happy with her strangeness. I wonder what that feels like. My finger rises of its own accord and traces the shape of the words.

'What does it say?' asks George, craning his neck for a peep.

'It says you should bloody well learn to read,' growls Arroner.

He pushes it across the board towards Eve. She picks it up and reads it, her voice trembling a little.

'*The Two-Headed Nightingale. Twice the Beauty! Twice the Thrills! By Special Appointment to Royalty.*'

She looks up, confused.

'Royal patronage, that's what,' snaps Arroner. 'They only went and got a visit from some

286

bloody baronet or other, didn't they? Presented her with a ruby the size of my eye, didn't he? No doubt she lifted her skirt for him, and all.'

Eve's hands hold steady on the paper and she reads on.

'*Also Featuring for the General Delectation of All Comers: the Thaumaturgic Thespianism of* . . . Oh!'

'Yes, indeed,' snarls Arroner.

'What?' asks George. 'What *is* it?'

Arroner snatches the bill from Eve's hand and reads aloud.

'*The Thaumaturgic Thespianism of the Celebrated India-Rubber Man, in an All-New Entertainment.*'

George still looks blank. Arroner rounds on him this time, so that it is now his face which is splattered with furious saliva.

'It's Bill, you idiot. Dear sweet innocent Bill has jumped ship like the rat he is and has gone to this new — this new . . . ' He strangles the paper in his fist. 'This is how I am repaid for all my generosity! I'll kill the ungrateful little sod.'

'I'll not leave you, Mr Arroner,' I say.

Arroner ignores me, pacing up and down the red-tiled floor.

'A woman with four legs, and not afraid to show them off. A pretty face to boot.' He glances at Eve as he speaks. 'Why couldn't we get a bloody lord? I'd settle for a Member of Parliament. All the years I've toiled. The money I've lavished on you all.' He stops in his tracks, hands clasped behind his back and surveying us like so many empty beer-bottles. 'We can compete against

287

Cow-Horned Women, but this? All I have is old rubbish and unsightliness. Shiftless ugly freaks, the whole damn lot of you.'

'Thanks a million,' grunts George. 'If I'm so ruddy ugly, maybe I'll go and join them as well.'

'You damn well won't.'

George gets to his feet and squares up to Arroner.

'Oh, won't I?'

'I'd like to see you try. Worthless without me, you are.'

'We'll see about that. And maybe I won't go alone when I go, neither.'

'What! You . . . '

Arroner's voice soars to new heights of fury and his face blooms a dangerous purple. Eve speaks, so softly it has the strange effect of making him quieten.

'We shall endure, dear Mr Arroner. Wherever there is heard the call for sensation, for entertainment — '

'Stow it,' grumbles George. 'You might get by, genuine article like yourself. Me? The minute I roll up my sleeves I'm marked as a gaff. As for him . . . ' He nods in my direction.

'George. There is no need for these hysterics,' says Eve, cleverly not including her husband in the accusation.

'Yes, George,' adds Arroner, breathing heavily and wiping his shining face with a gaudy handkerchief. 'Listen to my wife. Calm yourself.'

'You'll drop us like dog turds. You've just said as much.'

'You will keep a civil tongue, George.'

'A civil tongue? You can talk, you money-grabbing old skinflint. What you're about is filling your pockets and no-one else's. It's a sorry state when that idiot gets paid the same as me.'

George jabs his thumb in my face. Arroner narrows his eyelids, folds the handkerchief with great care and tucks it into his waistcoat pocket.

'Why should he not?'

'You even ask? That dead fish doesn't know what to do with what he *has* got. Now, I — '

'George.'

'He gives me the fucking creeps.'

'George, your profanity is most upsetting. Besides, the public continue to marvel at our good friend Abel, even if in somewhat reduced numbers. In my books, that makes him a better man than you are. Especially in these straitened circumstances.'

'What? You have got to be kidding me. How can he possibly — '

'He demonstrates a respectful manner to his betters. In case you have not noticed.'

'I've done your bidding this past five years, Arroner. In this circus and out of it. Not a word of complaint.'

'But I *am* hearing words of complaint, George. Plenty of words.'

'He's half-asleep most of the time. Half-dead the rest!'

'And half the trouble you are turning out to be.'

'I've given you everything.' His voice shakes.

'And I have paid you for it all.'

'Not even half of what I'm owed, you bastard.'

'George, I have asked you to moderate your

regrettable lapses into vulgarity. There is a lady present.'

He takes no notice. 'You've drunk the profits. Gambled away what's left.'

'Investments, George,' Mr Arroner replies, tapping the side of his nose. 'I am an investor, not a gambler.'

'You're a fool.'

'I believe I have had enough of this unpleasant and quite unnecessary display of histrionics. I must formulate plans to beat this new show at its own game. They'll not get the better of Josiah Arroner. I shall retire and enjoy the more stimulating company of my associates in investment matters. They conduct a far more pleasurable conversation.'

He screws his silk hat on to his head and leaves the room, shoes stamping an angry rhythm on the hall tiles. We sit around the table, staring anywhere but at each other. I rise, slowly.

'I shall go and prepare for tonight's show,' I say.

'Yes. Why don't you run off and play, you pointless excuse for a man.'

I laugh. 'You cannot hurt me, George.'

He grabs my wrist. 'Not so fast,' he growls. 'You done cleaning the house, meat-head?'

I shrug. 'I swept the rooms, both upstairs and downstairs.'

'George,' says Eve, a warning vibration in her voice.

'What? You starting on me, too?'

'No. But you speak as though he were your servant.'

'Well? What else is he good for? You won't catch me pushing a broom around when we've got a half-wit like him to do it.'

'He is one of us.'

George snorts. 'We'll see.'

Eve glares at the flames of the kitchen fire. The room is quiet again.

'I'm having a bloody drink,' grunts George. 'While the cat's away. Come on, Abel. You're having one with me.'

'I will not,' I say.

'What do you mean? Get a drink inside you.'

'George, let him be. He has said no.'

'Since when did you become his knight in shining armour? Let the man speak for himself. Unless you've become his bloody keeper.'

'We spend too much time moping over our glasses as it is,' I say. 'We must work harder and drink less, especially now there are rivals.'

'Oh, lah-di-dah. Listen to Mr Temperance.'

I sigh. 'But I shall have one drink, for comradely feeling, if it makes you happy.'

'Oh, don't do it to please a lowly creature such as myself, reaching down from on high to bestow your beneficence,' he sneers.

I shrug again. He looks at me oddly, but only for a moment. Then he glares at Eve.

'Haven't you got something better to do than sit here eavesdropping on men's talk?'

She throws him a look, gets to her feet and stalks out. He shoves a glass in front of me.

'That's better. Just the two of us. No women to get in the way, eh? Get this down you.'

I take the proffered glass, and it seems to put

him in a more jovial frame of mind.

'Mr Arroner was wrong. We have a very good show. We will prevail,' I say, taking a mouthful. 'You are a good performer.'

George places his glass upon the table very slowly.

'Am I, Abel? Am I indeed?' His voice betrays none of the merriment that was present a moment ago. 'I thank you, dear Abel, that you take it upon yourself to notice my stumbling efforts.'

'George, you are very skilled.' I smile encouragingly. 'You have a great talent.'

'But?'

I stare at him. First his throat and then his cheeks flush, pink as fresh-cut pork.

''But?' I do not understand.'

'I have great skill, *but*. That is what you want to say.'

'Not at all.'

'Great skill, but I am a drunkard. Great skill, but I am lazy. Great talent, but not as great as your fine self.'

'No, George.'

'Great skill, but I am lecherous.'

'I do not mean any of that.'

'Do you imagine for one bleeding minute that I can't see right through you?'

'See through what?'

'Don't talk to me like I'm a bloody fool, Abel. I know what your game is.'

'George, I do not have a game.'

'Playing the innocent. Might fool those bastards upstairs, but it doesn't fool me.'

'Innocent about what?'

'All this rubbish about being a half-wit. I'm not taken in by the act, even if everyone else is.'

'But — '

'Don't interrupt,' he growls. 'Everyone fucking interrupts. Spying on me, that's your plan, isn't it?'

'No.'

'Going to run and tell your precious little Eve what I've been up to?'

'Have you been up to something?'

'Not me. It's *you* that's making cow's eyes at the lady of the house.'

I feel blood rise into my cheeks, although I am not sure why. George laughs.

'At least you can blush. Didn't think you could raise that much blood.'

'I do not understand.'

'Be quiet!' he bellows.

'You are angry. It is best if I go.'

I half turn, but his hand grabs my shoulder and swings me round. Bile rises in my throat. He presses his face close to mine.

'You useless piece of workhouse shit. You mince in here from your stinking cellar, with your stinking spike manners, and dare to look down on me: me, a man born a piss-shot from this window. I am a man of this city; my father and bastard grandfather also. You should be grateful we don't chain you up in the privy yard like the dog you are.'

'George, I swear I do not understand.'

'I found you, you piece of mudlark scum. I *found* you. On the banks of the fucking Thames.

293

Washed up with all the other turds. And you speak to me like I'm dirt on your boot. Too bleeding good for the likes of me. You've no idea what it's been like. Day after day, forcing myself to smile when all I want to do is spit in your face and watch it run down your cheek.'

'You hate me because you found me in the river?'

I stare at him although I do not want to. I want him to stop so that I can follow Eve and get some peace away from this belabouring.

'You took Arroner's eye off me,' he hissed. 'Me. Since you joined us, it's the Modern Marsyas this and the Man With No Name that. He gives you top billing, and I'm left with scraps from the table. The years I've laboured for one glance from that man, one nod of praise. Yet over you he spews all his approval.'

'I did not mean to offend you.'

'You've no idea. All my plans to get his trust. Get rid of him and set up my own show. Have her, as well. Now some bastard's beaten me to it. I'm fed up with his miserly pennies. I want the pounds.'

'Do you want money? You can have some of mine.'

He lifts his fist and it hovers in the air over my head. He quails with the effort of holding it still.

'Make me hit you, eh? Is that your new plan? So you can go whining to Arroner and get me thrown on to the street? He's as much as said he's going to turf me out. I'll see you dead before that happens. I'll do what it takes.'

'Why are you like this, George? What did I

ever do to harm you?'

He ignores me.

'I knew one day I'd find the key to your fall from Arroner's bloody Heaven. Now I've got it. Don't think I haven't seen the way Eve moons over you. Arroner will kill you when he hears what I've got to say. He's a fool, but all I've got to do is point it out.'

'But there is nothing between Eve and myself.'

He grins unpleasantly. 'I don't care if it's truth or lies. As long as it gets rid of you. Then I'll have her.' He grabs my collar, leans close. 'I'll *have* her Abel. Hairy or not, she's got a cunt like every last one of them. She wants a real man. A man like me.'

He wraps his arms around himself and rolls his eyes upwards, licking his lips. 'Oh, George,' he coos in a girlish voice, running his hands over his body. 'Oh, George! Take me, bend me over, fuck me, now! That's what she wants,' he hisses. 'That's what she needs. Not a piece of your jellied eel.'

His hand sweeps between my legs and grasps the softness there, twisting harshly. After a moment, he shoves away, eyes filled with a revulsion I do not understand. There is still so much I do not understand.

'Limp as a dish-rag,' he spits. 'You shit-eater. Dead fish. You keep your hands off her. She's mine.'

'George, I want nothing of this.'

'No? Stow it where the sun don't shine, Abel. I'm no fool. I'm a man who makes plans, even if you're not. I'll take what's owed me and then

— well, we'll see. Shan't we?'

He strokes my cheek, so near I can see the grime of tobacco between his perfectly even teeth. He hesitates so long I am filled with the strange notion he is about to bite my nose off, but he pats me gently, spins on his heel, and is gone. I shake away the unpleasantness, yet it sticks to me. I am exhausted by the argument. There is nowhere to go except to my bed, and I am grateful the room is empty. The room swings like a headache. As soon as I lie down, I fall into a blank slumber.

My Italian master appears at my side. It is the balm I need. He is proof that I can seek and find answers.

'You have been gone so long,' I say to him. 'I thought I had lost you.'

He smiles, eyes warm. 'A good teacher should not lose his student.'

Here is the man who understands my confusion, this stumbling towards the truth of myself. He is a learned man: there is nothing he cannot uncover. I open my mouth.

'I have a secret,' I say bravely. 'I wish to share it with you, so that you can help me understand.'

'Understanding! A noble goal.'

My heart soars with hope. I lead him to the dissecting-room. It is so deep into the night as to be early in the morning, and we proceed slowly up the steps, finding the way to the anatomy studios with the help of the smooth banister. I pause on the landing and hold my breath; I savour the sensation of the air eddying around me, the hissing of blood in my ears. Yes, this is where I shall have my answer at last.

He wraps his coat about him, for although the night is warm enough outside, here the marble of the floors and table-tops chills the air. The waning moon, approaching the last quarter, is rising high enough to clear the trees in the gardens beyond the room and casting a pale gleam though the glass lights set high up the walls.

'Here?' he says.

'Here,' I reply, directing him to one of the tables.

On the bench before me is a wax model of an arm, newly finished, the fresh varnish perfuming the room with tart sweetness. Beside it I lay my own arm as though it were a second model.

'Look,' I say.

'Yes,' he replies. 'Our models are close to the life, so close it is sometimes hard to tell the difference. This is no secret; I know this already. You do not need to show me.'

I frown. He does not see what I am trying to show him. I must try harder, make it clearer.

'But you do not know the truth about me,' I continue.

'The truth? You are my student. You study under me. The Plato to my Socrates,' he smiles. 'You will learn, and become an anatomist yourself. What other truth can there be?'

'My secret, the one I wish to share. You alone can understand; and you will explain to me. I seek an answer to the riddle of what kind of man I am.'

'Lazzaro, my good man,' he declares, his teeth chattering a little. 'Must we talk here? Can we not go somewhere a little warmer?'

I ignore him. He is my teacher. He must listen.

'See: this is what I struggle to comprehend.'

I hold a scalpel and make a swift vertical cut into the skin of my lower arm. It is easy to see what I am about, for the brightness of the late moon makes it unmistakable. He ought to see it now, but still he asks questions.

'God in Heaven, man, what are you doing?'

His voice trembles. I make an incision from the inside of my wrist to the elbow, and transverse cuts at each extremity, like the good student of anatomy I am. Then I peel back the flaps of skin and fasten them to the board with silver-headed pins. They catch the light, and the water swimming in my eyes multiplies their number to many flickering dozens. The pain balances me on its tightrope.

I progress with the grave dignity of every other dissection I have undertaken: my hand moves with the same care that no detail is passed over in haste. Presently, the muscle of the *flexor carpi radialis* is revealed, fresh and glistening. My master holds his hand over his mouth, but it does not stop him from letting out small cries of surprise and fear.

'I am like no waxen anatomical model you have ever seen. I am like no other man you have seen opened. You understand, for you are my master.'

He sucks in air, sharply. We are embraced by a welcoming odour, a mixture of earth and animal musk. My flesh laid bare is as peaceful as any other piece of man I have seen on these tables, yet infinitely more beautiful.

'You are — '

The colours shake like oil on water, which does not hold one hue but changes as it moves; each quiver of exposed muscle sends a sheen of deeper colour across the surface, the scarlets and magentas anatomists only dream of, more lovely than anything a sculptor can create. He does not take his eyes from me; his whole body entirely still.

'I am impossible,' I say. 'I should not exist, but I do. Tell me how.'

I want him to grant me the balm of his answers; I want to possess them so passionately that I ache in my head, my breast, my belly. I am consumed with hopefulness: all I need is the key and all the doors to my being will be thrown open. At last he speaks, the words tumbling out in a rush.

'Lazzaro, what are you doing? Oh God. You are — ' He gulps and returns his attention to my arm. 'You are killing yourself.'

'I am not. Observe. No blood flows.'

He gasps, stares. The radial artery is whole, and I slip a pair of flat-ended tweezers beneath, lifting it for him to see for I know his question and am answering. We watch the gentle throb of liquid moving within.

'But the smaller veins,' he whispers. 'They must be severed. There is always blood, even from the smallest cut.'

'Here there is none.'

I lay down the tweezers, pick up a scalpel and draw it across the untouched skin of my upper arm: the cut wells up with dark liquid which seems about to spill to my elbow; one drop, then two, trail down the skin; then all is halted. I take in a sharp lungful of air and shiver, like a horse shaking off biting insects. My muscles gleam with moisture, and there are a few dark smears on the board beneath my arm, but nothing else. He stares at my arm as though I am some foreign thing he does not understand.

'How can there be no bleeding?'

'I do not know. You are the learned man. I want you to tell me.'

At last I lay down the blade and lean over my handiwork, and I hear my master gasping for breath. I lift my head and look at him. His eyes alight upon mine, and then dart about, unable to settle.

'Master, I do not understand how I can do this and live. I must understand. I am collapsing under the weight of my unknowing. Tell me. Please.'

'I do not — '

'You are a man of science. Surely you have the answer.'

He takes a step away, blinking as though waking from darkness into a great light.

'This is not — what I was thinking. I do not . . . ' he breathes. He grips the table-edge, knuckles pale. 'This is self-murder.'

'No,' I whisper. 'Anything but!'

'You are not what I thought,' he gasps, looking me up and down, his gaze drifting to my lap, where the blood that will not spurt from my wounds has poured into the *corpora cavernosa*, rendering my lower parts disgracefully firm. 'You *disgust* me. I do not know why you should force me to witness this salacious display of your deviant nature. You are a monster.'

And with that, he is gone.

I sigh. 'So you cannot help me.'

I do not know how I can have been so deceived; but the sensation is familiar. I can do no more. I wet the tips of my fingers and pull out the holding pins; then I lift the corner of peeled-back skin and bring it across the muscle, folding skin over flesh as tidily as a man folds his cravat. I bring the two long edges together and watch them knit, red paling to pink as I heal. My arm is dry, like smooth-planed wood married to fine-nap velvet.

I thought that if I studied with great doctors of physic I would uncover the answers at last. If a renowned doctor of anatomy cannot explain the mystery of my healing, then there exists no man wise enough to do so. Master Calvari wanted me with the hunger of one who needs a pupil to puff up his reputation, a mirror in which to show off his sagacity. The fortune-teller wanted me with the hunger of the prurient. Alfred wanted me with a hunger he dared not satisfy. On to the blank canvas of my self they painted their need and left no space for me.

★　★　★

I have failed. Wherever I have been, whenever I have been, whomever I have begged for help, I have found no answer to the riddle of myself. There is none. I am washed clean of hope and

301

do not know how much longer it can be borne. I am so lost in the forest of myself, shrunk to a leaf stamped into mulch by the trampling of my memories: I am crumbling, flickering, guttering out.

I want to grow old, and sicken, and ache, and stumble, and die, like everybody else. I want to feel the tickle of worms, the soft drift of earth as it rots the wood I'm wrapped in. I want to go back to dust. I ache for rattling breath, loosening teeth, blotched skin, rheumy eyes, stooped back, yet all of it eludes me. I am suicide's slave, following it like a kicked dog. It is all I want, and it is not permitted me. I hear Death's lies, tempting me: through wine, through knives, through every tower and balcony I have ever leapt from.

Come and join me, it teases. *We are old acquaintances. You have been glad enough of me, through all your times.*

I am left with only the pictures, the dreams, the memories: bright, colourful, confusing, making no sense. However hard I try I can mould no meaning back into them. I am worn out by uncertainty. I have trusted and had that hope dashed. No-one has been able to satisfy my hunger for self-knowledge, and after each disappointment I have tumbled into despair, as surely as I fell from the tower in that insistent memory. What a fool that I did not grasp its significance. Indeed, I rise, I fall. Unendingly.

Now there is Eve. She is solace, peace; she calls to me and I ache to answer. I wonder what she has found on her journey, what anchors she has forged for herself. I have seen the way she touches people's hands and knows the whole of them. She could plumb every part and gift it to me, so I would have no secrets any more. She could rope me to this present in which I find myself. All I need to do is say yes. Why should I let the events of the past soil the future?

Yet if she finds out what I am, who I am, will she turn aside from me also? Perhaps I can dare to hope that she will read me and read me true. With her help I can swim up from my depths and surface into wakefulness and understanding. I shall say yes the next time she asks to read my palm. I will not let myself be cast down. I will thrust my hand into hers and beg forgiveness for my cowardice, and say, *I am ready.*

★   ★   ★

Eager to find her, I peel myself off my sodden sheets and stumble to the kitchen. It is empty. Seized with a powerful thirst, I coax the fire in the range to light again.

'There is not much in the way of wood left in the basket,' she says, and I turn to find Eve watching me.

'No,' I say.

'George has gone.' She smiles. 'I heard the door slam.'

'Yes.'

I wonder at how mute I have become, when so many smart words were dancing in my head only moments ago. I lift the kettle, but my hands are trembling, so I put it down before it falls.

'Abel, sit down. You're all of a lather.'

'Yes.'

'Did he speak so harshly?' she asks with a small note of fury in her voice.

'Who?'

'George.'

'Oh. I had quite forgot.'

'Well, you are the talkative one, and no mistake.'

I look at her and see the kindness I have been too frightened to trust. No longer. I open my mouth. She grasps the handle of the kettle and hefts it over the fire.

'I believe *I* shall be making our tea from now on, Abel,' she says. 'The kitchen-girl has gone; and with her the plates, and knives, and spoons.'

'Are we truly in trouble, Eve?'

She raises her shoulders, and then lets them drop.

'My husband is an angry man. There is this new show, and it is the talk of the city. However, I shall endeavour to put it from my mind and direct my reasoning towards a more productive conclusion. It does not do to dwell on unpleasant thoughts, does it, Abel?'

Her eyes turn a key in mine. My mouth is still open, so I shut it.

'No,' I say.

I must find the right moment to speak. She returns her attention to the range, raising the shutter, examining the flames and talking as she does so.

'New acts, new thrills. I declare I am quite fatigued with all this bluster and fiddle-faddle.

Some peace would be pleasant. What think you, Abel?'

She glances at me hopefully.

'I — Eve, there is much I would say.'

My clever speech shrivels. She nods, and returns to peering into the fire. Lit from beneath, her face shimmers like the sun, her radiating curls its beams. When she straightens up, she carries the light with her.

'It is fired up well enough. I shall make tea. We shall sit awhile and drink a cup, and talk of anything you wish. Ah, there are barely enough leaves for one person. I hope Lizzie brings some back. There is coffee.'

'Coffee? Let us drink coffee, then.'

I take it from her, grateful for the distraction. As I spoon a measure into the smallest pan left in the place, I see a new picture, plucked from my mind's throng: a flat expanse of gritty sand; three stones set in a triangle with a smouldering stick set between them which I shuffle forward as it burns down. A small copper pot is wedged between the stones, sucking up the heat from the wood. I am hunched over the little fire; content.

'What are you doing?' she asks, and I am back in the under-stairs kitchen, stirring water and coffee grounds in a little iron pan.

'Making coffee.'

'I did not know it was made like that.'

'Nor did I. But you made me think of Lizzie when you spoke her name, and when I see her stomach-dance, it brings about a desire for coffee made this way. And a memory,' I add, more quietly.

She smiles. 'That is not what men usually desire when they see that dance.'

I heap sugar into the brew.

'It will be very sweet,' she says.

'Coffee without sugar is a marriage feast without dancing,' I reply, watching the pot begin to seethe. 'And burnt coffee is a wedding night without weeping. Some things must be so.'

She bares her teeth and laughs sadly. 'Where is that from?' she asks.

'I do not know. The smell of the coffee brought the words into my head. I am sitting next to a small fire, and above me the moon is slung on to its side.'

She stops laughing. 'I felt that strange magic,' she whispers, 'when you were playing the pipe. I was fairly transported by it. I did not know you could play so well.'

'Neither did I.'

'You are too modest.'

'Am I?'

'What other skills are you hiding?'

She runs her hand up and down the table-edge, as though it is an animal and she is stroking it.

'It seems that my hands are full of knowledge, but they conceal it from me,' I say, feeling a thrill to be opening the box of my self to someone who listens with sincere attention. 'Then I undertake a new task, and I discover they know how to accomplish it. I have not yet come upon something I cannot do.'

'You can do any job you set your mind to, I think.'

'Perhaps I can.'

She takes a considered breath. 'I shall speak honestly with you, Abel. You are not the only one with mysterious skills, for I have discovered one also. I can read men through their hands.'

'Yes.'

'I believe I can use this to help them. To help you. To help many others. I have plans, Abel. I have my face' — she laughs — 'I have my fascinating life, and it is no mean achievement.' She tilts her chin in a mixture of pride and defiance. 'I shall write the book of my life and present it with a fine frontispiece and it will be the sensation of the age. I shall write a yard of books. I shall be my own woman. I *am* my own woman.'

She laughs again; her eyes are bright, and hold mine longer than is customary for women. I lift the pot and pour the syrupy grime into two cups.

'Then let us drink to success. See. I did not think I could make coffee this way, but my hands are guiding me.'

'Such a tiny amount?' she says.

'Coffee is not for quenching thirst. That is the task of water. This is a different refreshment.'

I seem to be a book of proverbs. She does not notice, so I pinch the cup between thumb and forefinger, lift it to my lips, take a noisy sip. She does the same and sucks too hard, choking herself.

'Gently,' I say. 'The first time must always be gentle.'

She drops her eyes and takes a more careful taste.

307

'Its perfume transports me to another place.'

'It is indeed an evocative aroma,' she agrees.

I close my eyes, and this time am taken to a riverbank, floodwater shimmering over emerald fields, flashing like a thousand knives laid together side by side. On the far side is a huddle of mud-brick dwellings shivering in the noon heat, more than I can count at a glance. The place seems deserted, except for the spiralling twine of smoke from a cooking fire.

I shade my eyes and scan the line of crumbled walls, soft at the edges like kneaded dough without a mould. In the distance, beyond the irrigation, the desert spreads its red cloak into the west, league after league without end. I make my way towards the village, the ground yielding beneath my feet as I walk. A short distance down-river a boy stands in the water up to his ankles; he lifts a long cane and thrashes the sodden ground with it, raising a slow shawl of spray.

'Abel?'

I fly back into the room.

'Yes?' I blink.

'Are you well? You were like a man turned into stone. Where were you gone to?'

'You knew I had gone somewhere?'

'A great distance, by the set of your features.'

'Men call me an idiot for this way of mine.'

In my ears I hear *dead fish, dead man, corpse-kisser.*

'You do not seem like a fool to me. Thoughtful, rather. Different, of course.'

'Yes?' I look away, waiting for her to throw names.

'Abel, remember I am different also. I have fought to feel no shame.' She lifts up one of the locks of hair spilling from the side of her nose. 'It has been a long war with many battles. I shaved myself once — I thought to please my husband.' She grimaces. 'I will not do it again.'

'I am glad,' I say. 'For you would lose more than your fur. I should not like to see that.'

As I speak it, I know it for the truth. She pauses, and stares at me most intently.

'You *are* different to the others,' she says, and does not hide her pleasure. 'Abel, I am very glad indeed that you are my friend,' she adds, leaning across the table and brushing the back of my hand with her own.

I quiver with anticipation. I want to be read, but the fear of being thought grotesque remains. The look of disgust on the face of my Italian master swims before my eyes.

'Ah,' she murmurs.

'What is it?' I ask, fearing her response.

'I am not sure. I felt it before.' She shakes her head, and her hair swings about her face. 'I can read you: like the others, yet nothing like them. They unwind a few years and come to the end of their spool. You are — '

I wait for *monstrous*.

'Marvellous,' she sighs. 'Even a brief touch and I can see you stretching back and back. You were a slaughter-man.'

'Yes, but everyone knows this. Even George.'

'Before that, a clock-mender.'

'Yes.'

'And before that, an anatomist of sorts.'

'I was!' I gasp. 'I have told no-one of it.'

'Those few things I have uncovered after a moment's touching. There is a great deal more. In all the pictures I see you grow no younger. The images change; you are unchanging.'

'Now you will tell me they are perverted imaginings.'

'No. Why would I do that?'

'Everyone else has done.'

'Have they?'

'If you see what I contain, what I am, then you will push me away.'

'Why?'

'Because I am full of horrors,' I whisper.

'I do not think I could hate you, Abel. If that is all you fear — '

'It is not all. I cannot make the pictures stop,' I say, glancing at her and then away. 'They pursue me everywhere. I fear that if you open the book of me, I will be overwhelmed. That I will never be able to shut them away again. I will drown in the flood.'

'Abel, my friend.'

'I think I have changed my mind. I am sorry. One minute I want to understand the secret of myself, the next I do not.' Then it comes to me. 'Eve, these memories of mine. Can you take them away?'

'No! All I can do is read them.'

'But I do not want them.' I am visited by a stabbing image of a tent in a fair, an old man demanding to gut me of my memories and then to leave me burst open and helpless. 'If you read me, I am afraid that you will know more than I do, that it will be too heavy for me, that I will not want to know your answer. I am afraid it is what I guess. I am afraid it is nothing like I guess. I have been this close before, I think. I do not remember, but the fear tastes familiar.'

'That is a lot of fear.'

We smile at each other, as though for the first time. I bathe in its simple warmth, feeling myself washed strangely clean. I lean forward and wipe the stub of my thumb along her moustache. She does not start away.

'You have coffee stuck to your lip,' I say. I think of George, and if he came into the room, now. 'Eve. Do not tell your husband we have drunk coffee together.'

'I tell my husband very little. But why should the drinking of coffee be a secret to be kept?'

'You are a woman, therefore you understand. He is a man, and will not.'

The room settles into the warm silence of companionship.

★   ★   ★

Eve does not grasp at me with lip-licking curiosity nor does she thrust me away in horror. The word that comes to my weary mind is *safe*. I lie on my bed, concocting plans of how I may endeavour to find her alone again, and soon, and talk more. Conjuring romantic dreams of myself telling her how beautiful she is, and seeing her look upon me with more than friendship — with love. In such a dream I find her, fall to my knees and bury my face in her skirt. I inhale the delicious spice of her, something I know but cannot name.

'Abel, you are the only one who does not wish to change me.'

'You are Eve. That is enough.'

'My dear Abel. This is a greater gift than you know.'

'Eve, I — '

'You know I can help you.'

'I know. I am ready.'

Her smile brushes my heart with an intimacy so intense I am made breathless. I gather her to me as though the action may restore breath to my lungs. As I do, her fur melts away and her face is replaced with that of another woman, whose hair is so dark a brown as to be black, coiled in braids about her head.

I know this woman. I have unloosed her hair a hundred times. She laughs, and as she does so, changes once more. Her jaw sets, teeth grinding against each other as she is seized by a dreadful pestilence.

Her whole body labours to expel the poison, pushing the foul matter into swellings which crowd about her neck: the size of hen's eggs, the colour of raked ashes. In her armpit are further tumours, so great she can no longer keep her arm close by her side, but instead holds it away from her.

I watch her hurled back and forth by the violent fever and can do nothing to draw her to safety. I wish to be spared this torture, but cannot close my eyes. Words of prayer burst from my mouth: that I might keep her by me; that she might be returned to wholeness through some miracle of healing. An answering rattle bubbles from her mouth, breath creeping narrowly between the swellings in her throat.

Her teeth clench in a grimace that might be frowning or laughing. It is the smile of coming Death, which reveals what lies beneath the skin. Her head rolls from side to side and she lets out small piercing cries of surprise, hands grasping and ungrasping as her whole body wrestles the sickness. I try to catch her fingers and soothe her, but I cannot keep hold.

At last she is seized by a spasm as though a dog has bitten her in the lower part of her belly. She stretches her mouth wide and releases a long squeal; then the shriek is snuffed out and the room aches with silence. A crackling sound comes from her lips: the snapping of burning twigs. Her tongue spikes the filthy air and a corrupt stink buffets me as her bowels loosen.

I look upon the terrible face before me. This is not my beloved; it cannot be. This female has a quill pen of a nose, harsh jawbone, eyes fixed in a furious glare. Her mouth stretches wide in a final curse, tongue as grey as a ram's. I try to push this slug of a thing back into the mouth, but it will not fit.

I look from her blotched and pestilent skin to my own untouched flesh; I press my mouth to hers and suck at her last venomous breath in the hope that I might also be infected. But for all my desire to join her in the mortal grasp of the fever, I am unable to follow.

The voice speaks: *Would you do this again?*

Have Eve melt before your eyes in sickness? I know its truth. Every woman I have touched, and every man also: all have shrivelled, died; and I have looked on, unaltered, and unable to hold them to this life for one breath longer.

Like the Morning Star, Eve has risen in the dark night of my existence. She warms me with the bright flame of understanding. All I need to do is stretch out my hands and receive the comfort she offers so freely. But how can I cause her the pain I have inflicted upon countless others? How can I inflict it upon myself?

★ ★ ★

I wake up. My courage stutters. It is dark, and I am alone.

EVE

London, November 1858

'A prime space, my dear. A prime location,' he said, loud enough for any passers-by to hear. 'Sheltered from the wind. That is what is needed by persons of our standing.'

My husband tipped his hat on to the back of his head, winking at the fearsome man guarding the entrance and pushing a shilling into his handshake. The gate-keeper peered at me.

'What's that?' he growled, pointing at my heavy veil. 'We don't like women here.'

'That', said my husband loudly, broadening his shoulders, 'is my wife. A Non-Pareil of the Female Race. The only true and genuine Lion-Faced Woman, and Star Attraction at Professor Arroner's Marvels, which may be viewed — '

'Yes, yes, we've heard of you and have seen it all before,' our Cerberus muttered. 'Get along now, there's folk waiting.'

We made our way past men armed with staves who looked this way and that along the street, as if something admired or detested were about to appear round the corner and they must be ready to spring into attack or defence. I trotted at his

315

side with a sprightly step, for his stride was longer than mine and not obstructed by tight-laced stays or the thick quilt of petticoats through which I waded.

My husband thumbed his coat lapels, clapping the shoulders of many a fellow as if they were all of his acquaintance and handing out playbills. The first man said, 'Seen it,' the second, 'Old hat,' and plenty more remarked on there being 'new thrills to be had'. After a while even he tired of the interminable humbug, and led me to his chosen spot down a passageway barely the breadth of my shoulders.

A crowd of men far larger than my small self were streaming in, turning sideways and making themselves thin as doors to shuffle down the alleyway. I saw the most nimble transform themselves further, into Barbary apes, finding footholds in the bricks and perching in the empty mouths of windows. I did not know so many could be forced into so restricted a space. You could not name it a square: rather, it was a pocket of dank air, bludgeoned into smallness by grimy walls.

'Why are we here?' I said, sliding my hand beneath the veil to sweep aside my eyebrows. They had refused to take the curl overnight and insisted on curtaining my eyes.

'You will see, soon enough.'

'I see nothing of any note, save a company of folk such as one might encounter in any public bar.'

He barked out a swift laugh. 'Ah, this is not *any* public place. Nor are these any men.

316

Patience, Mrs Arroner. We are here for your instruction and edification.'

My heart sank a little. He rarely if ever took me out with him, and over breakfast had described this event as a diverting change, one where I might be entertained rather than providing the entertainment. The word 'instruction' cast it in a far less interesting light.

Still they packed in. The air seethed; I almost wished myself under the Baptist's paper mask, for the stink of glue would be better than this choking fog of sweat and beer, and flesh never washed. I clutched my veil to my nose and for once was grateful for its thick folds. My husband gripped my shoulder as though he guessed I wished to be away.

'What is this place?' I coughed.

'Be quiet,' he said, his voice strangling oddly. 'You are my wife and will conduct yourself as befits that elevated position.'

'But, Mr Arroner — '

'I said, be silent. Be obedient to my wishes.'

'Always, dearest,' I said, with as much sub-mission as I could muster.

He stared at me and it was as though the look pierced my veil and my fringe of disobedient hair all the way to the depths of my soul.

'I wonder?' he murmured. 'George has whis-pered some pretty tales, I do declare.'

'Has he indeed?' I declared. 'Of course, George is a trustworthy man.'

I turned my head to look forward. He grasped my arm above the elbow and squeezed so harshly I let out a small cry.

'Do not toy with me, wife. You are mine, remember that,' he hissed. 'I'd see you stuffed and mounted in a glass case before I'd let another man touch you, do you hear?'

'Yes, dear husband,' I squeaked, for his grip was unyielding. 'But I am true to you. I do not know where George — '

'Be quiet. Your education is about to begin. I hope you find it bends your mind towards contemplation of how a wife should disport herself appropriately.'

As he spoke, the rumbling chatter of the mob was cut short. Although it did not seem possible, people shrank to the sides to make more room, creating a clearing in the forest of bodies. My husband straightened up and loosened his grip a fraction. Then the two men were dragged in. For all I thought my life had cooked me tough, I was peeled raw at the sight.

They were Negroes, arms tied behind their backs, mouths stuffed with rags. One had skin the colour of porter, and was so ragged as to be near naked; through the gag he was mumbling words I was neither able nor desired to hear. His neighbour wore a shirt and breeches that had once been expensive, but were now torn and bloodied; his face was paler and so swollen I was sure he could not see anything. I was grateful he could not see me.

They were shoved to their knees; collars were padlocked about their necks and fixed to a chain that ratcheted through a ring in the flagstones. The man in the shirt struggled to his feet only to be clouted back down, letting out a sound I did

318

not think possible from the mouth of a man, till I saw how his jaw swung like a kicked gate.

'What is this?' I hissed.

'It is a good show,' said my husband, hitching up his trousers by the waistband. 'Observe.'

'No.'

'Ah, is the famous prima donna piqued that no-one watches her today?' he sneered.

'What sport is there in watching two unfortunate Negroes? There is more interest by far in our entertainments.' I laboured to make my voice light. 'We are staring at them as though this were the zoological gardens. Look at them. The poor souls.'

He tossed back his head. 'Souls? They have none. All men know they thrive on witchcraft. Savages.'

I gave no answer; I shuddered behind my curtain, where he could not see. My stomach turned.

'And besides,' he continued. 'This is not the show. That is about to commence.'

His words heralded the truth of it, for at that moment a man in a lemon-yellow waistcoat stepped out of the wall of bodies and held up his hand, hooking the other thumb into the pocket of his vest. It was so quiet I could hear the rattling gasp of the chained men, and wished I could not.

'Gentlemen!' he proclaimed. 'You have heard the word put about. You have gathered for this choice exhibition, for you are men of special discernment and particular bent. Have I ever disappointed you?'

319

The audience shouted its approval of this fellow, who made his pitch as well as my husband.

'So, sirs, be seemly, and place your bets in the usual fashion.' He waved his hand and cried, 'Ladies!'

Three women appeared from the masculine throng, squatted on the cobbles and spread out their aprons. An overture of coins struck up, clattering out of pockets and into the skirts, to an accompaniment of pointing and the shouting out of numbers and words so fast I could not follow it. My husband let go of my shoulder.

'I am going to place a bet,' he remarked casually. I took a step away, thinking to make my escape whilst he was gone, but he extended his arm and pointed the stub of his index finger at the ground. 'Stay,' he said.

With that single word, he melted into the crowd. My head swam. I wondered if they wagered on which of the Moors would faint the first, for each of them seemed close to it. More and more money found its way into the women's aprons, and when it seemed there was no more to be had, the mob settled into a greasy calm, like the slick around the hull of a steamer. My husband's breath warmed my ear.

'Do not worry, little wife. I have placed a clever bet. I am sure I will go home with a heavy wallet.'

Then the dogs were brought out: two of them. The first was a brindled cur the colour of stewed tea with a neck as broad as its shoulders, its eyes glittering in the long night of its head. Its

320

companion was a pasty grey and, if anything, its shoulders were even broader. They waddled forward, a pair of bow-legged gentlemen of the canine world, neither panting nor whimpering, but patient at the end of their ropes. I barely marked the men who held them, and wish I had examined them, to see if they were any different to my husband. Afterwards it was too late.

'Shall we not get started?' my husband hissed impatiently to low growls from our neighbours. 'How dare they hush me,' he murmured into my ear. 'Do they know to whom they speak?'

The women folded up the bags of their skirts and jingled through a doorway I had not noted before.

'What is going on?' I asked, not wanting the answer.

A weight descended on to my shoulder. I looked, and there was Mr Arroner's hand. So innocent, so protective it appeared: the pale white skin, the dimples on his fat knuckles, the neatly pared fingernails and the wedding ring glinting in the beams of the low sun. I was held there as surely as the two men in the arena before me. A small grunt of revolt escaped my lips and his fingers slid down and resumed their unyielding grip around my arm.

'Quiet,' he said gently.

My flesh was gripped silent, and before I could cringe with the sudden stab of pain, everything changed. A breath was taken in by the whole company and held tight. All I could hear was the muffled moaning of the Negroes and the scalding wheeze of the dogs. Then the handlers untied them and coiled up the leashes.

The brindled dog took a small step forward, but froze at one word from his master. I did not hear the command that released them, but command there was and it made the dogs ball up tight and then hurl themselves forward. The brindle went for the man in the tattered shirt; the grey took the naked Moor, jaws locking round his throat.

'Like a rat,' breathed my husband.

He might hold me at his side, but he could not make me watch this horror. I turned my head and concentrated all my attention on the sleeve of the stranger to my right. I was sure that if I peered very hard through my veil, I could count every thread in the coarse weave. My arm was released and I felt sensation return to the muscle. That, at least, was an infinitesimal blessing. My stomach tilted at the idea that I could even think of blessings at an event such as this and I bit my lip with shame. Almost at once I felt a warm sensation at the back of my head as my husband grasped the scruff of my neck and slowly twisted my head so that I faced forwards.

'Look. Learn.'

'No,' I begged.

'Wife. You will not make me look foolish. Understand?'

When I did not respond, he dug his fingers into the bone behind my ear and my moan seemed to provide the answer he sought.

'You will know your place. Do as you are ordered.'

He held me in the prison of his grasp.

Concealed beneath my veil, I squeezed my eyes shut. It was the only act of rebellion I could muster. The animals worked in silence; the crowd did not. They grunted, cheered, clapped; the square heaved with the thud of fist into palm, the gagged shrieks of the quarry. I was surrounded by men's bodies surging forward, stretching their necks so as not to miss one moment.

But for all I closed my eyes I could not shut out the sounds and smells: the crunch of gristle; the privy smell of shit and pissed-out beer. I clenched my teeth and growled, so low a sound that it was lost in the baying of the mob; thus I blotted out as much of the racket as I could. I sensed rather than saw my husband leap up and down with excitement, but not once did he forget himself enough to release the grip on my neck.

At a shout from the dog-wranglers it stopped. The cheering crested and then subsided into a grumbling calm. Cautiously, I opened my eyes and saw that the animals had stopped, turned into statues. The brown licked a dry crust from its muzzle, but when his master grunted the tongue flicked back into its mouth.

'Best dogs in the world,' breathed my master.

His thoughts fluttered into me through the skin of his palm. Against all my will, I was forced to read every thrust of his vile excitement, cramping my belly into a sickening tangle. I pulled away and at last he loosed me.

'Here endeth the lesson,' he said, and patted my shoulder.

I rubbed the back of my neck and felt the bruise flushing through my fur as the blood seeped back. His voice came to me from very far off, as though whistling down a long tube.

'Oh, did I hang on to my pet too hard?' he added. 'A man forgets these things in his exhilaration.'

The dogs stood obediently as they were tied up once more. To the side I noticed a group of lads, making a great show of pointing and crying, 'Ho! Such bowls of blood! Nay! Buckets full!' for each seemed determined to outdo his brother in indecent delight. One youth, seemingly no different, turned his face aside; his shoulders heaved and he raised his hand to press against his mouth to keep back the torrent.

But it was no use: his fellows straight away saw his frailty and goaded him with louder shouts about 'the throat torn out, the crunch of bones', until he voided his stomach on to the cobbles to laughter and accusations that he must be a babe, a tot and, worst, a girl. All of the lads were cowed with shame at his parade of tender feeling, remembering and hating their own tears when they first saw one of God's creatures killed. Now they were grown, they were determined to show no mercy to any one of their set who might show such weakness.

The women then reappeared; the money was counted out and distributed to its new owners. The pale dog glowed with pride, rubbing against its master's leg, tongue lolling from the side of its mouth like a piece of wet, pink rope. I was surrounded by a chorus of voices describing 'his verve, his bright eye, his spunk'. With a sick realisation, I knew this beast had been declared winner. *Winner*. I did not want to reflect on how this decision had been reached. The women, skirts empty now, slopped the cobbles up and down with long sticks wadded with rags. The bodies were put into sacks, and weighted down with stones for their short journey to the river.

I felt strangely tall, as though my neck were stretched long as a giraffe's, and I was looking down upon the proceedings from a great height: a distance so immense and comforting I could almost make believe I was not in this ghastly place. But there was no true escape. I was here. I had not screamed out *stop*. I was as guilty as every man present. The man in the golden waistcoat emerged once again from the wall of onlookers and held up a rectangle of glossy leather. He cleared his throat and all fell quiet.

'Gentlemen!' he boomed. 'Behold this wallet, found on the savage!'

He dipped his hand inside the purse and drew out a white paper of exquisite cleanness.

'See what was within! A five-pound note!'

The crowd exhaled, a wave of air that caused me to stagger.

'To the victor, the spoils!'

He thrust the money at the owner of the winning dog, who was promptly hoisted on to the shoulders of a pack of onlookers and paraded around the square. My mind began to squeal rusty cogs.

'But if the Moor was carrying a wallet and five pounds, how could he be a savage?' I said to my

325

husband. He ignored me, so I tugged his sleeve. 'Mr Arroner,' I continued; for all that my thoughts were reeling I was determined to be heard, even if only in this small matter. 'Where did his money come from?'

'Whose?'

'The Moor.'

He shrugged. 'He stole it.'

'Maybe it was his own. Why should it not be his own?'

Mr Arroner peered down at me and I squared my shoulders.

'How so?' he said.

'I have sewn enough shirts to know that his was a good one. Before you took me to wife.' I swallowed sourness, but forced myself to speak. 'And he was clean-shaven.'

'So?'

'So maybe he was no thief. No savage.'

He lowered his face and lifted my veil. 'My dear wife.' He looked at me properly for the first time that day — that week, that month: too long to reckon. 'He was a savage. Caught red-handed. There's an end to it.'

He dropped the curtain. Still I would not allow it. Some of the company had begun to gather around, listening to our exchange.

'If he was a thief, and this money stolen, then will not its true owner come searching for it?'

'You are too inquisitive.'

He returned his hand to the back of my neck, and squeezed.

'I believe that he was no savage,' I said quietly. 'He was merely different. Like me.'

'Dear wife, have you learned nothing today?' He stared down the curious glances of those around us. 'Yes!' he said boldly. 'Yes, I believe you know me, gentlemen!' He swept off his chimney-pot of a hat and brandished it before him. 'I am indeed Josiah Arroner, the True Originator of Arroner's Anatomical Marvels. One of those marvels accompanies me now. Veiled for her protection or for yours? Who can tell? You may view our unusual entertainments each day at — '

'Yes, yes, give it a rest,' grunted one.

'Nothing we haven't seen before,' said another.

'Off to see the Two-Headed Nightingale, so we are.'

'Surprised you aren't going there yourself,' snickered one fellow, thrusting a playbill at my husband. 'Look.'

My husband's hands trembled as he took the sheet of paper, gave it a cursory glance, and then handed it back.

'No. You keep it, mate. Might help you catch up.'

'Yeah. Lagging behind, as I hear it.'

They turned away, having had enough diversion for one afternoon.

★ ★ ★

As we made our slow passage away from the dreadful place, a slender man approached my husband and touched his arm.

'Mr Arroner, ain't it?'

'It is, sir,' he puffed.

'I believe I have found something for you, sir, knowing as I do your taste for the strange.'

'Indeed?'

He feigned indifference, but I could sense his curiosity was stimulated. The man leaned into his ear.

'I can get you a lady-boy. A real one. It's got a prick and a fanny; one tit small and one big.' He paused, and flicked his eyes about. 'It's in Birmingham, so the travel will cost you. But you won't regret a penny. It's real. Can dance a polka too.'

My husband drew himself upright, which was barely the height of the pinched man before him, and pushed out his chin.

'Sir,' he growled. 'Mine is a respectable exhibition. Educational.'

'It *is* educational.' He leered. 'Think of the pamphlets. The illustrations.'

'No, I will not have it. It is intolerable.'

'Not to mention the many other ways it can make you money,' he murmured.

'You disgust me.'

'Please yourself.' The man shrugged. 'I hear your shows have a lot of empty seats this season. This could be just the tonic you need.'

'There is nothing wrong with my audiences.'

'Not what I've heard. Come now. Think of the crowds it'll bring in.'

'Never. A thing like that should have its unnecessary parts cut off.'

'And cut off its income? We've all got a right to earn a crust.'

'What do you take me for?'

'A man who shows freaks for a living.'

'I am a married man,' he cried, though no-one was listening save myself. 'A gentleman. I have refinement and taste.'

'Like I said, suit yourself. No skin off my arse.' He paused. 'How about a Dog-Boy? I can get you a Dog-Boy.'

My husband sighed, jingling his winnings in the pocket of his breeches. 'I could have used one of those Blacks, you know. The Missing Link. What a wasted opportunity.'

'Oh no, Mr Arroner, not those two,' said the skinny man. 'They wouldn't of done it. Don't you think I tried to find out?'

'Indeed?'

'No. They wouldn't bend, not like Blacks should do. Not that pair. No choice there but dogs.'

The two of them sighed a little more about the waywardness of men, and then shook hands, with an agreement to meet again and discuss Dog-Boys.

'What a waste,' he confided in me on our walk home. 'I could have used them. I could have bent them to my will. A Black is a Black, after all.'

I tottered beside him, an obedient puppet of a wife with stick-like limbs, listening to the buzz of his conversation as it ebbed and flowed about my ears. I swayed along the pavement, almost wishing I might faint. But my body did not grant me such a peaceful escape. I stumbled into the path of other walkers, and did not care how they gawped at me; each of their faces revealing terrible teeth; their hands sprouting rending claws. The streets I walked down were entirely populated with monsters: a hell of ravening fangs, biting, tearing, devouring; scrambling over the backs of the weak, stamping those below into a mash of humanity, with no light in their eyes other than the beastly imperative: *Destroy!*

★ ★ ★

We arrived home at last; I barely knew how. Straight away I made an excuse about having to attend to the needs of nature and went to the privy. I bent over the stinking hole and voided my stomach until there was nothing left inside me. Then I washed my hands and dried them with extreme care.

Lizzie was in the kitchen, resting her enormous elbows on the table. I was never more grateful to see her. I sat down, very slowly, as though the chair were matchwood, or I were matchwood; I was not sure. I removed my hat and veil with great care and arranged them neatly upon the scrubbed board. My husband stood in the doorway, but did not enter.

'You will remain here, wife. I am going out,' he declared. 'To make better our investments.'

'Make sure you are not so over-invested you cannot stand,' remarked Lizzie. 'We must have our most excellent Master of Ceremonies for tonight's show.'

He stamped out of the house and slammed the door.

'I'll make tea,' said Lizzie and grunted to her

feet, swaying her bulk across the floor. 'Looks like you could do with a cup. There's some in. I'd make the most of it.'

'Yes.'

My voice seemed very small, the room very large.

'You all right, Evie love?'

'I do not know. He took me out with him. He never takes me out with him. I was excited. I chose my favourite hat.' I fumbled with the feathers trimming the bonnet lying before me. 'I cannot believe I thought hats were important.'

'Evie?'

'I have been sick. I am never taken ill.'

'Let's get you that tea. What has he done to you?'

I could hear far-off thunder in her voice.

'Nothing. He took me out: to a dog-fight.'

'Christ. If it was the one I think you mean — '

I found that my fingers had worried the cockade into shreds. 'He made me watch. I shut my eyes. I could not shut my ears.'

'The bastard. How could he take you there? There's been talk of it for days.'

She placed a cup of dark liquid before me.

'Lizzie, I am scared.'

'I thought I could wait for our luck to turn around as it has before. Not this time. Lizzie has had enough,' she growled.

'What will you do?'

'I'm making plans. I've got this to live off.' She cupped a hand around one of the rolls of flab around her middle and jiggled it. 'I shan't fade away just yet.' She cupped a huge hand around

331

my cheek. 'Now now, don't you fret for one moment. I'll not move a muscle till I see you fixed.'

'I won't hold you here.' I hoped I sounded braver than I felt.

'You have my promise. No, no tears. If you start now you won't stop. Save them for when you're good and safe. Oh, hello, Abel. The pot's not long brewed.'

She poured a cup for him and stirred in a hill of sugar.

'Come on, man, there's always plenty of room next to Lizzie.'

'I did not hear you come in,' I said, for lack of anything better.

'How he creeps about! Man or mouse?' said Lizzie in a good imitation of my husband's style. 'You don't mind me, do you, Abel?'

'You are a kind woman,' he said. 'You love Eve. That is sufficient reason for me to like you very much.'

I had never seen Lizzie so affected.

'You *are* a different man these days, aren't you?' She smiled at him. 'Anyhow, I have work to do if we are to eat well tonight. I am not prepared to starve just yet.'

She left, leaving Abel and me at the table. We sat in silence; one which was uncomfortable for me, but in which he seemed content. I could not rid my mind of what I had seen only a short while previously. Whatever I tried to think about in its place was swiftly overtaken by the sound of dogs, the baying of a mob, the excited shouts of my husband when he realised he had placed his money on the winner. I busied myself pouring more tea, adding sugar. It was stewed and bitter through the sweetness. If I could only break this silence then perhaps I could free myself; but the longer it continued, the less likely that seemed possible.

'Abel,' I blurted.

'Yes?'

'Please. Say something.'

He put his cup on the table.

'I would speak freely with you, Eve.'

'Do so, I beg you. I have never needed your words so much.'

'You are troubled,' he said. 'By your husband.'

'Yes. By what he thinks of me. Of us.'

'Ah, yes.' He raised an eyebrow. 'His crew of freaks, to do with as he pleases.'

The air hung between us, weightily.

'Abel, you are troubled also.'

'I am. There are things I would say to you. Ask you, even. But there are people in the house . . . '

'George?'

'Indeed. He wishes us ill. You in particular.'

'I know. He has been talking to my husband. Lies.'

'George has said certain things to me.' He shifted uncomfortably on his chair. 'He wants you.'

'Me?'

'To possess you. To remove Mr Arroner and take you for himself.'

It shimmered before me: a tempting vision, free of my husband. But . . . George? My fur stood on end.

'Never,' I declared. 'I know where my affections lie.'

'Eve,' he said, and I felt the weight of his hand travel up my arm and rest on my shoulder.

I leaned into the warmth and it flared into a heat that swept down my arm into my fingers. I surrendered to its wonderful comfort.

'Oh,' I said.

'Are you well?'

'Yes, oh yes! When you touch me it is like fire.'

'Am I to apologise?'

'Not at all. I forget how much pleasure I take from it. There is none other makes me so . . . '

He removed his hand, slowly, placed it in his lap and stared at it.

'See now. I said I would not speak tonight, with others in the house. But I cannot hide what I feel for you.'

I nodded, breathless and blushing, and was grateful for my fur. Every hair on my body stood on end, pricked and alert for what might come next. I tugged at my moustache. I took the deepest breath of my life.

'Abel, I have secrets also. I am making plans to leave.'

'You are?'

His eyes were lit with the brightest fire I had ever seen in them.

'After what I have been forced to witness, my mind is made up. There is no longer any safety with Mr Arroner.'

'No, there is not.'

'So, I shall go.' I waved my hand; I tried to make it a courageous gesture, but my arm seemed exceedingly heavy. 'I have money put by. I have my skill of palm-reading. Even my strangeness will keep bread on my plate, and I would rather eat crusts from a plate of my own than roast beef from one of his.'

My breath wheezed, my chest tight with the spilling out of my heart's truth.

'Yes,' he replied simply.

I smiled at him, and he looked at me as though we were seeing each other clearly for the first time. He smiled in return, and I bathed in its simple warmth; I felt myself washed clean. He opened his mouth to say more when the outer door slammed, speaking noisily of my husband's return.

'Where are you?' he roared.

I sprang to my feet, racing upstairs to meet him in the hallway, fired with a conviction that he must not find me alone with Abel.

'Dear husband!' I said, spreading wooden arms.

'Yes, yes, very well,' he muttered, shoving me aside. 'George!' he bawled. 'Where in hell are you? Where is Abel? I have plans.'

He tapped his temple with a broad forefinger.

'A new show in town? We'll see about that. It's all up here,' he said, leaning so close the spirits on his breath were unmistakable. 'I'm not finished yet. Not Josiah Arroner, Esquire. Plenty of fight left in me.'

He pushed me aside and yelled down the steps to the cellar.

'I said: Get up here!'

There was the sound of thumping and George

appeared, rubbing his face awake, Abel behind him.

'Where's the bleeding fire?' yawned George. 'I was asleep.'

'Sleeping off my food and drink?' he grunted. 'Into the showing-room with the two of you.' He pointed at me. 'You, Mrs Arroner. Downstairs and get a meat-skewer from the kitchen. If you please.'

'Is there such a hurry, dearest?'

'There is, wife, when I say there is.'

It took me long minutes to search through the drawers, now emptied of their valuables. I did not know why I was filled with such a sense of foreboding, but it seemed important for me to hurry. At last I found a skewer fallen down the side of the range, clearly overlooked by the last maid, and dashed back to the displaying-room. Abel was tied to the velvet chair, ankles strapped to the legs, arms twisted back and roped together.

'Ah,' purred my husband, snatching the spike from my hand. 'You are in time.' I wondered if he meant to draw out another chair and fasten me to it. 'We have managed without you, as you may observe.'

'My dear husband, why do you need to restrain him so?'

He rubbed his hands together. 'It is all part of the new act I have devised. I am still the guiding genius of this company. I'll show them. Think they can put me out of business? Me? Josiah Arroner? We shall be rich again. Abel doesn't mind. Do you, Abel?'

'It is an act,' said Abel, looking at me calmly.

I crossed the carpet, moving as swiftly as I dared without it seeming as though I was hastening to Abel's side. He was stripped to his under-britches. I had never seen him so exposed: for his turn in the show he only ever removed his shirt. His legs and toes were seeded with fine black hair; a dark mat covered the palm-span between his navel and the waistband of his under-garment; he sported a bear-lick of fur in the groove between his nipples. My husband shook his head, and drops of sweat spattered Abel's naked chest.

'It's all very well Abel cutting himself. But they think it fakery. Clever, but a trick nonetheless. Now we shall let them satisfy their curiosity.'

He brandished the skewer, placed its point in the inkwell at the joint of Abel's collar-bones and pushed hard. George stepped round to the back of the chair.

'Well, damn me.' He smirked. 'It's coming out the other side.'

I went also, but more slowly: indeed I was unsure that I truly wanted to see what I knew I would find. The skin on the nape of his neck was being pushed out into a small tent of flesh, as the metal nib probed for a way out. Then the skin opened. It did not tear: rather, it paused and then opened a polite gap just wide enough for the barb to pass through. I could not find enough breath; all the air had been stolen from the room.

'Is this how you preserve your investments?' I

337

said lightly, as though I did not care if I had answer or not.

'I'll do what I please,' my husband panted. 'I'll do more. I'll show them what he's capable of. No-one knows but me. We'll have wagers placed upon him. *How deep can he be cut? Gentlemen, place your bets!* We'll provide knives for hire. The deeper the cut, the higher the price. And the house wins, every time.'

He drew a knife from the inside of his waistcoat and waved it under Abel's nose.

'Aren't you afraid of me?' he hissed. 'Aren't you going to stretch your eyes? Grind your teeth? Aren't you going to beg for mercy?'

Abel gazed at him. 'Why?' he said, breast rising and falling slowly.

'Dear Mr Arroner,' I said, 'is there really such a need to vex him so?'

'If I am to feed and house him, then he needs to earn his keep,' he grumbled without looking at me. 'So, sir,' he continued, 'do I vex you?'

Abel continued to stare at him. 'No. But I am tired.'

'What!' he roared. 'You lie on my bed, stuff yourself with my food and drink, and you are *tired?*'

'Mr Arroner!' I said, still lightly.

The blade hovered; my husband gouged two lines in a letter X over Abel's heart and began to carve into the muscle. He watched the wound curiously, as if daring it to heal.

'Oh, will someone throw a towel over him!' my husband exclaimed. 'He is as shameless as a dog in heat.'

I saw the swelling in Abel's undergarments and flicked my eyes away; but could not keep them held off for long: I had dreamed of such a thing, had I not? If that made me a harlot, then so be it.

'You see?' barked my husband. 'There is no aggravation. Unless it be you, Mrs Arroner. So. How deep *can* you be cut?' he asked, pressing harder, voice climbing. 'What if I were to cut out your heart? Would you grow a new one?'

'It is all an act,' said Abel. 'All of this.'

'Go on,' urged George. 'Deeper.'

'I'll make you swallow knives whole, handle and all. Make men pay to feel your belly, the blades within,' he roared. 'Pay to watch you shit them out. You might fool them, but you can't fool me. No-one fools Josiah Arroner. No-one, d'you hear?'

His voice broke like a boy's. Moisture swam across his forehead, dribbling to the tip of his nose.

'In fact, we'll strip you naked. No britches to cover you up. Then we'll see the ladies gasp. Then we'll see the money come in — '

'Dear Mr Arroner,' I cried. 'Does it profit you to test him so?'

His hand paused. I looked at George, who was standing with his arms folded, head cocked, and observing the scene with a hungry interest. As though he sensed my gaze, he raised his eyes to mine and grinned, revealing his gleaming teeth. I made a big show of yawning and stretching out my arms.

'Ah, well,' I said, patting my hand over my

mouth. 'I am fatigued by all of this. I can see this sort of show any night.'

I turned, and walked away.

'Get back here this instant!' my husband screamed.

I carried on walking. Behind me, I heard the clank of the knife hurled on to the floor. I knew I must not turn round, nor show I had heard it.

★ ★ ★

I went directly to my room, and was never happier to be alone. I could hear the grind of argument downstairs; presently Lizzie's voice joined the mêlée. It swelled into a thunderstorm of shouting and thumping feet; then the front door slammed and the house grew quiet. I undressed, put on my night-gown and crawled beneath the covers.

Hours or moments later — I was unsure which — I was woken by a hand on my shoulder. A candle was waved over my face.

'Where are you, puss?' It was my husband's voice, but oddly choked. 'Puss!'

He beered his breath into my neck, grabbed my arm and squeezed where it still throbbed from earlier. I held my teeth in a clench; I knew. I must not make any noise at all.

'Here you are,' he hiccoughed. 'Hiding from me all curled up in your basket. What a pretty little pet it is. Pretty, pretty, pretty.' He blew out the candle. 'Who's going to be a good girl and let her husband climb in next to her. You are. Yes, you are.'

He set the candle on the night-table and poked me in the ribs.

'Want me to give you my heart?' he snorted, his hand growing sticky around mine. 'That's what women want, isn't it? Even you. Take my heart, then, and leave me nothing.'

He lifted my numb fingers to where his shirt was undone and pressed them into the flab covering his chest. I could feel the paddling of his uneven pulse.

'I caught you looking at him. But you're mine. A man needs something he can call his own.'

I wriggled against him, but he only held me tighter. I whelped against the pain and he ignored me, pulling up my night-dress and pressing his knees between my legs.

'What we need is a litter,' he slurred.

He grasped the hair on the back of my neck and clamped my face to his, tongue scrubbing against my teeth. I seesawed back to escape its anemone suck; he seesawed forward: back and forwards we went in a sweaty jig. His arms were huge: I struggled against the solid wall of him, but I was cemented between his fists. My jaws lost the fight to keep my mouth closed against him, and he eeled his tongue into me and licked, and licked.

He let go one hand and scraped at my throat until the buttons of my nightdress snagged and tore; he slithered his other hand through the forest at the fork of my thighs and prised me open, following with the hard pole of his secret parts, pushing and pulling in and out.

'Genius,' he grunted. 'Genius. Genius. Genius.'

After a few thrusts his body quivered and he stopped moving. A moment more and he rolled away, panting. I watched him wipe his lips, and then tuck his privates back into his trousers.

'Why do you stare so?' he whined. 'Why? I am your husband. Look at you. Look at the wife I chose. An animal. Business made me do this. This is not what I want. This is work.'

He lurched off the bed and staggered to the wall, spewing up the wine he had drunk. When he had finished, I heard him shuffling to the door, where he paused, the gaslight from the hallway silhouetting him so that he was merely the shape of a man cut from black paper and pressed to the face of the air. If I breathed out, I could blow him away.

I held my mouth shut for as long as I could, and he did not stir, dangling in the doorway on the hook of my breath. I grew dizzy but still held on, and only when the room began to sparkle did I breathe in at last. He shivered and floated away.

I lay, staring at the open door, and felt his moisture trickle out, for it seemed that no part of him wished to remain in contact with me. This thing I had desired so long, this thing I had dreamed of possessing had finally been given to me: I no longer wanted it.

I had been so cock-eyed. I fell in love with the mirror he gave me. I spent all my time seeking within it a kind reflection of my husband: like him, it sucked in everything and gave back nothing, reflecting only what it was given; and I fed it hope. I got out of bed and fetched it from the press. It was grubby with finger-smears I did not remember making.

Mirror, mirror, in the palm of my hand, I am the ugliest in the land.

I had spent so long chasing the will-o'-the-wisp of a safe and normal life with a husband and a halo of respectability, worshipping at the altar of romantic dreams. To think I believed Mr Arroner was the knight come to save me from my difference; that his ordinariness might somehow rub off on me, burnish me into an acceptable woman. I had been a deluded child. That portion of my life was finished with. Now there was Abel. With him I was neither strange nor normal, I was simply Eve. I had not seen this great gift laid out before me. Until now.

I raked my claws through my hair to see if there was still a bold girl hidden underneath. I lost her half a lifetime ago, and I was afraid that the breadcrumb trail had been eaten by beasts. My mind had been fly-paper, syrupy with the daydream dust of happy-ever-afters and a world where no-one noticed my fur.

There's no such place, said Donkey-Skin.

'You're back!' I laughed.

You just stopped listening out for me.

'You were right: I should never have married him.'

Tsk, tsk. Come, we have work to do.

'I am sorry,' I said. 'For not believing you.'

Sorry? It's not a word I know.

'I am finished with him,' I said. 'That husband of mine.'

About time. Where shall we start? Donkey-Skin giggled. *Make it good. Make it tasty. Tell* me what you've got.

So I told her. Told her of all the time I had wasted, praying for my husband to take me to bed. I might be called wife, but was let into his life only when he chose to make his pet more profitable. I had kept a candle burning for him too long and now it was guttered down to the stub. I was done with him.

You're being too coy, said Donkey-Skin. *Too sweet. Too reasonable. Stop pretending to be a saint.*

Come now, Evie, you must have something better up your sleeve. Have I taught you nothing?

I have been away too long for you to become such a milky maid. They call you a lion. So be one. Roar, unsheathe your claws, rake the life out of those you hate.

Come on!

I was angry with myself, for I could no longer hide the truth I had always known: by marrying him I had simply exchanged one confinement for another. When I left my mother, I believed that with my husband I might discover a new world. Not a perfect world, for although I was young I was not a fool; but a small space where I might safely open the doors of myself, and where this opening of myself would be welcomed, understood. I realised how foolish I had been.

Forgive yourself. How could you know what he was like?

I curled up in her words.

Blow your nose.

You were not like this as a child. You hissed

344

and spat and fought and shrieked when Mama tried to shave you. Even when you were spat on, shunned, called freak, monster, monkey, witch, bitch, sick, twisted, queer. Now you are crying because you've had your pigtails pulled.

Wipe your nose. Dry your eyes.

Where's your anger?

Give me more.

Yes, I was tired of being the sweet-natured maid who bore her foul features with a good grace. It was time to show myself the beast they thought I was. Time to drool and slaver; sniff myself in polite gatherings; cock my leg against expensive wallpaper; lick myself in the places people wished to look, but did not dare. I once longed to hear him sing my sweet songs of love but I was no longer romantic. It was time. Here be dragons: here be wolves.

That's better, but you're only getting warm. Give me salt. Give me heat. Shout and scream!

I drew the dream I wanted now: the one where I crept into his bedroom, climbed up the bed-frame, perched on the iron rail, swung back and forth on the balls of my feet, toes in a tight clench round the bar. I wrung my lips together until my mouth swam, squeezed out a creamy drop and let it string its way down from my mouth into his. Heard him gag, champ his jaws together, but not wake; whispered in his ear: *I'll sour your mouth with bitterness. Leak my poison into you. I curse you for what you've made of me.*

Donkey-skin clapped her hands.

Now, that's more like it! You are come back

to me! What fun we shall have.

Give me fire. Give me sweltering volcano.

Give it all to me.

I shall paw his windows-catches, crack a spoon on to his skull, roll his brain down a skittle alley, sieve salt into the hole that's left, tamp in tobacco and set a lucifer to the bowl, suck in smoke through the pipe of his nostrils, blow smoke rings through his ears.

I shall build buttons of his knuckle-bones, sew stockings from his skin, knit my hair into a noose for his neck, unrip his lungs and tread them to brawn.

I shall be skull-splitter, gut-twister, fire-belcher, breath-sucker, brain-squeezer, blood-dabbler, fire floating in my hair.

Till I am done with him. Till the Hounds of Hell drag him away, and leave a bloody ribbon on the floor —

It is time, said Donkey-Skin. *You are no longer a princess, you are a woman.*

'Don't leave me.'

Ah, but I must. Every moment from this heartbeat onwards is yours, to take, to keep, to make your own.

You've no need for me, nor mothers, nor magic.

You've found the right one for you. Don't make the mistake of letting this man go.

You are already one step off the ground.

'I will fall.'

I'll see your first steps safe. I am not cruel.

It is time for you to end this fairy story. You are halfway out the door. All it takes is to kick it

open and step on to the street.
  Do you have a box of lucifers?
  'I am ready.'
  I strike the match.

ABEL

London, November 1858

With all the might of a hundred lives, I strive to pull Mr Arroner from the heart of the flames, but he will not let off clinging to his precious money-box. I drag him by the wrist, so forcefully that any other man would have been pulled in my wake.

'You'll not take it from me!' he squeals, hanging on. 'It's mine! Thief!'

'I want to save your life, you bloody fool,' I cry against the roar of the gathering inferno. 'Let me help.'

'Help me? That's a good one. Help yourself to this, you mean.'

I pick him up like a stack of kindling and carry him, box and all. We proceed a few steps accompanied by the sound of clanking, only to have our flight arrested by the tightening of a chain that secures the iron coffer to the bed-post.

'Let go. We can come back for it.'

'Never!'

He laughs, a thin whistling sound. The fire is flattened out like a demonic rug, dashing across the floorboards from one side of the room to the other. It gobbles the bed-curtains, the quilted coverlet, the wallpaper, the press and all the linen stored within.

'If you wish, I will stay here and guard your money.'

'Leave you alone with my riches? I'm not stupid,' he caws.

'You *are* stupid. The fire will finish you off. It can't touch me.'

He struggles against my grasp, inhales smoke and starts to cough. A tendril of flame weaves round the leg of his britches, but he does not appear to notice. I am also wrapped in fire, but it laps me cool as a breeze from the river.

'You are on fire,' I try again. 'Drop the box.'

'No!' he howls, hugging it to his breast. 'You'll not get it, you hear? None of you!'

Flames scramble up the ladder of his body, from trousers to waistcoat to shirt. His hair is gone in seconds. The ferocious heat begins to crisp his skin and still he will not let go.

'You'll — not — beat — me,' he wheezes.

It is the last thing he says. He gags on the fumes, slackens in my arms. Still I try to haul him clear, but it is too late. I watch as his skin sears, peels back from his cheeks. When I am sure there's no hope I drop him, and he tumbles to the floor.

My clothes singe; the fire crisps my skin brown, then black, baking me to a hard crust. Memories flower, of myself in countless fires, my flesh unassailable. It breaks upon me that all my burnings have been a preparation for this moment. I love Eve, and I can save her with this gift.

This is the simple offering my Italian master could not accept, nor Alfred, nor any one of innumerable thousands. Why, I do not know, for it is a sun that suffuses my being, flooding me with joy.

It is time to leave. I pick up the iron coffer from where it has fallen to the floor and it sticks to my fingers. The bed-post is quite burned through so I carry it, chain and all, through the impossible heat to the door, which is so frail I can push it through.

The street is too bright for this late hour. I look at my body and realise I am the torch lighting the cobbles. I wonder how long it will be before I am consumed; then I remind myself that I cannot burn away, for it is another of my body's tricks. As I watch, the flames grow green, waver and die.

I look back at the house, for I have a fancy that Arroner is watching me, rubbing his hands together and chuckling: *Yes, I can see the banner! The Human Torch! He burns! He lives!*

It begins to rain, the drops sizzling as they strike.

★   ★   ★

She is suddenly before me. I try to ask her how long she has been there, what she has seen, but my jaw will not open. Hers will not open either. She reaches out to take my hand, but shrinks back from the charred thing at the end of my arm.

'Abel, can you walk?' she says at last. 'Come

350

away, now. Quickly.'

I follow where she leads. I do not ask where. Up many steps, into a room I fill with the scent of charred meat. My eyes hiss when I close the lids. I lie down and know that if I die this time, it will not matter.

EVE

London, November 1858 and onwards

That first night, I did not sleep, and he did not die.

*   ⋆   ⋆

I stood in the crowd and watched the house burn, unnoticed in the scald of the blaze. George hurled a few buckets of water, but it was more to prove himself innocent of any involvement, and he tired quickly.

The fire had much to devour: the costumes, the back-drops, the curtains, the props, the chairs, the rugs, the floors, the window-frames and doors. When I thought the roof was about to go, the front door fell open on a belch of smoke and Abel fell out with it, clutching a tin box.

'It's the devil himself.' screamed one woman.

Fire poured up his body. He teetered forwards with small stiff steps.

'Fetch water!' cried another.

No-one moved. As we watched, the flames swimming over his flesh flickered and went out. He steamed with blood. Lizzie and I looked at each other. I stepped forward and waved my hands over my head until I got the attention of our new audience.

'Ho!' I yelled. 'I am the Lion-Faced Woman! What a show we have put on for you tonight! See before you the Marvels of Professor Arroner's Famous Exhibition!'

They looked at each other, wondering if we could be so mad as to burn down our own house to entertain them. Lizzie danced a flamboyant polka, the conflagration her back-drop. George had slipped away, although I did not see him go.

'Come! Dig deep!' I yelled. 'Give generously! Have you ever seen such a marvellous and surprising show?'

Lizzie passed round an old hat of hers, and I heard the tumble of a few pennies. Behind me, the roof fell in and it started to rain. The people began to trickle away, already bored by the fading spectacle, and to escape giving us any more money. Abel's body was fizzing gently in the drizzle.

'Eve, my love, I don't think he can survive this one,' said Lizzie, tucking the coins into her bodice.

I wanted to sit down. I wanted to cry. I had not meant for Abel to be caught in it — not him.

'What'll we do?' I whispered.

'Let's go. Now,' she said. 'Too hot for me.'

I stepped towards Abel, but dared not take the cinder of his hand. He was black as the dead bole of a lightning-struck tree. Lizzie took us away from the fire. She seemed to know her way but I cannot be sure: my memory is as dark as that night. Abel stalked beside me, an automaton with rigid limbs. I was out of my wits, for how could a man live through that furnace, even a man like Abel? She led us to an empty attic room, and we helped Abel lie down. He passed me the box clenched beneath his arm.

'It is yours,' he croaked, and did not speak again.

The hinges had been so twisted in the fire that Lizzie was able to crack it open with her bare hands. It was full of money. The paper notes were charred at the corners, but the sovereigns were only warm. There were more of them in one place than I could ever have imagined. I sat beside him and I waited for him to die. I wept for my blind stupidity: all the time I had wasted on my husband when Abel was right before me. The only man who saw me for what I am and did not wish to erase any part of it.

Too late. I had been a fool.

⋆ ⋆ ⋆

The next morning Abel was still a living creature of sorts, his whole body scorched tough as a slab of overdone beef. I went into the yard, filled a pot from the stand and dribbled it, drop by drop, through the slot that was once his lips.

We divided the money. George discovered our bolt-hole, for I declare he was a man who could hear the particular tinkle of any coin he felt he had a claim to. Lizzie gave him one of her glares when he suggested I should get less, on account of how I was Arroner's wife and would be provided for in the will, and Abel none, on account of him being half-dead and a half-wit.

'All will get their equal share, and not a penny less,' she said.

'Who will stop me taking it all?' he grunted, lurching forwards and baring his teeth at her.

She folded her arms across the thrust of her stomach. 'Oh, George, I believe I shall.'

'You — ' said George and raised his hand.

'And I shall also,' I added and stepped forwards too.

'So, the cat's found her claws,' he sneered. 'All right, have it your way.'

Lizzie buried her portion in the valley of her breasts. George took his share and did not bother us again, there being no sign of further monies forthcoming.

'Well,' I said. 'Our business is done. It seems we shall make our adieus.'

'Oh no, Evie. I won't leave until I see you set. I promised, remember?'

'In faith, Lizzie, I shall — '

'I shall not hear of it.'

So she stayed. I barely noticed the passage of night to day and day to night, for I sat with Abel and ate only when Lizzie placed a plate into my lap or a cup into my hand. One evening she came back with the news that the police had found a man's body in the ashes of the fire. She peered at me, but I discovered I had no tears for my husband.

'It appears no-one is much concerned about the burning of weird folk,' she remarked. She gathered me into her vast arms and kissed the top of my head.

★ ★ ★

I watched Abel. Fed him water and milk when he would take it. He lay in a half-death, arms frozen in a clutch around the space where the box had been, as though he cradled a baby of air. It was just wide enough for me to crawl into and sleep; in the consolation of his wooden embrace, I whispered my confession.

'I did it, Abel. It was me who lit the match. I know what you did; how you tried to save him. I'm glad you didn't manage it.'

He said nothing. A half-corpse cannot speak.

I sniffed. 'I am sorry. I saw you come out, lit up like a torch. I have lost you.'

It seemed I could do little else but cry out the days, weep through the nights. Then one day he stirred. The black beetle casing of his old flesh cracked along joins I could not see, and came away like the shell of crackling on a piece of roasted pork. I lifted off the lid of his skin. Beneath he was pink and hairless as a baby. His eyelids split along their seams and he opened eyes pale and liquid as soft-boiled eggs.

'Your name is Eve,' he croaked.

'And you are Abel,' I said.

'Am I?'

He fell into a drowse once more. I held his hand, more to comfort myself, and with the holding I entered his mind. He burst into me, or I into him, in a headlong plunge so precipitous

356

my soul caught in my throat. I bobbed like a cork on top of the swelling tide of his memories, and at first I could get no purchase on the torrent of images. But either it slowed, or I became a better navigator, and I read him.

As carefully as I could, I swam into the sea of his lives. At first I stood in a slaughter-house, carcases swaying so close I could sniff the dangling meat, slippery against my skin. Then I stepped into a clock-mender's shop, awash with the kindly tick of a myriad pocket-watches, and felt the twitching of his fingers, aching to be at work. Next, a place filled with the deep peace of dead bodies, and the anatomists who worked upon them. And back, a wheelwright; and back, a blacksmith; and back, a soldier; and back, and back.

He was nested with lives, the skin between them thin enough to shine a candle through. The past poured out of his palm and into me, life upon life: I saw him stumbling through each, unchanging, with no understanding of his true nature, given glimpses which terrified rather than awed him. Wondering always: *Will this be a place I can rest awhile?* But he found no respite, only movement — and in one direction: forwards. Oh, the wonders he had seen, and forgotten. It was surely the cruellest joke, to live for ever and remember nothing of it.

He stirred in my hand, and came to wakefulness.

'You are reading me,' he husked, voice still rough.

'Abel,' I said as tenderly as I would to a child.

'Do you still wish me to stop? All you need do is say the word, and I shall.'

'No.' He ground his teeth. 'I must do this. Tell me: what have you seen? What do you know?'

'I have seen some of your lives. The most recent: at the slaughter-house before you joined the troupe; your friend Alfred.'

'Alfred,' he sighed. 'A lonely man. I had forgotten.'

'A fortune-teller also. Something of a mountebank. What greed!'

'Ah yes. I can still feel him pawing at my lives, trying to force his way in.'

'And before that, your sojourn in Holland, as a skilled watchmaker. Very skilled. And quite well-off, too.'

I pressed his hand with great gentleness and smiled. He gave a small one in return, his shining lips struggling to stretch into the shape.

'More,' he rasped.

'Before that, you were in Italy, and were a student at a school of anatomy. I see you standing next to a man who looks on you with an air of mastery. But he cannot tell you what you ache to know. It makes you confused.'

'Ah, yes. I recall him.' His eyes swam, and he closed the lids over them. 'As you tell me, I remember. It seems that through every one of my lives I have been nothing but a blank canvas on to which all have painted their need.'

'Blank? My dearest Abel, nothing could be further than the truth. You burst with stories. If your lives were painted they would fill every gallery in every city and still men would have to

358

build more to fit you in.'

'Yet I have forgotten.'

'Forgetting you have done something is not the same as not having done it.'

'Please.' He cleared his throat and nodded. 'I am ready.'

So I held his newborn hand and read his stories one by one as they surfaced like slow fish from the pond of his being. I told him the secret of himself, and very simple it was too: he had lived a hundred and one lives, and a hundred and one more. I was his Scheherazade and might never be done. He listened, and it seemed that with my telling he grew a little calmer, that his mind began to heal up its great breaches just as his body did.

★　★　★

Gradually we settled into our new home, a room under the eaves of a quiet house with a window that opened out on to roof-tops. I liked to lean on the sill and contemplate their slate expanse stretching into the distance. When it rained they looked like so many whales surfacing from the ocean of the city, and our home was a small boat making its way on that heaving sea.

I scrubbed the floors and windows, beat the rugs like any other wife and bore the stares of our neighbours as I went back and forth to the privy, or the pump, or the laundry. By and by they shouted, 'Hey missus!' and halloa as they passed and I said halloa back. One Sunday afternoon a woman from the room beneath us tied up my hair in blue and red ribbons and the whole household laughed, but it was kind laughter. By small degrees I became their 'kitty-cat' and they grew quite proud of me, letting me know how the whole of London was jealous because they alone laid claim to the residence of the one and only Pretty Kitty of Stepney.

Lizzie paid us visits when she was not too busy; and busy she was for she had a string of gentleman friends in thrall to her particular charms and they demanded a great deal of her attention. She told us how George had moved to Birmingham or somewhere equally far off.

'But don't you worry about him. He'll get into one fight too many some day. Lizzie's got friends in more places than you imagine,' she said darkly.

I did not enquire too closely what she meant.

'How is Bill?' I asked, to change the subject.

'He's quite the young gent.' She grinned with affection. 'Working the halls now. Got himself a nice little act with a dog. You know how everyone likes a dog.'

'We should catch him some evening.'

So she amused us with tales of her amorous admirers, each one more intent than the last on seeing her comfortably settled.

★　★　★

One night, some months later, I heard Abel crying out, and took his hand to soothe him. The orbs of his eyes flickered back and forth beneath the closed lids. I stroked my free hand up and

360

down the inner side of his forearm where the muscles flexed; I felt them straining urgently against some great force.

But I did not see more of his lives: this time I was assaulted with the vision of his attempted escapes into death. I saw him hurl his body into rivers and plague pits blistering with quicklime, devouring rotten meat and bread blue with blight, hanging from ropes which would not strangle away his breath, falling upon swords and spears and knives of every variety, seeking poisoned oblivion that swam like honey through his veins, and, over and over, throwing himself into tumbling falls from the highest buildings.

I tasted his need to break himself, and his desperation when each time his body renewed. Falling and broken, injured and healing, without end. The frantic quivering of his frame continued for many minutes, and I wondered whether I should try to rouse him; but at last the fit ceased, and he let out a gasp of breath. I echoed the breath, for I had been holding mine also. He opened his eyes.

'Is it time to go to work?' he hissed, blinking in the gaslight. 'Oh. It's you, Eve.'

'You were crying out.'

He lifted his hand, clasped in mine.

'Ah,' he nodded. 'If you have been reading what is in my mind, then you will know why. That I wish to die. That I have wished to die in every life. You will also have seen the countless times I have attempted it.'

He looked away from me.

'Abel, why?'

He grabbed my shoulders in an extremity of despair, greater than I had seen in him previously. 'I want to finish myself,' he cried. 'I want to stop, to rest. I have had lifetimes of restlessness. You have seen them, Eve. I am exhausted: I want to lie down and pull the earth up over me, to snuff myself out and be nothing. But my body will not let me.'

'But it is wonderful. You are wonderful.'

As I looked upon him, I realised I spoke the truth. He was all I wanted. It was so clear, so plain. With him, my difference was neither ignored nor made important. I was simply Eve. Furry, undoubtedly; a reader of hands, certainly But, primarily, Eve. I had always been defined by my queerness. Until now. He groaned.

'Tell me this: if there was a cure for your condition? If you could be made smooth and hairless? What would you do?'

'I would smash the bottle containing the elixir,' I said with a passion.

He held me at arm's length.

'Then we are truly different, for I would drink it. Sincerely, I would leap at it.'

'Why?'

'I wish to be the same as every other man. To bleed, to sicken, grow old and die. I give up.'

'Are you so unhappy?'

'I am so very tired.'

★　★　★

That night I lay in bed listening to the shuffle of his quiet feet across the floor, the hiccough of the

362

gas as he turned off the tap. As he stretched up, his nightshirt lifted and I glimpsed his thighs, twined with dark hair; I glimpsed also that masculine part of him which never stirred. For all that we had shared a bed since our escape from the fire, we were as chaste as babes. The mattress eased under his weight as he lay down beside me.

'Abel?' I murmured. 'Are you sleepy?'

'Eve,' he answered quietly.

I leaned across and kissed his mouth. His eyes swam, and with his forefinger he traced the downy curve of my cheek.

'Eve — '

'Abel, I spent one life being coy with a man who did not love me. I will not be such a fool in this my second life.'

I pushed up his shirt, skimmed my hand across his chest, delighting in the snag of hair circling his nipples and streaming downwards to his navel, swirling thickly around that sweet cave; the dark arrow leading downwards further still into the thatch of crisp hair nesting — limpness. I palmed the flesh, rolled my hand around, under, hefting the weight of him, but he remained unmoved.

He sighed. 'Your touch pleasures me, but I cannot — I would like to — '

He ran out of words. I could think of none to fill the space between us. My boldness shrivelled and I took back my hand. Although I was ashamed to admit it to myself, I resented this lack of vitality, which left me empty of the fulfilment I sought.

'It is not important, Abel,' I said, and it was almost true.

'Do you think I wish this softness? Do you think it is because I do not desire you?'

'I am used to it. Why should any man desire me?'

'Eve, you do not understand.'

But I did. It was no great surprise. My romantic dreams had died during my brief marriage, that fortress of unhappiness. I was determined not to be deluded by frivolous dreams with Abel. Here was the only man to delight in my difference. He was my dear friend, and a companion I needed more than I did any physical communing. If he did not lust after me, then so be it. I would not allow myself to be disappointed.

The following morning I found him searching through our meagre store of possessions.

'What do you need, Abel?' I asked, still sleepy.

He grunted in reply. I thought of how he used to need reminding of the smallest things each day. How he used to cling to that paper of his, reading it assiduously. Even though he now had me, perhaps he still needed its security.

'Do you need pen and ink?'

His arms fell to his side.

'I can get paper if you wish, so you may begin a fresh document of your lives.'

'No,' he croaked. 'Not that.'

'What is it? What ails you?'

I got out of bed and padded across the little rug, placed my hand over his where it gripped the table-edge and I felt the roiling of his distress.

'I need knives,' he gasped.

I took a step back, and our hands separated.

'No, Abel. No more cutting. That was another world. You don't need to display yourself to an audience for sixpences.'

'If you want me, I must have blades,' he whispered.

'Abel, no — '

He regarded me with sad eyes. 'Don't you understand why?'

'No. You don't need to hurt yourself.'

'It is not hurt.'

'It is!'

There was a pause.

'So, you will not help me?'

'Not with this.'

'I thought you understood. But no-one does. Not even you.' He put on his cap and boots.

'Abel?'

'I am going to find work. Your husband's money will not last for ever.'

His feet thumped down the stairs. I swept the room, turned the mattress and scrubbed the floor. Then I sat at the table by the window and continued writing the story of my life. I was resolved to join the throng of brave folk who set out the narrative of their lives; I had been much inspired by the *Life of Olaudah Equiano* and hoped that my story might have just as eager a reception. However much tastes might change, there was still curiosity even if such tales were dressed up in fancy words like 'autobiography'.

Then I finished the sewing, cleaned the window and peeled the potatoes with the tiny

365

knife I kept tucked in my bodice. I did not understand why Abel still sought to cut himself now that he was free of Mr Arroner and the Freak Show. I could tell him his history any time he wanted: I should be enough for him. He was mine.

The room was quiet.

I sat down, heavy with the weight of my shameful thoughts. He was *mine?* I was no better than my husband if I considered Abel to be my possession. Very well. If he needed blades, then I would let him have them, and would strive to understand. I laid the potato knife on the board, where he would see it, and when I heard his unmistakable tread upon the stairs I raced to open the door. He was smeared with blood, and I started back.

'There is a new slaughter-yard at Bethnal Green. They need a man like me. I have not misplaced my skill, it seems. I will earn my keep, Eve.' He laid a small brown-paper packet on the table. 'A piece of liver,' he said. 'It will taste good.'

'Abel . . . ' All my breath flew out in a rush. 'About this morning. I am sorry.'

'Sorry?' His gaze flickered briefly. 'Oh. It is no matter.'

'It is,' I said, my chin pushed out. 'I did not listen to you.'

'No. You did not.' He said the words without anger, but still they stung me.

'Let me listen now.'

He began to unlace his boots. I watched his lips work up and down as though bursting with words. As he pulled the boots off he seemed to reach a decision.

'You think I do not desire you?' he said. 'Let me show you.'

'Yes.' I swallowed.

He stood and folded his arms. 'Loosen your stays.'

'My — '

'Do it.'

I was silenced. I began to undo the buttons at my breast but I had only managed two before he took a step forward and gently pushed my hands aside. He unlooped the remaining buttons, releasing each from its tightly sewn hole in so leisurely a fashion that I cried out with the pain of wanting him to release me more swiftly. He paused, breathing on my neck just below the ear, stirring the long curl.

'There is no need for haste, Eve,' he said.

I was stilled. He shrugged the blouse from my shoulders, reached round and loosened my corset-laces, unleashing caught breath. The hair on my back flustered in moist swirls.

'That is better,' he said, his voice the brushing of a soft broom. 'Now, take off that corset.'

I obeyed, leaving only my chemise. He regarded me most intently, and I could not look away.

'And your chemise. All of it.'

I unpeeled damp cloth until I stood naked. He took my hand, and I felt a rough sweep of command surge into my body, swelling my longing. I tried to draw my paw away for I wished to compose myself, and not suffer the torture of this darting arousal between my legs. He held on fast.

'Lie down.'

I stretched out on the bed in the full light of

the sun slanting through our high window. With great care, he unbound my braided hair, smoothing his fingers through the weave till I was quite undone. I had never felt so stripped, even when I had been shaved. I trembled beneath his hands.

'I have a gift for you,' he said, and reached into the pocket of his jacket, for he was still fully clothed.

He drew out a small dandy-brush, such as those used to groom horses. At first I thought it was packed with hog's hair bristles, but as he flourished it before my face I saw that it was set with a multitude of delicate steel tines. I took in a frightened breath, for it looked a cruel instrument. He took my wrist, laid the brush against my shoulder and with a delicious ease drew it down my arm towards the elbow.

'I declare, Abel — ' I said.

He held a finger to my lips, and continued. The tiny metal points tickled through my fur; every particle of skin was brought to quivering attention. He continued the sweep from elbow to wrist, the teeth gliding through my tangles, unknotting me so gently I did not feel the slightest tug. Donkey-Skin's combing had never been so delectable. My flesh sparkled. He continued with my other arm, smoothing and flattening, plying the brush just as cleverly, then bade me turn on to my stomach.

Starting at the nape of my neck he swept the length of my spine to the swell of my hips; and further still, down my thighs to my ankles. It felt as though the frailest of kittens' teeth were grazing the skin; not harsh enough to be a scratch, more a sharp sweet caress which dissipated as soon as it passed over. All my blood rose to meet the touch in a loss. My body sang. I stopped seeking for words and stretched out beneath the inquisitive brushing, melting into the bed until I thought I must be spread as thin as the sheet I lay upon. The whole time he held my wrist, and through our joined flesh I felt his arousal mounting to match mine.

He stopped, and I turned to see if anything was amiss. As I watched, he began to undress himself. Snapped away his braces and undid his shirt, very slowly, from the neck down to the navel, each flip of the button revealing a thatch as dark as the boot-black hair on his head. I watched him ram his fingers into the gorsy clumps ringing his nipples, squinting at the tiny buds there, stroking his luxuriant pelt over and over. Lizzie in all her voluptuous beauty had never so entranced me.

He unpicked the buttons of his fly, wrestling his thumbs into the waistband and pushing his trousers down, down, revealing thighs bulging with smooth fur and the sleeping flesh that nested in its bristling curls; indeed the Pan I had dreamed of, lacking only a satyr's priapic vigour. I sighed: he was giving me more pleasure than I thought it possible to bear and I would not push him aside again.

'I am sorry,' he said sadly, indicating his slumbering flesh. 'I cannot.'

'Am I so very ugly?' I asked, my throat full of stones.

'You are more beautiful than there are words

to speak it in any of the tongues I know. This is my curse.'

'Is there no way?'

'There is. But you have already said you will not help.'

Suddenly I understood what he meant when he said he needed knives. I understood what I had only glimpsed before, why he had covered his lap with a scarf, why George had made so many lewd jokes. I sat up and took his hand in mine.

'Abel, I will help. I am yours.'

He curved his lips in a half-smile, slipping his hand across my breasts, tantalising my skin until I squirmed beneath his touch. Then he withdrew for an achingly long moment, and returned with the paring knife. He took my hand, and his yearning erupted through my whole being. The air crackled, shifting like a change in the wind across a field of wheat, or the ripping snap of a sail swinging as a boat tacks to one side.

'Yes,' I said. 'Do this.'

He opened up the flesh of his arm. Together we gazed into the familiar wetness and waited. Then a sudden movement drew my eyes downward: that part of him I thought incapable of motion was rising in a slow journey upwards, lengthening into a glistening rod crowned with a roseate head.

I had never seen Mr Arroner naked, only felt him the once; what Abel presented to my gaze was beautiful, and thrilled me with a fierce curiosity. My free hand rose and I touched the tip where the tiniest of slits wept tears of clear liquid, carried the finger to my tongue, tasted the sour and salt of him. His body shuddered and his need rocked through our handclasp. With a great effort, I wrenched my eyes away from the enchanting sight and looked up into his face. It only occurred to me then that I had never seen him smile before: his features were transfigured into life, vitality, comprehension.

'You see,' he said. 'I do need this.'

'You do,' I hummed.

'Please.'

He held out the knife; I took the proffered handle and unsheathed it from his fist. He gripped the blade tightly and moaned in pleasure as it sliced his palm, hips jerking forwards.

'Abel, I — '

He laid a sticky finger on my lips.

'Beloved,' he gasped. 'I heal quickly.'

His wounded arm showed the truth of it, for the sinews were already weaving their thick mat, and as swiftly as the limb healed, his lower branch began to wilt.

'I do not wish to heal,' he stuttered. 'Not yet. Help me, Eve.'

'I promised, and I shall.'

He circled my wrist with his fingers, and his fear swam into my veins: fear that I would fail, as everyone else had failed him when faced with his strangeness. He throbbed with emptiness, with yearning for completion. I was chastened: set against his, my own fear was as thin as water. I lifted the knife and slid into the gash, opening it wide again; he threw back his head and his entire frame stiffened, including that part I passionately

371

wished brought back to life.

He laughed. 'Ah, yes!'

I dug a little deeper.

'Yes!'

I dragged the blade the length of his arm until he lay open, pulsing from elbow to wrist. When the wound was deep enough, I wrapped my fingers around his cock, pulled him towards me with the slightest of tugs. We fell on to the bed, grinning, the knife held tight in my hand.

★ ★ ★

Our days passed into weeks, into months, the rhythm of our lives bounded with the new pleasures we discovered in ourselves. One such night we lay in each other's arms after taking delight in each other. He was kissing the top of my head, and I was running my forefinger in damp circles around the cup of his palm. Something tickled up my arm, cold as an icicle.

'Are you sad, Abel? Even at this moment?'

'Oh.'

He pulled his hand away.

'Abel, there is something you are hiding from me.'

'I am not.'

'You are. And you are still a poor liar.'

'Very well,' he grunted. 'It is true.'

'What is it, Abel? I promised I would not force you, and I shall keep my word. But let us have no secrets.'

'I am ashamed of my feelings.'

'Which feelings?' My voice grew small. 'The

ones you have for me?'

'No! I am selfish.'

'About what?'

'When you are gone, what will I do?' he moaned.

'My love, I shall not leave you.'

'You will. Eve, I shall live. One day you will die, and I will be alone. I will lose myself again. All that you have returned to me will be lost and forgotten. All this sweetness. It has happened so many times, whatever I do. I shall prove it to you. Do you remember that paper of mine? The one I kept in my shirt?'

'Yes. It was burned,' I said. 'By George.'

'You see? It is gone.'

'What?'

'Everything. It has happened over and over. I have recorded myself on paper, wood, clay, stone — then lost myself as many times. Burned in innumerable fires, robbed by legions of thieves, stripped by nations of slavers. Or I have just been careless, losing my written lives to mice or drunkenness. And after you are dead, I will have to start again. I will fail. Again.'

'Abel — '

'I will sink back into my fog of unknowing, forever wondering what and who I am, in flight from my memories as they batter me with their hail. I cannot go back to that; not now I have this peace you have granted me.'

He set his teeth, and pouted his lips like a child.

'Abel, do you still wish to die?'

'Yes. I am a coward. I know it.'

'You must not do this. Promise me.'

'No. I have a plan, and you cannot stop me. This is a new world: it has furnaces to boil me into molten steel and trains to grind me into pieces. I shall find steam engines to devour me and spit me out in infinitesimal pieces, so that not even I can put myself back together again. And when you have gone, you cannot prevent it.'

'I can,' I said quietly.

He stared. 'How?'

'I am taken.'

I placed his hand low on my belly and we felt the tiny bud stir in its warm silt.

'But . . . ? Oh.'

'I was not sure at first. But I have missed three of my monthly courses. I know.'

'Oh, Eve. I am sorry. I did not think that I could — '

'Sorry? Abel, I am happy,' I said. 'I could not be more delighted. We shall have a daughter: I feel her dancing, already. She will be as hairy as me, and as healthy as you. Indeed, perhaps she will inherit both our particular qualities. If I were still in the Freak Show, I would be frightened, it is true. I think of how my husband would have displayed us, the Lioness and her Cub. I would never have been free of him, licking his lips the better to count the money showering him, calculating how many times he must get me with child to buy him a racehorse, a mansion, a baronet's crown.'

'Oh.'

'Things are different now. Abel, we have found each other. I am becoming myself for the first

374

time, and am filled with exhilaration. What a journey! I want you at my side to celebrate each step.'

'I wish to be nowhere else. But for you it will be short — '

'I do not think so. See me, Abel. Standing at the prow of the ship of my life, the wind strong and salty. My hair billows like a sail and I cast myself free. What adventures await us.'

He stared into his lap, not persuaded. I pressed on.

'Think of this wonderful age of discovery! All the marvels we shall witness! We shall share all our adventures, and when I am old, you will bury me. In a lively place, near to music and laughter. I shall be a long time dead, and shall wish for entertainment.'

'It will grieve me too much.'

'It will not. For then you will have to tend to my daughter, and watch over her, and find her a kind husband. You must tend to her daughter also; and in that way you will never lose me, for in each will be the quintessence of myself. I shall pass down your stories to them, and they will keep you steady.'

'But I shall have lost you.'

'No. One day my daughter will lift a cup to her mouth and you will see me in the gesture. One day my granddaughter will laugh and you will hear my voice; my great-granddaughter will grasp your hand and her fingers will read you: for I shall pass down more heirlooms than my fur. I will be eternal for you, my dear.'

He rolled on to his back and put his arms

behind his head. I watched his face as he took in my words, the frown lines gradually smoothing out. I could have taken his hand and read him, but a man needs his privacy and I would not abuse my talent by forever prodding into others' minds.

'Abel, I believe you are smiling.'

'I was about to say *I have been in this situation before*, then I realised I have not. It is completely new.'

He laughed.

'What is funny?' I asked.

'In the past, I remembered nothing and it filled me with fear, confusion, searching. I was forever wringing my hands and bemoaning my fate. I have just said the word 'new'. Perhaps I will forget this moment,' he continued a little more quietly, 'but I do not care. I am not afraid.'

He laughed again, and I joined him.

'How wonderful,' he said. 'Not to care.'

★ ★ ★

He said no more. I reached under the coverlet and took out the hand-mirror, the one thing I had kept when I ran from the fire. Its edges were ash-black and the scent of smoke was ground into the glass. I held it up and Donkey-Skin peered out.

It is never happy-ever-after, she said. *But it will always be interesting.*

I gazed at myself, content with what I saw. A face appeared at my shoulder, matching me

strangeness for strangeness, and kissed my neck.
'Dearly beloved,' he said.
I cupped his cheek, feeling the warmth of
blood, of breath, of love.

ABEL

I have been running for ever: on my way to meet someone. I look around hungrily for the woman who is waiting for me; the one who heals me, fills and empties me, whose hands take away my fear. I know her name, if only I could bring it to my tongue: but my mouth is filled with the sour air of my desperate flight. My memory paddles for the word that will make her real, but its fingers scrabble in emptiness. If only I could speak her name, the one I keep forgetting. She should be here.

Suddenly I am at the top of a tall building, one I know too well. It is the tower from which I threw myself, all those uncountable years ago. Once again, I scramble on to the ledge; my feet push away; my hands swim the air; and I fall. It takes longer, much longer to reach the ground, for I am no longer falling through air, but through something warm, pulsating —

I wake in her arms; in Eve's arms, the woman whose name binds me to a life I wish to lead.

'You were thrashing about, Abel, my love,' she says, sending a ladder of kisses into the deep pit of my fears. 'A bad dream?'

'A bad dream,' I sigh. 'Nothing more.'
For the first time, I am speaking the truth.

★ ★ ★

I am becoming Abel: this name, of all the names I have borne. The more she gives my lives back to me, the easier it is to bear. Any time I begin to lose myself, I take her hand and the telling of my tales becomes its own comfort. She gives me my lifeblood, freely. I swear: if you cut me now, I would bleed.

As the shutters are thrown back on each of my existences, I am illuminated, page by page, and with each the terror lessens until I am curious to discover the next, a child who demands a fresh story every night to send it happily to sleep.

With each new memory granted into my safe-keeping I remember better. I do not come blinking into each morning; rather I wake and know the room, my name, the name of my dearest Eve, and now our delightful child Rose, for so we call her. If I have a beginning, then it is so far back even Eve has yet to touch the depths of me.

I am discovering what I am, and what I am is an old man made new, stepping out into tomorrow with no fear of what might happen. I do not need to leap into emptiness: I have found the closest thing to home.

Eve is my harbour, my sea-anchor. I have surfaced from my own oceanic depths and this time there is no drowning, no plunging back. I breathe. She holds me steady on a sea which once had no guiding stars, no coasts in view.

Now I can see the coastline of beautiful lands; together we journey towards them without fear.

Such is my unending, unbeginning life. I was the first to fall: flesh and fire from Heaven's morning, crushed to cinders by the force of my descent. I was dark matter from that moment, but she has restored me to brightness. I fall at last into understanding; and, if I am forever fallen, then I am content to be part of earth with her. The peace of her hands has found out the peace in me. I have stopped fighting. I have stopped forgetting.

There is none other like me. There is none other like her. We are unbelievable, impossible. I fly as high as the Heavens which cast me out. I have run out my comet's course: she is the world I have sought out. Round her I have cast the loop of my orbit, and am held fast and safe; she is my Sea of Tranquillity, my Milky Way, bearded with Berenice's Hair. I am a new constellation, pegged out in the sky. I am joy. Complete. For ever.

We do hope that you have enjoyed reading this large print book.

Did you know that all of our titles are available for purchase?

We publish a wide range of high quality large print books including:
Romances, Mysteries, Classics
General Fiction
Non Fiction and Westerns

Special interest titles available in large print are:
The Little Oxford Dictionary
Music Book
Song Book
Hymn Book
Service Book

Also available from us courtesy of Oxford University Press:
Young Readers' Dictionary
(large print edition)
Young Readers' Thesaurus
(large print edition)

For further information or a free brochure, please contact us at:
Ulverscroft Large Print Books Ltd.,
The Green, Bradgate Road, Anstey,
Leicester, LE7 7FU, England.
Tel: (00 44) 0116 236 4325
Fax: (00 44) 0116 234 0205

REGENERATION

Pat Barker

Craiglockhart War Hospital, 1917, where army psychiatrist William Rivers is treating shell-shocked soldiers. Under his care are the poets Siegfried Sassoon and Wilfred Owen, as well as mute Billy Prior, who is only able to communicate by means of pencil and paper. Rivers' job is to make the men in his charge healthy enough to fight. Yet the closer he gets to mending his patients' minds, the harder becomes every decision to send them back to the horrors of the front . . . *Regeneration* is the classic exploration of how the traumas of war brutalized a generation of young men.

HARVEST

Jim Crace

As late summer steals in and the final pearls of barley are gleaned, a village comes under threat. A trio of outsiders — two men and a dangerously magnetic woman — arrive on the woodland borders and put up a makeshift camp. That same night, the local manor house is set on fire. Over the course of seven days, Walter Thirsk sees his hamlet unmade: the harvest blackened by smoke and fear, the new arrivals cruelly punished, and his neighbours held captive on suspicion of witchcraft. But something even darker is at the heart of his story, and he will be the only man left to tell it . . . Timeless yet singular, mythical yet deeply personal, this beautiful novel of one man and his unnamed village speaks for a way of life lost for ever.

THE SHOCK OF THE FALL

Nathan Filer

'I'll tell you what happened because it will be a good way to introduce my brother. His name's Simon. I think you're going to like him. I really do. But in a couple of pages he'll be dead. And he was never the same after that.' There are books you can't stop reading, which keep you up all night. There are books which let us into the hidden parts of life and make them vividly real. There are books which, because of the sheer skill with which every word is chosen, linger in your mind for days. *The Shock of the Fall* is all of these books. An extraordinary portrait of one man's descent into mental illness; a brave and groundbreaking novel from one of the most exciting new voices in fiction.